W9-BIN-603

Other Tor books

by John Farris

ALL HEADS TURN WHEN THE HUNT GOES BY
THE CAPTORS
CATACOMBS
THE FURY
MINOTAUR
NIGHTFALL
SHATTER
SON OF THE ENDLESS NIGHT
THE UNINVITED
WILDWOOD

JOHN FARRIS

ScareTactics

TOR
HORROR

SCARE TACTICS

Copyright © 1988 by John Farris

First printing: July 1988

A TOR Book

Published by Tom Doherty Associates
49 West 24 Street
New York, N.Y. 10010

ISBN: 0-312-93085-2

Printed in the United States

0 9 8 7 6 5 4 3 2 1

The Odor of Violets

I was completing my last lap of the day on the rutted cinder track when a man in a trench coat and a muffler appeared out of the fog and called my name.

"Mr. Mayo, sir?"

Not as if he knew me by sight. I was tempted to pass him by with a curt shake of the head, since at the time I was nearly three months behind on my car payments, and ripe for repossession. But immediately after calling, tentatively, to me, the man in the trench coat was taken with a fit of coughing, like a volcano trying to erupt. He leaned against the chain link fence surrounding the track and the Sprayberry College football field ("Home of the Purple Maulers"). Instinctively, as I jogged nearer, I felt that he was not going to threaten me with harsh reminders of past-due bills. He seemed to have no business being there at all, in the dank night air. Nonetheless, I stopped well short of where he stood, trying to arrest his cough, holding with one hand to the fence for support and clutching, under his other arm, a bulky manila envelope.

Jogging in place, I spoke to him. "Yes?"

He got control of himself and straightened, breathing hard. Light from the sodium vapor lamp above the end-zone gate, now almost invisible in the fast-moving fog, touched his face; it was a glowing, unhealthy shade of red, as if from St. Anthony's fire. Although we were early into February, the air growing chillier by the minute, he was perspiring. He had

3

a brown ruff of beard along the jawline, like a worn-out strip of welcome mat, and not much hair on his head.

"You *are* Jack Mayo—the author?"

His accent was softly southern; I was reminded of pleasant bourbon-saturated evenings in Key West in the company of Tennessee and dear, doomed Carson McCullers.

"Yes," I admitted impatiently, now paying more attention to the telltale envelope he'd brought with him. He was of late middle age; I assumed he was not a student here. At least I had never noticed him on campus, or heard that distressing cough before. Sprayberry was a rather small and thoroughly déclassé institution, near the sea's edge and forever on the brink of insolvency. "Who are you?" I inquired of him.

He spoke slowly, and in a low tone, as if constantly needing to strangle the urge to cough. "David Hallowell, sir. You have never heard of me. But I am a writer, too."

"I see," I said unencouragingly, and decided to forgo the last hundred yards of my final lap. I began doing exercises so as not to cool off too suddenly and risk taking a chill. "If you're interested in signing up for one of my seminars in creative writing, then I suggest that you contact the admissions office."

"No, I—I don't have time for that," Hallowell replied, and he smiled deprecatingly before he began to cough again, into a soiled wad of handkerchief. When he regained his voice he said, "But it doesn't matter. I have nearly finished it. My book, I mean. Another two weeks—three at the vereh most. I wanted you to see it now. Then my fondest hope is that you will be willing to advise me. I know nothing about the publishing business. I do not know what I should do next. Of course, it *will* be published. It's good—vereh good. Superb, in fact. Yes, it should be a vereh great success."

"Really?" I grunted, touching my toes, feeling fire in the tendons of my thighs, the old bursitis that plagued my right shoulder. I was amused and, I suppose, a trifle irritated by his presumption. "What is it you've written? A novel?"

"Yes, sir. That I have."

"You want me to read it, and find you a publisher."

I couldn't keep the sarcasm from my voice: too many years of practice at the expense of mediocre scribblers unable to retaliate in kind had perfected my killshots. He drew back a little, shifting the position of the large envelope until it covered him like a buckler. But I had no desire to shatter his pathetic dignity.

"I'm much too busy," I said, "with teaching. And then my own work——"

"Oh, I know that!" he said, trembling now. "It's only that I have admired your writing so much. I must have read each of the stories in *Tug of War* a dozen times. The craftsmanship, the complexity, the humor——your talent inspired me from the beginning of my own poor ambition, and I——well——" He thrust the envelope at me, holding it at arm's length. His eyes pleaded for me to take it. "I owe so much to you."

"Mr. Hallowell——"

"Please! You'll like it, I know you will. Here is my *life*, sir——all that has kept me alive these past two years."

The coughing again. I felt a twinge of alarm and then, vaguely, guilt for not accepting his manuscript, making him suffer all the more in the fog and the cold.

"Yes, I suppose I could find the time. All right."

He stumbled forward eagerly, pressing the envelope into my hands. Quite heavy, there would be well over three hundred pages, I thought. At least I could glance at it before dismissing his labor with a few noncommittal words. Up close I saw how bad his eyes looked, like runny egg congealing on a cheap plate, how thin and ragged he was. I could not imagine him straying very far from the Salvation Army shelter, much less finding the high purpose and energy it took to write a novel.

"You're very ill," I said. "Are you seeing a doctor?"

He shook his head. "It's my lungs. I was a sickly child, and at fourteen I was made to go to work in my uncle's mill, on the Alabama side of the Chattahoochee River. It was an old, primitive, turn-of-the-century place, and the air was always thick with cotton dust. I contracted brown-lung disease while still a young man. And, well, nothing can help me now." His face screwed up in an agony of pride and he whispered fiercely, "I will finish my appointed task, however. I already have the last few chapters in mind. Just a few more nights—"

"You really ought to be in a hospital," I said.

He smiled, astounded, perhaps deeply touched that I might care whether he lived or died. Tears flowed from his red-flecked eyes. He seized my free hand and shook it. I felt as if I were grasping the bony hand of Death itself.

"You can't know how happy you've made me, sir! A year ago I couldn't imagine even meeting you, and now—you're going to read my novel!"

"Yes, certainly I'll read it, Mr. Hallowell. But I can't promise anything—"

"You'll do what you can!" he cried, ecstatic, his weeping eyes wandering from my face; almost instantly he appeared to be in a feverish fugue state. He babbled. "You're a man of high talent, a good and generous man!"—as if these qualities must be synonymous. "I only regret I shall not be here to read *your* novel. I know it's going to be a masterpiece, after all the years you've spent writing it—"

"Well, I'm afraid I still have far to go," I said, an automatic response. "Now, you really must put yourself to bed, take care of that cough."

Even as I spoke, his efflorescence was fading in the voracious Pacific fog; and I was left standing there holding a torn and seedy envelope I had no real desire to open.

"Good-bye—good-bye, Mr. Mayo! My address is on the title page. If you could see your way clear—I'm so vereh anxious to know what you think—"

"I'll read it immediately!" I promised rashly, now talking only to a ghost as he vanished beyond the gate. I shuddered, then began to jog again, in the opposite direction and away from the sea, across the rolling campus to my studio in the faculty apartments.

After a shower and a light supper I applied myself to the chore of reading my students' work, fortifying myself at intervals with double scotches. I had put the envelope containing David Hallowell's manuscript far back on my already cluttered worktable. For the next two hours my mood worsened steadily as I looked for some gleam of talent in the pile of chaff before me. Influences in style ranged from Saul Bellow to Erma Bombeck and, yes, even hoary old Hemingway. I gave up when a headache like a spike between my eyes diminished my ability to concentrate. I drank the last of the scotch in the bottle (remembering, too late, there would be no more credit at the liquor store), and went to bed.

Scarcely three hours later I was suddenly wide awake on the Hide A Bed, roused from an unmemorable dream; I had heard, or thought I heard, a tortured cough. And there was an unfamiliar odor in my cramped studio, the sweetness of wild violets.

I got up and turned on a lamp, but I had no company except for the memory of David Hallowell's face in the fog. I felt amazingly refreshed on a short ration of sleep. It was half past three in the morning; I didn't want to go back to bed. I made coffee. The odor of violets faded gradually as I stood at my windows looking at the campus lights through slow spirals of fog. Then I turned to a bookshelf and took down a copy of *Tug of War*. I looked at the dust-jacket photo of myself—leaner and with a thicker head of hair in those days when I had been, in pugilistic terms, a "comer." I knew the brief biography by heart, my present state of futility summed up in the last line: *Mr. Mayo is currently at work on a novel.*

The collection of eight stories in my hand, my only published work, was thirteen years old. Each year's crop of "comers" had pushed me farther and farther into the dim background of the literary scene. The novel blithely referred to on the endpaper was not forthcoming. In thirteen years I had managed less than a hundred pages. Not one word for the past two years. I was still not well recovered from the depression caused by my fiftieth birthday.

I set aside *Tug of War* and glanced at my worktable, now seeing only the soiled envelope with David Hallowell's manuscript inside. I felt annoyed with him; he was terminally ill, yet he had nearly finished a novel while I could not write at all. Assuredly it would turn out to be a dreadful piece of muck . . . but his dedication, his belief that he had a story worth telling, merited respect.

I opened the envelope, and a thick bundle of yellow pages torn from legal pads fell to the floor. It was a holographic manuscript, and he wrote, like Eugene O'Neill, in a cramped, miserly hand; there must have been half a thousand words on every page. But he composed so painstakingly that every word was legible without a magnifying glass. I scanned the first page casually after finding the title provocative, turned to the second, sat down slowly on the Hide A Bed with that untidy bundle in my lap.

By daybreak I had read all of *Angels and Aborigines*. I had been powerless to stop reading. It was marvelous: a comic, picaresque *Lear*. Hallowell's protagonist, an old poet, and three randy daughters careered like tornadoes through his pages. He satirized (and often tore to shreds) academia, government, religion, the full spectrum of intellectual pretentiousness and cultural folderol of our times. I turned over the last, incomplete page knowing that David Hallowell was a literary titan. My first thought, with nothing more to read, was an earnest entreaty to the gods that Hallowell be allowed to live long enough to finish this masterwork.

My second, distantly corrupting thought was, *This is the novel I was meant to write.*

I had been almost childishly pleased to note that there were echoes of the old, the good Jack Mayo, in those pages. It was true, as Hallowell insisted, that I had served him in some small way.

After my morning classes I drove down from the hills to the old section of San Augustín. David Hallowell was living in a *barrio* by the sea where the dreary fog lingered at noonday. The streets were narrow, the houses ramshackle, with a few hang-dog date palms and rusting pepper trees in the sandy yards. There was truculent graffiti in Spanish on every side wall of *laundería* and *bodega*. It took me quite some time to locate him.

The squat Mexican woman who responded to my inquiry on Portales Street had a baby on one hip and toddlers clinging to her skirt.

"Dah-veed, *sí*, is living here." She looked hopefully at me. "You are friend?"

"We met only yesterday," I said.

"Oh. Dah-veed very sick, is always—*tosiendo.*" She translated the word for me by coughing into her fist.

"Yes, I know. Could you take me to him?"

She led me through her squalid house and out the back door to a *casita* set against the alley fence. There were chickens in the bare yard, discarded beer cans, and rusted parts of automobiles. A stench of garbage saturated the fog. I could hear the surf just two blocks away. I also heard him coughing as we reached the *casita* door. The Mexican woman shifted her fretting half-clad infant from one chubby arm to the other.

"All night he is like that," she said of the coughing. "I go make tea for him now." She smacked one of her toddlers, who was bending over poking a finger into a fresh pile of chickenshit, and returned to the house.

I knocked at the *casita* door. Muffled coughing, but no other response. I shivered in the damp grayness. The door was unlocked, so I let myself in.

There was, unexpectedly, a sweetness in the air: violets, a welcome contrast to the sour spoor of the chicken-blighted yard. The one-room *casita* was quite dark, shades pulled down over the remaining panes of glass in the door and the single small window. I could make him out lying in a narrow mission-style bed, huddled under a blanket, coughing pathetically, rocking the springs with the violence of his affliction.

"Mr. Hallowell?" I said. "David?"

He gave a start, one bare foot kicking out from beneath the blanket, and sat up, peering at the doorway.

"Yes—yes. Who is it?"

"Jack Mayo."

"Oh, Mr. Mayo! I apologize, sir, I—please, if you would give me a few moments—"

"Certainly. I'll wait outside."

"No! No! Stay! I'm just waking up. I work nights, you see." He was having difficulty getting his breath. "If you wouldn't mind—on the table there—a bottle of tequila."

I raised the window shade, letting in some pallid light. I poured a shot of tequila for him and, at his urging, a shot for myself, as he had a supply of paper cups to drink from. I didn't entirely trust his explanation of the illness from which he suffered, and I have always been more than mildly phobic about germs. Fortunately there was no atmosphere of the sickroom, because of the remarkably pleasant odor of spring violets. I saw none growing in the room, however; and no potentially flowering seed would have survived for long out-of-doors. Perhaps it was perfume, a recent female visitor—

When I mentioned the odor to him he looked puzzled. His face was flushed and glistened from perspiration, his eyes were unfocused as he sipped his tequila.

"Oh, yes, I did smell violets in the beginning, I suppose. But that was so long ago I've become used to it. I hardly notice anymore."

His explanation was far from clear, but I had no good reason to question him further. And my attention had been drawn to the pile of yellow paper on his writing table, beside a cracked pair of wire-rimmed reading glasses and a jar crammed with ballpoint pens, the cheap variety given away by every sort of business establishment. It was difficult for me not to pick up the new pages and begin reading on the spot. Instead I smiled at David Hallowell.

The tequila seemed to have temporarily suppressed his cough, although it lived on in his skinny chest, as a low dangerous rumbling. His complexion had cleared somewhat. My smile was unexpected; it caused him to flinch, and then he returned an abashed smile of his own.

"Was I right? It *is* good, isn't it?"

"I think you're a genius," I said.

He scratched his head and trembled; he began to weep and shake the bed in a paroxysm of joy and thanksgiving. A little overcome myself, I fed him more tequila, and wondered how his heart could stand up under the strain. Some of the tequila dribbled into the ruff of his coarse beard.

"But surely," I said, "others have told you that."

"No. Not another living soul but you has read a word of my book. I moved to San Augustín because—I knew that *you* were here."

Rather than watch him suffer through more agonies of gratitude, I turned again to his worktable, noticing a copy of *Tug of War* atop a pile of badly worn paperback dictionaries. I picked up the book, which obviously he'd rescued from a stall in a secondhand store. Just inside the cover was a recent clipping from the local newspaper, my photo accompanying an announcement of the summer writers' workshop I had established on campus.

By now the odor of violets was all but gone from the room; I could smell his trickling toilet in one corner, and the sordidness of the *casita* became oppressive to me. Obviously before David Hallowell settled in, the *casita* had served as lodging for numerous wetbacks. Chickens quarreled in the yard; a child wailed.

"How long have you been living here?" I asked him.

He shrugged. "I don't know. Three months? Closer to four."

"And where is your home? I believe you mentioned Alabama."

"Eufaula, Alabama. That was a vereh long time ago. I haven't been back since—" It was an effort, or an ordeal, for him to recall. "Anyway," he said quietly, "there's no reason for me to go back. Everyone dear to me has long since passed to his or her reward."

"You have no family?" He shook his head. "Oh, I'm very sorry, David."

"An insufficiency of the genes, I'm afraid. No Hallowell or Radburne was ever celebrated for longevity." He clutched his blanket more tightly around him, smiling wanly at his expected fate. Then he looked at me with the sweet, devoted expression of a setter dog. When it was I who should have been wagging my tail at him.

"You will be celebrated," I assured David Hallowell, "beyond your wildest dreams. Leave that to me."

"Thank you," he said. "My friend."

I was braced for tears again; but the Mexican woman came to the door of the *casita* with a little tray: she had brought tea, some sugared oatmeal in a bowl. I took the tray from her. She look worried.

"Eat nothing," she said. "Many days, no *comidas.*"

"I'll see that he has some of the oatmeal. *Muchas gracias.*"

David was willing to be fed. But after a few gummy spoonfuls and half a cup of dark, aromatic tea he could manage no more. He lay down wearily, eyes closing.

"I'll sleep for a few hours," he said. "Until my muse shows up."

"Do you have much more to go?"

"It's almost done," he murmured.

"With your permission, David, I'll take these pages you've completed." I hesitated. "You have a copy of the manuscript, of course."

"No. Couldn't afford to make copies."

"Well, then. I'll see to it. And I'll be back tomorrow."

He thanked me, coughed, pressed a fist to his mouth, and drifted off to sleep that way. I let myself out and all but ran to my car.

I read the twenty new pages then and there, in an excruciating state of excitement. They were excellent. The wasting of his body and quantities of tequila had not in the least diminished his art. He was Faulknerian in his prodigality. Oh, a word might be changed here and there, a redundancy deleted. Nothing more.

For the next four days I arrived promptly at noon. I had forsaken pride and borrowed a hundred dollars from a faculty colleague with whom I had had an affair and who still entertained some hope the affair might be renewed, although she was one of those women for whom the sexual act seems to have the caloric input of a two-pound German chocolate cake: she had put on forty pounds through trysting. I purchased cough remedies which had only a temporary flagging effect on David's consuming cough, more tequila, painkillers. And many legal pads: David was using up more than one a night in a rage of completion. Each day the odor of violets, mysteriously present, masked the odor of dissolution in the *casita*. I was frightened for David, nearly sleepless at night for fear he wouldn't, after all, reach the dizzying conclusion of his novel.

A week after our first meeting on the running track at Sprayberry, I let myself in, and took a few moments to adjust to the portent that the odor of violets was absent from the *casita*. David Hallowell lay very still on his back, his eyes open and staring, a slight smile of peace on his lips. His ordeal had ended. In his right hand there was a note to me.

We have done it!

It was signed, *David*.

I gathered up the last pages of *Angels and Aborigines* strewn across his worktable and stumbled sobbing into the chicken-infested yard. The Mexican woman, children dangling haplessly from her swirling skirt, hurried outside and, hearing me, began her own lamentation. The children, one by one, contributed their voices. Dogs barked mournfully up and down the *barrio*.

"He has no family," I told the coroner. "He was the last of

his line. And, except for Mrs. Cerador and myself, he had no friends."

I sold my car, one jump ahead of the repo man, raising enough cash to retire the note and afford David Hallowell a modest but decent funeral.

The night following his burial I assembled all of the yellow pages in my studio, changed the ribbon on my Smith-Corona electric, drank two double scotches to fortify myself, then began typing the book I had been born to write.

ANGELS AND ABORIGINES
a novel by
Jack Mayo

I made a few editorial changes as I went along. Nothing major. Ten days later I mailed the typescript to an editor who had almost forgotten I existed, at an august publishing house in New York. The manuscript went through the house like wildfire. It knocked them all on their asses.

Angels and Aborigines was published the following spring, in a first edition of half a million copies. The Book-of-the-Month Club ordered an additional quarter of a million. Word of mouth secured the number one position on the *New York Times* best-seller list two weeks after publication. The novel stayed at number one through six additional printings, for eighteen glorious weeks. The reviews—ah, God, the reviews! Each one a nutritious sweetmeat, a seductive paean, an exaltation of a unique talent! I swept all of my peers under the rug that season—Norman, Philip, John. Even they came forth with tributes for the literary event of the decade. The King Rat currently in residence at the Dream Factory snatched the cheese from all the other rats, paying an unheard-of sum for movie rights. Thirty-three foreign editions were planned. The appeal of my novel was universal.

My novel, yes. Mine by escheat, if you will.

I had known what I must do, even before David Hallowell was laid to rest. Because—to be brutally honest about the matter—if I'd simply arranged for posthumous publication of the novel, it would have done far less well with his name on it. Perhaps *Angels and Aborigines* would have been grievously neglected. Those things happen. The bald truth is, publishers and the literati take little interest in dead authors, particularly those who have had the bad fortune to die without first establishing a reputation that will, you might say, tide them over. In taking credit for what David had written I was, in fact, ensuring the widest possible circulation for a great book. I assumed the role of literary celebrity and, I must say, played it with panache. This was a requirement for bestsellerdom that had to be fulfilled. It kept me busy for months. And as I read and reread the novel (some of the more wittily salacious passages made for uproarious cocktail party entertainment), it became rooted in my soul that I was the true proprietor of the words I recited.

For my services as executive consultant to the film version of *Angels and Aborigines*, my Hollywood agent obtained a fee equal to half the national debt of Ecuador. Production plans and major casting coups were to be announced and celebrated at a wingding hosted by the producer and the director, a thirty-year-old *Wunderkind* who—bless his heart —had yet to taste failure.

Much of the fun of having a party in Hollywood is to have it at a *boîte* which is so desirable that code names are assigned to the famous few allowed by the management to make reservations. There is more fun in deciding whom not to invite, and delivering invitations only on the day before the event. The howls of pain and outrage from the uninvited thus are concentrated into a short period of time, and the maneuverings of the newly disenfranchised to be included becomes a frantic shadow dance up and down the corridors of Tinsel Town.

I adored it all: exiting from a massive silver limousine, the press of *paparazzi* and plain folk swamping the sidewalk outside Gepetto's, the monstrous energy of allure released inside the packed café, the director's acknowledged indebtedness to me for providing the "raw material" for his next megahit; the camaraderie of the charmingly maniacal actor, a two-time Oscar winner, who was to essay the character of Lordy Lambkin in the screen version . . .

"I wonder what David would have thought?"

I was near the bar, looking for a refill, when she spoke. Perhaps not to me. But I turned anyway because, in spite of the atmosphere in the chic café, the mild scentings of fresh flowers and drop-dead perfume all around, the odor of violets was suddenly pervasive.

The room was filled with glamorous, world-famous women, but even in their company the youthful creature watching me with a questioning smile was unique. Perhaps because she seemed perfectly at ease when everyone else was trying a little too hard. She wore her red hair pulled severely back from her forehead; it was gathered in a cunning Psyche knot. There was a sweetness in her oval face, but not naïveté. Her gaze was direct, coolly sensual, slightly mischievous. She wore an almost piously simple, rather old-fashioned off-the-shoulder gown of some neutral, crushed fabric that shimmered with exotic color, like sunlight in the sea, each time she moved.

"I beg your pardon?" I said, sniffing audibly. I couldn't help myself. Her scent was familiar, and although it should have been pleasing, I had an adverse, almost allergic reaction to it: my skin suddenly felt clammy, my heart raced.

She edged past an old man in pigtails and a pink leather suit and stood in front of me, never taking her vivid blue eyes from my face. She was drinking one of those abominable Fuzzy Navels. Her nearness, the pungency of violets, made my eyes water.

"David *wouldn't* have liked it," she said thoughtfully, lowering her long-stemmed glass after a sip. "All the hoopla. I think we would have been someplace else right now, working on a new book. Isn't that what *you* think, Mr. Mayo?"

"I'm afraid I don't know what you're talking about," I said, too fascinated to avoid her strict gaze.

"I'm talking about David Hallowell," she replied. "The author of *Angels and Aborigines*. The book you stole from him."

"What a preposterous accusation! I don't know any David Hallowell!" A skeptical dimple appeared on one perfect cheek. I glanced around to see if anyone had overheard us, but the party babble was at such a level that our conversation, thus far, had been private. "Who put you up to this ludicrous jape? Who are you?"

"I'm Dierdre. I was David's muse."

I began to laugh, although I felt panicky. Somehow, somewhere, this beautiful, merciless girl had known David Hallowell, and he had told her about the book he was writing. What was she doing here now, and what did she have in mind? I could only try to bluff my way out of this predicament without exhibiting any sort of anxiety and thereby allowing that her accusation might be true. But my nostrils had dilated; I was again nearly anesthetized by the odor of violets.

"I think," she said, "you've recognized me already. Although, of course, since David worked nights we were never introduced."

"Are you an actress?" I asked her, manufacturing an air of good-humored resignation. "You're quite good. I hope you're going to be in the film. Would you like to meet the director? By all means, let me introduce you. Because you're wasting your considerable talents on this crude and rather insulting—"

"I have several hundred pages of an earlier draft of David's novel. Handwritten, on legal pad paper. A draft you never saw. Post-office copyright. It proves beyond any doubt who wrote *Angels and Aborigines*." She said all of this without rancor, as if she had no interest in intimidating me; a rueful little smile appeared as she finished. One eyebrow was slightly raised, inviting the denial she knew it was not in me to attempt.

"You were—a friend of his?" I said, when I could speak again.

"More than that. Much more. I told you. I was David's muse."

There was a twitching muscle near one corner of my mouth that I couldn't control. "Oh, yes," I said, desperately playing along. "Your perfume—the odor of violets. Is that what the gods are wearing on Olympus nowadays?"

"It isn't perfume. It's my natural essence."

"And your name is Dierdre. Forgive me, I thought I knew the names of all the muses. Calliope, Thalia, Terpsichore— and so forth. Not a Dierdre in the lot, however."

"I'm an apprentice."

"Oh, well, that does explain it."

"With everybody and his brother writing or composing something these days, they need so many of us. The Association took on ten thousand new apprentices the day before yesterday."

"I hope they all look like you."

"We come in all shapes and sizes," she said, not smiling now. "Why don't you have that drink you came over here for? You look as if you're going to pass out, Mr. Mayo."

I could see no reason for her to continue this labored and unfunny pretense, the exercise in humiliation she seemed determined to put me through. Obviously it was money she was after.

"How much?" I asked Dierdre. "How much do you want to keep your mouth shut?"

Dierdre lowered her eyes, and sighed. "I don't think this is the time, or the place, to discuss restitution."

"All right, when?"

"I'll be in touch. After the next Association meeting."

"The Association? What is that?"

"I'll let you know. Later." She raised her glass in a mock salute, smiled guilelessly, slipped suddenly through a gap in a shifting group of bodies. I started to follow her, felt a tug at my sleeve, looked down. It was our producer, a hunchbacked albino renowned for his conquests of ravishing women.

"Come with me," he said. "Want you to meet someone." He named a prominent studio honcho.

"Do you know who that girl is?" I demanded of him.

He looked around with alert bunny eyes. "If she works in the Industry, I know her. Which lovely do you have in mind?"

"There—the redhead." But when I searched for Dierdre in the mob I couldn't find her. I turned back to the producer. "The one I was just talking to."

"You've been standing here by yourself for the last ten minutes mumbling in your beard. Frankly I thought you'd had a couple too many snorts."

"You didn't see—"

"You look devastated, Jacky. Want a woman? Pick one. I'll personally see to it she's delivered to your doorstep at the hotel by one A.M."

I said something to the effect that I could handle my own love life, and went with him. I did not ask him if he also smelled violets. But the hypnotic odor persisted, like an olfactory illusion, although it weakened by the hour as I lay sleepless in my bungalow at the Beverly Hills Hotel. Wondering what the outcome would be and if, after all, it was only money that Dierdre desired.

I cursed myself for having believed David Hallowell's assertion that only the two of us had ever laid eyes on *Angels and Aborigines*. The solitude of the writer's trade can be agonizing: we must all, from time to time, seek the release of the confessional. The amateur wordsmith is particularly unable to keep silent about what he is up to. He must talk about his aspirations incessantly, even to a stranger on a bus. "I'm writing a novel." And so forth. Dierdre claimed to have an earlier manuscript . . . what, exactly, was her game? And who *was* she? How could I find out? After an hour of pacing and cigarettes I concluded that there was nothing I could do until she put an end to my speculation by contacting me again. I would simply have to wait.

For the next three days I stayed close to the hotel, anticipating, dreading her phone call. It was impossible not to think about Dierdre for more than a few seconds at a time. Despite the very great threat to my well-being she represented, I was perversely attracted to her, so much so that I scarcely paid notice to the numerous starlets and harlots available in the sexual marketplace where I was staying. Had she and David Hallowell been lovers? If so, then I was envious—of a man in his grave, from whom I had already appropriated everything.

Everything but Dierdre.

I swam in the pool, and at poolside I had meetings with the screenwriter, a well-respected hack who expressed reverence for my novel and seemed to have a few worthwhile ideas for translating it to the screen. The gardens of the hotel were lushly in bloom, there was a heated scent of roses outside my bungalow, but no violets to soothe my riddled nerves.

Her call came as I was having my sideburns darkened by Alberto in the hotel barbershop.

"Do you know what day this is?"

"The twenty-fourth of February," I replied, my heart pounding. "Why?"

"I thought you might remember," she said softly. "Well, never mind."

"Where are you? I want to—I think it's imperative that we get together."

"Do you know where the Bistro is?"

"On Canon Drive."

"I'll be in front at five o'clock." She hung up without another word.

I was driving a vintage Mercedes sports coupe which the producer had made available to me during my stay. Like many of the paranoids in his profession, he was terrified of muggers and kidnapers. He belonged to the Beverly Hills Gun Club. He had weapons in all of his automobiles. He proudly had shown me the hiding place built into the driver's seat of the Mercedes, the push-button release that ejected into his waiting hand a pearl-handled pistol with considerable stopping power.

At the end of the hotel driveway, waiting for the light on Sunset to change, I checked to make sure the gun was still there. The butt slapped into my palm with a little metallic click. I didn't know then why I found that so satisfying, why it made my scrotum crawl with pleasure. I've fired pistols, but I'm not an aficionado. I had never conceived of the possibility that I could do bodily harm to someone.

Even though it was growing dark I identified Dierdre's flame from two blocks away as I drove south on Canon in the rush-hour traffic. I was on the wrong side of the street to pick her up. I made a left turn into the driveway beside the Bistro, waving the parking valet away. Dierdre got in. As slender as I remembered her; "so coldly sweet, so deadly fair." Byron, I believe.

She wore tinted glasses and a fawn-colored pantsuit. Her red hair was loose and flowing. She carried a big purse like a saddlebag. She didn't say hello. The odor of violets was chilly in the weather she brought with her, exhilarating as the bouquet of a great wine.

"Where are we going?" I asked her

"Up the coast. To San Augustín."

San Augustín. I hadn't been back since resigning my teaching position at the college, shortly after the acceptance of my novel. My throat tightened.

"Why?"

"It's been two years," she replied, looking straight ahead. "We owe David a visit, don't you think?"

I realized then why she'd asked me over the telephone if I knew what day it was. February 24. The day David Hallowell died.

"Is that necessary?"

She looked at me, two seconds, her expression neutral. "Yes."

I could have refused. In traffic it would take more than three hours to drive to San Augustín. But the long drive would give me my chance to find out everything I wanted to know about Dierdre; the full story of her relationship with David Hallowell. It was even possible that—for her sake—I could persuade her not to take any action against me.

And if I couldn't—

Unfortunately she was not talkative on the trip up the Pacific Coast Highway. She answered questions sparingly or not at all. She seemed to be under a strain, not the assured, tantalizing amateur blackmailer I had met three nights ago. Finally I gave up trying to talk to Dierdre, willing to wait her out. Without harming my perceptions the odor of violets had a beneficial, lulling effect on me. I drove north with the confidence that the situation ultimately would be resolved in my favor.

The fog was rolling in as we reached San Augustín. The cemetery in which David Hallowell was buried lay on the slope of a hill only two hundred yards from the sea. With the fog lights on I crept up the winding access road past drab and dimly seen monuments to small deeds and inconsequential passions. The fuming fog cut visibility to less than ten feet. I had forgotten where he was interred. Dierdre seemed to know exactly, as if she had made many visits, after dark.

"To the left up ahead. There's a stand of oak trees and a crypt with a plinth. He's just down the path from there, near a wall that's parallel to the cliff."

"Now I remember," I said, my sense of well-being wearing a little thin. I wondered, for the first time, if Dierdre was in on this alone; if she was, then what was her real purpose in bringing me to a wayside cemetery under cover of the winter fog? The situation I had felt to be within my control was now unappealing.

Nevertheless, I stopped the small car by the trees, leaving

the fog lights on. Dierdre got out immediately. The leafless branches dripped moisture onto the canvas cover. I heard the swish and boom of surf across the highway below. There was a flashlight in the glove compartment. Before getting out from behind the wheel I reached down and released the pistol from its hiding place, slipping it into my jacket pocket as I closed the door behind me.

I didn't know what lay ahead, in the fog; but Dierdre looked back at me impatiently, waiting. Not as if she had devastating mischief in mind. Her blue eyes were wide and unwinking, like eyes in a portrait.

"This way." She led me to David's plot along a narrow path of stepping-stones, her essence—as she called it— sweetening the dismal, dripping air. I cast the flashlight beam on the little bronze marker, flush with the ground, that I had purchased. The sight of it brought back memories but prompted no remorse, if that's what she expected. If not for me, *Angels and Aborigines* probably wouldn't have been finished. And in what anonymous grave, crowded close to unwanted and unremarked men, would he now be lying? I was tired of indulging her fantasies of revenge, whatever they might be.

"What do you want, Dierdre?"

She looked up slowly from contemplation of the grave.

"I was hoping," she said quietly, "by now you would know what you must do."

"For a start, I want those pages you told me about. The earlier draft. Name your price."

She frowned, then opened her purse. I tightened my grip on the pistol in my pocket. But all she brought out was another bundle of the familiar yellow pages.

"I have them here."

"Just drop them on the ground." She did so. "There are no more pages anywhere?"

"No."

"I wonder why I don't believe you."

She turned her face toward the sea, livelier than this

boneyard, but invisible. "I'm going away tonight. I won't be back. It doesn't matter if you don't believe me. What matters is that you make restitution, in David's memory."

"I'm afraid that would mean the end of my career."

"You might try writing something of your own," she said sharply.

The night breathed mistily on my brow, its chill sinking to the roots of my heart. I suffered a momentary pang of self-loathing, and I hated her for judging me. She was very young; how could she know what it felt like, to be out of the running all of your life?

I took a step toward her. Our eyes met in a dead heat. I was shaking from anger, and desire. Goaded by her essence, repelled by the setting of death in which my lust was manifest.

"If I had the right muse—" I said, now throwing her own joke back in her face. "Why don't you consider taking the job? I'll treat you better than David Hallowell ever could."

She shook her head slightly. "I'm not the muse you deserve. But one will be provided—once you've admitted that you stole David's novel, then done everything in your power to ensure him full credit. That is the will of the Association."

"Goddamn you! What difference does it make to David now?"

"It's the right thing to do."

I knew then that she would never let me touch her. That she meant what she had said. She was going away. But I couldn't bear the thought that Dierdre would be forever beyond my reach—the one who *knew*, unforgiving.

I took the pistol from my pocket and shone the beam of the flashlight full in her face. She looked steadily at me, not blinking, bold eyes with no appreciation of danger in them, no fear.

"That doesn't mean a thing," Dierdre said. "You can't hurt me. I'm immortal."

"You're crazy," I said. "Or we both are." I raised the pistol a little higher and shot her between the eyes.

Something seemed to uncurl from the fog like the lash of a whip and snatch the flashlight from my hand. Dierdre disappeared without a sound; I was blind in the fog. Moments after I fired the shot I was seized by a clonus—a series of violent muscular spasms. Involuntarily I dropped the gun, then went to my knees beside David Hallowell's grave crying incoherently, anticipating some lethal, otherworldly blow that would end my own life.

But nothing happened. No one was there. I had no company but the disinterested dead, who now included Dierdre among their number. The flashlight, still in working order, lay a few feet from where I was kneeling. Perhaps, unable to bear the sight of murder, I had flung it there myself just after pulling the trigger.

I picked up the gun again and crawled to the flashlight. I looked through the fog for Dierdre's body. The purse she had brought to the cemetery lay near the low brick wall at the edge of the cliff. Gasping for air, I went to the wall and looked over it. The beam of light, diffused by fog, afforded me a glimpse of her tumbled body fifty feet below.

I wanted to search her purse, find out who she really was; but I couldn't chance leaving a fingerprint behind. I gathered up all of the loose yellow sheets of the draft manuscript, frantic that I might miss one, thus leaving behind a clue that eventually would point the bird dogs of the law in my direction. When I was sure I had them all I returned in a deathly cold sweat to the Mercedes and climbed inside. The pistol was in my pocket. I planned to pull off the highway on my return to the City of Angels and fling it well out to sea.

Before starting the car I looked through the legal pad pages I had carefully gathered up. David had written nothing on them; they were blank. Dierdre had been bluffing. She had no evidence of theft on my part. A pathetic attempt at blackmail had cost her her life.

But was it blackmail that she had in mind? I could no longer be certain. Perhaps she had prudently left the incriminating first draft with someone else for safekeeping. In that case, I was as good as cooked.

I was too traumatized to do anything but put some distance between myself and the lonely cemetery. Back at the Beverly Hills Hotel I opened a bottle of scotch, drank from the bottle until I was dizzy, then swooned across the bed. I dreamed, ghoulishly, of executions. Dierdre's. Mine.

I awoke, in a fever of apprehension, to the odor of violets in the bungalow. I sat up, a sob in my throat. I heard the clink of a bottle neck against the rim of a glass, the soft gurgle of liquor poured over ice.

She came toward me illuminated in her own pure radiance, holding the glass out to me.

"Drink this," she said. "You probably could use it."

"Killed you," I said in a pitiful croaking voice; my heart was slowly squeezed to the size of a peanut by a fist of iron.

She was wearing a simple white shift with a gold ceinture. One shoulder was bare. She had bound up her abundant, cedar-colored hair. Her forehead, where the bullet had smashed it, was now unblemished. Her expression was businesslike, as if she were there only to serve me.

"I told you," she said. "I'm immortal."

I took the whiskey from her hand—real flesh and blood to my own, stony fingers—and gulped it. The fist that gripped my heart relaxed and blood surged to my nearly comatose brain. I found that I could breathe.

"I really hoped you wouldn't fail me," Dierdre said. "That you would want to do the right thing. But I guess it isn't in you, Jack."

She spoke mildly, as if rebuking a puppy that had displeased her. I said nothing, only stared into her bright, strict eyes. Was I dreaming? Insane? If this was insanity, I was willing to make the most of it.

"What do you want me to do now?" I asked, desiring

soak a handkerchief in scotch and hold it to my nose as I
went out to the living room, intending to ring the front desk
and complain.

It was sitting in a wing chair by the fireplace, facing me. If
it could be said to have a face. Watching me. If it could be
said to have eyes. It waved a hand—no, no, no, how could
one call such a barbed and bloated thing a human hand!—
leaving a phosphorescent wake of putrefaction in the air.
There was a seething corona, as of tainted, primordial gas,
all around it. The thing belched more gases and rumbled
and laughed at me. Yes, that sound could be interpreted as a
laugh, though it was so dreadful I knew I was condemned to
hear it repeated even in those few hours of exhausted sleep I
would be entitled to for the rest of my natural life.

"Long as you're up, pal," my muse said to me, "why don't
we get to work?"

nothing more than a smile of favor in return fo
capitulation.

She didn't smile. "You're strong. Healthy. Good
another twenty years, at least."

I nodded hopefully.

"Now you will get the chance to earn the fame you've
so cheaply."

"How?"

"You're going to *write*, Jack. Write, and write, and wri
As many as eighteen or twenty hours a day your muse will
with you, scarcely letting you rest."

"Doesn't sound so bad," I said, and reached out to pu
her into bed with me.

She drew back politely before I could touch her.

"Oh, no, Jack, it won't be me. I have another assignment.
You'll be getting a different muse."

"Who?"

Dierdre looked away from me. "The muse you deserve,"
she said. "The Association is adamant about that."

"That isn't fair! I deserve you! I'm famous! I want—"

Her celestial light dwindled to the size of a rubied ladybug
in a corner of the dark room, turned scintillatingly and took
wing, flew through the wall. I tumbled frenziedly out of bed
and went to the spot where she had disappeared, standing on
a chair to reach it. The spot was warm and glowing to my
touch; an essence of fresh violets stung my eyes. And then
the ravishing odor faded. I felt deserted, bereft. And a little
frightened.

I poured myself another three fingers of scotch. The clock
on the mantel in the living room whirred and chimed, four
times.

A noisome odor was seeping into the bedroom, perhaps
from outside the bungalow. An effluvium of Southern
California's patented smog, mixed with—oh, God—dead
cat and overripe refuse and spoiled eggs, almost everything
unpleasant and sickening that memory could recall. I had to

Horrorshow

1

The ☆Star-Light☆ Drive-In

Nealy Bazemore stopped on the way to his shift at Lockheed for breakfast at the All-Niter Trucker's Haven, which he did whenever his wife overslept or was out of town visiting relatives. The waitress he'd been casually hitting on, Taryn Melwood, was talking to some freak at the other end of the counter: young guy, tall and gaunt, but who could tell for sure about his age the way he wore his hair, and there was some gray showing in his straggly beard. He looked well-traveled. Taryn smiled as if she were really interested in whatever line the guy was handing her; but that was part of her job. Nealy fidgeted until he was able to catch her eye. Taryn came down to his end of the counter after drawing a mug of coffee for him.

"Running late this morning," she commented.

"Yeah." Nealy glanced at the bearded guy and the greasy blue backpack beside his stool. "Get all kinds off the road, don't you?"

"Hero? He's not so bad. He's from England, how about that? Been in here off and on the last couple weeks."

"Say what? 'Hero'?"

"That's what he says to call him. I can't pronounce his regular name. He's into all kinds of interesting stuff: astrology, and, you know, reads palms. Anyway, what are you having this morning, Nealy?"

"What do I always have, darlin'?"

"Coming right up." Taryn bustled off to relay his breakfast order to the kitchen.

Nealy only had a few minutes, and Taryn was always busy at this time of the day, so when she served him his eggs over easy and sausage links he said,

"Gaynell's gone on down to Columbus to help out while her sister-in-law's low from her gallbladder, and Gaynell's mama has the kids. I got me two tickets for George Strait at Six Flags which I hate to see go to waste, so like I was wondering—"

Taryn didn't say anything, just glanced at him in a lively way before picking up another order and hustling it down near where the bearded Englishman was getting up from his stool. Taryn gave the shabby traveler a quick smile and a shrug to indicate she didn't have the time to talk or get her palm read.

Nealy watched them, his lip curling. *Well, tough luck, pardner. You're just not that little gal's type.*

Nealy had known Taryn, his wife's third cousin, most of her life, and had coveted her since she was a ripe fourteen. She was coarsely blond with brown roots, kept her hair that way on purpose, and it didn't look tacky because she was young enough to get away with anything. She had big dark brown eyes and made them appear bigger with a lot of eye makeup, but she never bothered with lipstick. Her lips were naturally red and so well-shaped it gave him palpitations when he thought about kissing her.

The bearded guy passed behind Nealy with his backpack, and Nealy smelled him: not dirty, exactly, but pungent, an outdoorsman's taint as if he slept in the woods. Nealy's eggs got a little cold because he couldn't concentrate on anything but Taryn and her teasing non-response. She took her time getting back to him.

"You're not through with that?" she said, looking at his plate.

Nealy nodded and reached for a toothpick. Their eyes met. Taryn gave a little what-the-hell shake of her head and shoulders and smiled and said,

"What time?"

"Six-thirty?"

"I'm in *love* with George Strait," Taryn said severely, as if that let Nealy out. But Nealy felt close to bursting just the same.

"You living over at the Walking Ford Trailer Park?" he asked.

"Uh-huh. Don't come in, though. Place is chockful of double-wides, and they all look alike. I'll meet you out by the main entrance. Still driving that silver-and-black Subaru?"

"Best damn truck I ever owned," Nealy bragged.

Nealy made it through the day without much on his mind but Taryn Melwood. He showered and shaved again when he got off work, polished his boots and put on a string tie. He bought a case of chilled Bud Lights and headed on down 41 to the trailer park, arriving promptly at six-thirty. Taryn was waiting for him, wearing a cute skirt that showed all of her kneecaps. With trick-or-treat eyes and her hair standing out from her head in a calculated tizzy, she looked, the way most of them looked at eighteen, like all of those hard-boiled female rock stars on MTV.

"That hat you got on is just like George Strait's!" Taryn exclaimed, getting into the cab beside him.

"Yeah, well, does it look as good on me as it does on ol' Texas George?"

Taryn was in a generous mood. "Nearly as good."

"That's okay, honey, I'll take second place in your heart anytime." Nealy reached behind him for a beer. "Want one?"

"No, and you don't neither. Drinking and driving don't mix, Nealy."

"Honey, I'm gonna have just this one, then I won't pop another top until after the concert."

Taryn sat close to the door with her arms folded.

"I hope not. My best friend Marlene's just a damn vegetable after what Ollie did to their Torino. Not to mention the kid who went through the windshield."

"I'll get rid of this one right now if it bothers you all that much."

"I just figure I got too much to lose, Nealy. No bout a' doubt it."

Nealy took one long sip, then threw the Bud Light can into a ditch; Taryn started to warm up to him again right away. Their date was all he could have hoped for, and George Strait put on a hell of a show at Six Flags. The crowd made him sing "Amarillo by Morning" twice. They stood down front and Taryn held on to Nealy with both hands, although her eyes seldom left the stage. Nealy wasn't unhappy about her devotion to the country singer, figuring that all the unrequited affection in her small body was just going to flow his way once they left the amusement park. Taryn clung to him all the way through the parking lot, and when they were alongside his Subaru, Nealy gave her a quick kiss, which she returned open-mouthed and with a little pelvic thrust to go with it.

"Hey, darlin'," Nealy said in a husky voice, "you want to come home with me tonight?"

"I kind of do," Taryn said, and they snuggled all the way back to Carver County, so close she had to shift gears. Taryn even shared a beer with him.

Taryn went straight into the bathroom when they reached Nealy's house. He opened another beer and went through a small collection of video tapes he and Gaynell kept way back on the shelf in their closet where the kids wouldn't be likely to find them. He put *Miami Hot Bodies* on the VCR, then took off everything but his undershirt and his pearl-gray Stetson. When Taryn came out of the bathroom wearing only a pair of lime-green panties she glanced at the action on TV and smiled.

"I don't need that to get in the mood," she said. She was slightly flushed all over, as if she'd been looking at herself in the mirror and biting her lip and fingering her nipples to make them hard. "I'm in the mood already, no bout a' doubt it." Nealy's own body temperature rose a couple of degrees.

Taryn sat on his knee and helped herself to his can of Bud Light. A little of the beer ran down her chin, and Nealy was quick to lick it off.

Taryn chuckled and was trying on his hat when they heard a car in the drive. She looked Nealy in the eye and said, "That better not be who I think it is."

But the dogs weren't barking, which was the tip-off. Taryn hit the floor running, shut herself in the bathroom, then thought better of it. She came out with her clothes in both hands, trailing her dusky pantyhose, dropping a Capezio. She was still trying to pick up the shoe, swearing under her breath, when Gaynell came in the door calling cheerfully to her husband.

"Dora wasn't near sick as she thought she was. Nealy? You awake? What's that moaning and groaning, honey, you looking at those sexy movies again? Shoot, those women can't do a thing I can't do better."

"Get your pants on!" Taryn whispered to Nealy, who was just sitting in shock at the foot of the bed with his hat covering his hard-on. But it was already too late to think about getting dressed; Gaynell was halfway down the hall. Taryn shook her head in exasperation, squared her shoulders, and when Gaynell reached the doorway and came to what looked like a skidding stop said sweetly, "Hello, Gaynell. I reckon I was just leaving, wasn't I?"

Gaynell got her jaw back in alignment and said to her sorry-looking spouse, "You *didn't*. Did you? Nealy Bazemore, you good-for-shit peckerwood!"

"Didn't do a thing," Nealy mumbled, as if he were drunk or dazed.

"And that's a fact," Taryn said indifferently, forgetting about her wisp of a bra and pulling on her blouse. There were red spots on her cheeks.

"Yet! That's what y'all mean! Didn't do nothing *yet*, just fixing to. Afraid to show me what you got under that hat, Nealy? And *you!* Taryn Melwood, you goddamn little tramp, it's high time somebody whipped your butt to a frazzle!"

"Not *my* butt needs whipping," Taryn said resentfully, staring her down while hastily buttoning the blouse over her breasts. "Just give me half a minute more and I'll be out of here, and we'll forget all about this."

Sensing her equal in Taryn, Gaynell turned on her husband, who was still sitting with his knees together and his hat in his lap. Despite his circumstances he couldn't keep his eyes from the TV, where an acrobatic redhead and two young men were coming to simultaneous climaxes.

"In my house! How do you get the goddamn nerve to hustle up this piece of trash as soon as my back's turned— bring her to *my* house—the bed *I* sleep in—"

Gaynell gushed tears like a dynamited dam, looked around for a weapon, seized an ornate metal-framed photo of her parents and started to heave it at Nealy. He went backward off the bed. Gaynell hesitated in mid-throw, saw that she would probably miss, and looked at Taryn. Gaynell was, in spite of her outrage, afraid of the girl, who she knew had a lot of meanness in her. Her third choice of a target was the TV, with its exhausted, groaning lovers. She hit the TV dead center but only cracked the protective screen. Gaynell wailed at her ineptitude, turned and ran from the bedroom.

Taryn balanced on one foot to slip on a shoe.

"Where do you keep your guns?" she asked Nealy.

"Den. Gun cabinet's locked."

"Gaynell any good with a butcher knife?"

"How the hell would I know?"

Taryn put her other shoe on. "You just may be about to find out." She parted the drapes, raised a shade, and kicked out one of the window screens.

"Hey," Nealy protested, "where you going, hon?"

"Nealy, you horse's butt. Want me to stick around and we'll all play Trivial Pursuit later? Here she comes back again. Don't call me. No use to tell her where I work, neither, because I just quit."

Taryn heard Gaynell start up again inside the house. Nealy yelled back at her, finally showing some balls, Taryn thought as she crossed the front lawn. Nealy's hunting dogs were in an uproar in their kennel. Taryn, walking fast, hit the road and didn't look back.

The night was warm, almost sultry. Not a breath of air stirring. There was a three-quarter moon overhead. Taryn paused for a look around. It was late, almost two-thirty in the morning. And here she was stranded a long way from the Walking Ford Trailer Park.

Taryn put her hands on her hips. The least Nealy could do was give her a lift home, but she wasn't about to go back into his house and wind up the innocent victim of a serious domestic disturbance. She looked at Gaynell's car, a white late-model Camaro she hadn't taken very good care of. The engine was still ticking. All Taryn needed, she figured, was the keys. Later she could call them and tell them where to find the Camaro.

She went reluctantly up to the porch.

Gaynell was loud and obscene, having reached that stage where she was practically begging Nealy to hit her. He'd hit her, all right, raise a couple of lumps, and by then Gaynell would be so turned on he'd have to fuck her, which was the other thing Gaynell was after; by morning they'd be lovey-dovey again.

Taryn looked through the screen door. Gaynell had dropped her purse on a lamp table in the living room. Her key ring was beside the purse.

Taryn opened the door a squeaky few inches, tiptoed inside the living room. Gaynell was screaming that if Nealy paid half the attention to her she deserved, then he wouldn't have to go scrounging for pussy on the side. Taryn smiled tensely. She snatched up the keys with a surge of elation and beat it; she didn't care if they heard the screen door banging shut behind her, but probably they hadn't. There was a lot of breakage going on simultaneously with Gaynell's recriminations. And good old Nealy had that fed-up tone of voice that meant he was about to take his hand-tooled leather cowboy belt to her.

To Taryn's ears the Camaro sounded like a cement mixer when she started it, but she didn't care about that, either. Unfortunately the damn car shook until her teeth rattled. Didn't Gaynell know about tune-ups? Not only did the Camaro handle badly, it was almost out of gas. Taryn headed south on the Etowah Pike toward an all-night Spur station at the intersection with U.S. 41.

The Camaro had a coughing fit just as Taryn passed the Mt. Pisgah cemetery and almost directly in front of the long-shut ☆Star-Light☆ Drive-In theatre, where she'd spent many Saturday nights when she was in middle school, giving and receiving sticky kisses and learning basic anatomy. The car coasted to a full stop a hundred yards past the barricaded theatre driveway. Steam was rising from under the hood. Taryn smacked the steering wheel and the horn honked feebly. She couldn't believe how bad her luck was tonight.

The pike was deserted; in this part of Carver County there wasn't a house or a light for half a mile. The front seat of Gaynell's car was a pigsty: cookie crumbs and styrofoam containers from Burger King and a plastic baby bottle with some soured milk left in it. Taryn was disgusted at the prospect of sitting tight until somebody came along to help her out. A couple of mosquitos were giving her fits. But it was a good two miles down to the highway. What the hell was she supposed to do?

Taryn rolled up the windows to keep other insects out and slouched uncomfortably, arms folded, teeth gritted, wishing she had a Coke and a joint. She stared through the bleary windshield at the pale oblong of the drive-in screen, trying to remember the last picture she'd seen there. Who she'd seen it with. Oh . . . it was that dumb jock Luther Phillips, who'd got her so hot and then had to go from car to car looking to borrow a rubber off somebody. Taryn made another effort to get comfortable, wondering what had happened to ol' Luther—

The windshield took on a glow and Taryn raised her head.

Lights of a car, or a truck, traveling north. Taryn gave serious thought to her options. Her heartbeat had picked up and her skin was prickly.

Uh-uh.

Trying to flag down a stranger on a deserted road could lead to a lot worse things than a couple of boring hours in a stalled car. Better to lay low and let him—or them—pass by.

Taryn scrunched down behind the wheel and waited. It was a pickup truck (she guessed) from the sound of it, maybe Nealy's. She wondered if he'd finished whupping that bitch Gaynell and was out looking for her. Maybe if she just sneaked a peak—but if it really *was* Nealy, he'd know his own wife's car; by now he'd have stopped and hollered for her. Also the truck was coming from the wrong direction, not from the vicinity of Nealy's house.

Taryn continued to lay low as the pickup idled opposite the Camaro. Now her heart was really thudding. The driver had turned his side-mounted spot on the parked car. If he was sitting up high in the cab of that truck, couldn't he make her out? Taryn slumped lower, her chin almost touching the steering wheel.

Finally—it seemed like half a lifetime to Taryn, with that big spot lighting up the Camaro—he got tired of looking at whatever he was looking at, and drove on.

Taryn breathed heavily, more shaken by the experience than she cared to think about. She felt trapped in the Camaro, bathed in sweat, itchy all over. *Maybe,* she thought, *this isn't the best place for me.*

Because someone else could come along any minute, looking for something to rob, and when he found her in the car—

Taryn raised up enough to look back over the seat. The pickup truck had disappeared on up the road; at least she couldn't make out the taillights, and she could see pretty well to the point where the road curved past the cemetery hill.

She grabbed her purse and got out of the Camaro, then remembered the keys and reached back inside to take them from the ignition. She had an idea, for what it was worth. There just might be a safe place close by, where she could spend what was left of the night.

2

One Dark Hour to Go

Before abandoning the Camaro, Taryn opened the trunk. Even without a flashlight she found what she was looking for, a tire iron. She took it with her.

There was no problem getting to the drive-in. The road was barricaded off the pike to keep kids from driving down there and parking, and to keep out those people looking for a place to dump trash. The main gates, she was sure, would be chained. But the road was unobstructed beyond the barricade, just a little weedy, with slash pine close on both sides. She walked watchfully by the light of the moon down the middle of the asphalt road, not wanting to turn an ankle in a chuckhole.

The box office was just that, a box not much larger than a telephone booth, and empty—no place to sit or lie down in there, and when she looked through the barred ticket window she heard a scuttling noise. Rat, maybe. Taryn shuddered and went on to the gates. The high wall of the outdoor theatre echoed the slightest sound: pebbles kicked away as she walked, a flattened aluminum can skittering over the blacktop . . . her own breathing, but maybe she just imagined she heard that.

It was spooky here, she had half a mind to go back. But

when she turned and looked toward the pike she could barely make out the Camaro parked there. She had come a long way. And she was suddenly afraid, achingly afraid, of being out here by herself in the middle of the night.

Just as she'd thought, there was a big rusted padlock on the gates. She used the tire iron, making a lot of noise as she pried the hasp of the lock out of the wood. She tried to ignore the noise and concentrated on thinking about the good times she'd had here just a few years ago, when the ☆Star-Light☆ was about the only place in the south county where, if you were underage, you could still have some fun. Part of the fun had been to sneak in for free, usually in the trunk of Walter Bevins's old Caddy. All of them just about suffocating if the line was long . . . but she didn't want to think about suffocating, she was feeling crawly up and down her spine, and beginning to panic.

The lock-plate screws pulled out of the old wood of the left gate and Taryn staggered back, dropping the tire iron. It missed her foot but grazed an ankle. Grimacing, she stooped to rub the anklebone and, in the midst of this movement, saw something, like a partially shielded flashlight beam in the pine woods beside the drive. But it came and went so fast she couldn't be positive what it was. Just a wink from a strong light.

Was somebody out there?

Oh, Jesus, Taryn thought, and she groped for the tire iron. When she had it she stood with her back to the gate, knees together, staring at the woods, breathing through her mouth, a habit carried over from childhood when she was unhappy or overwrought. But there was nothing more to see. Nobody drove by on the pike. She glanced down at the L.C.D. display of her watch.

Twenty minutes to four.

Only one dark hour to go, then the sky would begin to lighten and there would be southbound traffic, early birds on their way to the Perimeter to work, she'd get a ride home . . .

Taryn tucked the tire iron under one arm and pulled at the heavy rusted chain that held the gates together, cringing at the noise she made but desperate to be inside, not just standing there with the moon full in her face, casting a smudge of shadow against the fence boards, the faded remnants of old movie posters pasted there.

Eastwood, Redford. Those were some *real* men. She regretted the impulse that had prompted her to go out with Nealy Bazemore, even if they were related on his wife's side. All along she'd planned to go right home after the George Strait concert, although she was well aware of what that cuss Nealy had on his mind, but then something happened like it always happened, she couldn't help kissing him, and after the kiss she'd thought, *Well, just this one time, even if he is a married man* . . . shit! Now look. Stranded at the damn ☆Star-Light☆ with—

With nothing. Stop it. Nothing and nobody's here, you're all by yourself and it's maybe a little more than an hour to sunup, so stop! Just stop scaring yourself.

Straining, Taryn shoved open the heavy gates, slipped into the drive-in, paused for a few moments, trembling from exertion, then put all of her weight into closing the gates behind her.

There.

She felt better right away, at home here and oddly, nostalgic as she looked around at the acres of hard-packed clay in front of the single screen, which was dilapidated after more than four years of neglect, shot full of holes in a few places from kids using it for rifle practice. But she remembered how the screen had looked in the theatre's heyday, with huge misty images playing over it, films she hadn't paid all that much attention to except for *Rocky* and *First Blood*—when Stallone was featured at the ☆Star-Light☆ Drive-In she was there to see the movie, period. There had been in-car speakers once, but they were long gone, only a squat forest of iron pipes set in cement remained. To her right was the low building that once housed the projection booth and refreshment stand. The neon had been removed from above the long counter, the iron grill was down and probably locked. She assumed the projection booth was locked up too, but her tire iron would get her in.

As she headed for the building Taryn smiled, thinking about the time she and Jaymie Walraven had laced Becky Pratt's strawberry Frostee with Milk of Magnesia, getting back at Becky for putting caterpillars in Jaymie's popcorn— *caterpillars,* gross! She couldn't remember which of them had come up with the idea to spray-paint *Lost my cherry to Hilda Berry* on Steve Webley's car while he and Hilda were bare-assed in the back seat. But the worst, absolutely the *grossest,* thing that had ever been perpetrated at the ☆Star-Light☆—

Taryn came to a dead stop, freezing from the roots of her hair down to the small of her back.

The door of the projection booth a dozen feet away was not locked, as she had anticipated. Because the door was opening, even as she stood there gawking like a ninny at it. Creaking just a little on its hinges. Opening slowly, so slowly—

She was off like a shot, running a weaving course through the stuck-up pipe posts, just missing a couple of them, knowing she must not slow down to look back but more afraid of not knowing who might be after her, how close he was: so she risked it, glanced wildly over one shoulder and saw—Taryn stumbled to a stop, leaned against a decapitated post, and was choked with laughter, even as her heart continued trying to jump into her throat. She tingled all over.

The cur dog she had disturbed was still standing a few feet outside the doorway, looking at her, probably as scared as she had been. At a glance she realized he was too thin and pathetic to be any kind of threat to her—but there went her idea of spending an hour or so in the projection booth, not after that dog had been hanging around. More than likely the booth would be a flea circus, and flea bites were worse than mosquito bites anytime.

It crossed her mind then that there must be a hole in the fence somewhere. After four years, maybe several good-sized crawl holes. And she'd gone to all that trouble, breaking in through the gates . . .

Her heart was calming down and she wasn't breathing so hard. Taryn looked up at the screen and imagined Stallone bare to his waist, gazing down on her, the eyes of a man who knows he has what it takes, choice pectorals gleaming with sweat, *God:* where was Sly now that she needed him? Funny how after a big enough scare you could start feeling horny, just like that, and she mildly regretted that she and Nealy hadn't had the chance to get it on before Gaynell showed up. Never had any use for Gaynell, Taryn reflected. Nobody else in the family did either, really: "the bitch from Grinder's Switch," they called her, poking fun at her backcountry origins.

Taryn was still gazing at the movie screen when a sudden sharp yelp caused her to jump a foot. She looked around but couldn't locate the cur dog in the darkness beyond the projection booth. The door was still partly open; had he gone back inside? Then what was it made him yelp that way?

Silence, now; a silence she didn't particularly care for.

Taryn shuddered, crossing her arms, fingers digging into her forearms. From a long way off she heard the diesel horn of a train near the Carverstown yard of the Chessie Railroad. She needed to pee. But she felt embarrassed, for no good reason. It was just an unnerving thing to do, as if she could picture herself squatting and then suddenly the whole drive-in would be filled with cars, like the old days, head-lights focused on her and everybody laughing, *There's Taryn with her pants down!* She could even hear Stallone chuckling, *huh-huh,* up there on the—

Blank, empty theatre screen.

What an imagination! No bout a' doubt it, she was purely wasting her time with counter jobs. Ought to be out there in Hollywood right now, giving them the benefit of her good looks and talent.

Make up a movie, just to pass the time. Go ahead. What kind of movie would you like to be in, Miss Melwood honey?

Well, let me see. There's this champion stock car driver, only he's no good anymore after a bad wreck, lost his confidence or whatever. And, uh, then there's this rich girl, that's me, she's got *so much* money, but her life doesn't have any meaning. Uh, the stock car driver, who looks a lot like Bill Elliott, is down on his luck, and she needs a chauffeur, or maybe a bodyguard, because there's this real crazy guy who's been calling her up on the phone—

"Don't move. If you turn around I'll kill you."

The jolt of fear at the nape of Taryn's neck was powerful enough to pop her mouth open. *She hadn't heard a sound.* But he'd sneaked up so close behind her she could smell him—and his odor was instantly, powerfully familiar.

"Oh, come on!" she said, exasperated. "It's me! Don't give me a hard time, because I've already had—"

As she started to look around, a blow to the back of her head staggered her.

"Shit!"

"I said not to do that! Now, sit down. First we will have the Light. Then we will have the Truth."

"You really hurt—"

"Sit cross-legged, with your hands on top of your head. Do it now!"

He seized her by the back of the neck; a strong thumb pressed against her carotid artery. Taryn couldn't speak. Her knees locked and there was a surge of blackness to her brain.

Sensing she was going to faint, he eased the pressure on her throat.

Taryn took a shuddering breath which broke as a sob. She

sank slowly to her knees on the hard Georgia clay, then sat down as he had dictated. Because his tone of voice allowed no alternatives.

"Hands on top of your head!"

"Why are you *doing* this to me?" He was acting big-time bad drunk; but, no, he hated liquor, he had never taken a drink that she knew of.

"First the Light."

Taryn moaned.

"I haven't done anything! I ran out of gas. You saw my car—I *know* it's not my car, but I didn't actually steal it, I can explain—"

The beam of a powerful flashlight illuminated her. She gasped and bit down on her lip. She began to tremble so violently her teeth cut the underlip and blood trickled down her chin.

"Don't hurt me—love of God, *please*—"

"Are you a whore?"

"No. Yes! I don't know, just don't hurt meeee!"

He walked around her; then the beam of the flashlight was full in her face. Taryn shut her eyes tightly. Her bitten lip smarted.

"You're bleeding. But it was *Jesus* who bled for you."

Why, why, was he carrying on like this? "Oh . . . yes. Sure, I know that."

She heard something. A zipper. The sound chilled her.

"You need a lesson. You've needed one all your life. Isn't that true?"

"I don't know! Listen, don't make me do it! I won't tell nobody about this, I never told before. I never did! I just want to go home!"

"Open your eyes."

"It's too bright!"

He lowered the beam of the flashlight. Taryn blinked her tearing eyes. He was standing three feet away. His pants were open.

"Is it beautiful?" he asked softly.

"Uh-huh," she gulped.

"Isn't it the most beautiful one you've ever seen?"

"Is that—all you want?" Her eyes took in the flashy hunting knife in his right hand and saw that it was slicked with blood already. Dog blood? If he'd kill a poor homeless *dog*—she flinched, gagging on fear, the taste of her own blood. Her lower lip was swollen, it felt as sore and vulnerable as the naked breasts beneath her blouse. "If we—if I—do it—then you won't hurt me?"

"How do you know what I want you to do?" he said harshly.

Taryn guiltily lowered her head. The clay between her legs was soaked. She smelled the pee. But at least the odor was so strong she didn't have to smell *him*. Her trembling lessened. The shock of what was happening to her began to have a numbing effect.

"You can stand up now," he said in a disinterested tone of voice.

So that was all there was to it—he'd come already, from the pleasure and excitement of seeing her wet herself, from the aphrodisiac of animal terror that still racked her. She dared to raise her eyes, and was disappointed. No, he hadn't come, he couldn't even sustain a weak erection. So of course he wasn't going to let her go, not yet.

"Taryn, I want you to stand up."

"Okay." Anything to appease him. No telling why he'd gone crazy like this, but it didn't matter, *living* mattered; somehow—she couldn't think straight, but the impulse was sound—she had to get away. Yet she could barely stay on her feet. She had a cramp, couldn't stand up straight. Worst of all, she was soaking wet.

"Take everything off," he said.

"Oh, no," Taryn groaned.

"You have seen the Light, and you know the Truth. Now it's time for the Punishment."

"Why do you keep talking like that!!"

"TAKE OFF YOUR CLOTHES!" he shouted, and made

a quick, darting move with the knife that ended only two inches from her breasts.

"I'm going to! But you won't—you couldn't—please don't cut me! I'll do anything you want me to do so long as you don't cuh-cuh—"

She tried to unbutton her blouse. It was no use, her fingers functioned only as blunt hooks to rip and tear the material. His light drifted up from the ground to center on her navel and breasts. He looked at her for a long time while she hung her head, breathing through her mouth, trying not to be sick and add to his obsessive enjoyment of her humiliation.

"The rest," he said finally.

"I never thought you c-c-could do a thing like this t-to me."

"God speaks to me, and I obey him."

"You don't even go regular to—"

"Filthy, lying harlot! Strip yourself naked and *bow* to the will of the Lord God Almighty!"

She looked up tearfully but could not see his face. No matter; she knew it too well already. He who now named himself God. Past him the oblong theatre screen was bisected by the flight of an owl. Taryn took off her skirt and her lime-green panties and stood with her hands clenched over her breasts, hiccuping. The heat in her breast was turning to anger. With his free hand he was playing with himself. And that roused hatred—she *hated* him, and all the men like him in this world: liars, drunks, perverts, betrayers. The pitiful weak men who swaggered as they pretended to be strong, and just, and true.

"Why don't you suck that thing yourself?" Taryn said wrathfully. "Because *I'm* sure as shit not about to."

He dropped his penis and made a fist. Taryn fell back a step, staring at the upright blade of the knife in his other hand.

"*Run,*" he commanded, and she took to her heels, with no direction in mind.

The sudden freedom, the invitation to flight, was exhilarating. Weaving in and out among the iron posts, she ran faster than she had ever dreamed she could go. The night air seared her lungs. But he would follow; she knew that. It was part of the torment he'd made up his mind to visit upon her, a little part of the revenge on all the young girls he lusted after and was no good for.

As she ran Taryn had a glimpse of something that gave her hope and a desperate sense of renewal, the will to defeat him. He was going to spend the rest of his life in jail for this night!

The fence at the front of the drive-in on either side of the big screen was seven feet high. Taryn stood five-four; she knew she couldn't reach the top of the fence without climbing on something. But there it was, in the darkness, parked against the wall. A two-wheel trailer with a sign mounted on it, a portable marquee the ☆Star-Light's☆ owner had driven around town behind his station wagon to advertise the weekend double features: his last futile attempt to stay in business after the eight-screen theatre complex opened at the new mall.

Now Taryn chanced a look back and saw the beam of the flashlight slashing up and down through the dark as he jogged after her, confident she would succeed only in running herself into the ground. Taryn cut sharply to her left and raced toward the trailer. She mounted a soft rotting tire and pulled herself to the narrow tilted top of the marquee. As she stood on her toes reaching for a handhold on the fence the blinding beam of his flashlight isolated her.

She had one leg up and was pulling herself over when something like a piece of pipe or a club struck her hard in the ribs. She didn't fall, but the pain was so bad she couldn't summon the strength to push herself the rest of the way over. Then he was there: a hand clamped on her dangling foot and he jerked her down from the wall. Taryn screamed in pain when she hit the ground; a boot with a thick tread stepped on her throat. The light was full in her eyes again.

"You've had your chance to run," he said. "Now crawl for me."

When she didn't move immediately, he kicked her.

Taryn bucked and groveled, sobbing for breath.

He kicked her again, in the buttocks this time, once, twice—she began to crawl, pulling herself away from the marquee trailer, from his heavy boots. He followed slowly, kicking her from time to time, muttering under his breath. Then he went down on one knee in front of her and seized her by the hair, yanked her head up until her throat was taut.

She could see nothing but the bright light in her eyes.

"You're all dirty," he complained. "Time for you to wash in the blood."

Then Taryn saw the flash of the knife in his right hand, felt the sharp blade slicing through the skin of her hairline. Blood gushed down her face, blinding her.

She got up so slowly that at times she appeared static, posing grievously. Both hands were cupped to her forehead, filling up with blood as she tried to stanch the heavy flow from the cut that had half-scalped her. He had rocked back on his knees and was praying. Taryn stumbled away from him, crying, barely able to see where she was going. She fell twice, muddying herself in the red dirt, her own blood. After a few minutes she no longer heard him praying. It was her own voice she heard now.

"I don't want to die want to die want—"

On her knees again, the pitted theatre screen looming over her, wide as the sky, empty as a desert.

What kind of movie would you like to be in?

She was oblivious to him shuffling up behind her; she ignored the clutch of one hand on her shoulder because she was engrossed, now, in what she saw on the screen, the images of her life flashing by until the downward chop of his knife to the nape of her neck stopped the show with one last brilliant pulse of light that became a luminous river stretching on and on before her, forever.

3
Point of Fatality

He awoke at dawn with a headache, muscles cramping in his calves and wrists. He had the familiar sense of undefined anxiety that told him there had been an Occurrence.

Hieronymus "Hero" Flynn attended to his discomfort by concentrating on the rays of the unseen sun, the God Belus whom he worshiped, keystar of the Sabian religion. He had far to journey before he became a master; but his will was strong. He had made good progress in the treatment of his affliction during his three weeks' sojourn in this cosmically significant point of the Western Hemisphere, not far from a place called Carverstown, in Georgia.

By the time his body was more in concert with the human soul and his breathing had slowed to a just-perceptible six breaths a minute, the sky had lightened. He rose from his sleeping bag and hung it over a low branch to air it out while he walked down the path to the public area of Shoulderblade State Park. He had been living in the park since shortly after his arrival in the U.S., following long stays in Bolivia and the Yucatan.

The man-made lake was down several feet after a prolonged summer drought. This time of morning there were only a few solitary fishermen in the coves. A pale gold streak of daylight shone across the main body of water, and the concrete face of the dam three-quarters of a mile away was a soft rose shade.

Hero used the public toilet and rinsed his mouth, wincing at the sting from a bitten tongue, a typical consequence, along with a brutal headache, of the Occurrences. When he came out of the building the early, airy virginal odor of pines and other growing things had been diluted by the smoke from a breakfast cook fire, bacon frying. All was serene beside the lake except for the discordant yammer of a television turned too loud in one of the caravans parked in the area reserved for them.

As he did every morning, Hero took the path uphill through the pines to the Indian burial mounds, grass-covered hillocks approximately twenty-five feet high and scattered irregularly over a few acres. The site was several thousand years old but had never been more alive, cosmically speaking, due to certain conjunctions of benefic lights and planets and the energy these conjunctions discharged upon this particular plot of ground. It had been foretold by a Mayan priest he had discovered on the Belize-Honduran border that this site would be of vital concern to Hero if he desired to correct himself in this lifetime, to once and for all be free of the physical encumbrance that had persisted from a past life misspent in Babylon, some 3,500 years ago.

But today he found it difficult, perhaps because of the most recent Occurrence, to align himself properly with emanations from the unexcavated burial site, so rich in harmonics which enhanced his own earthly vibrations. He was saturated with the knowledge of another's death.

After twenty futile minutes of effort at concordance, uneasy from the sensation that he was urgently required elsewhere, Hero rose and returned to his modest camp. There he was instantly sensitive to the fact that something or someone had been prowling about—no, not an animal. He discovered no footprints to conclude that it had been a man, and as far as he could tell, his belongings had not been disturbed; yet a spoor remained in the air . . . he sniffed gently, downwind, nostrils vaguely offended by the lingering odor of smoke.

Tobacco, not wood smoke. It might have been one of the caravaners, passing through on a morning stroll, enjoying his pipe. Hero's fellow campers were, for the most part, a congenial lot. He did not, however, like the vibrations he was receiving here, where serenity had been the rule. Perhaps they were some of his own unquiet vibrations, left over from the nocturnal Occurrence.

But as he stood there motionlessly, absorbing all that the clear, ethereal morning had to describe, he began subtly to tremble, a quaking of anguish, reaction to an intuition of threat. In the jungles he had developed an ability to sense, even at a distance, where a jaguar had dragged its leftover kill through the undergrowth to lodge it in a tree for safekeeping until mealtime came around again. He was preternaturally attuned to violent disturbances of nature, down to the most insignificant clash of warrior ants from different nests. Crossing Chickamauga in the northern part of Georgia, he had suffered excruciating mental pain on that Civil War battlefield, smelled the powder and the blood as if it had happened yesterday and not more than a century ago.

He was suffering now, but still he had no idea why. It was some beastly imprint left in the delicate harmonic fabric he had woven in his temporary sanctuary, unwelcome knowledge of a feast or ritual of blood.

Hero shuddered. What did it have to do with him? Now he must move, find an undisturbed place where he might continue his meditations until, four days from now, heavenly configurations involving the burial mounds reached a climax.

When he opened his backpack to replace toothbrush, soap, and hand towel, there was a sudden flare just outside the angle of his vision. Startled, Hero looked up and froze, his hands clenching involuntarily. Fifteen feet away, stretched between the slender trunks of two young pines, he saw a giant, radiant web that he was sure had not been there earlier. The web was roughly in the shape of a wheel and divided into twelve sections, like the twelve houses of the zodiac. And on the wheel, positioned in the Eighth House, the astrological house of death, was a stellium of spiders that glittered like jewels in the sun's rays. He recognized the astral symbols by their colors: the great red god Mars, ruler of the Eighth House, was square to Saturn on the Ascendant. The white binary Algol, most malefic of stars, was aligned with the Dragon's Tail and combust the sun. There were afflictions everywhere he looked: but nothing disturbed him more than the Arabic Point of Fatality, which by his calculations was exactly in opposition to the Lord of the Fourth House—the end of things.

Yesterday he had idly solicited her birth date and hour, intending to present her with a horoscope delineation in lieu of the breakfast or lunch tips he could not afford. He had not yet got around to casting the horoscope, but he knew without a doubt, staring at the silken web and the twinkling implications of violent death stretched between the trees, whose nativity it was. Even the time of death was apparent to him, and the motive—

Sacrifice.

So that was the Occurrence, the seizure he could no longer remember, the cause of the disordered vibrations all around him! Hero sank slowly to his knees even as the angle of the sun was shifting, the pattern of the cosmic wheel dimming to his eyes. Poor girl, poor girl—a vision of Taryn Melwood came to mind simultaneously with the onset of another, uncontrollable Occurrence. There was pity in her eyes, pity for him, as she turned to the eastern source of the light that was about to consume her. Taryn pointed—telling him—yes—what, *what,* Taryn? But she was quickly gone, and nothing remained in his mind but the sere whiteness, a sort of blazing Eternity toward which his soul drifted while his body convulsed on the ground.

4

The Red-Haired Messenger

Gaynell Bazemore was awake not long after the roosters, sitting up with a cigarette and looking at her snoring husband in the bed beside her. All in all she didn't feel too bad about their most recent dustup—her ribs were sore where he'd popped her one, but she'd gotten him back: he had a humungous lower lip, and there was a little raw patch where she'd pulled another hank from his already-thinning hairline. After a brief slugfest they'd settled down to working it out in bed, their usual method for putting grievances behind them.

By now Gaynell had forgiven Nealy for slipping around, apportioning blame between herself (a little) and Taryn Melwood (a lot). A woman was a fool not to accept the fact that men were just going to go after pussy if it was available; and that little bitch Taryn was *always* available. Plenty of women found Nealy attractive, and why shouldn't they? In the ten years they'd been married, Nealy had never missed a day's work, or got drunk and hit her in front of the kids. He kept their house in good repair and was always nice to Gaynell's mother. Gaynell didn't have a single woman friend whose husband could compare. She had a lot to be grateful for; she just hadn't paid enough attention to Nealy lately. Made up for it pretty good last night, though. If it was pussy he was wanting, then by God she'd keep so much pussy in his face the next week or so he wouldn't be about to go whiffing the honey in another woman's hive.

The snoring stopped abruptly, and Nealy turned over

against Gaynell's bare hip. His nostrils twitched as he smelled her cigarette.

Without opening his eyes Nealy muttered, "You awake?"

"Uh-huh."

"It's Saturday morning, Gaynell."

"I just got to missing the kids, so I thought I'd run over to Mama's early and maybe take everybody to the waffle house for breakfast. That sound good to you?"

"Well, reckon I ought to get old Hitler down to the vet's first thing, have Doc look at that torn dewclaw."

"Want to give me a little sugar first?" Gaynell said teasingly.

"Whoo, honey, I just don't know if I got my strength back yet. Maybe I need to go back to sleep another half hour, you wake me up before you're gone on, hear?"

Gaynell got up and showered, brewed coffee, looked for her car keys but couldn't find them. That didn't bother her, she was always forgetting where she'd put them, but when she went outside with the spare ignition key they kept in a vase on the mantel and found her car missing, she needed about three seconds to get up a head of steam equal to her anger at seeing her husband buck-naked with a distant female cousin flaunting herself in a pair of lime-green panties.

"That does it, goddamn it, I'm calling the Sheriff and she's going straight to jail!"

Nealy scrambled up in bed, wide-eyed.

"Huh? What's matter?"

"She done took off in my Camaro, that's what's the matter!"

Nealy licked his sore and swollen underlip. "Taryn?"

"Just who the hell you think I'm talking about? Helped herself to my keys and drove right off! She thinks she can just help herself to anything she wants around here, but she's got another—"

"Hey, hold on, now, Gaynell. It was kind of late, and Taryn didn't have no way to get home—"

"I don't believe what I'm hearing from you! Too goddamn bad she didn't have a way to get home! What was she doing here in the first place?"

Nealy held up a hand. Gaynell heeded the warning and backed off to look for cigarettes. When she had one going she said, "Are you aiming to do something about this, or do I have to do it? I want my Camaro back, Nealy." She turned and went down the hall. Nealy hopped out of bed.

"Where you headed, Gaynell?"

"Call the Sheriff. Have her arrested for car stealing."

"Bull *shit*. Just give me a minute, we'll go and get your car back. No harm done."

Gaynell paused in the living room, hand on the telephone.

"Oh. You know where she's living these days?"

"Walking Ford Trailer Park."

"Just how many times you been over there to see her, Nealy?"

"There's no need to get cranked up again. Let me pull my pants on and we'll fetch the car. If she's the one that took it."

"She took it, all right." Gaynell frowned and then, unexpectedly, she laughed, snorting smoke out of her nostrils.

"What's so funny?"

"What's funny is I made it the last twenty miles home on the fumes. She couldn't've got far. Maybe three or four miles down the pike."

"Okay," Nealy grumbled. "I'm up now. We'll get a move on."

"You sure I'm not putting you out none?"

"Jesus, Gaynell."

Gaynell laughed again. "Bet you she had to walk some after all. I would like to seen her face when that tank run dry. I hope she had the good sense to leave my car where nobody could crash into it."

They drove south on the Etowah Pike toward Mt. Pisgah cemetery and the ☆Star-Light☆ Drive-In, Gaynell at the wheel of the Subaru pickup and Nealy sullen by her side sipping from a mug of coffee, still not fully awake. The sun was just up when they spotted the Camaro. Gaynell pulled up behind it and leaned on the horn, as if she expected Taryn topop up out of the back seat. To Nealy's relief the Camaro was empty; apparently she'd hitched a ride.

She'd also taken the keys with her. Nealy got out the five-gallon jerry can of gas he'd brought with them. Gaynell looked the Camaro over to see if Taryn had done any damage or removed something that didn't belong to her.

"*Hey! Hey!*"

Gaynell backed out of the Camaro and glanced at Nealy, who was putting gas in the tank.

"Who's that?"

"*Hey! Help!*"

"Kids," Nealy muttered, looking around to see where the voice was coming from. "There they are, down by the Drive-In."

"What do you reckon's the matter?"

"Don't know. Here comes one of them."

The boy, a redhead about twelve years of age, was running up the blacktop drive toward the pike.

"Sure enough in a hurry about something."

"Nealy, that little kid's got him a gun, honey."

"Lever-action .22, looks like. They're just out doing a little shooting, hope they didn't shoot one of their own by accident."

"Hey, mister!"

"What's the problem?" Nealy yelled back, but he had a bad feeling just then, a visceral coldness he couldn't explain.

"We got to get help!"

"*What happened?*" Gaynell called, but she had a look on her face, of unrealized terror, that must have matched Nealy's own expression. She'd always been a little afraid of red-haired children. In her scheme of things they were like black cats and one-eyed granny women: certified hoodoos.

"There's somebody dead in the drive-in! She's dead, all right! You got to get help!"

Nealy put the gas can down and took a step to Gaynell's side. She grabbed him around his waist and hung on for dear life.

" "Oh! My! God!" Gaynell said, her throat locking after each word.

Nealy squinted at the red-haired boy coming up to the pike, and at the other boy, who was standing just outside the gates of the ☆Star-Light☆ Drive-In with his own rifle over one shoulder and a thumb hooked inside his belt.

"She's dead! She's lying there dead! Somebody done stabbed her all over! Get help! Get help!"

"Oh, shit," Gaynell moaned. "Nealy, is he putting us on?"

"I don't think so. I might better go find out."

"Nealy—ohhh, Christ. I am not *believing* this! It can't be her—!"

"Shut up!" Nealy snapped. His color had gone bad. "Sit you in the pickup. I'll follow on the boy, and he just better be telling the God's own truth. If you see me in a little while down there by them gates waving my arms, you know to get on the CB and fetch the Sheriff out here."

"Oh, God!" Gaynell wailed, backing away from the Camaro as if it now represented everything that had ever gone wrong in her life. "Why didn't I have the good sense to stay in Columbus?"

5
The Set-Up

Lieutenant Bob D. Grange of the Carver County Sheriff's Department knocked on the boss's door and then after five seconds had passed, he let himself in. The Sheriff was sitting behind his desk with his face in his hands. He was still wearing the fisherman's vest, decorated with colorful little puffs of hand-tied flies, he'd had on when summoned to the office. Saturdays he always went fishing, so they'd known where to locate him in a hurry. He was listening, on tape, to what Nealy and Gaynell Bazemore had had to say an hour ago in Grange's own office. The Sheriff neither moved nor spoke to acknowledge the Lieutenant's presence.

When the tape was finished, he turned off the machine and looked abstractedly out the windows at the market-day traffic on West Fourth Street in the heart of the Carverstown business district. Sheriff John Stone was a tall man with bright blue eyes and an unusually large, leonine head that made his frame seem insubstantial.

"Bob," he said, "all my life I've tried to keep that little girl out of trouble. I tried my best, and I just don't understand how this could have happened."

"You know how sorry I am."

Still staring out the window, Stone reached into a desk drawer and fumbled for a small photo album. He held it in his lap and thumbed through the mylar photo protectors until he came to a snapshot of a woman with a head not unlike his own, a shoulder-length mane of blond hair and piercing eyes.

"Caddie and I never got along so good when we were kids. But I swore to her on her deathbed I'd look after Taryn."

"I know you did your best."

"I don't think she was ever a bad girl, even though she didn't show good judgment when it came to picking her friends. Like that woman she was renting from down there at the trailer park."

"The one that was busted for hooking two years ago in Chattanooga?"

"When Taryn turned eighteen, there wasn't much more I could do. She would have been just nineteen, come October." Stone swiveled his chair away from the window, looked up at Grange. Two deep brackets on either side of his mouth lengthened his face, saddened it. "What all have you got?"

"M.E.'s preliminary report just came over."

"Sexual assault?"

"Don't appear to have been rape."

"What else?"

"Taryn was—" Grange lowered his voice, as if that would make the brutal facts easier to bear. "Well, there was just a multitude of stab wounds. Any one of at least a dozen could've been fatal to her. Also she was beaten. Stomped hard enough to break some bones."

Sheriff John Stone's eyes went out of focus and he lowered his large head in an attitude of pain and sorrow.

"Have the body taken over to Daimler's when they're through with it. I'll talk to Ike Daimler later about arrangements."

"Yes, sir. The two boys who found her are in Arby's office, and the Bazemores are in mine."

"Let the kids go, they've told us all they can." The Sheriff got up. "I want to talk to the Bazemores. Give me about ten minutes, then we'll take another statement from them."

Grange nodded. "I didn't think too highly of what they were telling us the first time," he said, and followed the Sheriff out of the office.

In Grange's office Nealy and Gaynell Bazemore were sitting in a couple of thinly upholstered chairs pushed back against one wall. Gaynell, a caffeine addict, was on the fourth cup of coffee she'd had since arriving at the Sheriff's station. Her eyes were red and dry. Nealy twisted his hands slowly and chewed aspirin.

"Morning, Nealy," Stone said. "Keeping you all busy down there at Lockheed?"

"Yes, sir, they are for a fact."

"Gaynell, how are the kids?"

"Oh, Curtis is just growing like a weed since he had his tonsils out, and Kipper's the same old booger bear."

"Your mama making it okay?"

"Well, you know, her sciatica's acting up, but Mama's always been the bravest soul. You can't keep her down—you know Mama."

"I ought to. Best-looking woman I never married." He said this with an attempt at a smile, then sat on the edge of Lieutenant Grange's desk and sipped at the mug of coffee he'd brought in with him, which had Garfield the cat in a Santa Claus suit on the side. Stone looked at the Bazemores, mildly but with a slight air of disapproval that soon had Nealy so ill at ease he couldn't find the right attitude for his body in the straight-backed chair. The phone rang, but Stone ignored it.

Gaynell burst out, "I want you to know we're just heart-broken about this!"

Stone sipped coffee and continued to stare at them.

"Do you know who did it?" Nealy mumbled, keeping his head down and his eyes on the scuffed black-and-white tile floor.

"No." Stone put his mug down. "You know, I took Taryn into my own house when she had no place to go. It was that or the county shelter, nobody else in the family could do a thing with her. She was, what, barely ten years old? By then I guess it was already too late. Now, Roberta, if she hadn't of been bedfast, might have been a powerful influence, but it was all just too much for me to cope."

"Well, God bless you for trying to help her!" Gaynell said passionately.

"Nealy, are you fixing to be sick?" Stone inquired of the squirming man.

"No." Nealy cleared his raspy throat. "Reckon there ain't a thing left on my stomach to heave up."

"You're welcome to go out and use the bathroom, then come back."

"No, I appreciate it, Sheriff, but I think I'll be okay."

"Why don't you go on out anyway, take a turn down the hall, have you a drink of water, let your head clear, if you know what I mean. So you'll be ready to tell me the complete truth when you get back in here. Otherwise the two of you just might be sitting right where you are for the next couple days and I ain't crapping you negative."

Gaynell looked appalled. Nealy stared steadfastly at the floor, his clenched hands between his knees. The phone rang again. Gaynell, Mrs. Coffee Nerves, jumped slightly. Stone smiled bleakly at her. Gaynell's mouth turned down at the corners, and she looked hatefully at her husband.

Stone said, "Folks, I have been in law enforcement for thirty-three years. Set here thisaway the Lord knows how many thousand times and heard all the stories there is to tell. You want to know how many people have lied to me in thirty-three years? It's a simple computation." He leaned forward to emphasize his point. "They *all* lied. They lied a little, or they lied a lot, at least to begin with. Now, I hope you're just lying a little, Nealy. And that you honestly didn't have anything to do with Taryn's death."

Gaynell drew a breath through her teeth as if she'd put a hand to something red hot.

"How could you say a thing like that? Nealy was with me the whole night, Sheriff, and that ain't a word of a lie! I'll swear it on my daddy's—"

"The whole night, Gaynell?"

"Well—"

"Where were you when Nealy was getting it on with Taryn earlier in the evening? Out bowling?"

Nealy's head came up. "Sheriff," he said hoarsely, "we *never* got it on!"

"The autopsy'll find that out beyond a reasonable doubt. Now, then. You're the one that took her to Six Flags to see George Strait, which is where Taryn's roommate said she was going?"

"Yes, sir, I did. I, uh, left that out when we was talking to—"

"And Gaynell, you weren't home when Nealy and Taryn got there?"

"No, I was on my way back from Columbus."

"What time did you get to the house?"

"I reckon it must have been about two-fifteen."

"Where were Nealy and Taryn?"

"They was . . . in our bedroom."

"I guess you pitched a fit."

"That's right, I surely did."

"Mad enough to kill her, Gaynell?"

"I was, but I didn't," Gaynell said, and she broke down sobbing.

Stone let her carry on, staring at Nealy all the while.

"Then what happened?"

Nealy said hoarsely, "Taryn got her clothes back on and took off."

"You didn't give her the loan of the Camaro, then, so she could get herself home?"

"She sort of borrowed it off us without asking."

"And run out of gas down there by the drive-in theatre?"

Nealy nodded. "That must have been what happened."

"How long had you been dating Taryn before last night?"

"I never taken her out before. I'd see her now and then at the All-Niter, where she worked the counter. Sometimes I'd have me some breakfast there before the early shift."

"She talk to you about any of her other boyfriends?"

"No, sir. I don't have no idea who—" Nealy fell silent, thinking about something that intrigued him greatly.

"Whatever's on your mind could be helpful to us, Nealy."

"Well, I don't know how important—"

"Go ahead, son."

"There was this guy at the All-Niter, and he was coming on to her big-time. She told me his name was Hero, or else that was just a nickname, Taryn didn't know his real name. He was just one of those itinerants, you know, with a beard he never trimmed, and his jeans was so shabby he must have got them out of a church barrel. Had a big blue knapsack with him. Taryn said he was in the All-Niter a lot."

"Biker?"

"I don't know if he owned a bike, I never seen him on one. There was just something about him I didn't take a liking to."

"Sheriff, I'm the one needs go to the bathroom," Gaynell said, sniffing.

"Okay."

Nealy said with a little laugh that came off mean, "Gaynell just can't hold water when she's nervous."

Gaynell turned in front of him and began earnestly to kick his ankles and shins, swearing at him under her breath. Stone got up and pulled Gaynell away from her husband, turning her toward the door.

"All right, now, Gaynell, I don't want to have to put you in a holding cell until you cool off."

Gaynell lifted her chin and, without another look at her husband, who was wincing and trying not to rub all the places where it hurt, she went outside.

"I don't know what else I can tell you, Sheriff."

"You ever stop to think, Nealy, that one of these days you'll get hold of one who says she's eighteen when she's not? We're talking twenty years in this state."

"I heard *that*." Nealy's shoulders began to quake. He

sobbed, "I'm not ever going to forget what she looked like, lying there in the drive-in. God, I'm so sorry!"

"Would you recognize him again? The one Taryn called Hero?"

"Yeah, I'd know him anywhere. I just hope you can find the bastard."

Stone looked him over. Nealy already had it fixed in his mind that the bearded drifter had killed Taryn. Well, that wasn't so bad. "If he's around, we'll find him," Stone said. He sat again on the corner of the desk and took out his cherished corncob pipe, which he stuffed with a dark and evil-smelling tobacco from a leather pouch. He lit the tobacco with a kitchen match from another pocket of his fisherman's vest. There was a little dirt under one of his thumbnails. He stared at it, then used the other end of the extinguished match to clean under the nail. This time when the phone rang, Stone answered and spoke softly.

"Believe we're ready for a new statement," he said. "Also there's somebody we need to be looking for, Bob. Nealy'll fix you up with a first-class description."

6

Lime-Green Panties

Deep in meditation, Hieronymus Flynn was aware of the dog's presence before he heard the Deputy Sheriff speak; it was as if they were all underwater, he could make no sense of the words. Only the inflection of authority was clear.

"I said for you to get up now, and put your hands on top of your head!"

Hero began, with difficulty, to focus on the here and now. He was sitting crosslegged on a spongelike mat of pine needles and other woodland litter beneath tall, gently swaying trees. The sun was setting. There was a glint of light on the gold-toned badge and nameplate the deputy wore on his shirt, on the short chromed chain that held an eager German shepherd in check.

Hero smiled at the dog, which whined but sat back obediently. He had no such easy communication with the deputy, who faced him from ten feet away holding a walkie-talkie in his other hand.

"I want you to get up from there and do what I tell you, and I want you to be mighty quick about it!"

There was movement on the path behind the deputy, Don Maxwell according to his nameplate, and another uniformed man—older, shorter, pudgier, with impeccably styled gray hair—came into view. He wore lieutenant's bars on his collar.

"Harve," Maxwell complained to the newcomer, "he wants to give us a hard time. Been sitting there like he's in some kind of trance."

"Meditation," Hero said, his voice a little thick. "I've been meditating."

"You have a name?" the gray-haired Lieutenant asked him.

Hero pronounced it for him carefully, then said, "But most people find it easier to call me Hero."

"That so? Not from anywheres around here, are you, son?"

"I am from Sheffield, England."

"Um-hm. Stand up for us, please, Mr. Flynn. Just keep your hands in sight and place them on top of your head. If you make any kind of sudden move, Deputy Maxwell here will turn the dog loose."

"It's all right to let her loose," Hero said with a smile. He got to his feet, raising his hands slowly, as he'd been told to do. "She wouldn't harm me, in any event."

"Don't believe you want to take that chance, Mr. Flynn. This here's a trained attack dog."

"I practice kinship with all forms of life," Hero told him.

"What else do you do with your time? Which you seem to have plenty of to waste. Now, just turn around slow, hands on your head, I'm going to do a body search."

"Is something wrong? I don't believe I was disturbing anyone."

Hero, his back to the deputies, closed his eyes momentarily while the Lieutenant's stubby hands patted him down from his neckline to his ankles. He felt uneasy, not from being roughly touched, but because the position he found himself in—feet spread, elbows out, fingers laced on top of his head—was eerily familiar to him. In Bolivia the police had lined him up facing a wall, and beaten him senseless with rifle butts. But this wasn't Bolivia, and he couldn't be in any danger. No, it was *her* again. She'd been forced to stand like this, and then—dear God—

A shudder went through Hero, nearly staggering him. He saw it again, the oblong white space that mystified him, and Taryn's flitting, ghostly form, running, naked, across—but he couldn't identify where she was.

"What's a matter?" the Lieutenant said with a trace of contempt. "You enjoy it when my hand gets close to your balls like that?"

"I am not a homosexual," Hero said.

"You don't seem to have any kind of identification. Mind telling us just who you are?"

"My passport is in my knapsack. Also my traveler's checks—you will see that I am not an indigent—and my address book, with the names and telephone numbers of many friends and relatives who will vouch for me."

"What's that bracelet on your wrist? One of those medical ID's?"

"Yes. I have . . . a form of epilepsy."

"I see. You just stay standing there, Mr. Flynn, while I have a look at that passport and the rest of your belongings."

"I believe it is unlawful for you to search my knapsack without my permission."

"May I have your permission, Mr. Flynn?"

"By all means. I have nothing to hide."

Hero stood patiently. The dog growled, but not at him; a squirrel perhaps. There were mourning doves in the nearby trees, a buzz of boats on the sunset lake below, the shouts of children.

"Been in this country a little more than three weeks?"

"Yes, that is correct."

"How long have you been camping at Shoulderblade?"

"I believe I arrived on 27 July." Hero heard the click of the blade on the horn-handled knife he carried with him.

"Have any other weapons in your possession?"

"I don't consider the knife to be a weapon—only a tool."

The Lieutenant grunted skeptically. Hero's bedroll was shaken out.

Hero said, "She *is* dead, isn't she? But why on earth should you suspect me of doing harm to Taryn?"

Silence. He heard the Lieutenant walking up behind him.

"You can turn around, son."

Hero turned slowly and looked into the eyes of the gray-haired deputy.

"How well did you know Taryn Melwood?"

"I talked with her several times at the restaurant where she's employed."

"You been here in these woods all day?"

"I moved my camp this morning. I was closer to the public area before."

"You don't appear to have a radio. Maybe you overheard something about it while you were down there using the crapper."

"The—? Please, would you tell me what's happened?"

"Taryn Melwood was killed last night. A maniac got hold of her and cut her to ribbons."

Hero's eyes rolled back in his head, but this time he'd had sufficient warning and was able to block the seizure.

"Hey! Hey, sit down, Mr. Flynn, take it easy. You on some kind of medication for this epilepsy you got?"

"No," Hero said, but he accepted the invitation to get off his feet. The shepherd pulled Deputy Maxwell a couple of feet closer to Hero. "Medication interferes with my efforts to effect a healing through holistic and cosmic means. It could only delay or abort my progress. I've become sensitized to the onset of seizures, and quite often I am able to—"

"I don't feel like you're making perfect sense, Mr. Flynn. I'd like for you to explain how you knew Taryn Melwood is dead."

"I intuited the fact of her death during an Occurrence last night, and then again very early this morning."

"Explain what you mean by—"

"In everyday terms, I frequently have clairvoyant and clairaudient experiences."

"Oh, well, that flat does it. Mr. Flynn, you're going to have to come along with us."

"What do you mean? Are you arresting me?"

"No, sir. We just want to ask you some questions in town. But first I need to have a look at that campsite you occupied before you moved up here on the hill. Think you can remember where it was?"

"Yes, of course. I'll show you."

"Bring your backpack and your bedroll with you."

Hero gathered up his things and led them, in the lingering dusk, down the hill toward the lake and the public area. The caravan park was full. Men were pitching horseshoes to one side of the children's playground.

"Do any fishing while you were here, Mr. Flynn?"

"No, I don't kill creatures for sport. Nor do I eat their flesh."

"Must have been tough on you, finding something to whet your appetite at the All-Niter."

"Not at all. I ordered bacon, lettuce, and tomato sandwiches, and had them hold the bacon. Here we are."

The deputies looked around. They saw nothing to indicate that anyone had camped there recently: the area was immaculate.

"Didn't you ever build yourself a fire?"

"Fires aren't allowed away from the public area. But I seldom have need of a fire, no matter where I am."

"Donnie, turn Sugarpie loose here a minute."

"Yes, sir."

As soon as the shepherd was off the leash, she came up to Hero, sniffed at his desert boots and frayed jean cuffs. Hero regarded her with a relaxed smile. When Maxwell snapped his fingers the dog wheeled and began coursing through the area, pausing only to pee next to a stump. Maxwell snapped his fingers again. Sugarpie began doubling back, suddenly broke off, and stopped to sniff the needle-covered ground by a mossy boulder.

She barked, then began digging with both front paws at the base of the boulder.

The Lieutenant glanced at Hero, who was paying no attention to the shepherd. His gaze was fixed on the shining surface of the lake, as a powerboat towed a pair of skiers in the direction of the dam.

"Let's heave that rock out of the way," the Lieutenant said. "Mr. Flynn, you just stand quiet there. Move without my permission and I'll have to put Sugarpie on you, and I guarantee you won't find her as friendly as she's acted toward you so far."

"I can probably budge it myself, Harve," Maxwell said, inspecting the boulder. "Looks like it's been moved already. There's pine needles stuck to one side here." The deputy squatted, keeping his back straight, and slowly turned the boulder over. He whistled, and Hero returned his gaze from the distant shoreline of the lake. There was a lump in his throat, a tingling in his hands.

"Harve, come have yourself a look at this!"

Maxwell rose and took his revolver from the holster, stood facing Hero while the Lieutenant walked over to the boulder and snapped on his flashlight. He studied what had been concealed beneath the boulder.

"What are you looking at?" Hero asked them.

The Lieutenant reached for a stick and lifted a pair of heavily soiled, lime-green panties from the ground.

"I reckon you never have seen these before?" he said to Hero.

Hero shook his head.

"Or that knife that's lying there all gobbed up with her blood?" The Lieutenant's face was reddening from outrage. "Mr. Flynn, I'm placing you under arrest for the murder of Taryn Melwood." Hero heard the click of the hammer on the other deputy's revolver as he cocked it. "Donnie, will you kindly read this son of a bitch his rights after you cuff him?"

"Hands behind your back," Maxwell said, circling Hero carefully.

"This is a mistake," Hero said, his voice calm though his heart was hammering. "I could not have killed Taryn Melwood, or anyone else for that matter. I am not capable of violence."

"Maybe you had some help," the Lieutenant suggested.

"I had nothing to do with her murder! Someone, obviously, wants it to look as if I did! Given time, I should be able to discover who that person is."

"Is that a fact?" The Lieutenant walked back to Hero as the cuffs went on. He stared belligerently at their suspect. Youthful, despite the gray in his beard, his sun-parched face. "You are some piece of work, Mr. Flynn. I don't believe I've ever run across any such as you before."

"No," Hero said. "I'm quite sure you have not."

7

Sheriff John Stone, Please Leave Me Alone

They booked Hero at the Sheriff's station, a one-story brick building on West Fourth Street, opposite the County Court-house, at 8:45 P.M. He was made to shower and given a starchy prison coverall to wear—white cotton, a size too small for his six-foot, three-and-a-half-inch frame. He was placed in a holding cell, one of six, in the basement of the building. Hero was by himself; other cells were occupied by a couple of crackers sleeping off prolonged drunks.

He asked for and received his pocket-sized ephemeris, and a thin paperback book on the Sabian symbols.

At ten minutes after ten jail deputies came for him and he was escorted, handcuffed, to the office of Sheriff John Stone. There were two other deputies, in plain clothes from the department's homicide division, in the room with the sheriff. Their names were Boodleaux and Tucker. Boodleaux had a sandy complexion and a cliffhanger of a nose over a thick mustache. Tucker was portly, liver-spotted, and balding.

There was another German shepherd in the office, lying on a rag rug. Tucker called him "Beauregard" and fed him french fries from a McDonald's carton. Beauregard looked old and infirm, too old for active duty. He glanced at Hero without curiosity, lost interest in the french fries, and put his gray muzzle down between his front paws to doze.

Stone said, "Mr. Flynn, this is a formal interrogation pertaining to the murder of Taryn Melwood, eighteen years of age, resident of the Walking Ford Trailer Park, Carver County, Georgia. Before we begin, I would like to be sure that you're aware of your rights in this investigation. Were those rights read to you by the arresting officers?"

"Yes, they were."

"And you understand that you have the right to remain silent prior to obtaining legal counsel?"

"Yes."

"Do you wish to make a statement at this time?"

"I have been apprehended for and falsely accused of a crime I did not commit. I fully intend to cooperate with you in finding the true murderer."

"Is the identity of this person or persons known to you?"

"Not yet, I regret to say."

"How do you intend to cooperate with us?" Boodleaux asked him.

Hero tried to make himself comfortable in the metal folding chair they'd given him, but the crotch of his jumper was tight and there wasn't much he could do with his manacled wrists except keep his hands in his lap.

"It would be most helpful if I could be released from jail immediately. Then, if I had something of Taryn's—an article of clothing, a piece of jewelry perhaps, something she was wearing just before she was killed—I might then be able to visualize a likeness of the one who killed her."

Stone idly scratched the top of his leonine head, staring perplexedly at Hero.

"There's no way you'll be released from jail before the arraignment next week. Once you've been formally charged, I frankly don't see any possibility of bail. You're a long way from England, Mr. Flynn. Without friends or relations in Carver County. No visible means of support."

"I had four hundred dollars in traveler's checks when I was arrested."

"You still have them, in safekeeping. What I mean is, you're thirty-three years old according to your passport. You're not a student and you don't currently hold a job. Bail bondsmen wouldn't touch you, in the unlikely event the arraignment judge sets bail for your crime, which is one of the most vicious I have beheld in all my years in this office."

"I see. Then, if I may have something that belonged to Taryn—not to keep, just to hold in my hands for a few moments—I believe her soul has not yet left the earthly sphere, and she's tried to contact me—"

"Mr. Flynn, you are an epileptic, isn't that so?"

"Yes."

"Subject to fits."

"Seizures," Hero amended.

"Have you been treated for any other form of nervous or mental disorder?"

"I was—neurasthenic as a child. The debility was made worse by recurring nightmares. You see, in my most recent lifetime prior to—"

"Say again, please, sir?"

Hero licked his sunburned lips. "In a previous lifetime, in late eighteenth-century France, I was also falsely accused of criminal activity, and guillotined. As a child in England I recalled—too vividly—this experience." Hero paused, looking at each man in turn. He shrugged at their skepticism and expressions of bitter amusement. "But this wouldn't be relevant to my present circumstances."

"Because you were nervous, and had these nightmares, you reckon they caused your seizures? What kind of treatment did you have?"

"I was eventually subjected to electroconvulsive therapy."

"Calm you down some?" Stone asked.

"To an extent. But the treatment also opened certain pathemic channels, to both the past and the future, that had significant influence on my spiritual development."

"Are you a God-fearing man, Mr. Flynn?"

"I fear no gods. I enjoy the serenity that reverence for all life has given me."

"I'd like it if we could get back to the matter at hand," the Sheriff grumbled.

"By all means." Hero tried to smile. "That is the important thing."

"What precisely was your relationship with Taryn Melwood? Was she your girlfriend?"

"Oh, no, no, it was a platonic friendship. Taryn had—well, she was obviously a crude little person, but she was not unintelligent despite a limited education. She was always curious, open to ideas. I think she was fascinated by the fact that I had traveled to so many countries. She yearned to travel herself, to be more than just a waitress. I felt—rather protective of her, actually. My sun was well-placed on Taryn's Ascendant, you see, and my Saturn was posited in the Tenth House of her ill-fated nativity, which gave me a powerful but benign influence over her."

"What do you mean, 'ill-fated'?" Stone said.

"She had given me her birth date and time. Then—quite early this morning, I was warned in a vision that serious harm had come, or was about to come to Taryn."

"Maybe that was a self-fulfilling prophecy," Tucker suggested.

"I must say, this is all a dreadful waste of time when I could be meditating on the circumstances of her death."

Stone said, "We don't intend to loan you any of Taryn's personal effects. The Sheriff's department of Carver County doesn't set much store by mysticism."

"Hasn't the evidence for the existence of psychic phenomena been compelling for many years? Very well, then, I shall simply have to carry on through my own resources. Needless to say, I don't wish to spend any more time in a cell than is absolutely necessary."

"Mr. Flynn, we intend to have you examined by physicians familiar with your type of illness first thing Monday morning. Am I correct in assuming you take medicine to control your seizures?"

"I've explained why I do not take medication of any kind. It interferes with mental processes I've spent many years developing. Drugs would be quite harmful to me, really. The seizures have become less frequent as I grow older, and are usually—"

"While you're in our custody you will be required to take medication for your epilepsy, for your protection as well as ours."

"Against my will?" Hero said incredulously.

"Yes, sir, that is a fact."

"But—you have no conception of how damaging even a small dose of phenobarbital or Dilantin could be! My body is not accustomed to drugs!"

Stone reached out and turned off the tape recorder.

"Tuck, you and Boodleaux want to go out for some coffee a couple minutes, I'd just like to talk to Mr. Flynn for a spell off the record."

Beauregard the jailhouse dog got up from his rug and crept stiffly behind the men to the door.

When Stone and Hero were alone, the Sheriff reached for his corncob pipe and a humidor on his desk.

"Son, I do recommend that you avail yourself of the right to call your family over there in England, because here in Carver County you are in a shitload of difficulty."

"I prefer not to worry them unnecessarily at this point. Sheriff Stone, I—I simply must not be forced to take medication. I'll need a totally clear mind in order to be effective in finding out—"

Hero stopped suddenly. Stone had loaded his pipe, and his head was down as he put a match to the tobacco. He didn't look up again until he had the pipe going, blue smoke around his head. He was startled by the expression on Hero's face.

"Have you always smoked that brand of tobacco?" Hero asked quietly.

"Oh, I reckon for about the last eighteen years. You know, you just about can't buy it anymore. They keep a little supply on hand for me at the tobacco shop, but when that's all gone I'll have to be settling for a different mixture."

Stone took the pipe from his mouth, chuckling. "Changing your brand of pipe tobacco, it's almost as bad as getting a divorce. Now, look here, Flynn—"

"You were at Shoulderblade State Park this morning, weren't you?"

"From about five o'clock on. I fish there every Saturday A.M. when the weather allows."

"Then you visited my campsite, while I was at the public area."

"Beg pardon?" Stone said, and tapped the stem of his old pipe against his teeth.

"I have a very keen sense of smell, Sheriff. And your tobacco is not an odor I would likely soon forget. Since, as you say, it's so scarce, the odds are very much against another man using that same brand. Therefore you—but why, why should you wish to incriminate me, someone you've never seen before, by hiding her panties and that bloody knife where I—oh, God! How terrible! *You!*"

Stone settled back, perplexed, in his chair, pipe in one corner of his mouth. His hands were folded over his breastbone. An index finger slowly traced the outline of the badge on his shirt. He had the catlike ability to stare interminably without blinking.

"You're raving, son," he said softly.

The rank smoke drifting his way caused Hero's already dry throat to clog. Tears rolled down his cheeks, tears of pity for Taryn Melwood.

"I gave her a real chance once," Stone said, musing. "The chance to come and live with us and get her life straightened out. Roberta, she was in the first stage of Parkinson's then, and Taryn could've been such a boon to the both of us. But no, she was already beyond redemption, nothing but a little hellcat. Barely past the age of ten. I done my best to love her, but she didn't want *my* love. Boy, that hurt! It hurt deep, but I'm a forgiving man. Up to a point."

Stone aimed the stem of his pipe at Hero. "I'm not interested in you. Don't even want to think about you. And don't you believe for one second that you can mumbo-jumbo your way into some kind of mental incompetency plea. We have got you dead to rights, and you'll go to prison for the rest of your life for butchering that poor girl."

"But I didn't do it. *You did!*"

Stone got up slowly from behind his desk. He unstrapped his wristwatch and laid it down. Then he took his .357 Magnum revolver from a shoulder holster and placed it on the desk beside the watch. He came around to where Hero was sitting and slapped him twice, right hand/left hand, the second blow almost a chop to Hero's temple. It knocked Hero sideways out of the chair and he landed heavily on one shoulder.

"What you need is a good dose of that Thorazine to calm you down, maybe some more shock treatment, which I'll certainly recommend. Then nobody'll be inclined to pay attention to your crap! Not that they listen to long-hair religious freaks around here anyway. You're poor, you're foreign, and you've got mental problems. There's three strikes again' you already: you're dead to rights in Carver County, mister, and that's all there is to it!"

He picked the groggy Hero off the floor. Hero's eyes were back in his head; he was shaking, a powerful internal vibration, as if Stone had jarred to life some potent but seldom-used machinery. Hero slumped in the chair with a little blood leaking from his nose. It looked to Stone like he was in a fit, all the more reason to sedate him pronto. Stone wiped the dribble of blood away with his pocket handkerchief, then stepped back in shock and consternation. Hero had spoken, in a language the Sheriff had never heard before, and he'd been with the Air Police in six different countries when he was a younger man.

"Gargle as much of that shit as you please," Stone muttered. "But you're headed for the dumpster."

He sat down behind his desk again to wait, thumbing through a pocket New Testament. When Hero ceased his incantation in the strange tongue and his head sagged, Stone reached for the intercom button on the telephone console. Maybe, he thought, they should just get out a straitjacket and run the prisoner on over to the County Medical Center tonight. But the hospital had no facilities for the potentially dangerous, and Stone didn't care to risk losing his prime suspect. Also they wouldn't have a specialist around this time of night who could diagnose and prescribe for Hero's ailment. He looked harmless enough for now, slumped in the chair, his expression dazed. No trouble he could get into in a holding cell.

Boodleaux came in with the two jail deputies.

"Had him a temporary breakdown, nothing serious. Take him on downstairs."

"Did he have anything else to say?" Boodleaux asked.

"Yeah. He confessed to me that Mork from Ork told him the Queen of England killed Taryn with a Boy Scout hatchet."

Except for Sheriff John Stone, they roared with laughter. Hero raised his head slightly but it lolled like an infant's as he was lifted out of the chair and led, shuffling, from the Sheriff's office.

"Good night, Mr. Flynn," Stone said. "Pleasant dreams, you hear?"

8

The Bus to Georgia Avenue

One of the drunks in the cellblock was awake and throwing up violently in the toilet when the jailers put the nearly insensible Hero back in his cell. In a sitting position he teetered on the edge of the lower bunk. One of the jailers said, "Looks like he's fixing to fall."

The other said, "Let him fall and crack his skull for all I care." Then he yelled at the drunk with the heaves, "Jesus Christ, Bucky, try to get some of that in the hole, will you?"

The steel door slammed and Hero continued to waver unsteadily before folding up on his side on the thin mattress. His eyes fluttered open, closed, opened again with a look of dismay.

They were going to medicate him, and soon.

He must do something before he was chemically lobotomized, or he would surely be confined to an earthly prison for the rest of his life; and the karmic sentence he was already serving would be extended, through how many more, futile lifetimes?

As a slavemaster in Babylonia during the reign of the Kassite king Olur-Eshnu, Hero had garroted hundreds of slaves. He repeatedly cut off the flow of blood to the brain for short periods of time until, no matter how physically strong the slave was, he became, like so many latter-day punch-drunk boxers, docile and zombielike, no more than a dray animal incapable of coherent speech or intelligent thought, easily handled without chains, needing just the touch of a lash from time to time.

Perhaps one of the slaves on whom he had perfected this

submission technique—a slave so thoroughly forgotten that Hero could not hope, even with the aid of hypnosis, to recall a face or name—was here, now, reincarnated in the person of Sheriff John Stone—

But it was unproductive to dwell on the possibility, although Hero well knew there were no coincidences in life—or death. He was not concerned with the karmic debt the Sheriff had incurred by murdering his niece. An ordeal had been arranged for Hero, perhaps long before his most recent birth. He would need all of his wits and skill to survive and, somehow, reveal John Stone for the maniac he was.

Hero looked around at steel and concrete, smelled and heard the drunk moaning across the way. The brain-energy coming at him from that miserable individual was, texturally, like gritty, obnoxious smoke. He had to make an effort not to be contaminated, and he almost missed the slow clicking of toenails on concrete as Beauregard the jailhouse dog passed in front of his cell.

Hero roused himself and concentrated on the German shepherd, willing Beauregard to stop.

The old dog's brain waves were like soft, yellowing grass winnowed by the breeze of a mild season. Beau shivered and whined, but his eyes brightened as he turned his head to look at Hero on the bunk.

The Englishman had, since early childhood, enjoyed a gift: an ease of communication with all types of animals, including carnivores. He could also delve into the minds of humans, but never so easily, and seldom without suffering for it. Human brain energy was more difficult to assimilate. Frequently it was like a cyclone, with velocity but no coherence. At other times it could be a firestorm sweeping through his own mind, a psychological Armageddon. The horrors beneath the skulls of men were not lightly explored. What came to him randomly he was usually able to deflect. And metal—such as the bars of his cell—was always an effective barrier to clear channeling. The steel around him now somewhat impeded his efforts to slip deeply into the dog's subconscious, but there were no psychic barriers in the way. Beau, so close to the end of his earthly life, was not on his guard, wary and cunning; Beau had only his memories.

Hero sifted through these memories like a caressing wind while Beauregard's head dropped and his legs shook.

Easy, easy . . .

These days Beau slept on a rag rug in the Sheriff's office, probably because there was always someone around the station to look after him. But, Hero reckoned, he might have lived with—

Yes, there it was.

He saw, as if through Beau's eyes, a three-story frame house with a deep front porch and two chain-hung gliders. The house was painted a soft shade of yellow, with white shutters. On the left side was a driveway: two parallel strips of concrete with grass growing in the center. To one side of the walk a white concrete birdbath sat beneath a wide-spreading mimosa tree. A large glossy magnolia shaded one corner of the porch and the house.

But where was the house?

Beau moaned as Hero continued his reconnaissance through the dog's eyes. He felt a sympathetic pain—the dog's liver was diseased, failing. He wouldn't live more than another—*ah!*

The numbers on the mailbox by the curb were 322.

322 what?

Hero took Beauregard for a short walk down the block (how strong he was in memory, so alert and eager) to an often-visited fireplug. Hero received impressions of other dogs, a male, a female, no particular breeds. The sensation was voluptuous, electric.

No, Beauregard, forget about those other dogs. Where the hell are we?

Georgia Avenue, Southwest. According to the signpost across the street.

Okay, there's a good fellow. You've done your bit. Rest.

Hero withdrew from Beauregard's mind just as one of the jailers whistled and clanged a metal dish against the bars. Beau, though infirm, apparently still had his appetite. Or maybe he was operating on instinct. But he turned and did his best imitation of a scamper, almost tripping over himself as his back legs were slow to cooperate.

Hero settled back on the bunk.

It had been a simple matter to find out where Sheriff John Stone lived; getting there wouldn't be a problem. But what could he hope to learn at the house that might be crucial to his own defense in a court of law? If he did learn something, how could he present it?

Yes, Your Honor, I have traveled out of my body since I was a small child. We all do, of course, but few of us remember the experience; or else we choose to recast it as a dream . . .

No, what he learned at the Sheriff's home would not be of immediate or practical value. Still, Hero thought, one had to start somewhere.

It took him only a few minutes to prepare to leave his body. There was always the potential of danger: his body might be moved in his absence, so that he would not be able to find it when he returned. He dismissed the possibility. Carverstown was a small place, with a population of not more than fifteen thousand. Obviously he would not have to travel far in order to find the Sheriff's residence. In his absence from jail, if the sphere around his body was disturbed he could return in a fraction of a second. He would risk a seizure from the speed of re-entry, or a few hours of acute discomfort should he slide back into his body at a bad angle.

Hero, lying on his back, closed his eyes, slowed his breathing, and meditated on the address, 322 Georgia Avenue, SW. It was always best to know exactly where he wanted to go. Wandering about once he was free of the body could mean trouble. Violation of the ethereal envelope around this world would instantly plunge him into netherworlds, dimensions frightening for the creatures they contained, and frequently imcomprehensible to the human mind. But Hero was a skilled out-of-the-body traveler, always careful.

Tonight extra precautions had to be observed, so that he

wouldn't be seen by someone—Sheriff Stone, for instance
—who could recognize him. The *döppelganger*, although it
was not composed of flesh, was never invisible and appeared
quite real to the untutored eye.

With a slight tickling sensation, then a little *pop* in the
region of his breastbone, Hero separated from the flesh-
and-blood body and hovered momentarily, radiant, above
the still form on the bunk, connected to it by a thin bluish
cord of pure energy, like a laser beam but flexible. Although
he would be on the street in a few moments, only animals
and those rare individuals with clairvoyant powers would
realize that he was a wraith; they would be able to distinguish
the light-cord that connected him to his body in the basement cell at the sheriff's station.

In the next instant he had left the building and was
standing on the corner opposite the courthouse. Traffic was
slow. Next to Hero there was a glass-sided bus shelter with a
route map on it. He looked up the street and saw a sooty bus
coming toward him. On the side of the bus there was a
placard advertising a local mortuary: Daimler Brothers.

The bus doors wheezed open in front of Hero. He looked
at the driver, a husky black man wearing shades with
sapphire-blue lenses.

"Come on," the black man said. "What is you waiting for?
Ain't no more buses tonight, this here's the only one."

"Are you going to Georgia Avenue?"

The black man laughed. "If you say so. I'm just driving
this thing wherever it is the two of you wants to go."

"The two of us?" Hero said, looking around. He seemed
to be alone.

"Sho'. Why else ride the bus? Y'all don't need me to where
it is you're going." He snapped his fingers. "Man, you can go
anywheres, just that quick."

"I don't think I'm allowed to go with you," Hero said.

"Don't worry none about that pretty blue cord." Hero
never worried about the cord, which took care of itself. The
cord didn't become wrapped around lamp posts, tangled in
bushes, caught in revolving doors. It was always just *there*,

unobtrusively. "You is safe, long as you stays on the bus," the black man assured him. "And she do need to talk to you, hear?"

"Where is she?" Hero asked.

The black man jerked a thumb over one shoulder. "Right back there. Let's get on with it, now; I got a schedule to maintain."

As soon as Hero was aboard he saw Taryn Melwood on the bench seat in the rear of the bus. She was doing her nails. She put down the bottle of polish and gestured cheerily.

At the mortuary they had washed her body and closed all the wounds. Dressed her in something pretty, a shell-pink dress. With two strands of cultured pearls. Fixed her hair, re-shaped and made up her face. But the Daimler brothers hadn't done her nails for her. And, Taryn explained, she liked for her nails to look good.

"We're not supposed to be meeting like this," Hero said.

The bus pulled away from the curb. Outside, the court-house and all the other buildings along West Fourth Street began to vanish in a thick, dismal fog.

Taryn waggled the nails of her left hand so the polish would dry faster. "Listen, we have a problem, and we need to do something about it."

"*I* need to do something," Hero corrected. "And I'm not in a very good position to do anything."

"I'm going to help you," Taryn said.

"How?"

"Karma. Don't you recognize me yet? I mean, who I was back then?"

"Back when—?"

"Here's a clue. Babylonia, 1354 B.C. I was employed in the household of a merchant in the tin trade, but I, uh, got it on with the Master, and his wife decided to have me, what's the phrase? *Nun' sha telgrit.*"

"Turned into a zombie for the slave trade."

"Now do you remember me, Tawn L'uit?"

"I remember . . . a young nursemaid too beautiful to be . . . disabled so cruelly. So I . . ."

"Pressed a little too hard and broke my neck. Hey, don't give it another thought! You did me a favor. Now I'm doing you one."

"Why are you still here, Taryn?"

"I'm not, really." She grimaced and glanced out the rear window of the bus, at the gray void through which they were traveling. Not entirely a void, because it was occasionally punctuated by little streaking lights, like meteor showers. "I mean, where is *here*, for Chrissake? Anyway, I have a Dispensation, I think they call it, but only for a couple of days. Exactly two days, because once that first shovelful of dirt hits the coffin, that's it, I'm gone. You know what I mean. I hear the light's better over there. No old buses, either. Anyway, I'm trying to help *you*. I don't need any help. The nice thing about being dead is, there's nothing left to be afraid of."

"Why did he kill you, Taryn?"

"Do you like this shade of nail polish? It doesn't exactly match my dress, but I don't think it's too bad."

"Can't you answer any of my questions?"

"It won't help you if *I* answer them," she said matter-of-factly. "It won't help *her*, either."

"Who?"

"The next one he's going to kill, sure as God made little green apples."

"There's going to be another one?" Hero said, horrified.

"No bout a' doubt it," Taryn chirped. "Unless you're really on your toes."

"But I—I don't know what to do. *Help me*, you said you'd help me!"

The black bus driver looked over his shoulder at them and called out, "Georgia Avenue! This is the next and only stop."

Taryn, tongue between her teeth, concentrated on drawing a line of polish around the lower rim of her pinky nail. "Perfect! Okay, reckon I'm ready as I'll ever be."

"Ready for what?"

"For my funeral." She looked him sternly in the eye. "Be there. That's where we'll get him."

"How?"

"I'm still working on that one," Taryn admitted.

Taryn lifted her chin and showed him her profile. Despite artful applications of mortician's wax, knife wounds were faintly visible.

"Don't you think they did a pretty good job?" she said wistfully. "I ought to be in pictures, huh?"

"Boss," the driver moaned. "Time for you to de-part. This ain't no taxicab. I got me a schedule to maintain."

"Go on," Taryn said, giving Hero a psychic push. Close as they were, there was no possibility of them touching each other. "But stay out of his mind, Hero. It ain't pretty in there."

The bus doors whooshed open. Hero got up. When he looked again Taryn was lying down on the seat, wearing her pleated pink dress, hands folded below her breasts, a slight permanent smile on her face. Her eyes were closed. He walked to the rear doors and stepped down into the gray void. There was a twinkling of light like starfall and he felt himself tilting, as if he were standing on the deck of a ship in heavy seas. He instinctively knew he couldn't fall, but he reached out anyway as the neighborhood of Georgia Avenue warped into focus all around him.

He looked the other way and saw a pretty blond girl on the sidewalk a dozen feet away, staring at him. She was out walking one of those squat snitty little dogs with too much hair. The dog was barking its head off at the end of a glittering leash.

Hero discovered that he had a death-grip on a stop sign. He hung his head as if he were drunk. The girl scolded her noisy dog but quickly jogged him to the other side of the street. Hero continued to lean on the stop sign until he heard her well down the block, talking to the dog, whose name, apparently, was Cheezit. He looked up then, in time to see the girl dragging Cheezit up the walk to the front porch of the house at 322 Georgia Avenue—

The home of Sheriff John Stone.

9

Edie and Roberta

"Uncle, there's a drunk man on the corner. I don't think he lives around here. Anyway, I never have seen him before. Cheezit, now hush! I'll get you your bedtime snack."

"What was he doing?" Stone asked the girl. "Sitting on the curb? Lying down?"

"No, sir, he was sort of leaning against the stop sign like he was fixing to collapse." She shuddered eloquently. "He gave me the willies. Just sort of appeared out of nowhere. Cheezit and me was almost on top of him before we even noticed him." Edie went up on her toes to reach a box of the crackers her Pomeranian doted on and had been named for. She was a slender girl just into puberty, but her figure was developing fast.

Stone came up behind her, braced her lightly at the waist, and reached over her head to get the box down for her.

"Thanks, Uncle John."

"You're not feeding him too many of those things, are you?" Stone had bought Edie the Pomeranian as a Christmas present, banishing the faithful but failing Beauregard to his office.

"No, sir, I'm real careful about his diet after what the vet had to say." She scooped up her pet from the floor and nuzzled him. "Don't want to upset his tummy-tum, do we? No-no-no."

"Believe I'll go outside and have a look around for this drunk you saw."

Edie said disapprovingly, "The way he looked, he's mostly bum. Cinch he doesn't belong in this neighborhood. Now looky here, don't be biting my fingers half off. Okay, here's your treat, you bozo."

Stone took his roast beef sandwich with him and had a couple of quick bites on his way to the porch. The roast beef was delicious. Edie wasn't fourteen yet, but already she could cook with a flair that would be the envy of most housewives. She knew how to can jellies and vegetables, and was looking to win a prize in her age group at the county fair in September. Cooking was just one of Edie's God-given talents. She sang in the church choir and painted pretty watercolors and also ran the household, supervising the nigger who came in to clean and do the washing. Most importantly, Edie had taken on much of the responsibility for Roberta. Stone could afford to have a practical nurse only two full days a week, half day on Saturday.

Outside he scanned the street but didn't see anyone. Apparently the drunk who had startled Edie had moved on.

Stone heard Edie whistling as she left the kitchen and bounded upstairs. Although at the moment his spirits were weighted with rocks and sunk in dark waters, Edie was a ray of light even at those depths. She called him "Uncle," but they were not related. She had been a runaway from Tumblestone Mountain, Georgia, whom he had plucked off the streets two years ago, then taken into his own home. Edie had worked out far better than Stone dared to hope. Roberta adored her. And his own feelings—

Stone sat wearily on the edge of a glider with the Italian-bread sandwich in his hands. He had not eaten all day. In the kitchen he had thought he was ravenous, but after a couple of bites he just couldn't swallow any more. He blamed this lack of appetite on strain and fatigue. On arriving home from work he'd shut himself in his bedroom and had such a shaking fit he was frightened it would bring on a heart attack. Now he had difficulty focusing his thoughts on the girl, his angel whom he had rescued from the brink of Perdition. A young girl, forced out of her home, with no place to go—he had been in Law Enforcement for most of his life, and knew the terrible statistics, the fate of poor girls like Edie. He was so proud of her now—but when he thought about all that she meant to him, something corrupt and sickening welled up in his throat, he nearly gagged.

Taryn. Taryn was still in the way, though she had left his house more than eight years ago. He could never be truly happy with Edie until—but she was dead, damn her, finally—how long must he continue to suffer for Taryn's sinful ways, how long would he be cast down in the prime of his manhood because of what she had done to him?

Cheezit the Pommie was barking monotonously when he should have settled down for the night in his fancy basket-bed in the laundry room. Stone didn't have much affection for the dog, who was frequently underfoot and easy to step on. He'd always owned stalwart hunters or shepherds like Beau. But Edie had fallen in love, cuddling that little bit of fluff at the pet store; and he'd promised her any dog she wanted.

Anything, he would give her anything as long as she stayed with him!

Now that Taryn was close to being in her grave, her satanic grip on him released, he would soon be restored to his full dignity. And then he and Edie—

Why wouldn't that yapping dog shut up?

Stone went back into the house. The Pomeranian was at the bottom of the steps in the foyer, staring into the darkened parlor, his eyes bugged and froth on his lips.

"Stop that! Hell is the matter with you?"

"Uncle John?" Edie called from the top of the stairs. "He can't come up, I'm fixing to take my bath now."

"Well, I'm going to shut him in the laundry room so we can have some peace."

Stone gathered up the squirming dog with one hand and carried him back to the kitchen. Cheezit calmed down when the kitchen door swung shut behind them, though he was still uneasy. In the laundry room Stone put the dog in his basket. Cheezit looked at him with liquid, alarmed eyes, quivering and whimpering. Damn dog was nothing but a bundle of nerves, Stone thought. Edie spoiled him rotten. But then, Edie spoiled everybody—it was her nature to please. A lovelorn pang turned into a cramp and the bleakness of his soul appalled him. *Rejoice,* he thought, *why can't you be joyful now that it's done?* He took a stuffed Odie from the laundry room shelf and put it in the basket, company for the dog. He dialed fifteen minutes' worth of time and turned the dryer on. Damn foolish waste of electricity—but the sound of the dryer always lulled Cheezit to sleep. He left the light on too, and closed the door.

As Stone crossed the kitchen to drop his uneaten sandwich into the garbage disposal, he glanced casually at the cutting board and the carving knife he'd left there, slathered with mayonnaise. But it wasn't mayonnaise he saw. The knife was dripping blood.

He went rigid from shock, and his heart seemed to detonate icily in his chest. He was a moment away from screaming when he also noticed the catsup bottle Edie had taken off the shelf to fix her own favorite before-bed snack—a catsup, piccalilli, and white bread sandwich.

The scream was choked off. He stood there gasping, face lurid with blood, thinking: *Why did she leave the knife like that, for me to see?*

Because Edie suspected—everyone did—that he had killed Taryn . . . come across her lonely on the road on the way to his favorite fishing spot—and let it happen, *just let it happen!* Now every living soul he'd known in his life had congregated, they were all around his house but invisible as deathwatch beetles, and they were waiting for his scream of guilt; when they heard it they'd scuttle in like a horde of nightmare scavengers, drag him naked into the street and devour him.

How badly he needed to scream, to get the sickness out of his gut, this new horror off his mind! The effort not to scream and give himself away was the most excruciating labor of his life. It was worse than the night he'd dragged himself for three miles in subzero weather after breaking his right leg and hip falling off a cliff in Korea. Time seemed to pass almost as slowly for Stone now, until he could get to the light switch and throw the kitchen into darkness.

He was better in the dark, although the pressure in his chest, so rigid a cannonball would have bounced off it, made breathing an ordeal. Gradually his heartbeat subsided, regulated by the ticking of the wall clock.

The darkness discouraged them; but they wouldn't leave now.

They would continue to observe him, hoping for self-betrayal.

No, I'm too strong for you, Stone thought, nevertheless resisting the impulse to look around defiantly at those he had called friends, now there to mock and despise him. *None of you know what she did to me! But the bitch-child is dead, and you can die too, for all I care! All of you!*

But not Edie. No, no, never Edie! If he could only hold her now, just for a few seconds, and explain why he'd had to kill Taryn, she would understand, and forgive him with kisses . . .

She was taking her bath now. Just the sight of Edie would be reassuring; it was *necessary.* For a few moments he enjoyed his greed, his voluptuous sorrow. If he could get through the night, despite the lurkers all around him, and tomorrow, then the next day—

Taryn would be buried. Placed in earth for a silent Eternity. And in the ritual of her passing he would enjoy rebirth.

Stone left the kitchen quietly as the dryer stopped. Cheezit whimpered that it was a dream-complaint, the dog had gone to sleep. Stone went up the stairs to the second floor and paused by the bathroom. He heard water running slowly, not much more than a trickle, and Edie humming to herself. He put a hand on the doorknob. There was a punishing fire in his groin, but no hint of an erection. He had cold sweat on the back of his neck. No, it was the wrong time, no matter how desperately he needed the child's forgiveness, her lovely sympathy, her sweetly chaste embrace. He pictured her looking at him as he came in, her expression not glad but startled, perhaps frightened. He was afraid too, but deeply excited. What if she screamed? What would he do then? He felt confused, and angry at being confused.

He took his hand from the doorknob. His hand trembled. That made him angrier, so he struck himself sharply in the face, closing his right eye. He did it again. Still the fire burned in his testicles, there was no relief. Stone went down the hall and opened the door to the third floor, which consisted of unfinished attic space. Two bare bulbs hung from the rafters furnished light. He went cautiously across the floorboards to the mattress he'd placed there years ago, when Taryn had come into the house. He kneeled, then stretched out facedown and took up a loose floorboard.

Light from the bathroom below, passing through thick squares of opaque glass block, illuminated his face. He removed the bit of tape that covered the peephole he'd installed. It was a common wide-angle type frequently found in apartment houses and hotel room doors, concealed in a mortared corner of the glass block ceiling. The bathtub, with Evie in it, was directly below. She was sitting in the waist-deep water with her pale hair bound up, water running over a bare foot she held under the tap.

He had not spied on her for a while. He was shocked to see the size of her breasts, the caterpillar-like fuzz on her pudendum. *Child no longer.* Men would want her now. He was grieved and distraught. He squirmed on the mattress, maddened by the fire that smouldered in his groin and testicles, while his penis remained soft.

Edie cocked a foot on the side of the deep old tub and dreamily stroked the underside of her thigh with the soapy washcloth. She had used a touch of bubblebath, and the bubbles gleamed on her upstart breasts. Her nipples were not petite, as he had imagined them. They were surrounded by very large aureolae. Now the cloth was between her legs, and, *God, what was she doing?* Stroking herself with an insolent forefinger, eyes half closed as she gazed almost directly up at him, a mesmerized smile on her face.

Stone sat up clumsily, pain spearing through his head. He was salivating uncontrollably, like a sick animal. Grief and confusion racked him. Ah, not Edie! How could she torment him this way? She'd been so slender only a few months ago—so chastely made. Now look at her, whorishly involved with her own body.

The scream was building; he heard it in his head even as he clutched his throat, forcing it back, so that Edie and the lurkers wouldn't be alerted. He sat panting on the mattress he had long ago stained with his sap in a different thrall, thinking, *They are all whores and they all laugh at me.* Only Roberta had been faithful all these years, despite his barrenness.

He left the mattress and went haltingly down the stairs, right eye tearing badly, wiping away the saliva from his lips. When he opened the door Edie, barefoot but wearing her terry robe, was emerging from the bathroom. Her face was flushed, her hands were full of brushes and lotions for her body.

"Uncle John." Edie smiled. "What were you doing up there?"

"Looking for—tax records." Her face blurred, but not before he saw her swift look of concern.

"What's the matter with your eye?"

He could smell her, so sweet from her bath. He longed for

the touch of her moist skin. He cried harder. "It's the dust," he said. "The attic dust always bothers me." He smiled then, knowing it was a bad smile, a dreadful smile like some strange fleshy thing suddenly growing in the middle of his face.

"Oh—well, good night, Uncle John."

"Good night, Edie." *Won't you come and kiss me, kiss me, bitch-child? (As soon as one is dead, there's another.)*

Edie came halfway down the hall toward Stone, but she hadn't come to kiss him. She had, in her innocence, misread what was torturing him.

"Uncle John, you've had such a terrible day! Why don't you try to get some rest? In the morning I want you to come to church with me. We'll pray together for her soul."

He couldn't answer; he was afraid of the sounds he would make, bearing no resemblance to human speech. Or else she would hear the vilest profanity, and run away in terror. He nodded, surreptitiously wiping his wet lips and chin, hiding his face from Edie, hiding the evil he knew burned in his eyes.

"I'll just look in on Aunt Roberta before I go to bed," Edie told him, and she was off down the hall, stopping at the door of what had been the master bedroom in happier times. Now the room was Roberta's, night and day, and she no longer left her bed. She had taken her last steps nearly three years ago. Stiff as a board, probably weighing no more than eighty pounds, she lingered on, while Stone slept in a small bedroom next to the attic stairs.

He went into his room now, closing the door. He didn't want a light. He sat on the edge of the bed, still salivating. Wipe it away, and it would start again. He gasped and panted. His painful eye was only a slit, and watering too. It felt as if the eye were growing bigger and bigger in his face, bright as a supernova. An all-seeing eye, scanning many things that had previously been beyond his ken.

The door to the room opened slowly. He stared at it, distracted, tantalized, wondering which of the lurkers was about to put in an appearance. But he wasn't prepared for what happened next.

It was Roberta. She stood in the doorway in her flannel nightgown, all skin and bone and pressed-down gray hair on her yellowed skull, eyes fiercely bright as she pointed accusingly at him. He scrambled up on the bed and crouched there on all fours, shaking his head at her: no, no—

No, lovey, it's Taryn's fault!

But how could he say that when Roberta had found him nakedly astride the ten-year-old girl, a hand on the back of her head, pushing her face into the pillow to keep her from shrieking while he—

"But it *was* Taryn," he protested to the form of his wife. "From the moment she came into this house, she tempted me!"

Roberta wasn't buying it; she never had. Her face burned coldly, like the moon on a winter's night. Her pointing finger did not waver.

Stone covered his face with a pillow, unable to bear the sight. He shook with sobs and then, at last, he screamed. The sounds were muffled by the pillow. He screamed until the bones of his chest were tender, his lungs exhausted of air, his stomach muscles in an iron cramp. And fell weightlessly off the bed.

The spectre of Roberta had vanished, his door was closed. He lay clear-headed on the floor, emotionless but in agony.

He became convinced that he was not yet alone. One of the lurkers he had anticipated was in the room.

Stone looked up. Light from the street painted shadows on one wall. The window was open, the night warm. He was wringing wet in his clothes. He got up clutching his stomach, his throat so raw he couldn't swallow. At least the horrid salivating had stopped.

He knew the spasm would pass; he had made it through his crisis, he would endure. He took a couple of steps toward the door, needing to go to the bathroom. Then he stopped, unnerved, fascinated. He had glimpses of a reflection in the mirror over the dresser, but the angle was wrong and it was not himself he was seeing.

He saw, instead, the bearded face of Hieronymus Flynn.

Stone lunged at the dresser and drove a fist into the mirror, shattering it. He turned quickly but saw no one in the small bedroom with him, only an odd, unexpected blue light that flickered for a moment by the open window.

He had no further capacity for surprise; there was no fear in him. Only a dull resolve.

You can't tell on me. I'll kill you first.

10

Dr. Dove

Hero was catching up on his sleep when the Sheriff came to visit him, at six-thirty Sunday morning.

A Negro deputy, as tall as Stone but a yard wider, let Stone into the cell and stood by. He was an albino, ugly as an oyster, with rusty red hair and eyes that looked like little pink bullets. He wore a hearing aid.

"Good morning, Sheriff," Hero said, before he even opened his eyes. "I hope you had pleasant dreams."

Stone told him to stand up. Stone's right eye was a monster. He looked as if he hadn't slept, let alone dreamed.

As soon as Hero was on his feet, Stone dropped him with a billy to the side of the neck.

"I don't know," he said softly to the writhing Hero, "how it is you did what you did last night. But it doesn't matter. You better believe I'll personally take real good care of you now." Stone looked at the deputy and pointed to Hero on the cell floor. "Cuff him, Horace, and let's get a move on."

The black deputy came in with shambling lopsided gait and reached down to lock Hero's hands behind his back. Hero was puking. When he finished, Horace lifted him easily, inserted a long ebony club between his back and his elbows, and maneuvered him toward the door with it. Stone stood by pensively, fingering his swollen eye.

"Where . . . taking me?" Hero gasped.

"Son, you need medical attention. You're about to get it."

"No! I demand . . . speak to a barrister! My right. You must allow—"

Horace chuckled softly, trotting Hero along in front of him with little adroit manipulations of the club.

"Deputy! Listen to me! The Sheriff . . . murdered . . . Taryn Melwood! He knows . . . I know, that's why he—"

"Save your breath," Stone said. "Horace has his hearing aid turned off. But it wouldn't make no nevermind to him anyway. I own him, body and soul."

Beauregard the jailhouse dog stood shivering outside the alley door. He sniffed at Hero as Hero was loaded into a cruiser. Thick wire mesh separated him from the front seat.

"I want to know—where we're going," Hero said. He could barely speak above a whisper, his voice affected by fear and the blow to the neck, which had raised a throbbing goose egg.

Stone shut his dog up in the jail and got in beside Horace, who drove through empty streets.

"You can't do this! You're trying to shut me up, but it won't work!" Hero began to throw himself against one of the doors, from which the handle had been removed. He tried to scream, but even if he'd had the voice for it, no one was around this early to pay attention to him. Stone stoked his pipe and lit up.

West of Carverstown they took narrow country roads

through sparsely populated hill country. The white belfry of
a ramshackle church glowed in sunlight. At a touch on the
shoulder from Stone, Horace roared off the blacktop and
drove toward the rising sun past a nearly dry pond that
revealed the metallic hulks of discards half-buried around
the shore. They were even more isolated here. Parched
fields that simmered even in the early morning were bisected
by the dirt road, now not much more than a wagon track.
Horace pulled off into a straggly clump of loblolly and the
Sheriff looked back at Hero in a thin cloud of smoke, his
abused eye smarting. Hero was rigid with disbelief and
horror.

"Why . . . are we here?"

"Pee break," Stone said. He tapped Horace on the
shoulder again.

Horace got out and opened the back door. When Hero
dug in his heels and wouldn't be moved, Horace exerted a
minimum amount of force and removed him from the seat
as easily as if Hero were a week-old kitten. Horace was
smiling peaceably. Stone looked at Hero with the stem of his
pipe clenched between his teeth. Sunlight kicked off the
nickeled steel of the service revolver in his shoulder holster.

"I don't . . . have to pee," Hero said, shaking.

Horace slapped him lightly and smiled again. His ebony
club was swinging gently from his other hand.

"You will never . . . be able to explain this to the satisfaction of my family," Hero said to Stone. "They will come.
And they will not be . . . without influence, even in this . . .
godforsaken place. You are making a fatal mistake, I assure
you." Hero dropped to his knees. "You will have to drag me.
Then you will have to shoot me in the back, because I
refuse . . . to run. Any worthwhile forensic scientist will
know . . . that it was nothing but murder, plain murder!"

Hero remained on his knees with his head bowed, listening to warblers in the nearby trees, feeling the heat of the
sun. He heard Stone walking slowly around the car, and

began to tremble. He smelled the sweetly obnoxious pipe tobacco, and gamier odor of the deputy's old boots. He looked up without flinching, though his cheeks were wet from tears.

"What is it going to be, Sheriff?"

Stone sighed.

"I thought I'd do both of us a favor. Just get it over with. But, no, hell, you don't want to cooperate. So I reckon it's time for you to meet Dr. Dove. Son, I'll guarantee before it's all over for you you'll wish you'd opted for a bullet through the heart."

Stone moved so swiftly then he was a blur to Hero, but he sensed a kick was coming. He couldn't throw himself to one side fast enough to avoid it. Stone's boot caught him in the groin and Hero felt nearly impaled; the agony lasted barely two seconds before he passed out.

The jouncing of the Sheriff's car down another bad road brought Hero back to consciousness. He was lying on the back seat with his knees drawn up; the effort to straighten his legs, just a little, was like dragging a white-hot anchor through his groin. Light through trees and the back window of the sedan struck him glancing blows; it was better with his eyes closed. The lower half of his face felt artificially stiff. He couldn't open his mouth. *Taped,* he thought groggily. But he was more attentive to each bolt of agony as the squad car jolted along.

Presently they stopped. Stone and his deputy got out and walked away, leaving him alone. Perhaps they'd thought he was still out. It represented a chance, albeit a very small chance, to get away . . . but he couldn't do it. There was too much pain no matter how carefully he tried to move.

He was weeping again, from frustration, when he heard footsteps in gravel again. A back door was opened.

"That him?" a new voice said.

Hero opened his eyes and lifted his head, but he could make out only an indistinct face nearly shrouded in a mustache and beard longer and thicker than his own. The man's beard was nearly to his waist. His eyes were small as fish eggs, black and with a vaguely oily sheen.

"Why's he gagged?"

"He bites," Stone said.

"Take him inside," the other man said, and abruptly disappeared from the door space.

Horace took the bearded man's place. Hero bucked in pain as soon as he was touched.

"Reckon his balls still hurtin'," Horace said, looming over Hero and smiling. "Come on, now, I'll treat you gentle."

It surprised Hero that he was true to his word, but still Hero had to walk. Each step redefined his suffering. Horace allowed him to take his time, and Sheriff John Stone was nowhere in sight.

They were parked beside a low concrete-block building with a shingled roof. The walls had once been painted white, but the paint job had faded and peeled in places. It looked like a down-at-heels motel. There were several doors, regularly spaced, some with numbers on them. And all the windows were barred. Hero saw an old rusting ambulance in a field, a clothesline drooping with torn bedsheets. There was a pale face behind a partially lifted shade, staring eyes with no boldness in them. He smelled a sourness in the air, garbage smouldering in a pit, and heard chickens. The gravel drive he crossed with small dragging steps was littered with chickenshit and bottlecaps and discarded cigarette butts.

He was led by the patient Horace into a dank room with bright lights grouped in one corner, over a padded examination table and a rollaway table the top of which was crammed with instrumentation: an EKG machine and a console that resembled a VCR. The smell of garbage was behind him, but now his sensitive nose was treated to the slightly rotten odor of antiseptics. Hero tried to hold back on the threshold, but Horace put pressure on a nerve inside the right elbow.

"Have him lie down," the bearded man said. He was somewhere out of Hero's line of vision. "And keep a good grip on him until I've prepared the sedative."

Apparently Horace had turned his hearing aid back on. Hero looked up at the albino, his eyes wide with apprehension, trying to communicate with him. The pink eyes seemed incapable of reflecting emotion. Hero tried to make coherent sounds behind the plaster of tape over his mouth, then began frantically to shake his head. Horace applied a little more pain, and pushed him inexorably toward the padded table.

"I'm Dr. Dove. That doesn't mean anything to you, I'm sure. But there it is."

Hero stared at the man with the mountaineer's beard and long hair done into a ponytail. He had put on a white jacket. Under the jacket he was wearing only a T-shirt, with the notation *I dropped out at Club Med.* He had a syringe in one hand. Horace unsnapped the stained jail jumper Hero had on, exposing a bare flank. He held Hero down.

"I understand," said Dr. Dove, "that you're acquainted with ECT. Then you know there's very little to fear. Most of my patients benefit remarkably from the course of treatment." He showed Hero the syringe. "This is a fast-acting barbiturate; you'll soon be asleep. Once you've gone to sleep I'll administer another drug that temporarily paralyzes the major muscle groups, including your diaphragm. Then we can take that tape off your mouth, and a machine will do your breathing for you. That's the electroconvulsive machine you're looking at now. It will send a current through your brain for less than one second. When you wake up you'll probably have a headache, some muscle soreness, and, most likely, you'll experience a period of confusion. Not at all unpleasant, though. EC therapy also tends to eradicate memory—but nothing we can't do without, I'm sure."

Hero felt the prick of the needle even before the doctor had finished speaking. A sensation of ice-cold horror ripped through him like a storm wave. *They were going to steal his*

mind! —And all the memories he could do without, including, no doubt, everything he'd seen and heard at Sheriff
John Stone's house the night before. *No, you can't!* But it was
already happening, the wave of horror dwindling into a kind
of warm mist he found too comfortable to resist . . . but he
must, somehow he had to tell them both about Stone: a deaf
albino deputy, and someone else Stone apparently owned
body and soul, the bearded dropout Dr. Dove. It almost
made him laugh as his vision grew a little cloudy, and the
pressure of Horace's hands felt like a good-night caress.

He saw Taryn then, floating out there in the thickening
mist, composed and piquant in death, smiling regretfully.
Hero had failed her, failed blond Edie, failed all the young
girls he now saw laid out in neat burial rows, prepubescent
victims of Stone's ruthless mania.

I won't close my eyes, he thought. *All I have to do is stay*

> *awake,*
> *and*

11

The Mt. Pisgah Cemetery

With no apparent transition, no desultory period of restless
dreaming, he went from images of the dead to vivid
apprehension of the mundane: a dog's hoarse barking, a
distant radio playing a country song. He was indoors, not
outdoors, and there wasn't much light in his dark corner of
the world. But he saw streaks of pale sun, in barred patterns,
along a corridor. He smelled acrid, over-brewed coffee.

Water splashed from a metal pail. Mop-sounds. His stomach was empty.

His head hurt.

He was looking at the bars of a cell, but he had no idea of where he was.

The dog continued to bark.

Hero had random impressions of home, mother, university, a tawny-haired German girl who inspired a wistful pang for a long-extinguished romance—then, abruptly, a startling face, clear in the tiniest detail, filled his mind: scared him. It was a bleak, sunbaked Indian face. Obsidian eyes, only a few teeth to enliven the steady grin. Hero shifted his attention to a high Bolivian village. The air was so thin and sharp it was like breathing ground glass.

But I can't be there; I'm somewhere else.

Oh God where?

He couldn't remember. The dog was quiet now. He listened patiently to the sounds of mopping until he saw someone backing into view, sliding a galvanized bucket behind him on the concrete floor.

"Hello," Hero said. He moved then, shifting his weight, trying to raise a hand, but it was stuck fast in something; his entire upper body was immobile. He looked down curiously and saw that he was wearing a dirty buckled sort of—

Straitjacket!

"Good mornin'," said the man with the mop. He paused to wipe his forehead. He was black, with a raised wrinkled scar darker than the rest of his skin diagonally down his forehead. He wore a wrinkled jail jumper and unlaced docksiders. "Man, it's too hot already, ain't it? How you be this mornin'?"

"I don't know," Hero said. "I can't—I wonder if you'd be good enough to tell me—where I am?"

"Whoo-whee! Don't recollect where you is? That be some toot you was on."

"*Toot?* I don't understand—"

"They got you restrained that a' way on account of the
d.t.'s, I reckon."

"But I—I don't drink." Hero was sweating; he felt
queasy. "Am I in jail?"

"It ain't the Ramada Inn, Jack."

"Well, I—I need to get out of here."

"Shittt, don't we all."

"What time do you have?"

"Left my Rolex in my other suit, but I reckon it's going on
eight-thirty."

"I see. And—" He was very much afraid to hear the
answer to his next question. "The date?"

"Well, let's see. Was it the twenty-first today? That's right.
August 21. Now I got to get on with this floor, nice to be
talking to you, and I hope you feels better."

"Wait! Who do *I* talk to, to get out of here?"

"The judge, I reckon. That's tomorrow, though, nobody
gets out today."

"What's tomorrow?"

"Tuesday."

Hero nodded, sweat dripping from his forehead. His
beard itched on his cheeks, but he couldn't scratch it. His
nose felt sore, inflamed, and there was an ache in his groin.
Tomorrow was Tuesday. *Today was Monday.* Did that matter?
For some reason he felt that it mattered very much, although
he couldn't think why. Something to do with the harmonic
convergence? Yes, possibly. That called to mind cool pine
woods and a shining lake. Where recently he had—or was
that in Bolivia? Confusion. His mental processes were in such
disarray he was close to tears.

"Help," he said softly, then yelled it.

"*Help!*"

Before long a man wearing a badge and an Atlanta Braves
baseball cap showed up. He was eating a fried egg sandwich.
There was a dog with him, an aging German shepherd
watching for crumbs of the sandwich to fall his way.

Beauregard.

"Come out of it, huh?" the jailer said. "But you got to stop that yelling, boy."

"I must know why I'm here and what's happened to me! Why have I been restrained like this?"

"Doctor's orders, I reckon. Just came on a little while ago myself. You squawking because you need to use the john?"

"No! What doctor? By whose orders have I been placed in a straitjacket? What am I charged with?"

The jailer chewed a mouthful of sandwich, looking skeptically at Hero.

"Murder. Now I ain't believing you don't remember what you did to that girl."

Stunned, Hero slumped back on the bunk, staring at the jailer and Beauregard the jailhouse dog. The dog's name had come to him instantly. Associated with it was another name: fear-provoking, a different fear from that he experienced being trussed up like a criminal psychopath in an asylum.

"*Stone.*"

"Sheriff Stone? You can't talk to him, won't be in until afternoon. The funeral's this morning at eleven-thirty."

"But he's—" Hero couldn't complete the thought. He was shaken by an emotion too terrifying to verbalize.

Blood.

Blood on his hands, and—

A girl who sat in the back of a bus, wearing a shell-pink dress, doing her nails a slightly darker shade of pink.

Once that first shovelful of dirt hits the coffin, that's it, I'm gone.

"Where? Where is this funeral?"

The jailer wiped his mouth with the back of his hand. "Mt. Pisgah cemetery. That's where all the Sheriff's family is laid to rest. What's that to you, anyhow?"

"It's imperative that I—be there."

The jailer grimaced and put a finger in his mouth to explore a sensitive tooth. "You are one crazy son of a bitch.

And I got better things to do than stand here talking to you. Make any more noise, and we'll put the gag on, that's a promise."

Hero didn't reply. His eyes were wide but vacant as he stared at the patterned sunlight on the floor behind the jailer. Sunlight, but he seemed to hear thunder.

We've got a problem, Taryn said, after the sound of thunder. *—And you're in jail.*

Hero shook his head.

"But it's not my fault," he whispered. "They—"

A different voice. *"I understand you're acquainted with Electro-convulsive therapy?"*

"What are you going to do to me?"

EC therapy tends to eradicate memories. But nothing we can't do without, I'm sure, the doctor had said.

Cemetery. Mt. Pisgah cemetery. But where in the name of God was—

"Hurry, Hero," Taryn said to him, her voice barely audible behind the thunder. "Reckon I'm as ready . . . as I'll ever be."

"I can't!" Hero wept, thrashing helplessly on the bunk. "There's no way I can get out of here!"

But then his erratic movements slowed to a random twitch or start, and some residual of drug or high-rolling current crisping God-knew-what in the deepest layers of the brain reacted post-operatively. He was drenched in grayness, a non-speculative existence on the dullest levels of perception and sensation.

Until the dog returned.

Thunder rolled across the town; rain silvered the opaque unbreakable window glass in which a thin wire screen was embedded. Beauregard stood shivering expectantly outside the bars of his cell.

No, Hero thought. *It's night already. I'm late, too late.*

Beauregard whined and licked his graying chops.

Old dog. Soon you're going to die. What do you want with me? I can't help you, any more than I can help myself.

Then Hero sat up slowly, looking into lively amber eyes that reminded him of . . . Beauregard threw his head back and barked ecstatically.

"You're getting it," Taryn said, coming to him, once more, through the thunder and tumult overhead. *"But for Chrissake, Hero, shake it up—move your ass!"*

"I don't know if I—"

"Just do it. Doesn't depend on memory. It's all instinct. Affinity. You haven't forgotten. Do it!"

"Beauregard?"

The dog looked alertly at him.

"I don't know—how far. Can you—"

But there was no more to be said. He felt himself sliding forward out of grayness, swift as an eel from an undersea cave, powerful as a crossbow arrow, free at last from the confining straitjacket, the close-set bars of his cell.

Beauregard jumped as if the floor had become electrified and landed on his rump with a sharp cry. Yes, it hurt. Hero felt the gritty action of joints inflamed by rheumatism, absorbed all of the shepherd's reluctance and fear as he scrabbled with worn nails to regain his balance.

Easy—it's only me. And we're getting out of here, now!

Through Beau's eyes he saw the jailer with the Braves' cap at one end of the corridor.

"That you, Beau? Flea nibble your asshole?"

Beau turned his head for a quick look inside the cell, where the form of Hero lay inert on the bunk.

Come on, Beau, while you've got his attention.

Beauregard trotted stiffly down the corridor, whining.

"What's matter, big boy?"

Beau brushed past him and turned right. There it was, the way out: a steel door, steps, another door, the alley—he went paws up on the door, scratching, deep pain in the old bones, tongue lolling. He looked back at the jailer.

"Okay, okay, it's raining batshit out there, but when you gotta go—"

Beau let himself down slowly and they waited until the

door was opened, then went haltingly up the short flight of steps, the jailer trudging along behind.

"Worse than a little kid," the jailer grumbled. "I can see why the Sheriff don't want you home no more." He unlocked the alley door, and Beau squeezed outside into a blast of rain.

Hero had no idea what time it was. Daytime—that was all he could tell, with the sky so dark and a hard rain falling. But how much time had passed, was the funeral over? Beau looked back at the jailer, who was standing in the doorway waiting for him.

"I told you it was plenty wet out. Why don't you just get back on inside here? Won't be the first time you peed on the floor."

Run, Hero commanded.

Beau took off down the alley, going toward West Fourth Street.

"Hey! Get back here, damn you, Beau!"

Beau skidded a little at the mouth of the alley, and looked around. At the courthouse, the bus stop on the corner—

Over there!

The rain was licking down Beau's black and yellow fur, getting into his ears and eyes. He gave his head a shake, then trotted obediently to the bus stop shelter. A matronly black woman with a shopping bag gave him the fish eye. Beau looked up at the route map on the side of the shelter. Hero studied it disappointedly. He saw nothing to indicate where Mt. Pisgah cemetery was located.

Beauregard shook and sneezed.

Sorry, old fellow. What time is it?

Beau lifted his head in the direction of the courthouse clock.

Ten-twenty A.M.

No way to ascertain if the old clock kept accurate time, but if it was right—

They still had time. But now what?

Beau sneezed again. The black woman raised her rolled-up umbrella menacingly and said, "Shoo!"

Beau turned morosely and started down the street, directionless and already a little lost while Hero pondered their dilemma.

The florist's delivery van ("A little sunshine on the darkest days") was almost past them when Hero was seized by inspiration. He brought Beau up short. Beau complained of the pain in his rheumatoid hindquarters.

Follow the truck.

Beau loped across the watery street, slipping once as he dodged an oncoming car. They tracked the van for five blocks, steadily losing ground as Beau's stamina flagged, but always keeping the van in sight. Beau's heart was pounding alarmingly. Hero saw the van turn into the driveway of a well-maintained antebellum mansion. There was a discreet lighted sign beside the drive. *Daimler Brothers Funeral Home.*

Come on, Beau, that's it!

Beau was limping and out of breath as they started up the drive. The rain hadn't let up. He cringed at a crackle of lightning almost overhead. His feet were sore.

Behind the hedge.

There was a modern garage at the rear of the mortuary. Near an entrance with a canopy over it four limousines were parked. Farther back, behind the mortuary, a silver-and-black hearse waited with the rear door open. The van was parked and the driver was unloading tributes, perhaps for another funeral later that day.

Beau crept along behind the meticulously clipped privet hedge, came to a stop with his ears pricked forward.

Several employees of the mortuary appeared, trundling a coffin toward the hearse.

That has to be Taryn.

They loaded the coffin into the hearse, added several baskets of flowers, and returned to the mortuary.

Now.

Beau limped up to speed and crossed the gravel drive. He went around to the back of the hearse, hunkered, then leaped with all his remaining strength into the hearse and crawled toward the front, burrowing into a mound of flowers. He lay there shivering beside the coffin.

Hero wondered if Beauregard's tail was sticking out.

He heard footsteps, voices. Beau kept his head down. The back door was slammed. Three men got into the front seat of the hearse, and it drove away from the mortuary. One of them lit a cigarette. Someone else turned on the radio. Bob Seger. "Betty Lou's Gettin' Out Tonight." Hero thought that Taryn might have approved of that choice of music, rather than something lugubrious from Handel. One of the men began discussing the sexual proclivities of his girlfriend.

"Smells in here," another man complained.

"Yeah."

"Like a wet dog."

"Yeah."

Beau's nose was twitching. The flowers.

"Jesus," said the man with the perverse girlfriend, "She's too damn hot to be a minute over seventeen. But she can't get it on until you paddle her little ass."

"Does she call you daddy?"

"How did you know?"

"Lucky guess."

Beau sneezed.

"Shit!"

"What was that?"

"It's a goddamn dog!"

Beau showed his teeth.

"*Big* fucker! Pull over, Pete. Right now!"

"How did a dog get in here?"

"Just get it out. Don't look too friendly. Okay, big fella. We're not going to hurt you, don't get excited. Make it fast, Pete, before the cortege catches up with us, old man Daimler'll have our asses."

The hearse stopped. Beau laid low. When the back door was opened he scrambled up, growling.

"Look out, here he comes!"

Beau jumped from the rear of the hearse and landed in a ditch half-filled with water. Pain shot through his left hind leg, and he howled.

"Come on, let's get out of here."

The hearse pulled away. Beauregard, unable to move, stood shivering in the water.

Beau. Please.

Slowly, agonizingly, Beau crept out of the ditch and halfway up the embankment, where he lay down, unable to go any farther. The hearse was not in sight. But across the road there was what looked like an abandoned drive-in theatre.

They lay there for a few minutes while cars drove by in the rain, their tires sizzling on the blacktop. Then Beau lifted his head again.

The cortege was coming toward them, headlights aglow.

Can't be seen, Beau. He'll know you.

Beau worked his way back down the embankment and lay there as the four mortuary limos passed, traveling about thirty-five miles an hour.

Now, Beau, follow them.

But Hero wasn't sure Beau had it in him anymore. His progress was slow getting up to the road, and there he was so hobbled he could no longer run. The limousines were disappearing around a bend in the road.

Keep going, Beau. Don't quit now.

The old shepherd's heart was beating wildly. A car slowed, a woman rolled down her window partway. "Poor doggy." But the car drove on and a van, coming up fast, threw a wave of water over them. Beau shook himself; then, as if the dousing had done him good, he hobbled his way into a steady trot.

There it is!

A wrought-iron gate with an arched sign over the turn-in: Mt. Pisgah Cemetery. But there were no burial plots in sight. The road wound uphill through woods.

Can't be far. Beau, Beau, we have to get there before—

Beau growled resentfully, but he kept moving.

It seemed to take them a very long time to reach the top of the hill and Hero had his first glimpse of the cemetery, the hearse and limousines, the small group of mourners seated beside Taryn Melwood's coffin under a canopy. There was a minister in a gray suit and clerical collar. His voice came clearly to Hero through the sound of rain falling in the surrounding woods.

"The Lord is my light and my salvation; whom shall I fear? The Lord is the stronghold of my life; of whom shall I be afraid?"

Beau paused again, panting, his head down. It seemed to Hero that he had driven the dog mercilessly for the last half hour, and that Beauregard was about to collapse. He saw the leonine head of Sheriff John Stone in the front row of mourners and young Edie beside him, her head bowed.

Now that he and Beau had reached the graveyard, Hero had no idea of what to do next.

Don't let them put me in the ground yet.

"Taryn?"

Come on, Hero. The best part of the service is about to begin.

Beau took a shuddering step toward the gravesite, and fell over.

Get up, Beau! Hero begged him.

I'll help. And something passed through the dog's exhausted body, a wave of energy like a caressing hand. Beau perked up; he lurched to his feet and lumbered toward the gravesite, seeming to gain strength as he went. They hadn't noticed him yet; all heads were bowed as the minister prayed.

Then one of the men from Daimler Brothers, inattentive and bored with funerals, looked around at the charging shepherd.

"Holy shit," he said under his breath, and backed up against a co-worker as Beau gathered himself at the perimeter of the canopy and leaped atop the flower-covered casket, sprawled there, almost sliding off into the laps of the mourners.

The hand of pure energy that had reached out to him from the gravesite and coaxed him to his feet now kept him from falling off the casket as mourners scrambled from the front row of folding chairs.

Beau looked into the eyes of Sheriff John Stone, and was not chastened. Beside Stone, Edie was transfixed, gloved hands over her mouth.

"Get that dog out of here!"

Beau turned his head. Through a break in the hillside trees the screen of the ☆Star-Light☆ Drive-In theatre faced them, shabby but clearly visible despite the rain.

Hero focused on the screen, trying not to let his attention be diverted although quite a lot was going on. Hands reached out for Beau, who snapped and snarled, and Sheriff John Stone was backing Edie away from the casket while he reached for the off-duty revolver on his hip. But he had to reach awkwardly with his left hand; his right arm was around Edie. While he was trying to draw his revolver and shoot the animal he had only belatedly recognized as Beau, Gaynell Bazemore glanced at the drive-in screen.

"Nealy, look! That's Taryn!"

Taryn, stripped naked, running for her life—no mistaking her, the picture on the screen was bright enough to be seen through the rain, and clearly focused, even though what was happening seemed to be happening at night.

(She had one leg up and was pulling herself over when something like a piece of pipe or a club struck her hard in the ribs)

This they saw in closeup, and Taryn's contorted face as she reacted . . .

(She didn't fall, but the pain was so bad she couldn't

summon the strength to push herself the rest of the way over. Then he was there: a hand clamped on her dangling foot and he jerked her down from the)

"Uncle John!" Edie gasped, her voice no more than a shocked whisper. "Is that you?"

They were all watching the drive-in screen, Stone included. He had momentarily forgotten the revolver in his hand. His lips were taut in a grimace of disbelief. Beau lay shivering on the casket while Hero, as fascinated and horrified as anyone there, concentrated on projecting what Taryn had wanted them all to see of her last living moments.

(She got up so slowly that at times she appeared static, posing grievously. Both hands were cupped to her forehead, filling up with blood as she tried to stanch the heavy flow from the cut that had half-scalped her)

"Oh my God, I'm dreaming this!" Gaynell Bazemore shrieked, clutching at her husband.

(She fell twice, muddying herself in red dirt, her own blood)

Stone turned slowly away from the spectacle on the ☆Star-Light's☆ screen, chaos in his face, his swollen right eye bulging from his head. He lifted his revolver and aimed it at Beauregard, at the casket he had closed himself with Taryn inside.

(She was oblivious to him shuffling up behind her until the downward chop of his knife to the nape of her neck stopped the show)

Edie screamed hysterically.

Stone turned and stared at her and then at the drive-in screen as several mourners gasped. He saw himself driving the eight-inch blade of the hunting knife again and again, furiously, into Taryn's body, saw his face in closeup so clearly little splatters of her blood were visible on it.

Stone shook.

The minister was beside him, one hand on his wrist, holding the revolver down.

The show at the ☆Star-Light☆ Drive-In started all over again.

Stone jerked away from the minister, the gun firing wildly, scattering the mourners who were still on their feet.

Beau lifted his head and howled to the heavens.

Stone went down on his knees beside Edie, laughing and crying, embracing her. When she shrieked and tried to get away from him, he pulled the trigger of the revolver snugged up against his chest and with one shot blew his heart to bits.

12

Beau R.I.P.

His parents flew over from England the day they let Hero out of jail, and picked him up at the Sheriff's station in Carverstown.

His father owned a box factory and rental property in Sheffield; his mother decorated store windows. They were handsome, prosperous people who had never understood their son very well, but they loved him ungrudgingly nonetheless.

"I should think," his father said, "you might be ready for a lengthy visit home after this unpleasantness. Haven't seen much of you, these past few years."

"All right," Hero said, with uncharacteristic diffidence.

"Shouldn't we visit a doctor before we leave?" his mother suggested. "Really, Hero, you look dreadful."

"Feeling pretty well, though," Hero said. "I admit I could use a rest . . . oh, dad. Before we head for the airport, I must make some stops."

"What for?"

Hero pulled a piece of paper from his pocket which Bob D. Grange, the acting sheriff of Carver County, had given him.

"We're going first to 1263 Audubon Street." He read off the directions, and after three wrong turns they found themselves at the veterinarian's where Hero had been told he could pick up Beauregard's remains.

"What in the world—?"

"Mother, please. I made some promises."

The Flynns looked at each other as Hero got out of the car. Derek Flynn shrugged.

"I'll need a hand, dad. He weighed upward of eight stone. Lucky you rented a Cadillac."

"We put him to sleep last night," the vet said. She was a pleasant woman in her mid-forties. "There was just too much wrong with him, and he was in constant pain."

"I know," Hero said.

With his father he carried the box out to the car. The trunk of the Caddy was smaller than he'd anticipated, but they were able to wedge the box inside and tie the lid down.

"Where now?" his father asked him. "This won't take long, will it? We've a plane to catch at six-thirty."

"Right. I need a shovel. Noticed a hardware store just up the street."

They were at Shoulderblade State Park shortly after two. The trip uphill with Beauregard was hard on Hero's father, who had let himself go sadly to pot since Hero had last seen him; but the view from the site Hero chose was, to his mind, well worth their effort.

"I'm sure it can't make any difference to the dog," his father grumbled. But he pitched in willingly to help with the digging.

"Why is this so important to you, dear?" his mother asked.

Hero put down the shovel, and stretched. He had begun to love this place, and was sad to leave. But in the digging of this grave he was laying more than Beauregard to rest. The weight of 35 centuries was off him at last, no more than dust. He could think, now, about what he must do with the rest of his life. Until he and Taryn met again.

He smiled at his mother. "I'd like to be able to explain that to you," he said. "But for now . . . I wouldn't know where to begin."

The
Guardians

1

Major Starne Kinsaker was a tall man with a stiff, dour, seamed face, straight yellow eyes and straight lips, and a neck shrinking down into his collar like a turkey's, or, more accurately, a vulture's neck. His hair was straight and gray and dying off; his forehead was paisley with age spots, and his cheekbones shone like weathered, ivory knobs. But his hands were large; they looked strong and reliable. Jim Practice wasn't sure how old the Major was—somewhere in his late sixties. He wore high, obviously expensive horse boots, and jodhpurs, as if he had just come in from a ride.

An awesome face, in a way. Since Practice had been working for the Governor, he had encountered the Major many times and now he found himself studying the man with heightened interest, wondering in the back of his mind what the Major could want with him.

He had rung the bell outside the opaque glass doors of the Major's office suite in the Osage State Bank Building, expecting at least a token delay before being admitted, but the Major had answered the buzzer himself.

"Please come in, Mr. Practice."

Apparently the Major hadn't gone to much expense in furnishing the anteroom. There was a desk with a gray typewriter stand beside it and three straight chairs against one wall. The lone adornment was a narrow vase full of wilting iris on the desk. As he followed, Practice wondered if Kinsaker had some sort of unhappy surprise waiting so close to the Governor's Day Dinner. After considering the possibility, Practice disallowed it. If the Major had found a hold that would effectively break John Guthrie's back, he would

123

go ahead and break it without ceremony, or make his deal, which would amount to the same thing. Jim Practice would not have been called in either way.

Major Kinsaker's office was a large one, and by contrast with the cheerless room outside it had been furnished with a great deal of care. Six windows overlooked the center of the city. Most of the furniture had the look of heirlooms. There was even a tall cabinet clock behind the Major's desk, between the windows.

"Will you sit down?" Kinsaker asked, his hand resting on the high back of a leather chair in the middle of the carpet, facing the desk.

"Thank you, Major. Do you mind if I build a smoke?"

"Not at all." The Major bent his gaze on Practice with a hint of interest as he took out cigarette papers and tobacco. "Not many men go to such trouble anymore," he said, as if he approved of the ritual.

"I suppose I'm contrary in some ways," Practice replied. He liked the routine; it was comforting to him. He also told himself that he enjoyed the taste of the cigarettes he made.

Kinsaker moved slowly through the sunlight that intersected his desk and approached a door-front cabinet. Watching him, Practice recalled a brief conversation he had had with Governor Guthrie not long ago. He had made some sort of slighting remark about Kinsaker, and Guthrie looked up at him tiredly in the dwindling hours of the night.

"I don't think you have a right to think of him in that way," Guthrie said, then softened his tone. "The Major can be mean, and he can be kind, but for all the contradictions, his kindness is no less real than his unattractive qualities. Let's remember that."

The Major opened one of the cabinet doors and light from the windows shone on the liquor decanters massed on a shelf inside. Probably, Jim thought, there was a small refrigerator in the closet hard by the liquor supply. Gracious living, he told himself, his nerves chased by a spook of annoyance as the Major turned to him.

"What will you have, Mr. Practice?" he said, his hand gripping the shelf below the array of cut-glass bottles, no expression in his narrow eyes.

Practice spent a few moments carefully shaping up his cigarette, taking perverse satisfaction in letting the Major wait for his answer.

"You know all about me, Major. I assume that, anyway, because I don't carry any secrets of my own around with me. You know when I was weaned and where I was baptized and how many girls I coaxed up into the barn loft before I was fifteen years old. I work for John Guthrie, and that's all in the Blue Book, sixty-two thousand dollars a year, which is two thousand dollars more than the Governor himself makes. You know these things about me, so you know I can't drink. That's the first thing you must know about me."

"Then I won't drink, either," the Major said, turning away from the cabinet and closing the doors. He moved slowly, precisely, but with an underlying gracefulness and ease.

"Go ahead, it's nothing to me."

Practice had slipped into the drawling habits of speech that he adopted unthinkingly when under duress, or annoyed, because he had allowed the man to goad him, to try him. He had come to listen, he reminded himself; no more.

He struck a match and held it to his cigarette, then broke the match. Because the chair was just out of arm's reach of the desk and an ashtray, he kept the match, toying with it. For some reason he didn't want to get up out of the chair, go to the desk, and deposit the match; the notion of standing, stepping, then turning, and turning again to sit in the rather low chair seemed awkward, obscurely humiliating. Which could explain why the chair had been placed at that particular point, where a man might sit and talk with Major Kinsaker and feel as isolated from him as if he were in the next room.

Without appearing to notice the match, the Major walked around his desk and picked up the ashtray, handing it to

Practice, who set it on one of the wide armrests of the chair. The Major continued unhurriedly to the far side of the room with an air of reflection and detachment, and Practice turned his head to follow his progress for a few moments.

He was aware again of something remotely demonic about the man; another age and the Major might have made a first-class sorcerer. But he sensed now a part of what Guthrie had been trying to tell him, that Major Kinsaker was far from the malevolent, grasping man he was sometimes made out to be. His attitude was one of willful loneliness, apartness, perhaps with a faint distaste for but enchantment with the lives of ordinary men. The Major's family, among the original settlers of the state, had been wealthy for generations. Besides the Osage Bank, Kinsaker owned land, utilities, and diversified industry. He lived in a comfortable house in the oldest part of town, owned one car, rarely traveled outside the state, and had been married only for a short time. Practice had a hunch that his chief inspiration was a craving for intrigue. The dikes were crumbling all around him, but he didn't act like a man about to get his feet wet or be drowned.

The far wall of the Major's office was blank, except for a series of framed photographs of a young girl—as an infant in a snowsuit, as a child astride a Shetland pony which the Major held by the halter, as a blooming thirteen-year-old. They were the first pictures Practice had ever seen of Major Kinsaker's daughter, Molly. Shortly after her thirteenth birthday Molly had died after a fall from a horse; her death had been an almost fatal blow to the Major.

"I know many things about you," Kinsaker said. "I've looked into your beginnings. By the way, your father is married again. The girl is seventeen—and you have another half brother."

"I'm not interested in my father," Practice said, disliking the sour taste in his mouth; disliking the Major, who knew his life by the inch, his every stupidity and failure. "I haven't seen or spoken to him for twenty years."

"I don't blame you," Kinsaker replied, still without emphasis in his voice.

"What do you want, Major?"

Practice's bluntness provoked a frown. "I know about you—your promise and your failure. But I'd like to know more; I'd like to understand your relationship with John Guthrie. Why does he trust you and no one else?"

"We've never put it into words, Major."

Kinsaker came toward him, then changed direction and stood over his desk, a hand on the ornamental lamp that was suspended above it. "Two men are trying to kill each other," he said. "You stand between them, through no choice of your own. Possibly you could help them."

"I don't think so," Practice said.

His tone seemed to disrupt Kinsaker's thoughts, and he turned again to the windows and the warmth of the sun.

"John Guthrie is mistaken if he thinks he can hold the reins of the party and hold office effectively at the same time. It can't be done. From what I've seen lately he's overburdened already, very nearly a spent man, with half of his political life ahead of him. His only possible achievement will be such a severe disunity, such a chaotic reversal of loyalties, that the party will literally explode under the pressure of its internal quarrels. There may be no hope of peace for another fifty years. And fifty years is only about half the time it took, Mr. Practice, for my father and me to build our party from nothing to what it represents today."

"Your party is an anachronism," Practice said. "Even a man as popular as Guthrie will have his hands full building a winning ticket for the next election."

"Leaving my personal feelings aside for the moment, I think John Guthrie is a brilliant politician with an erratic streak in him. He's willfully, unaccountably being a fool. He doesn't understand power *or* the party. I hoped that we could be in some accord once he was elected Governor, but he takes no man's advice, except that of certain irresponsible and politically ignorant men even younger than himself."

The Major paused, nearly trembling with outrage. "He's like a child-god playing with lightning. He's going to burn us all badly, for no reason except an almost psychopathic rejection of me that I've done nothing to deserve."

Practice blinked, fascinated by the glimpse of the molten core of the man. Then he found his voice.

"What about those personal feelings you mentioned, Major?"

"They have nothing to do with my politics."

"Which is hard to believe. You see, Major, I don't recognize John Guthrie at all when you talk about him. And I've seen him almost every day for six years—"

"I'm John Guthrie's godfather," the old man said, cutting Jim off. "His family and mine have been interlinked for two hundred years. I was, at one time, the only older friend he had. He trusted me as he now trusts you. I taught him to ride, to shoot, and to drink. I taught him a few things about responsibility, duty, and honor. When he had calmed down and burned away some of his excess energy in his own pursuits, when he was ready for grooming, I planned his political future. I can only say, when he won't speak to me or admit me to his house, that I've been betrayed."

"And yet you spoke as if you might be killing him. What did you mean?"

A vein scrawled on the Major's right temple was throbbing in an ugly way. "I gave him the lightning. And he can't let go of it." He faced Practice squarely. "I'd like to think that you see this, too, that you're disturbed. He is, he must be, your friend. I've said nothing to you I wouldn't say to the Governor, if I had his permission to see him. If he were here, I'd ask him why he had to hurt me. I'd hope we could have the matter out and arrive at a workable compromise. Perhaps—but there's been too much bitterness. Compromise is the best we could hope for. The worst . . ." He lowered his head slowly. Where his face had been hard before, it was now granite. "The worst is upon us because of John Guthrie's insensibility. I will defend myself."

"How can you do that, Major? He whooped it up when he was younger, but he didn't make any fatal mistakes. You couldn't break Guthrie with scandal, or you would have done it by now. That's as much a part of politics in this state as a goat roast. For what it's worth to you, I have a suggestion: challenge John Guthrie to a duel."

The yellowed eyes didn't waver. "Are you as big a fool as he is?"

"Duels have always been fought over what is petty and trite and unbecoming in human nature—over nothing. The two of you, as far as I can see, are deadlocked over the vanity that passes for honor in your school. Give him the party, if that's what he wants, Major. Don't wait for him to take it all away from you. You're too old to go down so bitter; it isn't pretty, it isn't graceful, and it doesn't suit you. Respect yourself. Get out and let John Guthrie play with his lightning. Because it doesn't mean a goddamn thing. Because with all your tradition and dignity and estates by the Mississippi, you don't mean a damn thing and neither does he as long as you insist on vindicating this measly little power shuffle. It's embarrassing, like seeing a couple of kids wet their pants in public. What's it good for? The felicitations of stupid, dishonest, and greedy men who aren't good enough to eat dinner on your back porch. No matter what happens, Major, the Kinsaker name and the Guthrie name are going to reek. Whatever's between the two of you—and it's got to be more than anyone's saying—let it go, or shoot it out, just the two of you, and have done."

"How do you let go of a man who has you by the throat?" the Major asked, in a lower tone, with a grim hint of humor.

"Maybe you try to buy off the second-best man," Practice suggested.

For an aging man, the Major moved lithely, his fist raised; and Practice, somewhat astonished, merely sat still under the threat of that fist. Then, slowly, the Major lowered his hand.

"I thought we could talk," he said harshly, "without cupidity or postures. Is it comfortable for you to distort everything? Is it the only way you can live? We have nothing in common, sir, no way to speak to each other."

"I'm sorry for wasting your time, Major. You asked me to come."

"I don't think our time is wasted. Perhaps you might be able to say you know more about me than you did, and in your relationship—whatever it is—with our Governor, such knowledge may be useful to you and to him. And I know about you, sir. What was elusive and unfocused is clearer now. You have a certain hollow ring, an insincerity that belies your physical directness. Your angers and disillusionments burn themselves out at the greatest depths, where they cause the least pain."

"I'm not partial to pain," Practice said, stubbornly meeting the Major's eyes, resenting him and the implied superiority in his "sir," yet at the same time feeling oddly craven. "Who is?"

"Perhaps I am," the Major said, and for a moment his eyes seemed to clear. "Because I've deliberately sought it, in an area you find sordid and futile. Perhaps I've found all human relationships sordid and futile, but I haven't denied them. Pain has made me cautious, temperate, wiser than I might otherwise have been. But you never searched for pain."

"I didn't have to. I was born barefoot and running, and I stayed a runner. My old man kept my head knotted until I was old enough to take his club away." He shoved his way up beside the Major then, making room for himself, and they stood eye-to-eye, Practice feeling rude and sad and exposed. "Have you ever known an alcoholic, Major?" he asked.

"I've known men who drank themselves to death."

"I mean men who haven't had that privilege. Those who don't take the stuff anymore. A man like that is a sort of monk, with his own monastery, nobody inside but himself. The sun is high up in the windows, higher than he can touch, but at certain times of the day a little pool of it lies on the floor where he passes on his way from morning to evening prayer. It's a queer, dim, chilly but oddly satisfying experience, Major. It's not like life, though, don't make that error. It's no more of life than the existence you seem to have led. I suppose I've said too much, so I apologize for my assumptions. In a way I like you. In a way you scare the hell out of me. I didn't think that was possible any longer." He paused, feeling a little exhausted with the effort of talking to a man who looked at him with the motionless, fierce expression of a bird of prey. "Do I worry you as much as I did before you called me up here?" he added with a meaningless smile.

"I'm afraid," the Major said, in the gentlest tone he had used all afternoon, "you don't even interest me anymore."

2

The interview had left Practice edgy and displeased with himself, and all the virtues of a fine spring afternoon couldn't help him forget the sense of foreboding the Major had seeded in him. A special sort of man, Practice thought, who had created himself and was sadly lacking for company. I will defend myself, he had said. *I will defend what I must be.*

Practice walked the two blocks to the Governor's mansion, twirling his hat on his fist, and as he reached the grounds, the clock in the city tower chimed four. A flock of starlings flew low over the mansion and out across the river, their wingtips like jet velvet as they passed through the nearly invisible rays of the sun.

He walked slowly up the drive of the mansion, knowing that the Governor was probably upstairs, but not wanting to see him just yet. He would be unpleasantly tense because

A.B. Sharp was reportedly going to make one of his rare appearances at the Governor's Day Dinner that night, and John Guthrie badly needed Sharp's support in his struggle with the Major. But Sharp was old, and his ties, though tenuous, were with Kinsaker. Sharp apparently was disposed to smooth out the intraparty dispute without taking sides. That was all Practice had been able to learn, although he had applied himself diligently to the problem of A.B. Sharp for several weeks.

One of the mansion shepherds, a tawny yellow brute, was stalking moles in the soft earth beside the stone wall at the edge of the bluff, and Practice paused to rub behind the dog's ears. He boosted himself up to a seat on the wall. From there he could see out over the river and well up the valley, where the river was running high. Despite the exhalation of lavender, rosebud and white dogwood blossoms, the crocus and the iris and early tulips in the flower beds that sectioned the lawn, he could smell faintly the fresh coat of white paint on the outer walls of the eighty-year-old mansion. He gazed up at the Victorian roof, where the sun was striking against the copper rain gutters and shingle trim, and then at the cool-looking, high, bent windows, warped like water in their bays.

The mansion occupied a small part of one of the many hills of the capital city. It was built almost too close to the edge of the bluff, below which ran mainline railroad tracks and the silt-thickened river. Years ago steam locomotives had thrown up enough smoke and soot to make the mansion a thoroughly unpleasant place to live, but John Guthrie had seen to it that the old and neglected place was restored and improved before he moved in as Governor. Opposite the mansion, on the next hill, was the Capitol building, nearly a replica of the one in Washington, particularly in regard to the massive dome, which rose high above the city and its hills. In between the mansion and the Capitol was parkland, which slanted down into the earth-fold between two hills. On the bank of the river was an old shoe factory, but the factory didn't obscure the Governor's view when he looked out of his bedroom-study window on the third floor. Across the way was the Capitol, floodlighted by night and white as salt.

Christopher Guthrie, the Governor's six-year-old, came around the corner of the mansion, his head a golden red beside the long, knuckled shadow of an elm. He and Practice saw each other, but with the sure knowledge of good friends, made no fuss in recognition.

Chris looked back over his shoulder, then reached up on tiptoe to place something in the bole of the elm. The shepherd crossed in leisurely fashion to the boy, with his heavy curved tail swinging, and Chris sank both hands into the ample skin of the dog's nape, tugging furiously.

"C'mon, Josh, you'll give it away."

The dog turned his head and grinned at Chris. Then, alerted by the gray shape of a squirrel in the rose arbor, went loping off with his nose down.

Chris sauntered in Practice's direction, pausing to give a redbud tree a good shaking. The lavender petals whirled silently down through depths of sunlight that sluiced through the tight lacing of branches above. The lawn was almost buried under fallen petals, and Chris squatted, giving them a stir with his forefinger.

"Lucy'll give you heck for shaking that tree," Practice observed.

"Did she see me?"

"She doesn't have to see you."

Chris looked up, his face very still, a quizzical turn to his lips. His eyes were deep blue, almost lidless, penetrating. He shook his head furiously at a wandering bee.

"I'm tired of playing with Lucy," he complained. "Let's go shoot something. When are you going to take me to the fort?"

"What fort?"

"Near school."

"Oh. That's no fort, Tiger Hunter. It's part of the old prison. Nothing inside but rats."

"We could shoot rats."

"I'd take you," Practice said, "but your dad and I are working tonight." He decided to have a cigarette.

"Is that so?" Chris replied, his favorite expression of the week.

"Chris!" Lucy's voice called. And Practice lifted his eyes from the cigarette he was rolling.

"Don't tell her we're here," Chris said.

"Too late, I think. What are you two playing, anyway?"

"Hiding buttons. I'd rather shoot something." Chris dipped into the pocket of his jacket, and Practice saw a brass button as big as a milk-bottle top gleaming in the boy's palm for an instant. Then he felt Chris's hand at one cuff of his trousers and Chris was standing back guilelessly with his hands at his sides.

"C'mon," he said. "Lift me up."

Lucy Childs appeared around the corner of the mansion. She was a tall girl who wore a rust-colored sweater and skirt, with a long-sleeved yellow blouse, the cuffs almost as deep as gauntlets and secured by little brass arrows. There was a gleam of ornamental brass slanting at one slender wrist. She wore her black hair long and full, and her skin seemed to have soaked in the lambent moisture and light of spring, so that it glowed as tenderly as the boughs of the dogwood all around her.

For a moment Practice forgot his cigarette, and a small unconscious smile appeared on his frequently melancholy face. Lucy had been born with the kind of style that many women spend a fortune and a lifetime trying to achieve: like Dore Guthrie, the Governor's wife, who adored Lucy, envying her flair but without malice.

"You're getting warm," Chris said to Lucy with an uncharacteristic giggle.

Lucy began to move in a wide circle, approaching them slowly, sizing up every likely hiding place. Practice continued with his cigarette, not taking his eyes from the girl. Her gaze flickered over the elm, then returned.

"Cold, cold, cold!" Chris shouted as Lucy reached into the bole of the elm and drew out the brass button. Lucy laughed delightedly and Practice shuddered at the sound of her laughter.

"You know something about Lucy?" Chris asked as Practice gave him a boost up the wall.

"What?"

"She was crazy once."

Practice looked at the boy. There was nothing in Chris's face to indicate he was troubled by what he had just said. Like as not, the meaning of the word was vague to him, but Practice wasn't willing to let the matter drop.

"Where did you hear a thing like that?"

"In the kitchen. I was playing with the mousetraps and I heard cook talking to her cousin."

Practice drew a long breath. "Lucy was real sick one time and had to go to the hospital."

Chris nodded, occupied with the scuffed toe of one of his shoes. He knew about hospitals.

"Why did cook say . . ."

"Cook was wrong, no matter what she said. Listen, Chris"—Practice glanced up to see if Lucy was within earshot—"remember the time you had that strep throat? When you couldn't swallow or talk?"

The boy's penetrating eyes were on him. "Yes."

"Well, when Lucy was in the hospital, she hurt as bad as you did. But for a longer time."

"A month?"

"A year. Two years. That was a good while ago, but she still wouldn't want to be reminded of it. Just remember how you felt when your throat was sore."

Chris's tongue prodded his cheek. For a moment his

expression was quite tragic, then he swallowed forcibly and began to brighten, wriggling in anticipation on the wall.

"Don't tell Lucy where the button is."

"Don't tell Lucy what?" she asked, joining them. "Hi, Jim."

"Did you see me put the button in the tree?"

"No, but I know how your mind works, pal. About ready to go in? It's story time."

"Find the other button."

"I'll just do that," Lucy said spiritedly. She retreated a couple of steps and surveyed them both carefully, while Practice grinned and Chris applied his own brand of hex, crossing his eyes and fingers and ankles.

Lucy's eyes were green, with a suggestion of serious mischief in them at the moment, but usually her expression was serene, nearly smiling. On more trying days the fine humorous softness tended to disappear, replaced by a fitful sadness, and if the mood continued for a long period, her face hardened as if she were trying consciously for self-control. When their relationship had been different, he had tried to help Lucy, comfort her, and gradually the color would come back into her face. Lucy had never let anyone else be close to her at such times.

For months after Lucy had come to the mansion to look after Chris—with excellent references, after her year and a half of therapy—she had been friendly but withdrawn, and Practice, intrigued by her contradictory nature, stirred in a way nearly forgotten during his bitterest years, had at last penetrated Lucy's reserve. He found that she could be dependent and adoring. At other times she would glory in self-possession, and be as untouchable as a swan.

One night their romance had become openly physical. They faced up to the most unpleasant details of their fragmentary lives, and concluded that they were stronger in each other. Then, without warning, Lucy began to draw away from him. The relationship was now in delicate balance, still comfortable in many ways, but without the eager physical intimacy they had enjoyed. Practice didn't know why she wanted it so, and at first nursed a bruised sexual vanity, but she had shamed him out of this mood. He was puzzled by the vision of an oblique, distant Lucy, but he kept the threads of their relationship intact, there being nothing else he could do. Despite her attitude of firm restraint, and of irresolution, Practice felt that Lucy still needed him, that she was watching him with great concentration, critically and expectantly. His own desire and needs were far from consistent. He just didn't know what was expected of him. His one proposal of marriage had been conclusively refused.

Lucy had moved closer, and, with a look at Chris to see if he was giving anything away, took one of Practice's hands in her own and turned it over.

"No button," she said. "You've got me this time, Chris."

Chris yawned and appeared uninterested in the game and in them.

"Here," he said, reaching into Practice's cuff. "Can we go in now? I want to ask Mother something."

"She's probably busy, Chris. She just came home an hour ago, and she has to get ready for the dinner tonight."

"I don't care," he said stubbornly, and got down from the wall.

Lucy looked sadly after him.

"Dore's probably made some wild promise to Chris and forgotten all about it. But he never forgets. I'd better go in with him."

"Why don't I stop by after the rally tonight?" Practice suggested. "We can look in the fridge for some of that crock cheese and maybe work up a Perquackey game with Dore."

"Oh . . . I don't think tonight, Jim."

"What would keep you?"

"Well . . . Fletch said he was coming over, some family business he wants to discuss. His life insurance or something like that."

"Shouldn't take all night."

"Please, Jim, couldn't we make it some other—" She seemed about to become annoyed, then smiled automatically. "What about tomorrow night?"

"Sure, Lucy."

He watched her as she walked briskly away after Chris. Lucy's brother Fletch—Dr. Fletcher Childs—was an avid amateur politician who hankered to run for Lieutenant Governor in the next election. It wasn't likely he would leave the rally and the informal smokers that followed until the early hours of the morning. Practice shrugged, still annoyed with Lucy and all the rubble she had diligently stacked between them the past few months. Not a wall, exactly. He could have walked right into it and knocked it down and come face-to-face with her. But he was afraid to try.

Paul Dunhill, the Governor's secretary, came out through the kitchen entrance to the mansion and stood in the drive for a moment, trying to fit another batch of papers into an already gorged briefcase. He flicked away the hair that was forever hanging down to the rims of his eyeglasses and looked around. Probably half blind in the twilight, Practice thought. But Paul saw him and beckoned furiously, an unmistakable gesture. The Governor wanted him.

Practice lingered long enough to finish his cigarette. The land was gathering shadows and the gold of evening. Far across the river, tractors and discs were driving out from the turned fields to the barn lots, and Practice could almost smell the brown clods and the sweetness of elm and sycamore. He had come from a different soil, where the smell was grease and ashes and unwashed bedding. His old man had farmed a hundred and forty acres in the bootheel and Jim Practice was just so much slave labor, a cut above the croppers because he got to sleep on the porch, almost in the house, after the new woman came. Then he didn't get much sleep at all, because her brothers trickled down one by one, a couple of them from the reformatory, and ran him off. He could have taken the beatings because he was big-boned and strong, held his own despite the fact that there were four of them, but his old man didn't seem to care one way or another and he couldn't, wouldn't, stand for that.

He had never returned, although a time or two he was tempted to stroll through the brick and tin-roof town and show off a little. That was after the war, when he had his Captain's bars and the two longish rows of ribbons that included a silver star. He might have been tempted again after his graduation from the state university, because he'd learned how to wear clothes and was driving a used Buick, but he stayed away; and the mild urge never troubled him again, particularly after Steppie, his wife-to-be, came along. She wouldn't have made the trip, even for laughs.

He got up then, the seat of his pants cold from the stone wall, and fired his cigarette butt away, down the steep bluff, its limestone outcroppings dyed black from a century of coal smoke and cinders. The horn of a diesel blatted on the tracks below. He looked idly down at the blue and silver streamliner, knowing where it was going—first Kansas City, then the mountains. It would be nice to see the mountains in spring, he thought; and quite suddenly and painfully, for the first time in months, he wanted a drink.

3

He used the gray and white marble stairway at the front of the house to get to the Governor's apartment on the third floor, taking it slowly, enjoying the elegant emptiness of the front hall, with its gleam of old silver and fireplace brass and figured tile and cool fabrics. The carpet before the high double doors of the apartment was gold; there were a couple of high-backed Italian chairs against one wall for those rare individuals awaiting a call into the Governor's private quarters. The doors were oak, very heavy, but moved with minimum effort.

Inside the suite was an entrance hall, with two closets and gold-on-white silk wallpaper; the carpet became a claret shade. Through an arch Jim entered the sitting room, where three windows looked out over the river, now with a red glaze from the setting sun. Sun motes through the windows picked out highlights of gold thread in the draperies.

The Governor's bedroom was on the left, his wife's opposite; in a niche behind the entrance hall was a small kitchen. The sitting room was empty, impeccably arranged, silent; not even the two antique windup clocks whispered to him.

Practice had expected to find the Governor waiting there. When he didn't see him, he crossed to the bedroom door and opened it without troubling to knock.

Dore was in the bathroom with her husband, and, from the sound of their voices, they were having an argument. Practice hesitated, then went in, shutting the door behind him.

There was not much light in the bedroom. He intended to

go out on the small north balcony until Guthrie and his wife were through, but he found the doors stuck; they had been painted over. Sloppy workmanship, he thought, holding the draperies and gazing out at the top of an oak. He gave his attentions to the voices in the bath.

"I knew if I let you out of my sight for a few days you'd figure out some way to make an ass of yourself."

"I'm not listening to you."

"Every time my aunt and uncle come down here you're all over them trying to get invited to their house. All right. They had to invite you, and I had to let you go. You don't understand a damn thing about people like that, how they live . . ."

Her voice was squeaky, humble. "They're your folks and I've always wanted to know them."

"You couldn't sit quietly around for a couple of days and drink tea at the right times and talk about Flemish art and go out to concerts . . ."

"I'm not listening!"

"You had to get next to some wop concert pianist who haunts families like mine to make a living . . ."

"Oh, *that* isn't true at all. Paul is Polish! And he's a wonderful pianist."

"How would you know? Dore, I've got a headache. Let's forget it."

"He's recorded three albums! Your aunt said so."

"She's a sucker for greaseball *artistes* herself."

"Greaseball! You don't know what you're talking about, so shut up! We had dinner—the *four* of us had dinner—and I danced with him. After that we had brandy and Paul played exclusively for us. And I invited . . ."

"What?" Guthrie said ominously.

"I . . . invited . . . *Paul* . . . to . . . to . . ."

"Good goddamn." There was a sharp silence. "Uninvite him."

"W-why?"

"Oh, stop. *Why?*"

"He gave me his card, Johnny. Honest, he's so nice. You'll like him. He wrote on his card: to one of the world's *loveliest* women."

"When the hell are you going to learn?" Guthrie said. "Uninvite him."

"Okay," Dore said tearfully. "Johnny—we got along just fine. Everybody liked me, Johnny."

"All right, Dore, go put on some clothes."

"Don't you want me to . . . to give you your bath?"

"I'm tired and I want to soak, that's all."

"Aren't you glad everybody got along? Johnny? I didn't do anything wrong. And I missed you all the time."

"Dore, get out of here."

"Are you sick?"

"I think so."

"What can I do?"

"Just go, Dore."

"Do you want me to fix you something to eat before we go to the Governor's Day . . ."

"No. We? *We* aren't going."

"We . . ."

"I don't want you along tonight, Dore. It's going to be a rough evening."

"I won't bother you."

"I didn't say you would. But you can't go, I won't have time to . . ."

"Jim can sit with me."

"He's not going, either. There's something I want him to do. Now, go put on your clothes and write a letter to that goddamn pianist who was sucking up to you."

Her voice was shrill. *"People will think . . ."*

"Dore!"

"Just answer one question. When did you stop caring whether I lived or died?"

"Get out, Dore. I can't say a damn thing to you when you're acting like this."

Practice sighed and turned toward the Governor's desk, a

cherished leftover from his college days. Over the desk, in defiance of the order and tranquillity wrought by the decorator, was a display of cheaply framed documents and photographs: John Guthrie as a law student, as a jazz musician in the murky Chicago night haunts of the late thirties, as a pilot in the RCAF during the battle for Great Britain. John Guthrie had lived hard in his youth without being pretentiously glamorous, and had survived the excess of his energies to fight a more subtle and involved battle with Starne Kinsaker.

It was not the kind of fighting he had a taste for, Practice thought. It pinched at his nerves and soured his blood, so that he was given to sullen and irrational moods. Politics had made his reputation as a man, but had shackled him to a curiously crippling half-life at the same time.

Practice didn't hear Dore, and thought she must have come out of the bathroom, seen him, then made her exit through the kitchen to her own bedroom. After waiting a couple of minutes, he turned around and almost jumped.

Dore was standing in the middle of the carpet, completely nude, her shoulders hunched, one fist pushed up hard against her forehead, between her eyes. She was sobbing without a sound, digging her toes into the carpet.

In moving the draperies to get at the balcony doors, Practice had allowed a shallow stream of light into the bedroom. It angled sharply across Dore's body at the small dimple of her navel, so that he could see the straining muscles of stomach, thighs, and calves. Even in such an unbecoming pose there was something quite gentle and tender, almost childlike, about Dore's body. It was as if no eyes but hers had ever seen it, as if she had never borne a child or loved a man.

She was twenty-eight, and her hair had probably been a natural, if streaky, blond before she started sitting in at the beautician's three afternoons a week. Dore had a figure which Lucy had once wryly described as "colossal": long legs, just enough hip, and high, slightly elongated breasts that kept their shape and their rise without support. Her eyes were big and sooty blue in a catlike face that might have been prettier; an unfortunately carnal mouth diminished the effect of softly planed cheeks and jaw.

But there was something timorous and indefinite about her sex that a man would rarely identify, and that was a shame. Perhaps because of a confusion of emotions, she made the obvious choice and dressed to be sexually meaningful, was afraid of her purpose, and thus a failure. Frequently she believed that people were thinking badly of her—an intercepted smile or misunderstood wink would crush her—but she'd only try more frantically to be liked. Perhaps the moment might come when she could slip away from the party; Practice had seen her at such moments because he spent his time observing, not participating. He had seen her sitting under the trees in a dark landscape, staring at nothing, and when he could arrange to do so, he went out and sat with Dore and silently shared a cigarette with her. He sat with her not out of pity but in recognition, because in a distorted way the fact of Dore's life repeated his own. Knock, knock, and you went in where you didn't belong, in your best clothes, and somebody dumped a bucket of slops on your head.

Practice heard a gasp from Dore, and then there was a momentary silence. She hurried across the carpet and he looked up in time to see one bare leg vanish, as she drew the door to the bedroom closed behind her.

He crossed to the bathroom and rapped on the door. "Governor?"

"Where the hell have you been? Come in."

The firm which had redesigned and redecorated much of the mansion had installed new fixtures and a slip-proof tile floor in the Governor's bathroom, but otherwise had left it much as before. The carved oaken panels of the ceiling were bleached to a paler shade, along with the wood of the deep glass-fronted cupboards. The glass was leaded, except for a clear diamond center pane, one to each shelf, for displaying the Governor's collection of family shaving mugs. The bathtub took up all of one wall of the room.

Guthrie was lying full length in his tub, water chest-high, his head supported by a plastic float that resembled a horse collar.

"Any news about Sharp?"

"No," Practice said, clearing a bench opposite the bathtub. "He's not in town yet."

"But he'll be at the dinner tonight."

"He made that piece of news known two weeks ago. There hasn't been another word from him or his associates."

"Damn it, Jim," the Governor complained, "I don't think you've done much of a job this time."

Practice looked swiftly at him. Guthrie's eyes were closed, but he looked unrested. Shampoo lather was dripping from one ear, foaming over his thick, dark shoulders and chest. He checked a curt reply. The afternoon had been a bad one, and he didn't want a fight with Guthrie to cap it off.

"I've done my work, John. A.B. Sharp is even more eccentric than your old friend Major Kinsaker. He doesn't own a telephone. All of his mail goes directly to his lawyers. You can't drive within a mile of his house. I tried. Not many people even see that old boy from one year to the next."

"But he can swing a quarter-million votes in six important districts. Ever since I can remember he and the Major have had a common view about politics, although maybe they don't say a dozen words to each other, week in and week out. The Kinsakers have always held the land next to Sharp's up there in Greenbard, and they both wear the old school tie, so I suppose a gentleman's agreement was a natural and unspoken thing between them. What do you suppose'll happen, Jimmy, if old A.B. has decided to dissolve his gentleman's agreement with the Major?"

"After that, the deluge."

The Governor nodded, and massaged his eyes with fingers

that trembled as he raised them. Practice frowned. Guthrie
was a shaken man and the sight disturbed him.

Guthrie was so dark he looked purple under the eyes and
down from the ears where he shaved and under his still-firm
jaw. At the age of forty-eight his hairline was slipping back
rapidly, giving him a lofty forehead and a shine at the
temples. His black eyes looked suspicious when he scowled
and sensual when he smiled. The sex in his face came from
those eyes, from a straight chin with an arrogant commalike
notch at its base. He wore glasses more often now, and they
added a certain dignity and maturity to his appeal; and his
hair feathered up from a brushing in a way that made
women want instinctively to reach up and smooth it down.

"I have dreams at night, Jimmy. The two of us, the Major
and myself, on a landscape as bleak as the moon, trying to
kill each other. Some nights I win; some nights he kills me."
For a moment pain glinted in his eyes; there was a vulnerable, scared twist to his mouth. "I don't have a taste for blood
anymore, Jimmy. But how can I stop now?"

"Maybe it's not up to you. A.B. Sharp may have the
answers." He hesitated, and then added, "I think the Major
already knows what Sharp is going to do."

Guthrie floundered in the tub, removing the float from
his neck. He stood up.

"Hand me a towel, Jimmy. When did you see the Major?"

"This afternoon."

Guthrie took the proffered towel and began drying himself.

"What did he have to say?" Guthrie asked, not as casual as
he was pretending to be.

"It wasn't what he said; it was the way he looked, like a
man with a barb sunk deep in his guts."

"Then he'll quit." Still half wet, Guthrie reached for his
robe. He was perhaps an inch shorter than Practice and
carried ten more pounds, but not well; he was sinking into a
ponderous belly. He stood flat-footed beside the tub, wrap-

ping the robe around him, then slid his feet into slippers and went into the bedroom. Practice rose slowly and followed.

The Governor was standing at the west windows, the draperies gathered in one hand, his face looking clean and as white as bone in the pale light from the sky.

"No, he won't quit," Practice said.

Guthrie remained standing by the windows until the light had failed appreciably. He shook himself once, all over, as if something was clinging to his back. Then he sat down in front of his little-used baby grand piano and spread both hands over the uncovered keyboard.

"Jimmy, I'm getting to where I hate life," he said tonelessly, and smashed his fingers against the keyboard with all his might. "Fix me a drink?"

"Sorry," Practice said, drawling. "Not one of my better days."

The Governor glanced up at him, then rose and went to his liquor cabinet. After making his choice, he disappeared into the kitchen for ice.

"I can't say what it is that makes me feel this way. The family doesn't like it, of course, this bloody scrimmaging with the Major; it isn't gentlemanly at all. But then it's been a long time since I cared how they felt about anything. Maybe it's because I've always taken it for granted that I was an exceptional man. I've been righteously arrogant about it. Well, being Governor doesn't take an exceptional man, no great intellect, no qualities of saint and mule skinner. All it takes is a tremendous ego, a rind like a pineapple instead of skin, and some of the commoner traits of the fanatic. All I've brought to the job was ego. Unfortunately, my skin is not always thick enough. I can handle any man in an open fight. What I can't tolerate is"—he returned to the bedroom, holding his glass high in one hand, squinting at the color of the whiskey—"the damned undertow that's always trying to sweep me out where I can't keep my head above water, where the crabs are waiting to take a pinch of flesh here and a bite there. And when they've had their flesh, come and gone in the dark, the big boys move in. It's the sharks that take their meals in chunks, until the bones are clean."

He sat on the edge of a chair, with his oversize bare feet sticking up from the carpet, and reached into a pocket of his robe. "Come here, Jimmy."

By the time Practice had approached the chair, Guthrie had unfolded a sheet of paper and was holding it in his lap.

"Switch on the light."

Practice did so and looked down in puzzlement.

"Where did that come from?"

"Crank mail. Wastebasket stuff."

"But you kept this one." He pursed his lips. "Mind if I take it and use the glass on it?"

"No, go ahead."

Practice accepted the leaf and carried it to the desk. There he weighted down each corner of the yellowing paper and turned on a powerful desk lamp.

He was looking at a four-color drawing on fairly heavy, smooth paper, in dimension about six inches by nine inches. The left side of the paper was unevenly frayed, as if it had been carefully torn from a book, a book of fairy tales, he guessed, although neither the title of the book nor the page number was left. The reverse side was blank, except for some of the same brownish-red smears which decorated the margins of the drawing.

The drawing itself featured a scaly, blue and green dragon with a lashing, arrow-tipped tail. The dragon, crouched in front of a cavern, was bleeding from a sword puncture approximately where his "heart" might have been.

The sword-wielder was a young, apple-cheeked, blue-eyed knight in armor. He held the huge double-edged sword by the hilt with both hands, and had raised it for another swipe.

Someone had carefully pasted over the dragon's head a photograph of Governor John Guthrie.

Practice didn't know whether to laugh or not. He picked

up the magnifying glass and carefully studied the brown-red stains in the margin. Under closer scrutiny two and a half fingerprints—or was one a thumbprint?—became clear. Again he studied the pasted-on photograph, which probably had been cut from a newspaper. No prints showed around the photograph or in the two streaks of glue that bound it to the sheet. He removed the weights and picked up the paper, sniffing the glue.

"What do you think of it?" Guthrie asked. He had started a cigar and the air around his head was a drifting blue.

"Childish. But . . ."

"I know. The fingerprints. That's blood, isn't it, Jimmy?"

Practice frowned. "Hard to say. The fingerprints are nearly as old as the paper itself. The paper is good quality; it wouldn't age quickly unless the book were left open to the air. I'd say the page was torn out recently. I'm sure the picture of you was pasted in just a day or two ago. The glue still has an odor."

"What about the fingerprints?"

"I'm no expert. I remember most of what they taught me at the state patrol school. Chances are these are the fingerprints of a woman—or maybe a child. Do you have the envelope?"

"No. There was nothing on it but a typed address: Governor John Guthrie, the Capitol, and so on. And a *personal*, underlined three times. Postmarked here in the city, eleven o'clock Monday night."

"When did you receive it?"

"Today. Paul opens most of the mail marked personal, unless it has a name on it which he recognizes. He opened this one, thought to tear it up, then had one of those cases of the shivers he gets from time to time. So he had to show it to me. And bring up . . ."

The Governor took his cigar out of his mouth and sat glowering at it.

"Bring up what?"

"You know how Dunhill is," the Governor growled. "He's a damned superstitious old lady. Always reading more into these crank notes than anyone else would. For some reason the Hilda Brudder thing has been on his mind again. I ran him off before he could rehash the whole case and get himself thoroughly hysterical."

Practice nodded, his eyes on the storybook dragon and knight, wondering what tale the drawing had illustrated. Was the knight one of King Arthur's or some unknown Prince? Or even a commoner proving his mettle? His knowledge of fairy tales was sketchy; there had been few books in his father's house.

With a faraway look in his eye, Practice put the drawing carefully on the desk and began hunting in one of the drawers for an envelope.

The Governor smoked silently in his chair, his eyes closed again. Perhaps he was thinking of Hilda Brudder, who had been the first of little Chris's nursemaids. She had been a part of the Guthrie household from the day Dore brought Chris home from the hospital and in a panic gave the baby over to Hilda's care. Hilda had the instinct for raising children which Dore seemed to lack entirely.

Hilda was a big-shouldered, round-faced woman who had spent the pre–World War years of her life in Bremen. She spoke competent English, had the constitution of a dray horse, and liked nothing better than to spend her free time tramping around the woods or, in winter, to skate with surprising deftness on the frozen ponds and streams around the city.

As soon as Chris was able to walk, she began taking him to the park at the edge of the city. Shortly after Chris's third birthday Hilda was killed.

Two women found Chris, alone and hysterical, wandering on one of the paths, with blood in his hair and on his face. At about the same time, Hilda was discovered at the edge of the lake, sitting cross-legged, slumped against a tree. She had been shot cleanly through the neck. Chris hadn't been able to say much. Apparently he was sitting in her lap when the bullet struck. The subsequent investigation turned up no information. The Commissioner of the Highway Patrol, a good friend of Guthrie's, concluded that Hilda had been killed by a stray bullet from someone hunting in the hills and woods above the lake. Several hunters who had been in the vicinity were tracked down and questioned, but all denied shooting in the direction of the park.

After that, Chris had had a succession of nurses with whom he had been moody and uncooperative. Lucy had done a lot for the boy in the year and a half she had been at the mansion, and if Chris remembered Hilda Brudder at all he never spoke of her.

"Why should Dunhill bring up Hilda Brudder?" Practice asked now.

Guthrie got to his feet and stuffed his cigar into an ashtray.

"You know what he thought at the time. Some nut was taking a whack at Chris and got Hilda instead."

"He should have given up that idea by now," Practice said. "If someone had been gunning for Chris, he could have killed Chris right after Hilda."

"Sure, I know. Dunhill's an old lady." Guthrie gestured with one hand. "That thing . . ."

"What do you want me to do with it?"

Guthrie shrugged. "Throw it away, I suppose. Still—it's weird."

"Most of the vicious mail you get is the Dear Bastard, I'm going to kill you, sort of thing. This is more complicated. The fantasy involved is no spur-of-the-moment inspiration. I'm curious about these fingerprints, the bloodstains—if they are bloodstains."

Guthrie had gone to his closet and was standing with the door open, choosing a suit.

"I'm curious, too," he said softly.

"You don't have any idea who it came from?"

"No idea. See what you can come up with, but don't waste a lot of time."

"I'll get on it in the morning."

"No." Guthrie took a dark gray suit from the closet and held it up to inspect it for creases. "Do it tonight. Bill Dylan's probably still in his office. Give him a call."

Bill Dylan was the local agent of the FBI, who ran a one-man office in the Department of State building.

"Why Dylan?"

"If you start sleuthing around with that drawing and those fingerprints, word'll get out. Oh, it's nothing; I know it's nothing. But the thing is ridiculous enough to make me look damned silly, and I've got enough on my mind without a lot of people giggling behind my back."

"Dylan it is," Practice said, sealing the drawing into a clasp envelope. "I'll call the Commissioner and have him send one of his boys over to drive you to the rally."

"Won't be necessary. Luke can drive."

"If I'm not going, I want somebody I can depend on to be there," Practice said obstinately.

Guthrie sighed. "Suit yourself."

"I'll either be at Lex's Steak House getting my dinner while Dylan does my work or here at the mansion," Practice said. He went out, the yellow clasp envelope tucked under his arm.

4

Bill Dylan turned the rust-stained page Practice had brought him, then laid it atop the envelope and settled back in his chair, gazing out of the window of his tenth-floor office at the flow of traffic in the street below.

"Why bring it to me?" he asked Practice. "I've seen political cartoons more threatening than this."

"The bloodstains, for one thing."

"Can't say for sure that it's blood."

"Assuming it is. The whole concept is grotesque and a little frightening. I'd like to know who sent it. Maybe he's somebody I should talk to."

Dylan stood up and began rolling down the sleeves of his shirt.

"Whoever the sender is, he's probably eager for attention. He might as well have signed his name."

"Are those fingerprints good enough for a trace?"

"I think so," Dylan murmured, holding the paper up to the light again. "And your man, or your woman, if that's the case, must have known that. Of course, the prints might not be those of the sender."

"Can you work on it for me, Bill?"

"Officially I can't. But . . ." The FBI agent glanced at his watch. "I'm already keeping half the file clerks in this place on overtime. I could drop this off at the state patrol lab on my way to dinner. Truscott owes me a favor. Shouldn't take long for his department to test these stains and photograph the prints. I'll send a set of photographs over to the ten o'clock plane and have the girls downstairs check the classifications through the state files. Are you in a hurry for the data?"

"I'd like to get this thing cleared up."

"It'll take six hours at the most to run through the state files. Probably two days by wire from Washington, if the subject is still living. I wish I had the envelope. Guthrie shouldn't have thrown it away."

"More likely his secretary. Thanks a lot, Bill. The Governor appreciates this."

Dylan grinned. "The hell with him. It's his duck blind I'm interested in. Best location on the lake."

They went down together in the elevator and parted on the terrace of the new state office building. It was full dark and the neon of the Congress Hotel on the hill flashed redly in the sky. The air had turned chilly and Practice wished he had remembered his trench coat as he walked in the direction of the hotel. He had no plans for the evening other than a leisurely dinner at Lex's, the best steak house in town. After that, it would be several hours before he knew if the fingerprints on the drawing had turned up in the limited files of the state's investigation bureau.

A man in a winter topcoat and muffler dashed down the steps of the Congress Hotel's main entrance in front of him, and Practice called, "Fletch! Dr. Childs . . ."

Fletcher Childs hesitated, then gathered himself and hurried on for a few strides. Then he stopped and looked cautiously around. He smiled.

"Oh, hello, Jim. Didn't recognize—thought it was one of my patients. Didn't want to get started on gallbladder diets in the middle of Tenth Street." He was a tall, stooped man with the kind of prim, professorial face reminiscent of Woodrow Wilson. Dr. Fletcher Childs, however, preferred horn-rimmed glasses, which he continually had to adjust on the bridge of his nose. "I'm in a flap. Haven't dressed and the dinner starts in three quarters of—suppose Lucy's on your mind, too. Why don't you walk over to the parking garage with me, if you—hell of a thing, I admit I don't know what to say to her."

"What's on your mind?" Practice said noncommittally, puzzled by the doctor's reference to his sister.

They waited for a cruising taxi to pass and hurried across the street.

"Why would he just run off?" Dr. Childs muttered. "Suppose I frightened—I might have said something—but no; I remember, I didn't say . . ." He flashed a look at Practice, who was keeping pace with him but not without effort.

"What I said was," he went on, as if he were simplifying a point for one of his classes at the medical school: " 'Lucy? Is that you, Lucy?' And I flashed my light in the garden, because it was dark. The moment the light touched him, he threw up his arm, over his face, then turned and ran. Right through the shrubbery. Made a terrible mess. I had to call the nursery and have them send a man out. And Lucy . . ."

"What about Lucy?" Practice asked patiently, knowing Fletch Childs well enough to let him run on. He might circle the point of his story several times, but he always landed on it dead center.

Dr. Childs raised a hand to steady his slipping glasses. The two men had stopped just inside the entrance of the city parking lot, and the doctor burrowed deeper inside his muffler with his chin, as if an icy wind were scouring the street.

"She just sat there in the swing, long after the boy had run away, with tears on her face, looking after him, crying. Hardly said a word to me. She looked very unhappy. Didn't stay that way for long. You understand? Came into the kitchen while I was having my medicine and kissed me on the cheek and went up to bed. She was all right then."

"This was last weekend, when Lucy was off," Practice said slowly.

"Yes, yes. I dozed off about nine o'clock in my room, but the alarm woke me at ten of twelve. Time to take my medicine. You understand? And I heard voices in the garden. Low. Couldn't make out what was said. But I recognized Lucy's voice. Didn't think anything of it. I thought it must have been you."

"I was out of town."

"Remembered. The other voice got louder, but he wasn't —talking. More like making a speech. Reciting. Is this clear?" Dr. Childs angled a look at Practice, as if he suspected him of skepticism. "Finally got on my nerves, high-pitched voice, almost hysterical. Took my light and went out by the kitchen door. Just to see—to see . . ."

"To see if Lucy was all right?"

"Yes. That's it."

"She *was* all right? Except for the tears, I mean."

The doctor nodded, almost losing his glasses.

"Who was it? Had you seen him before?"

"Well, no," Dr. Childs said, and peered at his wristwatch. "Never really *saw* the boy—until last Sunday night."

"How do you mean?"

He fidgeted. "Once before, when Lucy was home, he came. Knocked on the door. He wouldn't come inside. They stayed on the front porch for about an hour."

"Did Lucy tell you who he was?"

"He was a friend, she said. A friend who—no—she didn't say *friend*. Someone who needed her." The doctor nodded soberly into his muffler. "I suppose—you understand? When she was in nursing school, all kinds of people came to see her. People with troubles. Too many troubles." Abruptly he turned away. "Forty minutes," he said fretfully. "Important night. May I carry you . . . ?"

"I'm just going across the street for dinner, Doctor. Do you know what this boy looks like?"

Dr. Childs shook his head. "Tall. Taller than you. And thin." He took several quick steps up the ramp to the parking levels, then turned and looked back. "Very white face. Like a clown's. Hard to say—that face, that voice. You understand? Maybe it wasn't a boy at all."

In a few moments he had disappeared up the ramp and Practice turned thoughtfully toward the street, chewing on the end of a paper match in the absence of a cigarette. Dr. Childs's disjointed story had given him several things to think about, all concerning Lucy.

The parents of Lucy and Fletcher Childs had died when Lucy was very young. Fortunately her brother was considerably older than she, had finished medical school and his residency, and was able to make a home for her—a home inevitably dominated by young doctors and medical discussions, so that Lucy grew up wanting to be a nurse. She was also somewhat timid and lonely; and Fletch, who could spare her little time, was strict about her upbringing. She saw very little of boys until she enrolled at the state university.

Then she was, for the first time, on her own, exposed to the attractiveness of university life, enrolled in a difficult school that demanded long hours of work and study. She had no trouble with her books, but the hospital work itself left her with little energy in reserve; a lot of things that other girls in her class took for granted came as a series of small shocks to Lucy: death and affliction and the selfishness and fear of individuals who found themselves threatened by both. She weathered two years, and matured. In her third year she fell in love with a surgeon, who had a minimum of conscience as well as a wife and two children at home; and when he was done with Lucy, as he had finished with others like her, she was very near a collapse.

Fletcher Childs hadn't been able to stop the affair from developing, although it was rumored later at the hospital that he had expertly removed four of the surgeon's front teeth with the first and only left hook of his life; but he'd recognized the signs of impending mental breakdown and taken Lucy from the school, not long before her class was due to graduate.

He turned to a longtime friend, Dr. Edward Mackerras,

who was in charge of the state mental hospital. Mackerras was hesitant about recommending either the state hospital or a private institution for Lucy; after several talks with her, he decided to invite her to live in his house on the grounds of the state hospital. There she would be under observation for as long as they both felt was necessary, yet she wouldn't be exposed to the routine of institutional life.

Lucy had spent a year and a half with Dr. Mackerras, working part-time in the hospital dispensary to help her therapy. After an initial period of depression and isolation, she had begun to take an interest in the problems of the other patients, and by the end of her stay had several unofficial "cases" of her own—to Dr. Mackerras's secret satisfaction.

Lex's hadn't filled up yet, and Practice was shown to a booth at the back. He had scarcely looked over the menu and begun his usual debate—prime ribs versus T-bone— when he felt someone standing over him.

"Hi," Steppie said. "Saw you come in. Room for me?"

"Why not?" Practice said casually, but he wasn't in the mood for his ex-wife's company, and he hoped she wouldn't stay long.

Steppie sat down opposite him with a rustling of some very expensive dress material. The cocktail dress was pale orange, a shade she wore well, and showed most of her bare arms and a good half of her bosom, without showing her true age.

"How long's it been?" Steppie asked. "Six weeks? I've meant to call you. Keeping busy?"

He nodded, and she raised her glass to her lips, looked at him over the brim, and regretfully finished the last of the drink she'd brought with her.

"I thought you'd be married by now," Steppie said with lofty good cheer. "So I heard—you and Fletch Childs's sister. The delicate-looking kid who wears clothes so well. No? No marriage yet? Say, Jim, let's get out of here. You can order your steak in the bar and buy me another one of these, and we'll have a nice talk before I have to run. Doesn't bother you in the bar, does it?"

"No," he said wearily.

"Come on, then. I don't like this crowd I'm with, and if they see me come in with my ex, they'll leave us alone. Be a sport, Jim."

Nothing changed about Steppie, he thought, as he followed her from the restaurant into the adjoining bar. You followed wherever Steppie might go. You jumped out of airplanes or spent the night in a tree house or made long-distance phone calls to political figures in Moscow. That was being a sport.

They took a booth in the bar next to the rotisserie, and Steppie firmly waved off a couple who seemed inclined to join them. He ordered the T-bone and settled back.

"So you've actually stayed on the wagon," Steppie said teasingly, holding up a fresh daiquiri to the light. "How about it? Do you sneak one or two before you go to bed? Why don't you take a little sip now? One sip won't hurt you. Please."

"Don't be so goddamn childish, Steppie," he said sharply.

"Sorry," she murmured, and withdrew, her gaze wandering around the interior of the bar. She looked forlorn, and he felt ashamed for a moment, wondering if it was yet another act or if he had hurt her. With Steppie it was hard to tell.

"I was hoping we could be friendly, Jim. I mean that." She gave him a haunting look he remembered well. "I'm not very happy," she continued in a low voice, as if she were at a confessional. "No, I'm trying to be serious. You get that suffering look on your face as if I'm talking bull, and I'm not."

She reached out and took his hand between her own, and he didn't try to pull it away. Her own were icy, and not solely from holding the daiquiri. He realized they were being observed, talked about, and that the hand-holding would assume a disproportionate significance in the gossip of the city during the next few days. Somehow Lucy would find out, but at the moment it didn't make much difference to him.

"It's just a phase, Steppie," he said.

"No, it's *not*," she insisted, turning her wrist slightly so that she could see the face of her watch, then leaning toward him to intensify their contact. "Oh, I knew you'd be like this," she said, shutting her eyes for a moment and looking decidedly more youthful. A strand of hair had worked free of the comb and was dangling; she shook her head like a colt. "I've felt this way for a long time, Jim. At least a year. I want to get free of this town and everybody in it."

"Eight years ago I couldn't drag you away."

"I've changed since then."

"Have you?"

"Yes. Will you listen to me? Stop sitting there with that cynical mouth and really listen to me, because I'm in earnest."

"I've won my right to be cynical, Steppie."

"I know," she said. "Believe me, I know it." Her hands gripped his more tightly, then relaxed. "I want to sell the shop and be free of this town. I want to move somewhere else. San Francisco, New York. Meet new people . . ."

"Start a new life," he said.

"Yes. Start . . ." She blinked, and her expression grew a little cold. "Well, then, if you're going to take it this way . . ."

"Go on, Steppie. I'm listening."

Her head was down and a bitter smile appeared.

"What's the use? I thought it would be a cinch. I've been planning this for weeks. Just walk right up to you and say, 'Jim, I still love you and I need you. Marry me again and let's get out of here and . . .'" She stopped, her voice dry, and swallowed a couple of times. "It isn't very goddamn easy," she said, almost whispering.

"And this isn't the place." He felt the touch of her hands then, for the first time, and a painful wrenching in his chest, through his heart. "Steppie, how can we sit here and talk about love? I don't even *remember* us very well. Don't you realize that? I went almost all the way down. Any farther and it would have meant sleeping in doorways and eating in soup lines the three or four years it took my kidneys to rot. That bad, Steppie. And where the hell . . ."

"Stop it," she said: there were tears in her eyes. "Stop, I know what's next."

Do you? he thought. And do I believe you now, that your hunger to escape is as pure as mine, or is this more playtime, more calculation, the surefire approach? Was I as good as all that, Steppie? He thought of the years away from Steppie, the other man she had married, all the other men besides himself.

She withdrew her hands and reached into a small purse for a handkerchief, which she held unobtrusively in one fist to dry the eye that was tearing most.

"Whatever you want from me," she said, "I'm ready to give. I want you back, so bad you don't know. Jim"—she looked up again, her eyes gleaming with tears—"something's hap-hap—I swear, if you marry me, I'll be—I'll try . . ."

He looked down at the table, not able to bear much more.

"I can have children, still. At least two. I want children, Jim."

"Steppie. It's *all over*."

For almost a minute he heard nothing but the voices around him in the crowded grill, a few fragments of conversation. He wouldn't lift his eyes.

"I know how bad I was," Steppie said, a note of urgency and contrition in her voice. "I couldn't help it, because you—you let me be that way. I think I was always hoping you'd treat me the way I deserved to be treated. But now I . . ." She drew a sharp breath. "All right. I guess I'm not up to her standards, am I? Little Lucy, she's a—a dish, that's for sure. Jim, I can see why . . ."

Practice heard the rustling of her dress as she stood up and quickly sidestepped out of the booth. His hands were clenched, separately, on the table. Then she was standing beside him and a hand with surprising strength in it gripped his shoulder.

He raised his head and felt a little stunned at the look of terror in Steppie's eyes as she bent to whisper in his ear, *"Something awful's going to happen to me!"*

He started up, but she was already moving rapidly through the rear of the bar, thrusting her way through knots of men, who glanced after her in astonishment. Practice hesitated, still a little shocked by the look in her eyes and the anguish in her voice. Then he hurried after Steppie, pushing against the same men, who yielded resentfully a second time, to the back entrance where an arriving couple blocked the door.

By the time he reached the stairs of the alley he saw Steppie by the light of a printer's shop across the way, sitting in the back seat of an old Cadillac limousine, a stiff smile on her face. The limousine pulled quickly away with the smooth roar of a well-tended engine. But not before Practice had a glimpse of Major Starne Kinsaker in the seat beside her.

5

He had a two-room apartment in an old brick building that was located midway between the waterworks and a Catholic cemetery overlooking the river, where no funerals had been held for at least thirty years. From his bedroom window Practice could see the water stack, which had been abandoned when the city outgrew its capacity.

One window of his apartment was open, and the curtains, which Lucy had picked out for him, billowed occasionally in

the strong evening breeze. He lay on the bed with his feet up
on the iron headboard and smoked. On the back steps of
the building a milk bottle toppled, rolled, and broke.
He shifted his weight on the bed, holding his cigarette at the
tip end as it burned closer to his fingers. He was remembering a marriage.

The Army had claimed him at seventeen, and he was at
Schofield when the Japanese attacked Pearl Harbor, already
a seasoned soldier; his first three stripes came quickly after
that.

Following the war, he finished at the state university in
three years, attending all sessions. For extra money he
parked cars and drove a milk truck. Before he was half
through his undergraduate courses, he knew he wanted to
be a trial lawyer. He went out with a lot of women, some of
them perpetual students, practicing intellectuals, not too
predictably cynical to be boring as yet. All the relationships
were casual, beer and two hours of bed, the sort of thing that
made younger men grind their teeth with envy; and because
his background was more glamorous than that of other
bachelor vets—two battlefield commissions—a lot of the
prettiest girls went out of their way to cross his path.

Steppie Saunders never went out of her way. They met by
accident, parted friends, ran into each other a couple of
more times, started dating.

Steppie, the only daughter of a fairly prosperous automobile dealer in town, was the *enfant terrible* of a generally rich
and lamebrained crowd. By her senior year she had two
broken engagements behind her and a reputation for sexual
liberality which she in no way deserved; the truth was, boys
didn't last long enough with Steppie for any real intimacy to
develop. She had a sharp tongue, an eye for the ridiculous,
and no hesitancy about speaking her mind. On the other
hand, when she thought she was overmatched, she could be
gracious and devoted.

Practice never intended to fall in love with her. She was a decided contrast from the girls he was usually involved with. And, when he met Steppie, he was bone-tired. The war had sapped him, and five years of uninterrupted study had dulled his purpose. Her light touch and amusing, sometimes childish viewpoints were refreshing.

Things began to go sour when her father died. Steppie and Wilbur Saunders had fought ferociously all her life, but in a complex way she was devoted to him, and his death was torture for her. Practice was then angling for a place with a good law firm in Fort Frontenac.

"I won't leave Osage Bluff," Steppie had told him.

"Why?"

"Because it's always been my home."

"I can't afford to turn down the chance," he protested.

"You'd better turn it down."

He hadn't argued with her, because of her dead father and because he was a little uncertain of himself in the face of her ultimatum. His first mistake—the others multiplied quickly after that.

"Why don't you take over the auto agency?" she said one morning, when he was still sounding out job opportunities in the capital. There weren't many.

"I'm a lawyer, honey. I don't know anything about selling cars."

"Of course not," Steppie said impatiently, "but you'll learn. I can't bear to see the agency sold. It's been in the family for fifty years."

"I'm a lawyer," he said stubbornly.

"Jim, let's get down to hard facts now, baby. Certainly you're a lawyer. You have a degree to prove it and you've passed all those difficult state examinations. I'm proud of you. But you don't have to beat your brains out in some little office for coolie scale the next fifteen years to prove a point. I want a few things out of life, Jim."

"You've got the house, his car, and his insurance."

"His house, his car. And damned little insurance. I want a house of my own, a *new* one. The agency is mine, Jim, and I'm not letting go of it, not just to salve your ego. Why, you can make ten times more money at the agency than you'd make as a lawyer. Let's just keep our heads about this."

He had his weaknesses; Steppie was only one of them. The memories of a redneck boyhood were still painfully real to him. Money, or the promise of big money, weakened him further. After a show of indecision, and a great wrestling with his conscience, he took over the automobile agency.

The funny thing was, as soon as he had done so, Steppie wasn't the same Steppie anymore. But he didn't become aware of this all at once. He was too busy. The new house was going up in the best part of town; he was learning the business, or doing his best to learn it; and nearly every night he and Steppie were entertaining or being entertained.

It took him just sixteen months to steer the agency to the brink of bankruptcy. He was not a businessman; even if he had been, the endless alcohol-fogged nights that stretched well into the following days would have numbed him to the point where making a go of the agency was a near impossibility.

Besides his own inexperience, he had inherited another handicap; Wilbur Saunders had been something of a cheat, and there was no backlog of goodwill to speak of. Practice tried to lure vanished customers with a heavy advertising campaign; unhappily, the new model was a lemon. Not even the shrewdest dealers were moving it that year.

He was working fourteen hours and staying out most nights until three, and one day he carried a bottle to work with him from the party the night before. Thereafter, a full pint accompanied him to work every morning and went, empty, into the trash can at night. The pint became a fifth. Vaguely, he understood what was happening to him, but he couldn't help it. The liquor put a necessary fire into him. Only because of the liquor could he go down every day to the agency, which had assumed the proportions of a devouring ogre in his mind. He and Steppie were in debt up to their ears; home was no refuge, only another battleground.

The end of their marriage came at one of the interminable parties where everybody knew everybody else, much too intimately. They were Steppie's "crowd"; he was a gander among swans, honking as loudly as anybody but somehow not in unison. He had suspected her for months—this man, that man—she was too friendly with some of the bastards she'd known most of her life, and had dated. They were probably all having a good laugh behind his back. The shame of failure had blighted most of his confidence; the liquor had turned to pure jealousy and hatred in his veins. No, he hadn't caught her, but by God he knew there was something, had to be.

That night he was playing the game he had rigged; sulking with his liquor in one corner of the house, pretending drunkenness so they would leave him alone, so Steppie would feel safe. The drunkenness, however, became a fact and he lost track of great chunks of time. He knew only that it was very, very late and that he hadn't seen his wife for some time. He went in search of her, through the crowded rooms of an unfamiliar house, feeling a barely discernible anxiety that had nothing to do with a possible infidelity on Steppie's part. He felt that he was going to die, that he must tell her before it was too late, and his anxiety became a paralyzing dread.

His search took him to a small back bedroom on the second floor of the house, and there was Steppie sitting on the edge of a bed with the straps of her dress down. A man was bending over her, one hand on her shoulder. It looked to him as if she were getting dressed after being on the bed, at least the covers were disarrayed. There was no surprise in her face at his appearance, only a weary resignation.

What he had to say to her brought a scowl and then a murderous look.

He might have saved them both if he had dragged her from the room and out of the house in full view of everyone present. But he could only hang on to the door frame, gasping out filth, while the man protested and tried to restrain him.

Steppie rose from the bed and came toward him, slit-eyed and filled with wrath. She pushed the man aside and began talking to her husband in a high but controlled voice. She demolished him on the spot, or rather she completed the demolition that was well under way. He didn't see the people in the hall behind him, and he didn't know how still the house became as her voice carried.

Even while the carnage was going on, he had the insight that she was begging him to be a man, to make her stop. He tried. He gathered his strength and for a few moments his mind functioned, and he started toward his wife. Then he broke down again inside, and tears gushed from his eyes. There might have been a moment of horror in her own eyes, but he didn't see it; instead he turned and fled from Steppie, beating his way down the hall with an incoherent stammer, desperate to be free of the house and the faces that swam in the air around him, desperate to hide from her, and all the truth she had told.

They were his last moments of clarity for some time.

Six weeks later he woke up in an unfamiliar room with a clear blue sky outside that made his eyes ache. He fumbled on the floor beside the bed for his bottle, and, finding no bottle, struggled up from the blankets in a panic to see John Guthrie sitting in a chair nearby, watching him. Guthrie was wearing boots, Levi's, and a corduroy hunting coat. His glasses flashed in the light of the lamp behind his chair.

"Welcome to the fourth day," he said.

"Fourth day?"

"Your fourth day without a drink. For a man in your condition, you've put up some good scraps." He touched a hand to a lump on his chin and grinned. "Three good scraps." He turned his head toward a small kitchen in the cabin. "The liquor's in there, if you want to try to get it. If you try, we're going to go 'round again."

Practice looked at a half-shattered mirror and a broken chair and sank back onto the bed.

"What do you think you're doing?"

"Playing Christus, I suppose. How do you feel?"

"I ache, I ache! Steppie."

John Guthrie rose and crossed slowly to the bed.

"There is no more Steppie," he said. "She came to me and asked me to handle the divorce, but I wouldn't do it. Tried to talk her out of it, but nobody's ever talked to that kid and made it stick. She's in Reno now, on the fifth week of her six weeks' residence. I'm a little sorry for you, if that's worth anything."

"I don't care what you feel, you son of a bitch." He closed his eyes then and dozed off. When he woke it was dark, and there was a smell of broiling steak in the cabin. His sore stomach muscles contracted. He could barely move his body at all.

He began trying to reconstruct the last few months, but each effort threw him into such profound despair that he gave up trying. Then he struggled up again to a sitting position, and hung on to the frame of the bed, gasping.

"Need help?" Guthrie asked.

"You'd better give me a drink," Practice said, "because if you don't, the first chance I get I'm going to kill you."

Guthrie's chair scraped on the floor. The next thing Practice knew, Guthrie was standing over him with a glass of whiskey in his hand. Practice's throat muscles worked but there was no saliva; he was dehydrated.

"I'll give it to you, and a full quart besides," Guthrie said, "if you still want it after you hear me out. I'll give you the quart and take you back to Fort Frontenac and drop you approximately where I dug you up out of the mud, and let you rot there. You'll rot, all right, because you're an alcoholic. That's the worst of your problems. You've lost your wife and fumbled your way to the door of bankruptcy court, but this"—and he held out the glass—"is your big problem. I don't even say you can lick it, I don't know that much about alcoholism. But I have a friend who does, a real sweet retired M.D. who's made a specialty of rehabilitating problem drinkers at his farm up in the northeast corner of the state. I've told him about you, and he's willing to take you on. The question is, are you worth the effort?"

Practice tried to reach for the glass but the strain on his arm was too much and he fell back, gasping. "I'm not worth the effort," he said.

"I don't know you very well," Guthrie went on. "My firm was ready to give you a job until Steppie steered you into the automobile business. Maybe we would again; maybe I could use you in the Attorney General's office. I'm not making any definite offer because I haven't seen any real signs of life yet." He put his face closer to Practice's. "You hurt, don't you? Good."

"You bastard."

"Because when you stop hurting you're a goner. Let me tell you what really hurts, boy. You castrated yourself in front of fifty people, and that kind of shame is forever."

This time Practice got his hand up to swing at the glass of whiskey, and it spilled on the floor.

Guthrie hit him across the face.

"Maybe all that's left for you to do is break even," he said. "And to do that you might have to go down to the last inch of your guts. Smell the booze? It's a smell you're going to have to pretend doesn't exist."

"I'd like to kill you," Practice muttered.

"Why?"

"Because you've had it all handed to you, every goddamn thing. Money, family, everything."

"Ahhh . . ." Guthrie said in disgust. "Chicken guts. How'd you ever get through the war, Patsy?"

"I was good at it," Practice said through his teeth.

"You were good at it. So good that a spoiled brat with a shrewish tongue could shoot you down in a mess of bloody feathers. Patsy, have I ever wasted a week! I've got better things to do than sit here nursing you and mopping up your chin after you've puked up more of that self-pity you're bloated with. Get on your feet. I'm taking you back to Fort Frontenac, Patsy, where you can bury yourself."

Practice found strength he didn't know he had and shot out a hard right at Guthrie's face. His fist hit high, on the man's temple, and snapped his head around.

Guthrie looked back, grinning, and spat on the floor.

"So you hate me? That figures. I'm a better man than you."

"Not when I'm sober."

"*Any*time, Patsy. I had my woman trouble once, and it was worse than anything you can think of. But I didn't go down into the bottle to get away from it. Get on your feet. I'm tired of you stinking up my place."

Practice put his feet over the side of the bed and sat up, trembling, but he didn't take his eyes off Guthrie.

"Who won?" he asked weakly. "You said we had some scraps."

Guthrie smiled, a little cruelly.

"I whipped your ass good."

"You'll never do it again."

"I figure," Guthrie said, "that even with you in top shape, you're no better than equal to me, and I give away years."

"I'm better," Practice said, "because I want to kill you. And I will."

"Don't you believe it."

"I want to kill you for sticking it in my life, for bringing me back. For holding whiskey under my nose, then slugging me with the bottle. Oh, I've got lots of reasons."

Guthrie went away, then returned with a pair of Levi's and a shirt. He threw them contemptuously at Practice, who put them on. His muscles screamed and his hands trembled. But he dressed, and stood on his feet, with tears streaming down his face.

"Did she send you to find me? Was it Steppie's idea?"

"Steppie wrote you off," Guthrie said evenly. "The idea was my own—a bum one."

"Maybe," Practice said, wiping his wet face on his sleeve, "maybe she shouldn't have written me off."

"How do you feel now?" Guthrie asked in a different tone of voice.

"Sick." He was weaving on his feet, but still standing, thinking about Steppie and about his life.

"Could you eat?"

"I don't know. I'd . . . like to try."

"Sure. I bought some vitamins and some salt tablets. They're good for what ails you. Look, it's five hours to Doc Merrill's. If we leave after dinner we can make it by one in the morning. He's expecting you. When you're able to work, he'll put you to work. Farm labor. Who knows? A couple of months—maybe you won't be Patsy anymore."

"How much—will it cost?"

"Who knows?" Guthrie said with a little smile of satisfaction. "Who knows how much it'll cost?"

Seeing Steppie at the steak house had awakened a beast of a mood, and it was crawling all over him; he didn't have the will to throw it off.

A sound came to Practice. It was familiar, but he couldn't place it. Then he remembered the weak plank on the back porch and how his weight caused it to give. Part of his mind focused on the porch and the dark kitchen, but he didn't move. The sound wasn't repeated. Instead, he heard the rusty action of hinges as the screen door was slowly opened.

He sat up carefully, aware that any sound he made would be heard. The screen door was let softly into its frame. He reached out and pulled open the drawer of the nightstand beside the bed. He hesitated, trying to remember the position of the revolver inside. Then he put his fingers around the butt and drew it out. He shifted the revolver from his right hand to his left and turned his head toward the doorway of the bedroom.

With his thumb he cocked back the hammer of the revolver, and waited.

"Jim?"

He sighed and put the revolver aside, then reached out and turned on the lamp. Chris Guthrie appeared in the hall and looked at him with bright, tired eyes.

"What are you doing here, Chris? It's almost eleven o'clock. Who's with you?"

Chris walked silently in and crawled up on the bed. Practice put the revolver back in the drawer. The boy's lips were trembling.

"Did you walk all the way?"

It was over two miles from the mansion, and Chris had been to his apartment only once before, when Lucy had stopped by with him for a few moments.

Chris nodded.

"Does Lucy know you're gone? She doesn't, does she?"

"Can I stay here?" Chris whispered.

"Why don't we have a cup of coffee together? I was going over to the mansion a little later myself. You can go along, and we'll talk to your dad about it."

Before the coffee was ready Chris's head rested on his crossed arms, and he was sound asleep. Practice went out quietly and called the mansion. Lucy answered.

She was astonished when he told her where Chris was, and then alarmed.

"Jim, he's never done anything like this before! How could he get out without anyone knowing it? I put him to bed at seven and he went right to sleep."

"Probably he was faking. I don't suppose it's too difficult to come and go without being seen, especially if you're friendly with the dogs. I'll bring him right home. Not," he added, "that he wants to come."

Lucy was silent for a few seconds, and then he heard her sigh.

"I know, I know. I've been trying to put off having a talk with the Governor, but Chris's running away is serious. Jim, you didn't fuss at him, did you?"

"I was glad to see him. I've been putting Chris off myself lately. I think I'll get in touch with Riley at the Air National Guard and see if we can't arrange a plane ride for Chris early next week. He's been promised and promised."

"Good for you," Lucy said, and the tone of her voice warmed him.

He was going to ask her if she had been in her room when Chris went out, because the child had to go through Lucy's room to reach the hall, but he decided it would sound like a reproach. Obviously she had been somewhere else.

He put on his coat and gathered Chris up, then carried him down the back steps to the garage. Chris stirred, but his eyes didn't open.

On his way up the hill to the Governor's mansion Practice saw a light burning in Bill Dylan's office high up in the Department of State building, and reminded himself to give Dylan a call; he had forgotten all about the dragonslayer and the fingerprints.

The back gates of the mansion were open, as usual, and he drove up to the garage. His headlights passed over Trudy, one of the mansion shepherds. The dog was straining at the rope that restricted her, and her eyes glared in the light. Her ears were almost flat against her head. Practice got out of the car and heard a low, shocking growl. He went cautiously over to her. He'd never seen any of the dogs act that way, and momentarily he wondered where Josh was.

Trudy stared at him as he hunkered down beside her, then renewed her efforts to be free of the rope. Saliva mixed with blood fell from her lips; she was nearly half choked.

Practice reached into his pocket for a knife to cut the rope.

Crouched over Trudy, with the knife open, he had only a moment's warning, a sizzling sensation of imminent danger as the male shepherd attacked from the dark. He was bowled over by the snarling dog, separated from the knife.

Practice had a horrifying impression of bared teeth and glittering eyes, inches from his own face. He had both hands on the ruff of the shepherd's brawny neck, hanging on for his life, but he had no hope of subduing the powerful animal, who must have seen the knife in his hand and acted instinctively to protect Trudy. Or maybe he had mistaken Practice for someone else.

"Josh! No!"

He jerked his face aside, just avoiding the dog's jaws; then Josh identified him before he could try to bite again. Behind them Trudy strained at the half-severed rope, broke it, and was off like a shot, silently, low to the ground. Josh whirled and followed her; Practice was a distant third. From a corner of the lawn, in the darkness of the rose arbor, he heard a terrified shriek, and saw a figure lunge toward the wall a dozen feet away. But Trudy was on him and the man went down, still screaming.

A frightened face appeared at one of the back windows and Practice shouted, "Lights! Turn on the garden lights!"

He was halfway to the arbor when Trudy suddenly yelped and whimpered. The man rose up against the sky, careened, plowed through several bushes, and mounted the wall in a bound. He was tall, Practice saw, but he saw nothing else. There was no moon. The man disappeared over the edge of the bluff, and Practice could hear the clatter of dislodged stones as he made his way down the steep facing.

The lights in the garden flashed on, right in Practice's eyes, and he was momentarily blinded. He cursed and made his way to the wall, peering over it. He could still hear the man's progress, but there was nothing to see but the blue-white image of floodlights dancing in his eyes.

He turned back. Luke had come out of the kitchen in his nightshirt with a shotgun in his hands.

Practice waved him away. "Call the patrol," he said. But he knew it was unlikely that a search would turn up the man. Once he reached the railroad tracks below he'd get away.

Something on top of the wall caught Practice's eye, and he took out his handkerchief. It came away bloody from the stones, quite a bit of blood.

Apparently Trudy had nicked a vein in the man's arm or hand. He looked for Trudy and saw her lying motionless in the arbor. Not far away Josh lay. Practice knelt and turned the big yellow shepherd over. Josh was dead; his throat had been hacked. He went to Trudy. There was a long cut across the bridge of her nose and a stab wound in her chest was welling blood, but she was conscious. He changed his mind about the blood on the stones; it could easily have been Trudy's.

Practice looked up again to see Lucy approaching in pajamas, slippers, and a robe.

"Oh, no," she said, horrified. "Oh, Trudy."

The dog had been a particular favorite of Lucy's. She dropped to her knees, then looked up at Practice, her face colorless.

"What . . ."

"Somebody was hanging around out here, looking for a way into the mansion. Or maybe he'd been in and was on his way out. Josh apparently surprised him the first time, but Josh always was too softhearted for his own good. Not Trudy. I think she may have gotten her teeth into him."

"Did you see the man?"

"Just barely. He was tall and thin. Fast on his feet."

Lucy put her hands under Trudy.

"Help me, Jim."

They moved the dog into the garage and Practice had Luke call for a vet. In the excitement he had forgotten about Chris, and now he looked in the car. Chris was curled up asleep on the front seat.

"I'd better get him to bed," Lucy said, staring at Chris as if she were in shock.

"Are you okay, Lucy?"

"I think I am. Would you carry him for me?"

She followed, as Practice took Chris up to bed. The boy sat up and complained sleepily as Lucy took off his shoes and clothing, then went right back to sleep.

Elizabeth, Luke's wife, looked in at the door, her hands fluttering with excitement.

"Police here."

"I'll stay and keep an eye on Chris," Lucy said.

"No, I think you'd better come."

She stared at Practice, troubled, then looked away.

"All right, but I have to change first."

"Lucy, where were you tonight? When Chris ran off?"

She was very pale, but her eyes met his, somewhat defiantly.

"I went out. For about an hour."

"To meet someone?"

She gathered the robe more tightly about her throat with one hand.

"Yes, to meet someone," she said evenly. "I suppose I shouldn't have"—she glanced down at the sleeping Chris— "but I didn't know he . . ."

"Forget it," Practice said wearily. "It's none of my business." He turned away from her abruptly and went downstairs to talk to the officers.

Highway patrol and city police had arrived almost simultaneously. Practice glanced at his watch; not quite ten minutes had gone by since he had seen the intruder vault over the wall. The grounds were now being painstakingly searched.

Practice gave a brief account of the incident and Captain Mike Liles of the highway patrol issued orders over a telephone. A tight net would be drawn around a ten-square-block area, south from the river. But a thorough shakedown of the railroad yards would take time, and if the man hadn't been too badly hurt, he could have traveled a mile or more along the tracks within five minutes.

Liles made a second call, relayed by radio to the troopers assigned to the Governor's Day Dinner. Four more cars were automatically assigned to the armory, and in another minute additional men would be inside the hall, their eyes on the Governor. The routine was well established.

Liles's third call was to the patrol laboratory, and a field investigation truck was dispatched. He went off to check on his men, who were going over every window and door of the mansion, looking for signs of possible entry. He came back with the servants in tow just as Lucy joined them. She still looked unpleasantly pale to Practice, but seemed composed and alert.

Luke and his wife had been asleep in their room and hadn't heard anything until the scream awakened them. The cook, an old black woman named Mary, was hard of hearing and hadn't known that anything was wrong until a trooper banged on her door.

"Where were you, Lucy?" Liles asked.

"In my room. I wasn't asleep. I was waiting for Jim to bring Chris home."

Liles's eyebrows went up slightly at that, but he didn't comment.

"Did you hear the scream?"

"Yes. It wasn't loud, of course. With my door shut I can't hear much of anything, not even in the next room." Her eyes flickered to Practice, and she touched the tip of her tongue nervously to her lips.

Liles nodded. "You didn't hear either of the dogs barking?"

"Trudy doesn't bark, she growls. Josh barks all night long, at everything. I may have heard Josh, but I didn't pay attention if I did."

One of the troopers came into the sitting room.

"We've checked the first two floors, Captain. No sign of entry anywhere. About all that's left is the Governor's apartment . . ."

Lucy stood up so suddenly that the chair she had been sitting in toppled over.

"My Lord," she said shrilly. "Dore! We forgot all about Dore!"

7

Practice was out of the sitting room almost before Lucy had finished, with Captain Liles and three troopers in his wake. He reached the third floor and the door of the Governor's apartment far ahead of the others, and was twisting the knobs ineffectually when they caught up.

"Dore!" he shouted, then turned.

"Should we try to break it down?" one of the patrolmen asked helpfully.

"These doors are solid oak," Practice said. "Luke?"

"Suh?"

"Bring your spare key."

Luke went back down the stairs in bowlegged haste, and they milled around tensely until he returned. There was no sound at all from within the apartment.

Practice snatched the keys from Luke's outstretched hand and tried two of them before finding the right one.

The sitting room was brightly lighted, but empty. Practice threw open the door of Dore's bedroom and looked inside. The covers had been neatly turned back on the bed and a table lamp was lighted, but there was no sign of Dore.

"What was that?" Liles asked, lifting his head and frowning.

Practice listened and heard the sounds, too, the faint crashing of piano keys.

He ran out of Dore's bedroom and across to the Governor's door.

The discordant sounds of the piano were louder. Practice pounded on the door, then looked through the ring of keys again until he found one that would fit the lock. He opened the door slightly and peered in.

"My God!" Liles whispered, and withdrew, his cheeks reddening.

Practice shut the door.

"Lucy, get a robe out of Dore's closet. Mike . . ."

"We'll wait downstairs," Liles said, and quickly herded his men from the Governor's apartment.

When Lucy had returned with a robe, Practice opened the door again and they went inside.

Dore Guthrie didn't look up from the piano at the other end of the bedroom. Her hair was hanging in her eyes and her tongue was clenched between her teeth in concentration as she brought her hands down again and again on the keyboard. She was wearing red silk stockings and a short nightgown and one leg was tucked under her on the piano bench. There was a reek of whiskey in the room despite the air coming in through smashed French doors leading to the balcony.

"Oh, Dore," Lucy murmured, and Dore looked up slowly, her hands poised over the keyboard.

The room had been smashed to pieces. Drapes were pulled down, covers were torn from the bed, pictures hung in tatters from crooked frames, lamps were overturned, and furniture was slashed so that gobs of upholstering oozed from the wounds. The whiskey odor came from broken bottles beneath the overturned liquor cabinet.

"Hi," Dore said, and a shy, sticky, lopsided smile appeared on her face. She seemed about to topple from the piano bench, but put out a hand to steady herself; then she beat her stiff fingers methodically and unmelodically against the keys. "Chopin," she explained giddily, and reached for a glass on top of the piano. She hit it with the side of her hand and it fell to the rug.

Practice crossed to the balcony doors and went outside to look over the railing. From a nearby oak a man who could jump and who had little to fear might reach the railing and pull himself up. Most of the glass was scattered inside, on the carpet. He shut the remains of the doors and stepped over the dragging draperies.

Lucy was trying to put the robe around Dore's shoulders as Dore flailed at her.

"You jes let me alone!"

"Dore, don't be that way."

"I'm gonna sit right here on his highenmighty panno stool 'til he gets home 'n' gonna have it out with 'im."

"Did you do all this, Dore?" Practice said sharply. She looked up at him, then guiltily at the wrecked room. She shook her head, her eyes widening in a protestation of innocence.

"Thass way it was when I came in."

"Did you see anybody in here, Dore? Anybody at all?"

Her eyelids fell and she gave a little shrug and almost collapsed. Lucy held Dore up and helped her put on the robe.

"Iss all over," Dore sobbed. "All over." She struggled up suddenly and lurched to the middle of the room, looking around as if she were just becoming aware of the damage.

"Oh, God!" she wailed. "God! Gonna think it was me!" She stumbled again, and Practice put out a hand to hold her. She clutched at the front of his coat, tears running from her eyes. "Gotta help me, Jim. I didn't do it. Gotta believe me. Only came in five, ten minutes ago."

"I believe you, Dore. Somebody climbed up to the balcony and smashed his way in. Didn't you hear anything?"

She shook her head again, several times, her eyes on his face, her legs buckling. Lucy put a hand gently on Dore's shoulder and Dore turned quickly, her teeth bared. She pointed a shaking finger at Lucy.

"You did it!"

"Dore . . ."

"Sure, make me look bad! Bad with Chris, bad with John,

bad, bad! Chris doesn't want me, John—do you come up here an' get in his bed, Lucy? Is he sleeping with you?"

Nothing happened in Lucy's face except that she turned a little paler. She didn't take her eyes from Dore's face, and Dore couldn't tolerate the condemnation she saw there.

She covered her own face with her hands and sobbed, "Well, who is he sleeping with? It isn't me!"

"Go to bed, Dore," Lucy said in a voice like a lash.

Obediently, Dore stumbled off, peeking from between her fingers, and Lucy walked stiffly after her.

Practice called downstairs on the intercom, and presently Captain Liles entered the Governor's room. Practice showed him the balcony doors, and they went out on the balcony with a flashlight. There were traces of mud on the fresh paint of the railing and half a footprint on the floor.

"A size thirteen, maybe fourteen," Liles muttered, examining the mark. "Let's say he came in over the wall from the bluff side, ambushed the one dog, climbed the tree, and took a jump for the balcony. He must have arms like a gorilla. Then he popped out the glass, came inside, and—what's missing? Maybe the wreckage is a cover."

"The Governor will have to tell you that," Practice said. "Offhand I'd say he only has about five hundred dollars' worth of personal jewelry. No papers here that would be valuable to anyone."

"Well," the Captain said, "much as I hate to, I'm going to have to interrupt his politickin' and get him over here."

"There's a call for you, Mr. Practice," one of the troopers said, and Practice went inside. He took the call on the bathroom telephone, where he could shut the door and not be distracted.

"Jim? Bill Dylan. What's all the excitement up on the hill?"

"Looks like a simple breaking and entering," Practice said, wondering to himself exactly what it did look like. "Any news for me?"

"You're in luck; the prints were on file here. I've got a dossier, and I'll send it over by messenger. The prints belong to Billie Charmian, black, female, age about forty-two. Occupation listed as 'singer.' Her last known address was Fort Frontenac."

"Criminal record?"

"No. Cabaret entertainers are required to be finger-printed in this state. That's why she's on file."

"Billie Charmian, huh?"

"That's it. Ever hear of her?"

"No, I haven't. But Guthrie might know who she is." He thanked the FBI man and hung up.

Liles's troopers had taken over the bedroom, and there was nothing more he could do there.

Lucy was coming out of Dore's bedroom as he left, and she elevated an eyebrow and lifted her hands in a gesture of resignation and amusement. They went downstairs together.

"I've got to see about poor Trudy," she said. "I wonder if the vet has come?"

"Dore calmed down?"

"Yes, she apologized for—for certain things. After that, she was good and sick to her stomach." Lucy's lips quirked sardonically. Then she became serious. "Jim, who could it have been? Someone with a long-standing grudge? The Governor's bedroom is a complete wreck."

He shook his head. "Hard to say, Lucy. Listen, from now on, I want you to keep an even tighter check on Chris. Lock his door after he's in bed, if you have to."

She nodded ruefully. "I've already started."

"And have a talk with the principal of his school tomorrow. Make sure that someone has an eye on him every minute he's there. I know they watch the kids pretty carefully, but . . ."

Her eyes flashed with sudden alarm. "Jim? What are you thinking?"

"I don't know. But there's been a lot of violence around here tonight. Only a dog was killed, so maybe most people won't find it as shocking as I do. I'm going to be damned sure, though, that nobody gets within a block of this place from now on without an airtight reason."

John Guthrie came in the front door of the mansion, a mixed coterie of lawmen with him. He shed his coat and dropped it on a convenient chair. He looked as if he had just fought to the limit against a more experienced man, and was sulking because someone had cheated him out of his victory celebration.

"Jim! What the hell is this? I've got troopers coming out my behind."

"A prowler knifed Josh and Trudy, and broke into your room by way of the balcony. Better have a look."

Guthrie walked quickly to the steps, then stopped and glanced back at Practice.

"Dore . . . ?"

"She's all right. A little frightened, that's all."

"Who saw him?"

"I did. Just a glimpse."

"Liles, your men pick him up yet?"

"No, sir."

"My God. What did he want?"

Captain Liles was getting red in the face from his trips up and down the stairs.

"Sir, could you check your valuables? We'd like to know what's missing."

Guthrie nodded. He went to a high walnut bureau; Practice and a trooper helped him set it upright. A strong-box had fallen from a bottom drawer, but the lock was intact. The Governor recovered his jewelry box from beneath a pile of shirts, and opened it.

"Nothing missing," he said, looking around again. "I wonder if I have any whiskey left?"

"There's a bottle in the kitchen."

Practice and Captain Liles followed him to the kitchen, where he poured a stiff shot of whiskey over ice and sat in the corner on a stool, next to the refrigerator, his tie loosened and his socks falling down around his ankles.

"I wonder if you'll get him," he said vaguely.

"We may," Liles said. "I've got twenty men out, and Chief Robards has called in all off-duty detectives. Do you have any ideas, Governor?"

Guthrie shrugged. "Most men have enemies. I have more than my share. It's human nature to want to do in your enemy, but because we're civilized, we tell ourselves that it's not really possible, that violence is an oddity, a freak, rather than a way of life."

"According to Jim," Liles said, "the prowler may be hurt. One or both of the dogs got him. I've stationed a man at both hospitals. Now I'd like to know if we can let the press have the full story."

"No," Guthrie said, scowling.

"It might make the difference between getting this man and not getting him."

"Sorry, Captain. I don't want any headlines. Just give out a statement to the effect that there was a prowler; he got away; and there's no evidence he was inside the mansion at all."

"Yes, sir," Liles agreed reluctantly, and excused himself.

"Well?" Practice demanded, after Liles had left.

Guthrie smiled wryly. "Well, what?"

"Did you see A.B. Sharp?"

"He came in ten minutes before the dessert was served, wearing a moldy old tuxedo with lapels that pointed up past his shoulders, and took his seat. He sat there smiling all through the speeches with his hearing aid turned down, and afterward there was a great milling around, with Sharp in the middle. He put one hand on me and a hand on the Major, and said, 'Well, gentlemen, don't you think it's time you started considering the party instead of yourselves?' Then he invited myself, the Major, our immediate families, and any friends whom we considered indispensable to his farm next weekend. And there the Major and I are going to cut for high card."

"That's all Sharp had to say?"

Guthrie nodded. "Word for word. The next instant, so help me, he vanished. The whole evening reminded me of the tea party in *Alice in Wonderland*. The Major, the white rabbit, who looked just like A.B. Sharp, and little old Alice, that's me."

Guthrie's glass slipped from his hand and smashed on the floor. He looked at it wearily.

"It's all over, Jim. If the Major were going to win, there wouldn't be any conference at Whitestone Farm next weekend. The Major knew. I watched his eyes while Sharp tendered his invitation. Terrible eyes, aren't they? I never realized it before. The old, yellow eyes of a proud and brutal man, whom I happened to love once. He forced the knife into my hands and now he's too proud to ask me to pull it out from between his ribs. My God, if I were half of that man! You don't see it, I suppose; you never knew him. Should have seen him, Jim, after the war, in his full-dress uniform. Tall and straight, by God, not a line of that uniform wrong, brass and gold and gleaming boots. He carried a sword that Marshal Pétain himself gave him, beautiful damned thing, Swedish steel and razor sharp, with a hilt of gold that flashed in the sun. I suppose I had the Major in my mind's eye the day I headed for Canada to join the Air Force . . ."

"Where did you know Billie Charmian, John?" Practice asked casually.

"Billie?" He frowned. "Where did you hear that name? She called herself that. She was Wilma, Wilma Croft . . ."

"Ted Croft's sister?"

"Yes. She joined the band the winter of '38 in Chicago. Sang with us for a while." Guthrie swallowed, rubbing his forehead. "I'm having a letdown here. Suppose I ought to get to bed. Billie—she was only seventeen, but she had the voice. Could have been one of the great ones. Ted never encouraged her, though. He was far gone, that winter. T.B. Died late in the spring. I couldn't get to his funeral." He lifted his head abruptly. "What about her, Jim?"

"Bill Dylan called a few minutes ago. Those were her fingerprints on the crank letter."

Guthrie stared at him.

"Billie? She sent that thing?"

"I only know that her fingerprints were on the drawing. What can you tell me about Billie, John?"

He was still staring at Practice blankly. Then he closed his eyes and put his hands over his face.

"Tell? I haven't seen her, or heard from her, in almost twenty-five years. I haven't heard anything *about* her."

"Her last known address was Fort Frontenac. She's been licensed to sing in nightclubs in this state since 1945."

"Fort Frontenac? That's where Ted lived. I was part of a combo playing in a dive down on the riverfront when he was putting his last band together. Nineteen thirty-seven or thereabouts."

"How well did you know Billie?"

There was an irritable edge to his voice. "We played together, lived apart. The original group had Ted on clarinet, Darby Post on drums, and Liberty Leeds playing bass. Later on Ted added Phil Petigo, a tenor sax, and somebody named Kelvin on trombone—he never amounted to much. Darby and I were white, the others black. Billie probably hadn't been with us more than three months before I quit to join the RCAF. I didn't know her well"—he lifted his head and stared at Practice—"but I knew her well enough. She would never send anything like that damned picture. Billie was a shy, quiet girl, and she read a lot. Ted took care of her, good care. He wouldn't have let her travel with the group, but there was no one in Fort Frontenac whom he trusted to look after her. Even knowing how good Billie was, Ted didn't want her to sing, but she begged him for months until he gave in. She was only seventeen, as I said."

"What happened to her after her brother died?"

"I don't know, Jim. Went back to Fort Frontenac, I suppose. I don't know why she didn't become a star. Everybody who heard her sing loved her. She sounded like the original Billie to begin with, but she was developing a style of her own in those three months. Nobody singing today sounds anything like her. Maybe Dinah Washington did."

Guthrie fell silent and looked uneasily at the floor.

"I think I'll move in with Dore tonight," he said. "Too much trouble to put the spare bedroom in order."

"What do you want me to do, John?"

"Do?"

"About Billie Charmian?"

Guthrie stood up, avoiding the glass on the floor.

"What does she want?" he asked vaguely. "Why would she do it?"

"I'd have to ask her."

"No. No, don't. Don't stir up—" He hesitated.

"Don't stir up what?"

"Maybe," Guthrie said, "she needs help. Who knows? Maybe there's something I can give her."

"According to the drawing, she wants your head."

"There is no reason for that, Jim!" Guthrie shouted. More quietly he added, "Believe me. No, I'm positive Billie isn't responsible, even if those are her fingerprints. All right, then. Find her if you can."

"If she's still in Fort Frontenac, it shouldn't be hard. If she's been moving around, it'll take more time. The envelope was postmarked here in the city, but that may not be significant."

"Don't take much time, Jim. I need you here. Give it tomorrow, and if you don't find Billie, come on home. If she wants something from me, she can ask, instead of playing games. And now I'm going to bed."

Practice walked with the Governor into the sitting room and stood a few moments by himself after Guthrie, with an irritable "good night," had entered Dore's bedroom. His thoughts returned to Billie Charmian and the grotesque image of knight and dragon which had come to John Guthrie stained with her blood. Practice had no answers, but, thinking about the puzzle, he felt challenged and absorbed for the first time in months—almost his own man.

8

Gene Ogden had been one of the better first basemen in the National League until aging legs retired him at thirty-three; now he had law offices with two other men in a prosperous black settlement of Fort Frontenac. Practice looked about wistfully as he waited for the girl to announce him. There were several good paintings on the walls and just enough Swedish modern furniture, with neutral shades of upholstering, and from somewhere the homely smell of brewing coffee subtly softened the effect of uncompromised efficiency.

The girl came back with a tapping of heels. She smiled at him.

"Won't you come in, Mr. Practice?"

Gene Ogden rose up hugely from behind his desk and reached over it to shake hands; for any other man it would have been a strain, but Ogden's reach reduced the desk to child's size.

"Good to see you again."

He had added a mustache and horn-rims since Practice had last seen him, but the athlete's body looked as solid as ever. Ogden's skin was caramel-colored and his thinning hair reddish brown. There were a few trophies around the room, and several photographs, including one showing

Ogden with the President of the United States and Governor Guthrie.

"I came in about four to get some book work out of the way," Ogden explained. "Have you met my partners? I'll see if they've come in . . ."

"You don't need to bother, Gene. I only have a few hours, and I may have some trouble locating the person I came to see. I was hoping you could help me."

"Do my best."

"Her name is Charmian. Billie Charmian. Does that ring a bell?"

Ogden frowned. "Just barely."

"She'd be forty-two, almost forty-three years old now. Charmian's a stage name, by the way."

"What does she do?"

"She was a singer, at least she was during the thirties. Sang with her brother's band, just before he died. I suppose you remember Ted Croft."

Ogden nodded.

"I'll call my wife. She's the authority on jazz singers."

He reached for the telephone and dialed. The receptionist came in with a tray and coffee service and poured two cups.

Ogden listened intently, then wrote on his pad, then listened again, frowning. Presently he hung up and swiveled around to face Practice, his big hands lightly grasping the edge of his desk.

"She told me to look up a man named Skandy. I've had some dealings with him. I hope this Billie Charmian isn't in his company much."

As he was putting on his topcoat, Ogden glanced casually at Practice and said, "The Governor used to play with Croft's group, didn't he? Way back when."

Practice nodded.

"Could you give me some idea why he's looking for Billie?"

"The Governor has a trunkful of relics from those days—pictures, arrangements, old recordings. Since Billie is

Croft's only surviving relative, as far as he knows, he thought she might like to have them."

"Skandy is going to say, 'You give me the trunk, I'll see she gets it.' "

"I want to talk to Billie myself. Alone."

Ogden shrugged. "All we can do is try."

The lawyer did the driving, and soon they were in an industrial valley webbed with railroad tracks and crowded with brick factories and stacks. Not a blade of grass was visible anywhere. The narrow business streets contained one- and two-story buildings, housing taverns and chili parlors. There were few white faces visible on the streets or in the asphalt play yard of an elementary school. Ogden's eyes were impassive as he wheeled his big car through the heavy traffic, but he missed nothing.

"Look at their faces," he said. "Look at their poor bodies. Place like this, it's the big reason I've got to get myself into politics."

He stopped once to ask directions, then swung into an alley that ran beneath a steep ashen bluff, and parked at the rear of a ramshackle factory building. The air outside the car was faintly acid, despite the sun and blue sky overhead.

They entered a dim hallway by way of a loading platform and turned up a flight of iron stairs worn to a glitter in the center. Some pallid light came through windows at each of the landings. Ogden paused once to catch his breath and grinned, then patted his middle significantly. They went on.

On the fourth floor Ogden indicated high metal doors with a tilt of his head and punched the buzzer mounted on the pocked and crumbling wall. From behind the doors Practice could hear the racket of hammering: mallet and metal.

A smaller door cut into the left-hand door opened and an old man with rough gray hair that matched his paint-flecked gray topcoat looked out at them. The din from within was louder, and Practice couldn't hear the conversation between the old man and Ogden. The old man apparently spoke in monosyllables and continued barring the way, until Ogden put a hand against the man's chest and gently pushed him back.

The man yielded without further argument. Ogden stooped and entered, then beckoned to Practice.

He found himself in a high-roofed loft that obviously occupied nearly all the space on the top floor. There were two grimy skylights and a bank of floor-to-ceiling north windows, somewhat cleaner, through which sunlight poured. Against the west wall a complex of scaffolding surrounded some unidentifiable monolith that looked like the remains of a pile of partially melted scrap iron. Looms and shuttles stood in the south end of the loft, near the doorway. Glittering mobiles of all descriptions hung from the rafters. There were tarpaulins in spangled patchwork on the dirty floor.

Two youths in blue jeans and sweaters out at the elbows were hammering away at workbenches, working over sheets of copper and aluminum. Far down the floor, near the windows, a man straddling a stone bench was working with a welder's torch on a spindly framework dripping with excrescences. The old man who had opened the door for them pointed at the welder and shrugged, then went back to a stool nearby.

"Skandy," Ogden said loudly in Practice's ear.

"What's all this?"

"His workshop. My wife tells me he's good, but I wouldn't know. I know one thing, she put me in hock for a month and a half to buy a small bronze bust of his. Last month he had a one-man show in Venice."

They walked slowly across the floor of the loft, past piles of scrap metal. The flavor of the torch was very much in the air, but otherwise the loft was cold and smelled stale. They paused before a huge mural, seeming to consist of numerous wires and gobs of metal strung together.

"Supposed to be his most famous work, but he won't show

it," Ogden explained. "Claims it'll never be finished. It's called 'The Work of Mankind,' which itself is never finished."

"Bravo," Practice murmured. The whine of a drill set his teeth on edge. "Tell me about Skandy."

"Okay, we've got time. I wouldn't want to interrupt him at his labors, he might turn that torch on us. He's forty-five years old, was born a block and a half from here, has no home at the moment except for a spare room somewhere in the building. There's a cot in it, for when he feels like sleeping, which he doesn't very much. Usually a chick on the cot. He sends out the young bloods to comb the streets for him; can't be bothered himself. He's made a fortune and given most of it away to politically inspired causes, and once he set out to walk barefoot across Africa, some kind of protest. He did time when he was younger. Politically he's either a Red or an anarchist. A lot of people love him. I don't, because in his free time he's also an unpredictable drunk. Fortunately he doesn't have much free time. I did him a turn once, or he would have lost this studio, so he may return the favor—if he's in the mood."

"If you knew where he was all the time, why the phone calls?"

Ogden grunted. "To find out if he was in the mood."

Skandy had turned off his torch and pushed back the shield that covered his face. He sat slumped on his stone bench in an attitude of abject misery. Then he got up slowly, peeling off his gloves and flexing his fingers. He shot a glance at Ogden and Practice, then nodded his head slightly.

The two men approached the artist.

"Who's he?" Skandy said, without preamble, to Ogden.

"A friend."

Skandy looked at Practice with an expression of such unforgiving suspicion that it was almost amusing. He had long hair for a black man, which was going dead white in streaks. With his fingers he combed crisp particles of burned metal out of his hair and then rubbed his nose.

"What do you want?" he said to the lawyer.

"Man here wants to talk to Billie Charmian," Ogden replied, slipping into street vernacular.

"No."

"I hear you and Billie is real close," Ogden went on, undisturbed. "She don't have none of her own to look after her, so you see to what she needs."

Skandy sat staring at his creation, which looked like a series of elongated S's with interlocking humanoid figures. He sat very still, his hands on his knees.

Finally he said, "Nothing I can add to what you hear."

"This man," said Ogden, "has got something of importance for Billie."

Skandy's eyes shifted a little, and then closed. A brief smile touched his lips, bitter, ironic. He looked at Practice.

"Are you death?" he said. "Did you bring her death?"

"No."

"There is nothing else she can use."

"Is she sick?"

It seemed as if Skandy wouldn't answer, and then he put out a hand and lightly touched the bronzework in front of him.

"What do you think of this?" he said gently, as if he were speaking from a dream.

"You're asking me?" Practice said, and felt Ogden's sidelong glance.

"Yes," Skandy breathed. "Judge it for me."

"I'm not a fit judge."

"Judge it," Skandy commanded softly.

"All right," Practice said. "You've tried to create a clean, biting tension within a rigidly defined space, and that's wrong, because you've defined space in terms of a preconceived torment—those figures. You've sacrificed line and freedom to a central idea of pain, sensed that it was wrong, and tried to correct with a melodramatic emphasis instead of a sweeping simplification. Because you're a professional, this

piece is technically exciting. And because you're a professional, it has to be called by its rightful name: clumsy,
aggravating claptrap."

Skandy had thrown back his head to stare at Practice, and
halfway through the précis the man's eyes narrowed in rage.
Then he swung back to look reluctantly at his work. His
lower lip trembled for a moment, as if a piece of the metal
had pierced him. Suddenly he bellowed in satisfaction.

"Conrad! You! Come here and get this thing out of my
sight."

One of the boys dropped his mallet and scurried across the
floor. Skandy was sitting with his head down on his chest.

"How did you know?" he said to Practice.

"I'm no artist. I like art. I read a lot of books."

Skandy sat still in contemplation before speaking again.
"Billie Charmian is a very sick woman. Heartsick, crippled
with arthritis, blinded by bad whiskey. She don't have a voice
to sing with no more. A week ago two men found where she
was staying. They wanted to know something about her life.
She wouldn't tell them. They twisted her knotted and
crooked hands until she screamed, and left her in agony on
the floor of her room."

"What men?" Ogden asked. "What did they want?"

Skandy shook his head. "Who knows? They was black
men who should have had a little reverence for our Billie
Charmian. Instead, they hurt her. But she couldn't tell them
nothing. She ain't seen the boy in years."

"Boy?"

"Her son."

"I didn't know Billie Charmian had a son," Practice said.

Skandy looked up at him with an unfocused anger in his
eyes.

"Call him that. He never loved her or worked a day to
support her. I wouldn't call him no son."

"What can you tell me about this boy?"

Skandy rose. "Walk with me," he said.

As they went slowly across the loft floor with Skandy between them, he explained about the son of Billie Charmian, whose given name was Val and whose surname was Croft.

"I knowed Billie when she was young," Skandy said. "Twelve or thirteen year old. A beautiful girl, too tall, a little awkward, shy. Never much to say. She was like that until her brother took her on tour. Saw her at the funeral, the spring of '39, and after that, around town. Complete change in her then; she was a drinker, a lewd woman. No one was surprised when she had the baby. There was always people to take care of her, though. One good man could have made a great talent out of Billie, but the men who had that chance, they was all small-time. Billie didn't work much; she liked the drinking, the fast life. So did I, and I still do; but I'm a man with my destiny in my own hands, and I never had that feeling about poor Billie. Something drove her, some devil inside that wouldn't let her be. First she went blind from illegal alcohol, then the arthritis struck her. Well, when it was plain she couldn't work, most people give up on her. Nobody cared. I took it on myself to care. Yes, I could care about Billie. But not about that boy. Nobody could be his friend, he made that plain. Do him good. Be kind to him. Obey his whims. And he'd stab you in the back before walking all over you."

"What happened to the boy, Skandy?" Practice asked.

"He left town four year ago, and I ain't seen or heard from him since. He stole two hundred dollars from me and left. Word was, he went off to California to be an actor. Some people, who thought they could use him to get to me, flattered him that way. But he wasn't no actor. Even a new name couldn't help him there."

"What name did he go by?"

"Val. Val St. George."

They left the studio and went down the iron stairs one flight, then entered a warehouse by a narrow alley lighted with a succession of fly-specked bulbs. The air was close and even chillier than it had been in the studio, and Practice shuddered.

"Who would be interested in her son?" Practice asked.

There was a hint of impatience in Skandy's voice.

"I've tried to tell you that the boy is bad trouble. Who knows what he's done? He started as a thief and a liar. Wherever he is, Billie don't know and I don't know. I hope we never find out."

They had come to a partition of the warehouse apparently made from scrap lumber, with two unmatched doors a few feet apart in the wall. Skandy opened one of the doors and they went in.

The room they had entered was a large one, warmed by an electric heater on one wall. The furnishings were simple: linoleum on the floor, several benches, bookshelves, a TV, and a sofa bed, but the effect was tidy and comfortable. To Practice it seemed the sort of room an experienced artist or decorator might provide for himself out of whim, seeing what he could do without spending more than a few dollars for paint.

A black woman sat nodding in front of the TV set, which was turned down low. She wore the blue and gray jumper of a practical nurse.

"How is she?" Skandy asked.

The nurse looked up. "I think she feels better today."

"See if she's awake."

The nurse rose and let herself into an adjoining room. In a few moments she reappeared, nodded, and Skandy left them alone, shutting the door behind him as he went in to talk to Billie Charmian.

"I thought you said he was a hard man," Practice whispered to Ogden.

"Most times he won't do more than curl his lip at white skin," Ogden replied. "But you handled him right."

"He wanted an opinion," Practice said.

Ogden chuckled. "He got it, too. Right between the eyes. Here he comes."

Skandy approached them, but his eyes were on Practice. "I don't ask who you are or what your business is with Billie," he said softly. "Just you remember she is a sick woman. I've told her you're coming in to see her, so she'll talk to you if she can. Don't stay more than five minutes. I mean what I say."

"Thank you, Skandy."

There was scarcely a ripple in the old man's face. He looked directly into Ogden's eyes for several seconds, a blood look that was without meaning to Practice, and then he let himself out and the nurse settled back into her chair in front of the television.

Billie Charmian's room was small. It contained a full-sized bed, a toilet, and a bathtub. There was a single window facing north, but the blinds were half drawn. The air smelled of rubbing alcohol.

She sat in a wheelchair near the one window, very straight, her hands useless in her lap, a scarlet robe across the lower part of her body, sunglasses masking a third of her face. She was neatly dressed; her hair was long and straight, blue-black with one wide streak of white past her right ear. Practice was startled by the lightness of her skin, tinged with yellow from years of sickness, lined but not dull.

For a moment Practice felt awed by something he didn't understand, then realized that it was the attitude with which she sat, cruelly immobilized in a way that trapped her energies without reducing them.

"Billie?"

"Who are you?" she said.

"I'm Jim Practice . . ."

"You're white. How do you know about me?"

"John Guthrie told me about you, Billie."

There was no visible reaction, but Practice was aware that something had happened at the mention of the Governor's name, an indistinctly painful happening.

Practice took out the drawing. He told her about the

envelope in which it had come; then he described the drawing to her, with its burden of bloody fingerprints.

"They're your fingerprints, Billie. Made long ago. Could you tell me how long ago, Billie?"

Her head had inclined forward slightly so that the sun was full in her face. She might have been asleep.

Practice sighed. "Years ago, Billie, you bought a storybook for a boy filled with the kind of tales that children like to hear and read. Like most mothers, you'd hold your son on your lap and read to him. One story out of all the others struck his imagination in such a way that he never forgot it. There was a meaning in the story that involved his own personality to such an extent that as he grew older, he took the name of the knight who slew the dragon. In fancy he became the white knight he never could be in truth."

For a blind, ferocious instant she bared her teeth.

"What did you tell him about his father, Billie?"

"From the first I made him know what it was to be a bastard, not black, not white, to be a never and a nowhere on this earth. For such feelings, for the way I made that boy suffer from his first living hour, the good God Almighty took away what I had left of self-respect, took away all love, and then my eyes, and then my voice, and then"—her voice had become a dark passionate growling—"my power to kill the poor bastard and the poor woman who gave him birth."

He knew that in a moment she would abandon herself completely to self-torture and lose all sense of his words, and so he stepped closer and said harshly, *"Billie! What did you tell him about his father?"*

She gasped, bending over in the wheelchair, and he put a hand gently on her shoulder, aware of what the slightest pressure would do to her. Gradually she straightened and the look of horror lessened in her face.

"Everything but the truth. That I loved John Guthrie. I never told the boy a thing about love."

"Have you seen Val, Billie? Talked to him? When was the last time you saw him?"

"Three years ago. A letter came. He said—said he would never come home until his father was dead. 'When my father is dead, then you can love me as you should.'"

"Do you have the letter he wrote you, Billie?"

"In my mind I see every word. Printed, as he would have printed it when he was a child."

"From where was it sent?"

A spasm of terror caused her mouth to slant downward in a grimace.

"From—from the insane asylum." She choked then, and from beneath the glasses two tears rolled down her cheeks.

There was a quick, insistent knocking at the door, and Practice glanced at his watch, frowning.

"Billie, tell me something about the two men who came to see you. They knew you had a son. Is that all they knew? Did you tell them that Guthrie was his father?"

"They couldn't make me tell. But . . ."

"What, Billie?"

"They found the letter, the letter Val wrote."

"I'll have to go now. But I want to know something else. Does Guthrie have any idea what's happened to you?"

Her lips thinned and she raised her head proudly, turning it a fraction of an inch to the right, then into the sun.

"He never knew."

9

The state hospital for the mentally ill was located on a large wooded tract in a small city not far from the capital, and Practice drove back by a route that would allow a stopover at the hospital. He had phoned from Ogden's office for an appointment with Dr. Mackerras. When he reached the grounds shortly before one o'clock, the sun had vanished and the sky was overcast with a hint of rain in the darkness to the south.

The assistant receptionist who took him back to Mackerras's office had the typical look of institution help: bland, country, and with muscles under her jumper. She smiled automatically and held the door open for him. Mackerras rose from behind his desk, which held the waxed paper and bread crust remains of a hasty lunch, and extended his hand. He was a small man, blond, with a lady-killer's profile.

"Hello! How are you? How's Lucy? Haven't heard from her in a couple of months."

"Fine," Practice said, and offered no additional comment.

Mackerras reached for a stack of folders on the side of his desk and selected one.

"This is the information on Val St. George. At the time of admission, three years and five months ago, he was nineteen, six feet two inches tall, weighed one hundred and forty-nine pounds. Malnourished, which condition could have accounted for part of his mental troubles. You see"—he put on a pair of reading glasses to leaf through the folder—"we put all incoming patients on a better than adequate diet, plenty of supplemental vitamins, and so forth, and some of

201

them respond so well to the improved diet that they can be discharged in a few weeks. Anyway, Val St. George was a light-skinned black, but not the type who could ever pass for white. Definitely Negroid features and hair. One unusual feature here, he was responsible for his own commitment."

"How's that?"

"He came to the institution and asked to be admitted. He was examined by one of our staff psychiatrists over a period of three days, diagnosed as schizophrenic, with manic-depressive tendencies, certain patterns of hostility not unusual for someone who finds himself a racial outsider. He claimed to be an orphan, and apparently investigation confirmed that as fact. We obtained the necessary court approval and he began treatment. He responded well to analysis and was discharged ten months and twenty-four days later as cured."

"Did you know him while he was here, Doctor?"

"Yes, I did. He was active in our drama group, as a matter of fact was virtually responsible for a good production of *Henry V*, and he played Henry with great style. I knew him through Lucy, as well."

Practice frowned. "How do you mean, Doctor?"

"Lucy, as you know, wasn't, by definition, a patient. She lived with my wife and me, helped out in the dispensary, and was free to come and go as she saw fit. While she was here, she took a personal interest in several of the patients—first there was the Indian girl with suicidal tendencies. They became good friends and I'm happy to say the girl was eventually discharged, perhaps Lucy had a hand in her recovery. I know that she was partly responsible for the rapid integration of personality which Val St. George demonstrated. He would gladly have given her all the credit. I don't think the boy ever had a friend in his life before Lucy."

"I see."

"She's never mentioned him to you?"

"No, she hasn't." He hesitated. "Dr. Mackerras, was there

any indication that Val St. George was potentially dangerous?"

"Dangerous?"

"Could he have killed someone at the time he was
admitted?"

"Nearly everyone is capable of killing under a given set of
circumstances. In the condition in which he was admitted,
Val St. George wasn't dangerous, either to another human
being or to himself. If he had continued to deteriorate
mentally, it's possible that a paranoiac syndrome may have
manifested itself, which, in turn, and I qualify again, *might*
have resulted in violence. On the other hand, if his schizophrenic tendencies had developed fully, it's likely he merely
would have regressed to an endurable level of adolescence or
childhood, and spent the rest of his days in that state—
within these grounds."

"But he's no longer here. As a matter of fact, he's been
free for two and a half years."

"Yes."

"Do you know where he is now, Doctor?"

Mackerras settled back in his chair. "No. We have no
record of his whereabouts."

"Suppose, after he was discharged, his condition worsened again. Could Val St. George have become markedly
paranoiac in two and a half years?"

Mackerras threw up his hands. "How can I say? All I can
do is speak from the record. He was discharged as cured, all
potentially debilitating tendencies arrested."

A buzzer sounded on the intercom and Mackerras looked
at it regretfully, then leafed through the folder and removed
a photograph. Practice took it, and briefly studied the
features of Val St. George, a petulant, thin-faced youth.
There was a date penciled on the back; the photograph had
been taken shortly after the boy's admission.

"I'm afraid I'll have to be on my way," Mackerras said,
rising.

"Thanks, Doctor, I appreciate your taking so much time."

"Tell Lucy we'd like to have her over for the weekend sometime—if she won't steal too many of my patients away from me." He smiled, but Practice wasn't able to return the smile.

The streets were wet from a slow misting of rain when Practice drove across the river bridge and turned in the direction of the Governor's mansion. In a way, he was relieved to have found out all he could about Val St. George. There was a small chance that the boy was not so dangerous as Practice had first thought. Apparently Lucy believed in him, or she wouldn't be protecting him so fiercely even after what she had seen in the Governor's bedroom the night before. It seemed almost certain that Val St. George had been the man in the garden and the man who had broken into the mansion, but almost wasn't quite good enough for Practice; there were too many inconsistencies in the character of Billie Charmian's son, as he had reconstructed it. Only Val St. George could tell him the truth, and Lucy must know where he could be found.

As he pulled into the driveway of the mansion he saw Mike Liles getting into the back seat of a state patrol car; he honked his horn and pulled up beside it.

"You might want to come along with us, Jim," Liles said.

"What's up?"

"Two boys have been missing from the Borden Private School since the lunch hour. One of them is Chris Guthrie."

10

"Where's Lucy?"

They had driven to the east end of town in less than ten minutes; Liles sat slumped in the back seat, a cold cigar at one corner of his mouth, his eyes on a pocket notebook. At Practice's question he turned his head slightly.

"According to Mrs. Guthrie, after Lucy drove Chris to school this morning she asked for the rest of the day off. Left the mansion about nine o'clock."

Practice tried to make a cigarette but soon gave it up; the car was moving too fast and his fingers felt cramped and cold. "What's the name of the other boy who's missing?"

"Hugh McAdams."

"How could they have left the school without being seen?"

"I don't know," Liles muttered. "One of my men has been camped by the gate since eight this morning. You know the school—seven-foot fence around the yard and building. There's only one way to go in or out."

They arrived at the school Chris Guthrie attended. Liles paused to have a few words with the trooper posted at the gate, then they hurried across the brick play yard to the entrance.

"Who knows the boys are missing?" Practice asked.

"The principal of the school, one of the teachers who's supposed to keep tabs on them at lunch hour, Mrs. Guthrie, and Dunhill, the Governor's secretary. Dunhill called me. He was a little upset, but I can't see where this means anything. Couple of kids playing hookey."

"Who's looking for them?"

"All of my men in the district and the local police. We

didn't put anything on the radio, though. Had the men
telephone in one at a time to keep things quiet."

They were met by the principal on the front steps. He was
a young, sandy-haired man named Stack.

"Glad you could come, Captain."

"This is Mr. Practice, the Governor's aide. How long have
the boys been gone, Stack?"

"Almost two hours."

"Have you notified the parents of the other boy?"

Stack seemed flustered. "I—I didn't want to call until I
had talked with you."

"I think you'd better call now. The boys might have
gotten tired of running around in the rain and headed for
the nearest fireside."

They went into the principal's office and Stack made his
call. No one was home but the maid. Practice leaned against
the doorjamb and waited, his arms folded, a small frown
creasing his forehead. The school had the familiar chalk-
and-polish odor of childhood; down the hall a mixed choir
was practicing.

"I was afraid to ask too many questions," Stack said,
replacing the receiver.

"You did fine," Liles said approvingly.

"I think I can tell you how they left the grounds," Stack
said, eager to atone for the reprimand of Liles's presence.
"Will you follow me?"

They went out into the hall.

"At lunch hour all the children line up outside their
rooms, then march together to the cafeteria in the basement," Stack explained. "It would have been possible for
Chris and Hugh to slip into the bathroom at the head of the
stairs, because sometimes there's a little confusion at that
point. We try to keep them orderly and quiet, but on a day
like this the kids are restless and mill around . . ."

He dabbed at his face with a handkerchief and opened the
door of the bathroom. There were four casement-type
windows in the north wall, about five and a half feet from the

floor. One was open, and underneath was a pasteboard barrel with a metal bottom.

Practice and Liles went to the window and looked out. A narrow brick corridor ran behind the school at the edge of the ravine. It was obvious that from the windowsill an agile boy could reach the top of the fence and let himself down on the other side.

Practice scanned the bottom land as far as the river's edge a half mile away. It was a poor area; some shacks were perched on the sides of the wide ravine and along the twisting gray tributary of the river. In a marshy pocket, within the shadow of Tournament Hill, stood the half-ruined old prison, a Victorian relic of iron-roofed towers and heavy oak and iron doors. The surrounding wall had long ago been reduced to heaps of stones and isolated gateways.

"Looks to me," said Liles, "as if they're off on a jaunt. They'll turn up before long. Jim?"

"It looks that way," Practice agreed. "But I'd like to know where they are."

"Should the Governor hear about this?"

"I wouldn't bother him just now. He's having a tough fight in the Legislature today—his road-tax bill. I think the kids will turn up in the next couple of hours—wet, tired, and unhappy."

Liles dropped Practice at the mansion and returned to his office.

Dore Guthrie met Practice at the kitchen door. She looked a little haggard without her customary heavy coat of makeup.

"Is Chris all right?" she asked expectantly.

"I'm sure he is," Practice said, but something was brooding in his mind, trying to take shape. "Chris and a buddy of his apparently got fed up with school and declared a holiday for themselves. How are you feeling?"

She glanced away. "I remember—some awful things from last night. I was . . ."

He nodded.

"This morning when I woke up, John was there." She sat on a high stool with her hands clenched between her knees. "He was looking at me—*staring* at me as if I were a stranger. I pretended I was still asleep. Then he—I felt his hands, touching me, all over, and I heard him crying. I didn't know what to do. I just didn't know what to do. Finally he went away. I wanted to hold him. But I was afraid to put my arms around him." She looked up at Practice, her eyes startled and fearful. "I was afraid if I put my arms around him, he'd disappear, just like that, and then everything—the bed, the room, the mansion—would disappear, too." Tears started in her eyes, and she wiped at them. "Everything. Chris. My— baby." She put her hands flat against her thighs and stared down at them. Her voice was low, but with a hint of desperate strength.

"Jim? What's mine? Is anything mine?"

"I'd have to answer that question for myself, Dore, before I could help you."

"He—was in love with me, Jim. I swear it. A lot of people would never believe that. Me. How could John love me? But I swear it. He did. And he . . ."

"I believe that, Dore."

"Well, what did I *do?*"

"You think he's disappointed in you?"

She threw her head back. "Well? Isn't he?"

He shrugged helplessly. "Dore, he's not—he's not happy with himself."

"Why, Jim?"

"A lot of reasons. You're a part of it; so is Chris. Chris baffles him. John can't remember his own childhood, and so he doesn't know what Chris wants or needs. I guess he blames you for not showing the way."

Anger appeared in her face. "I want to love him. *Him.* The way it was. I pleased my husband, Jim!"

"Now it's different."

"But I don't know *how* to love a little boy!"

The silence between them grew, and Dore shook her head. In the dimness of the kitchen, loneliness seemed to press down upon them both from the heights of the empty mansion. Dore put a hand in her hair and tugged fiercely, then her hand dropped.

"When I was in college," she said, "I had the same dream. Everything would disappear, a little at a time. And when everything I had ever wanted was gone, then I—I'd start to disappear, too. And nothing could stop me."

"That won't happen, Dore."

"Then where is Chris?" she said, hissing, and instantly began to sob. Without thinking, he took Dore in his arms and held her as soothingly as he could, a little perplexed by her weight and warmth.

"Don't let me disappear, Jim." For a moment she looked at him pleadingly, her eyes big, then she put the tip of her tongue catlike against her lower lip. "Don't let me . . ."

She lifted her shoulders and raised her head and kissed him. There was a thin cold edge to her teeth, and her tongue was ripe and quick. He responded easily, but at the same time was repelled and appalled by the twist of her shoulders, the lurid pressure of her breasts, and the digging fingers at the nape of his neck.

His resistance became obvious as his reason asserted itself, and Dore let him go, her expression at first annoyed, then bewildered, at last ashamed.

"Some people think I'm this way with any man," she mumbled.

He touched his lips where her kiss still burned.

"Stop telling me what people think, Dore," he said sharply.

She stiffened at his tone, and sat facing away from him, wounded.

"I'm going to go out and have a look around for Chris myself," he said more softly. "When he comes home, you can either bawl him out as he deserves or you can gush over him. I'd bawl him out. But a little later I'd find the chance to show him I loved him. If I were you, I'd just pick him up and hold him, and maybe tell him a story—the way Lucy does."

"I might do that," she said grimly, "if I could get him away from Lucy. I haven't yet."

"Then get rid of Lucy," he snapped, and carried the image of Dore's eyes—staring, surprised—with him as he went outside and hurried away from her, from them all, with a taste of rust in his throat and a tremor in his hand where it had brushed against her breast.

Oh, no, he thought. That would be just fine, wouldn't it, Dore? But I won't let it happen, not because I'm afraid of John Guthrie, or respect him too much. Not because I think you're a sulky child who needs a lick now and then to straighten up. But only because I'm afraid there's not enough of me for any man or woman to feed on and grow strong, and I fear anyone who tries.

11

He drove slowly back to the east end of town and Tournament Hill. The rain had quit, but if anything the sky was darker, the air more gloomy. At the top of the hill, the highest part of which was occupied by Major Kinsaker's house, he looked down from his car at the school and beyond to the mist-shrouded river. Suddenly he smiled and focused his attention on the old prison buildings. Chris had called it "the fort," and it was obvious that at some time or other he had gazed down from the windows of the school at the ruined buildings, wanting to explore them. He wouldn't be likely to go alone, though, and it must have taken him a while to find another boy willing to accompany him.

Practice put his car in gear and headed for the old prison.

The street ended two blocks from the prison site. Part of the ravine had been used by the city as a dump at one time, and jagged precipices of rusted metal loomed through the few slender trees that clung to the slopes above the creek. Practice made his way across the soggy ground by using a series of stones and flattened cans for a haphazard path.

As soon as he was within the wall line of the prison he wished he had brought a flashlight, but he wasn't willing to go all the way back to his car for one.

The heavy doors of the entrance to the larger of the two buildings were still secure on thick hinges, and he passed them by, looking for a window low enough or a hole big enough for a boy Chris's size to get through.

He used a pile of fallen stone to reach one of the windows and peered inside, but couldn't see much.

"Chris!" he called, and listened patiently. If the boys had come this far, the odds were they had made only a cursory inspection and then wandered off. Unless . . .

"Chris?"

He shrugged, pulled a sharp stone off the window ledge, and crawled carefully through, letting himself drop the seven feet to the floor below. He stood for a few moments under the window, until his eyes had become adjusted to the faint light inside. There were rents in the timber roof, and a couple of crossbeams sagged dangerously. Pools of water stood where sections of the thick flooring had tilted and sunk into the ground. In one corner there was a faint scratching, as if a rat had backed away at his intrusion.

He called again for Chris, more loudly this time, and waited, his eyes on a far doorway. Then he made his way across the floor and brushed aside cobwebs before passing through.

Light came weakly into the cellblock from several sources. Practice glanced at the rows of cells with their old-fashioned latticework iron. Some of them bulged from the pressure of stones and timber fallen from the roof. He listened intently, hearing the slow drip of water, and shuddered. It was cold and wet, and the stones at his feet were slippery from the drainage of water into the underground cells. He picked up a bit of wood and tossed it down the nearby stairwell, but there was no answering splash.

Then he froze, staring at an object on the floor ahead of him, just out of reach of a pale shaft of light from above. He made his way across the treacherous floor and picked it up—new and shiny, a school lunchbox. He lifted the lid and read the name of the boy printed inside: Hugh McAdams.

Hugh hadn't touched his lunch.

Again Practice called, feeling tension and alarm in his heart. He called out the names of both boys, but still there was no reply. Squatting, he examined the floor beneath the shaft of light. Some of the green slime had been scraped away near the place where he had seen the lunchbox. There were two long skid marks, as if one of the boys had fallen.

He rose and walked slowly toward the stairway, looking into corners, trying to see into the cells.

His foot hit something and sent it skidding across the stones. Puzzled, Practice struck a match and held it near the floor. A halo of light flickered over the boy's shoe he had kicked. He picked the shoe up and studied it.

One of the boys had lost a shoe. Then why hadn't he retrieved it and put it on?

Because he had been running and hadn't wanted to stop, or even think about stopping.

Practice made his way back to the stairs and struck another match. The stones here were dry, covered with dirt. He saw footprints in the soft dirt, the imprint of shoes and of a foot wearing only a sock.

But there were three sets of footprints. The third set was that of a man, and the prints obliterated some of the smaller ones.

"Chris!"

Practice hurried down the iron stairs, one hand on the railing for support, and found himself in a chamber with iron rings around the walls and half a dozen doorways. Iron doors leaned from sprung hinges. The sound of water dripping onto stone was louder, faintly echoing. Practice struck another match, looking around in dismay.

Then he heard the sounds, distant, regular sobs, ghostly and disembodied.

He plunged toward one of the doorways, then backed off, finding the passage choked with rubble. He started into the passage to the right of the first one, pausing to strike another match.

Some light filtered through the blackness at the other end of the passage. He went toward the light, but the sounds of his own hurried footfalls obliterated the cries.

The passage ended in a huge, many-pillared room filled with overturned, rotting benches. The light was poor and, cursing, Practice fumbled with his matches, listening again for the cries.

He called Chris's name several times, then dropped the burned-out match and struck another, turning, holding out his match, the light stabbing into the corners of the room, over the heaped shadows and tumbled stone, over the thing that hung heavily from the crossbeams by a rope.

He wasn't even aware of the match until it seared his fingers, leaving him in darkness. He didn't want to light another. He shook his head, dazed, and his fingers reacted automatically, scraping the head of another match against the side of the box. Flame dazzled him; he looked up slowly, at the rope, the heavy, lumpy burlap sack, slashed and torn and stained. He stumbled forward, not able to take his eyes from it. In the light of the match the stains seemed to turn red before his eyes. Blood dripped slowly from the soaked bottom of the sack to the stones below. There were three red pools on the floor.

He held the match higher. In the last flicker of light,

through a rent in the burlap, he saw the dark, mutilated head of a child.

For a few moments, in the darkness that followed, he thought that he must be losing his mind, because the dead child seemed to be calling out to him. Then he realized that the cries, echo-distorted, came from somewhere else in the depths of the prison.

Backing away from the sack that hung dripping from the beams, he took two more matches, and struck one.

"Where are you?" he shouted. But he had seen a doorway, and stumbled toward it.

Inside the passage, he heard running water. The passage sloped downward and, as he followed it, the cries were louder, desperate; the terror in the child's voice seemed to accelerate in concert with a different guttural sound: something heavy and metallic, like a manhole cover, dragging over concrete.

There was meager light in the passage from a tower window high above; Practice could distinguish the rippling of water in near darkness. Apparently all or part of the creek had been diverted so that it flowed under the prison and spilled down into an aqueduct, then was channeled through a sewer to the river. The aqueduct was about half filled.

He had two matches left. The scraping of iron on concrete continued; and he heard heavy breathing as the screaming abruptly stopped. Not hearing the childish screams anymore was unendurable: Practice screamed himself as light flared above his fingertips.

"I'll help you! Where—"

He had a glimpse of the far wall, an uncovered well near where the racing waters of the aqueduct dropped underground. And something was moving swiftly toward him, a shadow on the wall that could have been a beast or a man. He heard a terrible low grunting sound, and as the match flickered in a draft, saw the curved blade of an upraised sword.

He had no weapon, no time to think. It was combat again, always the unexpected—groping for the enemy in darkness, the swift, violent encounters where you killed men whose faces you never saw. Instead of backing up, which probably would have been fatal, he hurled himself down and forward in a rolling block, cut the legs of the sword-bearer from under him, heard a hard *whang* of steel on the stone floor as he went rolling toward the opposite wall.

He got up slowly and silently, holding his breath. His ribs were bruised and one hand smarted from skinned knuckles. He heard footsteps echoing, then nothing except for a soft splash, no louder a sound than a frog would make jumping into a pond.

Disoriented, trembling, he waited, not knowing if the other man had run or if, perhaps, there was more than one. Someone might be waiting, only a few feet away in the dark; a misstep, the slightest miscalculation, and he risked dismemberment.

When he moved he went quickly, sideways, crouching, brushing against the rough damp wall opposite the aqueduct. He could just make out the surface rippling of water again. And heard the child whimpering.

The well, he thought. He could barely make it out across the chamber.

But where was the man with the sword?

He knew he had to take the chance that he was alone now with the child in the well . . . oh, God, God, had it been Chris Guthrie hanging up back there in the bloody sack? The survivor might be seriously wounded or dying. He moved again cautiously across the uneven floor, pausing to listen, trying to see through the gloom to hiding places, frightened of the terrible swift sword, reluctant to light his last match and make of himself an unmissable target.

"Bastard!" he whispered, ashamed of his fear. "Bastard, if you're here, come and get me!"

The well. His right foot stubbed against the iron cover on

the floor. He looked down into the well but could see nothing. The nape of his exposed neck felt cold. He was sluggish with dread, but he had to light the remaining match.

12

"Who's there?" Practice whispered into the well, striking fire from his thumbnail.

Chris Guthrie, his face dead white around a puckered scar of a mouth, gazed up blankly at him from three feet of swirling water.

"Oh, God," Practice moaned, and threw the match away. He reached blindly into the shallow well, got his hands under Chris's arms, and lifted him, drenched and shivering, from the water, knowing that this would be the moment the attacker might have waited for: waited until he was certain that Practice, with the boy in his arms, could not defend either of them.

Practice turned, his back to the well, and wrapped the boy in his trench coat. He saw nothing, heard nothing but Chris's chattering teeth.

He hurried then, avid to reach daylight, feeling his way back to the room where the murdered boy hung from the ceiling, but not stopping there, clattering up the iron stairs, falling once but holding tightly to Chris. On the first floor of the prison he crawled up a pile of stone to the roof, where there was enough space between the beams to force his way through, and drew Chris up after him. He made his way to the back of the building where an earth slide had buckled one wall, and clambered down the slope to the ground. In the light of day he looked anxiously at Chris's face. The boy's lips were still a ghastly blue, and only the whites of his eyes showed beneath the lids.

He knew Chris might die if his body temperature couldn't be raised. He jogged across the lowland to his car, placed Chris in the front seat, and drove up the hill. Without taking time to think about what he was doing, he turned into Major Kinsaker's driveway and stopped by the front porch. In another few seconds he was ringing the bell and swearing under his breath.

The door opened a couple of inches and Steppie peered out.

"Why, Jim . . ."

"Don't stand there, let me in."

"I can't . . ."

"For God's sake, Steppie, this boy is dying!"

He shoved the door open, unbalancing Steppie, and carried Chris inside.

"Where's the bedroom?"

"Jim! Please! You can't . . ."

Without waiting for a satisfactory reply he started up the stairs, and on the second floor opened the first door he came to. He went inside, stripped the wet clothes off Chris, wrapped him in a blanket taken from the foot of the bed, and put him under the covers.

"Call Dr. Childs," Practice said to Steppie, who was staring at Chris's face. She wavered a little on her feet, and he smelled whiskey. "And get me some of that stuff you've been drinking."

When he saw that she wasn't going to move he looked around for a telephone, failed to see one, and went into the adjoining room. More than likely this bedroom belonged to the Major himself, but Practice spotted a telephone on the bedside table and didn't waste time looking around.

Dr. Childs hadn't come in that day, according to his receptionist, and she sounded miffed, as if she had spent an unhappy morning placating angry patients. Practice asked her who usually covered for Childs, and then quickly dialed that number.

This time the doctor, a man named McLemore, was in, and Practice quickly explained the situation. He was told to keep Chris warm and not to move him again.

The receiver of the phone clattered against the table, and Practice realized how badly he was trembling. He used both hands to set the receiver in its cradle, then slumped on the edge of the canopied bed, clenching his hands between his knees.

Steppie came toward him uncertainly, with a decanter in one hand and a glass in the other.

"Are they going to take him to the hospital?" she asked. "Maybe if they do the Major won't find out . . ."

"Damn the Major," Practice said between clenched teeth.

She poured some of the whiskey into the glass without spilling any; Practice took it and raised it to his lips. He seemed to realize then what he was doing.

Seeing his hesitation, Steppie said, "Go on, Jim. You need it."

He grimaced and put the glass down.

"Look at you, you're a mess," Steppie complained. "At least get off the bed."

He stood up, drawing a deep breath.

"Your bed now, Steppie?" he said, for no good reason; she looked at him hatefully, then shrugged, as if it weren't important.

"You made a spot," she said. "I'd better try to clean it up."

"Let it go. The Major won't care, for God's sake."

"You don't know him."

"Where is the Major?"

"I don't know, but he might come home any minute." She put out a hand as if to draw him away by the sleeve of his coat. "Bring your glass and—" She broke off, aware that he was staring at the wall opposite the foot of the bed.

"What's that?" he asked.

She showed her teeth in a grimace of distaste.

"I *told* you you didn't know anything about him." For a moment it seemed as if she might cry, but she checked herself. "Come out of here now."

He hadn't taken his eyes from the painting.

"That's Molly," he said, "the Major's daughter."

"Yes . . ."

Practice put a hand to his eyes as if he couldn't believe what they saw. Obviously the picture had been painted not long before Molly's death. The artist had posed her in a child's swing, and caught her in full flight, her long hair flowing behind her, an expression of oblivious joy on her face. She was absolutely, literally nude, fixed forever by the artist's brush in the days between puberty and sexual maturity.

The bedroom itself—wood-paneled, with thick carpeting —was a small museum. There were three glass cases of war trophies, maps, two gun racks, and a good-sized mounted telescope, which was pointed toward the river. The painting in any setting would have been startling, but in that room, with its faded mementos of a vigorous manhood, it was shocking.

Steppie swallowed, reluctantly looking at the painting, her expression squeamish.

"No," she said, "it isn't my bed. I'm not allowed in here at all. Only *she* . . ." Steppie made a motion toward the painting, then averted her eyes. "Oh, Jim, there's something in the Major's mind that . . ."

"Get out of here," he said. "Go sit with Chris. I have to make another call, and then I'll come."

Captain Liles wasn't available. Practice requested that Liles be located, gave the address of the Major's house, and hung up. He glanced once more at the painting, both fascinated and appalled, then joined Steppie in the other bedroom.

He looked down at Chris. There was less strain in the boy's face, but his skin was still cold to the touch. Practice knew Chris was in shock, but couldn't tell how bad it was. He wished Lucy were there. What had Chris seen in that prison? Had he seen his friend killed, or only heard his screams as he crouched in the well? For a moment Practice thought of Val St. George, but revulsion took over his thoughts.

Steppie sat dispiritedly in a chair beside the bed and poured herself another drink.

"What happened to him?" she asked without interest. "Did he fall in the creek? It's not so cold this time of year, why is he . . ."

"He's in shock. Someone tried to kill him."

"What?"

"Three years ago he was almost killed, but nobody believed then it was anything but an accident. Today the same man tracked Chris and a friend through the old prison. Chris got away. The other boy wasn't so lucky."

She stared at him with round, frightened eyes.

"The other boy is . . . ?"

Practice nodded. "Dead. Strung up in a burlap sack and run through a dozen times with a sword."

On the bed Chris moved restlessly, but no sound came from his lips.

Steppie doubled up as if a cramp had hit her, but in a few moments regained control. Practice paced nervously, occasionally stopping in front of the windows. From there he could see the school yard and the long, desolate valley where the old prison lay. And inside . . .

"How long have you been living with him?" he said, trying to get his mind off the murder.

"Two months. Maybe more. I've lost track. But I don't stay here all the time. I come when he wants me. Stay two, three days. Then I go."

"How did you get together in the first place?"

She looked down into her glass, frowning, as if she didn't

want to be questioned, but in some way was eager to tell him everything about her relationship with Major Kinsaker.

"He saw me, he wanted me, he sent for me. That's all."

"Not quite all. What are you getting this time, Steppie?"

Steppie squinted resentfully, then her expression became bland and a little smug.

"Nearly everything he has, when he dies."

"I can't believe that."

"Can't you? What else would he do with his money? There are no more Kinsakers. Someone's going to have his fortune; it might as well be me."

Practice was silent, and she turned her head sharply.

"Don't believe it, do you? Listen, Jim. He made out a new will when I came to this house for the first time. I've seen it. I know just where it is. Ninety percent of everything he owns is mine as soon as he dies. And Jim"—her voice became a husky, passionate whisper—"he is seventy-one years old. And any day, just any day now . . ." Her head dropped again and she stared blankly at the floor.

"What's going to happen, Steppie?"

Her mouth opened and closed petulantly.

"He'll die, I hope."

"He'll double-cross you somehow, Steppie. Can't you see that?"

"No, he won't! He won't dare!"

"Real easy for you. You come when he calls. Any hundred-dollar-a-day girl could do the same, and it would be a hell of a lot cheaper. What's going on here, Steppie?"

"Nothing you don't know."

"Then why are you so scared? If you're so certain he'll die soon and leave you a fortune . . ."

"Will you shut up?" she hissed.

"You asked me for help last night."

"Forget last night."

"You were serious enough. Are you trying to tell me you'd give up the Major, and the security he's pledged, for me?"

She hit her fist on the arm of the chair several times, her eyes shut.

"Where is that doctor? Why doesn't he come and get this kid out of here before the Major comes back?"

"What does the Major want from you, Steppie?"

"Don't be an idiot."

"Besides that."

"Stop it, Jim. I know what you think of me. But believe this, by the time I get out of here I will have earned every nickel I . . ." She sat erect and still for half a minute, her expression serious, almost stolid, a distant look in her eye. "You know, Jim, the Major hates Guthrie. Really hates him."

"I know there's bad feeling . . ."

"If he hates him, then why doesn't he go ahead and ruin him and get it over with?"

"He doesn't have anything on Guthrie that would . . ."

She turned her face toward him, but without really seeing him.

"Oh, yes, he does. And I know what it is."

Practice waited and then said impatiently, "Go on, Steppie. What are you talking about?"

She shook her head, perplexed.

"The Major could do it anytime he wants; he's told me so. He could send Guthrie to jail."

"How?"

Steppie smiled in a queer way.

"For killing Molly Kinsaker."

Practice stared at her, for the moment stunned; then his mind cleared.

"He couldn't have, Steppie. Molly died from a fall off her horse."

"That's what everyone thinks, because the Major made it look that way. The truth is, Guthrie killed her, or was responsible for her death. Molly Kinsaker was crazy about Guthrie; they were real saddle pals. This was back when the Major and Guthrie were still thick. Well, one weekend the

Major had some people up to the farm for a barbecue and all that. There was heavy drinking and Guthrie did his share. About noon on Saturday Molly talked Guthrie into a jeeping expedition down by the river bluffs. The Major wasn't well and didn't go, so Guthrie set out with Molly. He was driving and feeling no pain. Nobody knows just how the accident started, but obviously Guthrie was too drunk to control the jeep. Near the river they went over a forty-foot embankment, and Guthrie managed to keep the jeep right side up all the way down. At the bottom he ran out of luck, and they crashed head-on into some trees. Molly went out over the top of the windshield, headfirst into the trunk of a tree, broke her neck and shattered her skull. Guthrie was better off. His arm was hung up in the steering wheel and he stayed inside. You should see it, Jim, it's awful. Molly lying faceup on the hood of that jeep with her eyes staring at the sky, blood running down her face and all over the hood and right fender, her head twisted way over; and Guthrie trying to walk and staggering drunk with a sick smile on his face . . ."

"What do you mean, I should see it? Were you there?"

She shook her head. "It's all on movie film, Jim—the wreck, the tire tracks, the beer cans in the front seat. The Major has the film. He's made me watch it, several times." She swallowed hard. "It's so awful I—but I don't understand. They covered the whole thing up. They towed the jeep away and buried the oil and gasoline slicks and brought Molly's horse to the scene, so when the Sheriff and the search party reached the spot all traces of an accident were gone, and it looked as if the horse had thrown Molly against the tree."

"You said 'they.' Who else was involved, Steppie?"

"Dr. Childs. Fletch Childs. You know, the brother of that girl you're so crazy about. He found the wreck. He was out filming nature studies and heard the crash. I suppose he was so upset he just kept the shutter open and got those movies—but no—" She hesitated, biting her lip. "They weren't made accidentally. I mean, all the close-ups, the girl's face and those beer cans in the front seat. He filmed enough evidence to put John Guthrie in jail." Practice shook his head at that, but she didn't see. "But they didn't do it. They covered up. Why?"

She looked searchingly at Practice. "I know one thing. I know why he keeps running those films over and over."

"So he won't forget?"

"Because," she said in little more than a whisper, "because he actually enjoys them."

With no more sound than the click of the latch the bedroom door opened and Major Starne Kinsaker stood in the doorway. Steppie started, a small cry escaping her, but Practice only returned the Major's stare in the moments before the old man's eyes turned in astonishment to the boy lying in the bed.

13

The Major's reaction to the sight of Chris Guthrie was swift and unexpected. Before Practice could move, Kinsaker had pushed past him and was crouching on the edge of the bed, his arms around Chris, lifting the boy, blankets and all, to his thin, hard chest. He pressed his cheek against Chris's, one hand cradling the back of Chris's head.

A series of sounds like dry sobs broke from Major Kinsaker's throat.

Steppie had half risen from her chair. The sound of door chimes was startlingly loud in the house. Practice motioned to Steppie and she left the bedroom, her eyes a little feverish and still frightened. Practice crossed to the bed and put his hand on the Major's shoulder.

"What is it?" the Major said softly, still clutching the boy. "What's the matter with him?"

Practice noticed that the Major was wearing gray wool slacks and house slippers instead of his customary riding boots and habit, and because of the change seemed less rigid and formidable.

"Something very bad has happened, Major," Practice said. "Another boy, a friend of Chris's, has been killed— murdered. I think Chris would have been killed, too, but he managed to get away. I found him down in the old prison, hiding in the well of the aqueduct. He was half frozen, scared witless. I brought him to the nearest shelter I could find."

"It's all right," the Major said, and slowly lowered the boy to the bed, rearranging the covers around him, his eyes never leaving Chris's face. There were muffled voices on the stairs, as Steppie returned with whoever had been at the door.

"Who was after him?" the Major asked. "Did he tell you?"

"Chris hasn't been conscious. I hope he saw what happened. But I don't need to hear it from him to know."

The Major turned his head slowly, his hawk-yellow eyes burning.

"Were you there? Did you see the person?"

"Not well enough to identify him. I'd like to be able to tell you more, Major. But I'll have to discuss the murder with Captain Liles first. He should arrive here soon."

The doctor entered, followed by Steppie. He introduced himself and went briskly to the bed, a man with a brigadier's mustache and dewlaps. The Major walked stiffly away from the bed, past Steppie.

"Make some coffee," he said to her in a tone of cold command, and signaled Practice with his eyes. He looked at the door to his bedroom, hesitated, then walked across the room to lock the door with a key from his pocket. Practice watched him, then turned and followed Steppie out. The Major joined them in the hall. They both looked at Steppie as she went unsteadily down the stairs, a hand on the railing.

"I'm sorry she was here when you came," the Major murmured. "Awkward. My chauffeur has the day off, but I'll send her home by cab."

"We haven't been married for quite a while," Practice said.

"I'm fond of Steppie. But I suppose she told you."

"We've never discussed you, Major," Practice said, and knew as soon as he had spoken that the Major didn't believe him. He wondered how long Kinsaker had been in the house before making his presence known, and what he had overheard outside the bedroom door.

"I'd like to know what happened," the Major said. "A friend of Chris's has been murdered? How did it happen? What were the boys doing at the old prison?"

Practice had just begun to outline the story for him when two cars pulled into the driveway. Shortly thereafter he went over the details with Captain Liles and three subordinates, Detective Sergeant Prohaska of the city police, and the Major. As soon as he had finished, several of the men left for the old prison. Outside, rain was whipping down, and there was no heat in the house. The Major sat stiffly through Practice's summary, wordless, his eyes studying every man present but dwelling the longest on Practice.

They were interrupted by the doctor, who looked curiously at the policemen.

"Boy's strong as a bull. The shock is wearing off, but I'm a little worried about congestion in the left lung. Might easily turn into pneumonia. Which one of you is the boy's father?"

"I'll speak for him," Practice said.

"I'd like permission to move him to the hospital."

"I don't mind if he stays here," the Major said.

The doctor pursed his lips. "Hospital's a better place for

him. If pneumonia is brewing, it could explode anytime. Be real dangerous for him, right on the heels of shock."

"The telephone is in the hallway," Major Kinsaker said. "You'll want to call for an ambulance."

Captain Liles got ponderously to his feet, snapping his notebook shut.

"Wonder if I could ask the boy a few questions, Doctor?"

"I'm sorry, he's not awake. I thought a sedative would do him good. He may sleep until early tomorrow morning."

Liles muttered something under his breath, looking at the chewed end of his cigar.

"Bad break. Jim, I'm going to send a man along to the hospital with the boy. I'll have someone outside his door around the clock. Well, I guess I'd better get down below. Major, awful sorry about the disturbance."

"It's all right, Captain. A shocking thing."

"My job to get in touch with Guthrie," Practice said. "He and Dore will want to be at the hospital."

As they were leaving, he had a glimpse of Steppie's face in a doorway at the rear of the house.

The Major saw them all to the door.

Practice put a hand on the sleeve of Liles's slicker as they were walking through the rain to their cars.

"Just a minute, Captain. I have some more information about the murder."

They stood close together, with the rain dripping from the brims of their hats, as Practice told the story of Val St. George. Liles's face had an eager, excited expression as he finished.

"Damn! Why didn't you tell me all this earlier today?"

"I couldn't. I was hoping to find Val St. George myself and talk to him. That seemed easy enough."

Liles nodded. "So Lucy knows him. But where is Lucy?"

"I don't know. She left the mansion about nine this morning."

"Maybe her brother can tell us."

"I hope so."

"I don't like to ask this. Is there any possibility of an affair between Lucy and this St. George?"

Practice shook his head irritably. "There couldn't be. Don't you understand? Lucy thinks he's just another crippled bird that can be healed with the right combination of patience and fellowship."

"She should have spoken up last night," Liles said angrily. "It must have been obvious to her that this St. George fellow did the job on the Governor's room."

"I know she was thinking about it. But she didn't want to believe he could be capable of such violence."

"Let's hope she doesn't find out the hard way. All right, Jim. I'm calling men in from four other troops on this. I know the city police will cooperate fully. From the description you've given me, St. George shouldn't be hard to locate. I think we'd better start with Dr. Childs and work backward. He's likely to know where Lucy can be found. I have a couple of more questions. They may not be easy to answer, but it's my job to ask them."

"I'll try to answer."

"What does Val St. George have against John Guthrie?"

Practice hesitated. The information Liles had asked for was dangerous. If the wrong people knew, John Guthrie could be utterly ruined overnight, disgraced as few men know disgrace. Without turning around, Practice felt the pressure of Major Kinsaker from within the house; he wondered if the Major was watching them closely as they stood in the rain, engrossed in tragedy.

Practice knew that Liles was a good policeman, thorough and honest. All he asked was that those involved in an investigation be honest with him, so that he could do his work. In a few seconds Practice weighed all his doubts, and decided that the Captain must be trusted.

"John Guthrie is his father."

Liles's eyebrows drew together. "That's straight?"

"Yes. One thing more."

"My God. What else?"

"I don't think Guthrie is even aware of the boy's existence."

Liles's expression became bleak. "I'll be damned. This is a real bomb. A real, live, ugly—I never thought I'd find myself in the middle of one like this. No wonder you were so reticent inside the house. I was getting ready to ream you good for withholding information. Lucky thing I didn't." His eyes flickered to the front of the house. "If the Major even had a smell of this, he'd tear Guthrie's guts out."

"The trouble is," Practice said quietly, "I think the Major has more than a smell." He told Liles about the two men who had visited Billie Charmian a week ago and mistreated her.

"A couple of hardcases. So they know about the kid, and they know he was in the state hospital. Did Dr. Mackerras mention if anyone else was asking about St. George recently?"

"No. But they wouldn't have to go to him. I suppose a dozen staff members have access to patients' records. If the request seemed harmless enough, and the bribe was big enough, the dossier on St. George could have been made available to others."

Liles nodded. "More than likely we're not the only ones looking for St. George. He'd better be dug in real good. But don't worry, Jim, we'll get to him first."

"I hope so."

Liles nodded again and started off toward his car, where a patrolman waited behind the wheel. Then he turned.

"Thanks for leveling with me. I know it was a hard decision to make."

"Not so hard, Mike."

"I'm glad to know I'm trustworthy," Liles said, a brief sad smile appearing on his face. "Now I've got a nasty job to do, and I wish to hell there was a way to get out of it."

"Hugh McAdams's parents?"

"Right." His expression became savage. "That bastard St. George. Maybe he's off his rocker, but that doesn't make me feel any better. I hope he tries something when we're pulling

him in." Liles drew up his shoulders in a spasm of disgust
and hatred, wiped the rain off his cheek with the edge of his
hand, and said, "What about the Governor? How much can
you tell him?"

"I don't know," Practice admitted. "That's up to Guthrie
himself."

He stood beside his car until the dark blue patrol car had
backed out of the driveway, then he slid in under the wheel
and glanced for a moment at the Kinsaker house. On the
second floor, where the stairs would be, he glimpsed someone standing behind the curtains, looking out, and thought
that it was Steppie, but he couldn't be sure.

Just as he was leaving, an ambulance from the city hospital
came down the street with its red light flashing and turned
into the driveway.

 14

In the west, over the river valley, the darkened sky was
streaming back like smoke from the molten wreckage of the
setting sun, and except for a tatter of squall blowing out
along the ridges of the north, the valley lay clear of rain,
glistening and green.

Governor John Guthrie sat in a chair he had pulled close
to the windows of the sitting room, his back to Practice, an
untouched drink in his hand. He had been sitting that way
for almost half an hour, saying nothing, staring at the sunset
and the slowly clearing sky over the river.

Practice stood near the doorway to Dore's room, his
weight against the wall, a homemade cigarette burning itself
out between dry lips, his eyes on Guthrie's back. He was
trying to decide how he felt about this man, and it wasn't

easy, because he had discovered that his feelings for Guthrie were almost as ambivalent and contradictory as Guthrie's own life had been.

The resentment Practice had felt six years ago at being bluffed and bullied from the edge of disaster by Guthrie gradually disappeared as a bedrock dedication to living took hold, and from that time there was no recurrence of resentment or hostility. As he became more valuable to his employer, the balance of dependence shifted and became more nearly equal, so that what was left of his pride suffered no severe strains.

And yet, he admitted to himself, the more self-sufficient he became, the more remote he was from Guthrie. Their friendship was real, but passive.

He had always thought of Guthrie as a man firmly in control of his own life, who had by strength and foresight avoided the defeats and disillusionments that characterized the lives of most people. But in the past twenty-four hours Practice had learned differently, and was nearly as shocked as Guthrie must have been in the rare moments when his energy ebbed and the specter of Molly Kinsaker intruded on him. Somehow Guthrie had adjusted to a tragedy that would have killed other men, and Practice felt a grinding sympathy for him. The tragedy was harder to bear because it must never have been admitted. It was still a fresh wound which the Major wouldn't allow to heal, for reasons of his own. And John Guthrie must have lived for four long years wondering why. Why had the Major worked to elect Guthrie as Governor, even after Guthrie had split the party in a radical move? Why did Guthrie insist on stripping the Major of his power, when there was tragedy enough between them? He had never wavered once from his goals; his determination, at least in Practice's eyes, had never flagged for more than a few scattered hours during all the months of his term as Governor.

But the cost had been paid, every day. Dore had felt the emotional sapping first, and perhaps Chris had felt it, too.

Then Practice had seen the slow erosion of energy and resolve. For the last few weeks Guthrie had been running on grit alone.

He sat now in his chair with unseeing eyes, like a man who will never rise.

The attempt on his son's life, the new tragedy erupting from a nearly forgotten episode in his past, had engulfed John Guthrie. He was trying to fight, but he was weak. And Practice didn't know what he could do to help.

Guthrie slowly lifted his glass to his lips but didn't drink.

"Should be a beautiful day tomorrow," he said tonelessly.

Practice shifted his weight and glanced at his watch, wondering why he hadn't heard from Mike Liles. So far the state patrol hadn't been able to get in touch with either Dr. Childs or Lucy, and a worm of alarm caused Practice's shoulders to tingle. The taste in his mouth was still pure dirt, as it had been half an hour ago when he finished telling Guthrie about Val St. George.

The telephone rang and Practice scooped up the receiver before the bell had stopped. He listened for a few moments, his eyes on the reflection of the Governor's face in the darkening glass of the windows, then hung up with a murmured, "I'll tell him."

"That was Dore," he said to the motionless Guthrie. "She said that Chris is resting comfortably and wants to know when you're coming."

There was no answer and Practice scowled in irritation, then paced the wide room, hoping Guthrie would tell him to sit down, hoping for any sign or spark to indicate that the formidable engine that had driven the man for so long was about to come to life.

"A lot of people wondered why I married Dore," Guthrie said unexpectedly, in a low voice. "I was forty-one and I had a lot of women on the string, elegant women, brainy, good-looking, the works. I might have married a few of them. Instead, I picked Dore. She wasn't dumb, but she wasn't bright. Just a kid, too, packing around all that sex, but naïve as hell. I suppose people say I tumbled for the sex and didn't see another goddamn thing, but that's baloney."

"Sure," Practice said encouragingly.

"Baloney," Guthrie repeated after a while. "I married Dore because she was woman through and through, not some oversensitized and desexed bitch who has to cut a man's throat for every smile she gives him. Dore gave me every ounce of woman in her, without a thought of what she was getting in return. Because, you see, with Dore it wasn't an effort, she was born that way. It was her nature; and when I had Dore close by I could stop clanking around and let down my guard and stop thinking about what it was to be a man and just experience it. You know what I mean?"

"I think so."

"Well, that's over with," Guthrie said resignedly. *"Was* over a long time ago. Dore smarted up. She wanted to be like all the other women she saw. She listened to the trash they put out when they're all by themselves, and so she lost interest in just being a woman; she became some kind of godforsaken *creation,* if you get me. And I let it happen."

"You could change all that."

"Know what I feel sometimes? I look at Dore and I feel so disgusted I want to strip all those brassy clothes off her ass and put her back in blue jeans where she belongs. Better still, there's a place I know out West, a canyon deep in the Montana highlands south of Billings. Nobody ever goes there. I'd like to take Dore and sheep-dip her until her hair's back the way it was and all the goo melts off her skin. Turn her loose naked in the grass beside the river, until she gets brown all over, until she's natural again. I wouldn't mind a spell of that kind of life myself."

"Then, get going."

Guthrie reached down and set the glass with its untouched whiskey on the rug. His hand was shaking.

"What the hell?" he said. "When she hears what I've done . . ."

"She won't let it hurt her. She may be shocked by Molly Kinsaker's death and upset for a little while over Billie Charmian, but she'll get over those things because she has to—for your sake."

Guthrie rubbed his face, then let his hands fall into his lap. The glass in the window was gold from the setting sun.

"I never loved Billie," he said. "I seduced her, pure and simple. It lasted three days. I wanted her and I had her. She didn't resist. She cried after the first time, but then she wanted me as much as I did her." His face contorted. "God! She was a sweet girl."

"If it hadn't been you . . ."

"Don't say that. I could have cared about poor Ted Croft, dying. But all I thought about was going to bed with Billie. I think she loved me, but she let me go without saying a word. I never went back."

Guthrie rose from his chair and hurried into Dore's bedroom. He was gone for a quarter of an hour, but when he returned, he looked better. He had shaved and changed his shirt. There was a little crawl of blood near his left earlobe, where he had nicked himself, and the shaved moon of his jaw was a pale blue.

He smiled wanly at Practice.

"Know what I've been thinking? The boy might be killed when Liles's men try to arrest him."

"It's possible."

Guthrie nodded, absorbed. "I want him dead and wiped out of my life, because I can't face him." He sat down at a writing desk and drew out a sheet of paper with the Governor's letterhead, selected a pen, and sat staring at the paper with his fists clenched.

"All I want is to save something of myself."

"Do you think you can accomplish that by resigning your office?"

Guthrie glanced up in annoyance.

"I don't know. I don't know what I'll do or where I'll go when the boy tells his story."

"*If* he tells it."

"If he doesn't, the Major will. All the Major has to do is plant a few notions with the right newspapermen, and they'll dig up the rest."

"Use your head. Suppose Val St. George does talk and someone without authority hears him. It's going to sound like the ravings of an insane murderer with some imaginary grudge against you. Even the lowest type of newshound is going to think twice about accepting such a story, and proving it will be next to impossible. Without documented corroboration from Val St. George or Billie Charmian, there is no story, and I'm convinced only Billie's word could damage you conclusively. She'd never admit it. No paper in the state hates you enough to print a story based on St. George's confession, whatever it may be. Mike Liles will see to it that the boy's signed confession doesn't damage you. As for the Major, he'll have only the wildest suspicions, enough for a rumor campaign if he chooses. Survival may take some gumption on your part, but it won't be fatal."

Guthrie's face was bleak, but a hint of determination showed around the mouth. He sat straighter in his chair, staring down at the blank paper.

"Wherever he's hiding, the boy still has his sword right at my throat. Because, Jim, the Major might get in touch with him first. And when he does, he'll squeeze out every drop of information that's in the boy. If he needs evidence, he'll manufacture it and drop it right in the lap of an editor like Swenson. If the story sees print in just one edition, even if a retraction is forced later on and the whole shoddy affair hushed up, the boy will have realized his wish—he'll have my head."

The room had darkened and Practice switched on a table lamp, then drew the drapes across the high windows.

"The only way for the Major to get his hands on Val St. George is for Val to give himself up to him. That's not even worth considering. John, I'm not even convinced that the Major would smear you if he had the boy in his pocket."

"Why wouldn't he?"

"Because he's had other means of ruining you, these years, and he hasn't done it."

Guthrie looked up at him.

"You don't understand the Major. He could never bring himself to use his daughter's name for revenge against me." His head dropped until his chin was nearly on his chest. "Jim, how did you know what happened to Molly Kinsaker?"

"I only learned about it today. Steppie told me. She'd seen the movie the Major has."

"I've heard about that movie," Guthrie muttered.

"Why did you go along with it, John? The accident wasn't pleasant, but it wouldn't necessarily have meant the end of your political career."

Guthrie's mouth twisted. "I was very, very drunk. By the time I sobered up enough to realize what had happened, the story was already out that Molly had fallen from her horse. Even then I wanted to admit the truth, but the Major wouldn't let me do it. Only he and Fletcher Childs knew what had happened."

"What did happen? Do you remember?"

"It was five years ago. Sometimes I only see the accident clearly in nightmares. What really happened, and what happens only in nightmares—it's hard to say. Molly wanted to go jeeping. I felt fine when we started out . . ."

"What were you drinking?"

"Beer. We had a long lunch and I ate practically nothing, but I drank about seven cans of beer. That wasn't unusual, I could hold that much all right; but it was a boiling hot day and the jeep was bouncing all over the place; and before long I started feeling bad. I should have quit drinking, but I had just opened a can and I didn't want to waste it. So I drank the beer down fast, and—that's the last thing I remember, except for bits and flashes. The Major, with tears streaming down his face, forgiving me for killing his daughter." Guthrie's face was lugubrious. "I killed her all right, as surely as if I'd put a gun to her head. I was too drunk to drive. And yet . . ."

"What is it, John?"

"In some of the dreams I've had, I wasn't driving. Molly was."

"Molly? Could she operate a jeep?"

"Sure. She loved to drive, and she could handle the wheel pretty well, although she'd just turned thirteen. Sometimes, when we went out jeeping, I let her drive. She was begging me to let her have the wheel that day, too." Guthrie licked his dry lips. "That's what I remember. Or was it a part of the dream, too?"

Practice felt a prickling of excitement, but he kept his voice level.

"It may not be a dream. What do you remember?"

"The sun, shining in my eyes. The river. Clear blue sky. And Molly's voice. She was laughing and teasing me."

"What did she say?"

" 'Old—drunk.' " Guthrie's eyes were fixed in absorption on the carpet. " 'Move over, you old drunk, and let me . . .' "

"Drive?"

Guthrie looked up slowly.

"She was driving, Jim. I remember clearly now—the motion of the jeep, the sun stunting in the sky, and the river down below. We were on a high bank . . ." He swallowed and wiped his forehead where a film of perspiration had appeared. "And then Molly started screaming, and the jeep slid to one side. I almost pitched out. We were sliding out of control down the bank, and I—I . . ."

"What happened?"

"This is the nightmare part. My hands are stuck, stuck

tight somehow, and I can't reach the wheel. I know something horrible is going to happen, but I can't reach the wheel. Then the Major's face and his terrible eyes, and I hear him saying, 'I forgive you, I forgive you.'" Guthrie put his face down into his hands and sat quietly.

Practice looked at him abstractedly, thinking hard.

"According to Steppie," he said slowly, "the films which Fletch Childs took show you behind the wheel of the car, with your arm caught in the wheel. Could that be what you remember, John, when you say your hands were stuck tight?"

"I don't know," Guthrie replied, his voice muffled. "I was drunk. Anything could have happened. Maybe Molly wasn't driving. Maybe I only want to believe that she was."

"Maybe," Practice said. "At any rate, Fletch Childs saw the accident and filmed the aftermath. And in those films you're behind the wheel of the jeep." He fell silent, lost in thought.

The Governor raised his head and shook himself like a nervous horse.

"I—suppose I'd better be getting to the hospital," he said. "Dore will be wondering . . ."

"I'll call down and have the car ready," Practice said, and Guthrie nodded.

After the Governor had left, Practice sat alone in the apartment for some time, thinking about the death of Molly Kinsaker.

He tried to picture the girl in his mind as she must have been on the last day of her life: an exuberant, high-spirited girl, strong-willed, perhaps with a saving grace of humor. He saw Molly and John riding across the rough meadows in the jeep, going toward the river, following a familiar trail that Molly knew well. It was reasonable that she would be eager to take a turn at the wheel. And it would be reasonable that Guthrie, feeling the impact of the beer and the heat, would allow her to drive. Then—too much speed, the wheels slipping over the edge of a sandy embankment, the girl frantically struggling to keep the jeep upright as they skidded down. Perhaps at a crucial moment the inexperienced Molly had placed her foot upon the gas pedal instead of the brake and hurtled them into the midst of the trees.

"My hands are stuck, stuck tight somehow . . ."

Stuck where? Between the seats? So that at the moment of impact only Molly Kinsaker was flung from the jeep, across the windshield, headfirst into the wall of trees?

After the crash, silence. The birds have flown from the trees and are circling in fright high in the cloudless sky. Far away, perhaps, undisturbed by the noise, other birds are twittering on a perfect summer's day.

And across the field a man comes walking, slowly at first, as the impact of the tragedy he has witnessed drags after him. Then perhaps he breaks into a run and makes his way breathlessly to the periphery of tree shadow, where the hot odor of the jeep engine slowly escapes into the broad air and a dead girl lies faceup across the crumpled hood, staring sightlessly at the sky.

Practice squirmed uncomfortably in his seat. And after, for reasons known only to himself, Fletcher Childs rearranges the unconscious form of John Guthrie so that it appears as if Guthrie was behind the wheel of the jeep at the time of the accident, and then methodically films every gruesome detail to substantiate the lie he is going to tell.

15

As Practice sat in edgy contemplation, the telephone on the table beside him rang, and then rang again. It was the Governor's private line; the ring wouldn't be answered below. Probably Dore, he thought, wanting her husband, and picked up the receiver.

At first he heard nothing on the wire. Then, little by little, human sounds reached his ears, the sounds of someone at the limits of physical endurance trying to speak or to scream, to find relief in human contact, in any manner at all.

"Who is it?" he said sharply, with a sudden icy tautness from the nape of his neck to the small of his back.

"Jim—I need—you . . ."

"Lucy?" He hunched forward, pressing the receiver of the telephone closer to his ear, as if by sheer concentration he could bring her voice more strongly from the void in which she seemed to be speaking. "Where are you?"

"Lake Road," he heard indistinctly. "The Mill—then—Baldtree. Fletch . . ."

"Talk louder, Lucy, for God's . . ."

"Can't—say any more. Help—Jim . . ."

There was a plastic clatter in his ear, then the click followed by an instant's nothingness, and the long droning of an empty line.

He sat for a few moments with a grimace chiseled on his face, then got up quickly. *The Lake Road.* Apparently she had called him from the big reservoir forty miles south of the city, and Baldtree—that would be Fletcher Childs's summer place. Practice had heard them both talk about it, but had never been there. So that's where Lucy had gone after leaving the mansion earlier in the day. To be alone, or to meet . . .

He borrowed one of the mansion Cadillacs for the trip to the reservoir. It was an almost new, midnight-blue behemoth, with all the power he could ask for on the highway and plenty of weight for negotiating the narrow, precipitous roads in the woods above the reservoir shores.

He drove with only a part of his mind alert to the still-wet highway and the oncoming traffic. The feeling of oppression that had begun earlier in Billie Charmian's antiseptic room in the warehouse had settled on him again. The shadow of a boy whom he had never met raced through his mind, and he withdrew in glum horror from its touch. Because the boy wanted revenge against a man who hadn't known he existed, Practice's own life was involved beyond his control. For several years he had lived in a thin, dry atmosphere, in the midst of people, but without acknowledging their humanity. Whenever their personal failings had seemed to threaten him in some obscure way, he had withdrawn deep inside himself.

During the months at Doc Merrill's, he had attempted to strengthen his personality by simplifying it, and in gaining strength he had discarded all those emotions that make life unpredictable, confusing, and sometimes unpleasant. He had tried to make a simple equation of himself, so that each day would be a mathematical certainty, with only the variables of his work to provide stimulation. But those variables had nothing to do with him; they were pertinent only to John Guthrie and his career.

Lucy had known all of this, intuitively, and she had taken a chance on loving him. He had responded painfully—taking care to hide his pain—dutifully bringing out all the old words, the litany of love, while feeling guilty for desiring her. Maybe he had been relieved when at last she despaired of finding a reliable depth of passion and had left him, naked, distressed, but persistent out of ritual or some stubborn sense of obligation to her.

Out of the dark, alongside the highway, the tavern and roadhouse signs appeared, one on top of another, flickering across his mind. Anonymous places, with a car or two parked in front. The odor of taprooms welled out of his memory, his throat was dry. He could turn off at any one of the low, garish buildings and nudge the Cadillac against the siding. Inside, he would likely be alone; no one would try to talk to him. He knew just how he would do it: three cold beers to ease his thirst and then the first double shot of scotch, no ice. He had forty dollars in his pocket. Enough for two fifths and one of the cabins out back, deep in the pines. There were always cabins, with an iron bed and a faded pink spread, a cracked yellow dish covering the light bulb in the ceiling.

If he was lucky, he would never come out of it long enough to remember John Guthrie or Dore or Chris or Lucy.

Headlights hit his face like an icy deluge; he turned the wheel hard to the right and the other car roared by an inch away, with a howling horn, trailing off in a crazy weave of red taillights, as the driver left the pavement and then steered out of trouble.

The near miss had cleared his mind, and he sat up straighter. A headache was lodged on the left side of his skull, above the ear. Crazy bastard, he thought, and wasn't sure if he was referring to the driver of the car he had almost run down. He found himself thinking of Lucy and that curled smile of hers, reproving smile.

What do you think of when you think of me, Lucy?

A signpost rose up out of his headlights: Lake Road, next right.

He began to feel anxious again, wishing that he had called Mike Liles before leaving, to find out if there was any news of Val St. George. It was now almost seven o'clock. Six hours earlier, St. George had committed murder. Where was he now?

The Lake Road appeared. Practice slowed, turned off the highway, and accelerated. There was a bewildering pro-

fusion of signposts along the road, and for a few moments he had no idea where to go. Then he noticed a red
and yellow cutout windmill with an arrow, and took the road
pointed out to him.

He was driving as fast as he dared, almost too fast for
safety on the unfamiliar road. The mill appeared, an artifi-
cial creation with neon blades, apparently some sort of
restaurant. There were a few cars around the place. Again
he slowed, scanning the many signposts, and picked out the
one that said "Baldtree" in faded hand lettering.

The lodge was almost hidden from the road by the
thickness of trees around it. Practice had to back up to the
single gatepost and rutted drive that wound up the knoll to a
point overlooking the reservoir. He shone the spotlight of
the Cadillac on the mailbox and saw the name "Childs." But
from the road the house was unlighted and looked deserted.

He had driven within a hundred feet of the lodge before
he saw an old Plymouth in a lean-to garage not far away. It
was Lucy's car; she kept it at her brother's house in town and
rarely drove it anywhere.

There was a half-moon low over the hills south of the
reservoir, creating enough light in the black and yellow sky
for him to make his way to the front door without stumbling
over the stones of a neglected rock garden. He had taken a
flashlight from the dash compartment of the Cadillac, but
didn't turn it on.

He knocked several times at the heavy timber door of the
lodge.

"Lucy!"

Practice waited for several seconds, then tried the door
and opened it slowly. The air inside was warm and stale. He
fumbled for a light switch beside the door, found one, and
pushed the button several times, but there were no lights.

He thought he heard someone breathing in the room, and
shut the door behind him. Then brought the flashlight up
and the beam spilled into the large living room, traveling
over the kind of furniture that used to grace the verandas of
resort hotels thirty years ago.

"Lucy?"

He heard the slow hiss of her breath and then the beam of the flashlight found her, crouching in one corner, eyes staring intently and blinded by the light. Her lips were shaped in a snarl, and there was a sixteen-gauge shotgun in her hands, pointed directly at him. She didn't move or speak, but the breath hissed through her teeth from time to time and her head would jerk up and down as she tightened her grip on the shotgun.

"It's all right, Lucy," he said gently. "It's Jim. I came as soon as you called. What is it? What's wrong?"

She stared at him without changing expression. Her eyes appeared to narrow a little, and there was a tiny compressed sound in her throat that sounded like "uh-oh." Then with a rush her eyes lost their look of blindness and her face its frightening rigidity. The shotgun fell from her hands and bumped the floor. Practice swallowed hard. Lucy toppled forward on her hands and knees and stayed in that position for several moments, her hair hanging forward like a curtain.

"Oh, Jim," she said in a dry, weightless voice. "It's Fletch. He's dead. And Val killed him."

 16

After leaving the mansion that morning, Lucy had gone to her brother's house hoping that Val St. George might try to get in touch with her there.

She had seen him about once a month since his release from the state hospital, but always he had sought her out. Either he came to the house to visit her or else he telephoned and arranged a meeting. They never met twice in the same place. Lucy never had any idea when he would call, or appear, but she was always glad to see him.

The pattern of their meetings was invariable. Val St. George talked and Lucy listened. Sometimes he went on for hours, eagerly, excitedly, like someone who had been marooned, intolerably isolated from a friendly ear. He talked until his throat was a rasp, spilling out everything he had thought or read or dreamed. Sometimes he acted out skits he had written for Lucy, or sometimes he read passages from books that had attracted him, while Lucy sat by attentively, with an occasional smile or comment.

She never asked him where he had been or what he had been doing. She saw him as an appealing, lonely boy with a need for grandeur in his life, a boy with vision and imagination, and—yes—talent, whose unhappy existence was beneath the contempt of most people. She was certain that he had a job in a neighborhood where he could be as anonymous as possible, not an easy task in a city the size of Osage Bluff.

All Lucy knew about his life was what he chose to tell her, and she felt that some of the harrowing stories he related of his ghetto childhood were fabricated, substitutions for the story he could not bring himself to tell anyone.

He came to her full of pride, vanity, schemes, and plans, as well as a rich good humor, leaving his bitterness behind. Lucy knew that Val was often tempted to unload his frustrations and resentments on her, that it was sometimes a struggle not to do so; but to come to her for pity would be to admit a final defeat, and that he wouldn't allow himself.

The pattern of their meetings had only recently been broken. Three times in the past month Val had called her, and when she saw him, she noticed the change. He was not so quick to dominate the hours with jokes and ambitions. Instead, he asked a great many questions about her work, about the mansion, about John Guthrie and his wife and child. He seemed almost obsessed by John Guthrie; no detail of the Governor's daily routine was unimportant to him.

Lucy supplied what information she could, innocently wondering at the change in Val. When he saw that his interest in the Governor perplexed her, he quickly changed the subject for a while, but always, with the curiosity of a hound sniffing out a buried bone, would return to the same subject and probe, intently, a fixed, almost glazed look in his eyes.

The last call from Val had come yesterday afternoon. Would she meet him?

Lucy had hesitated; it meant breaking a date with Practice and leaving the mansion without telling anyone just where she was going; but the note of pleading in Val's voice made it impossible for her to refuse.

She had waited almost an hour on the lawn of one of the high schools for him, and then returned to the mansion, feeling both annoyed and disturbed. It was the first time he had ever missed a meeting.

And little more than an hour after that, staring at the wreckage of Governor Guthrie's bedroom, she had allowed herself to believe for an instant that somehow Val might have been responsible.

But why?

She lay sleepless most of the night. Then, after getting Chris off to school, she awakened Dore and received permission to take the day off—though Lucy was aware that the sleep-drugged Dore had scarcely heard a word she'd said.

She felt certain that Val would try to get in touch with her. But by one o'clock, as she waited in the living room of her brother's house, an unread magazine on her lap and a ticking clock working at her nerves, she was no longer so sure, and she was no longer as confident of Val St. George as she had been.

Lucy lighted one of her infrequent cigarettes and called Fletch's office, but his nurse told her that he hadn't been in all morning. She received the same answer at the university hospital. It was not his day to teach nor his day to play golf, even if the weather had made golf possible. Fletch was a man of established routines, and any deviation was unheard-of.

Possibly he had taken his fishing tackle and gone down to the reservoir. Lucy went up to her brother's bedroom and looked in the case where he kept his fishing rods and tackle, but nothing had been removed.

It was then she realized that water was running softly from a faucet in the bathroom, and she went to turn it off.

The yellow porcelain rim of the washstand showed small flecks of blood and in the bowl were streaks, as if a larger quantity of blood had been wiped up.

Lucy found it difficult to get her breath. Her eyes took in the snippings of catgut on the shelf near the washstand and a surgical needle. There were two unopened packets of gauze and an empty sodium pentothal ampule.

Stooping, she looked into the wastebasket. A small gasp broke from her lips. She reached down and pulled out the remains of a shirt she knew well, an iridescent blue, long-sleeved sport shirt with the pocket initials V.S.G.

The left sleeve of the shirt was ripped almost to the shoulder stitching and stiff with dried blood.

Lucy stood up, staring vacantly at the shirt for a moment, then a grimace appeared on her face and she dropped it, remembering Molly and Josh, the mansion shepherds.

If Val had been at the mansion and was bitten by a dog, where had he disappeared to? Why hadn't the police been able to find him?

Because in desperation he turned to the only man whom he might trust to give him medical attention and perhaps protection from the police: Dr. Fletcher Childs. Val didn't know Fletch, but he knew that Lucy's brother was a doctor, and from the looks of the shirt and the preparations that Fletch had made for emergency treatment, Val had needed a doctor badly.

Then where were they? Why hadn't Fletch called her?

In the bedroom she sat on the edge of the bed for several minutes, trying to think. Fletch would surely have driven Val to the hospital after treating his wounds. And at the hospital Val would have been swiftly arrested by state troopers.

But he hadn't been arrested; neither Fletcher Childs nor Val St. George had gone to the hospital.

She thought to call Practice, but remembered that he had left for Fort Frontenac earlier in the day and might not be back until tomorrow.

Lucy jumped up in agitation and went to the windows, staring out at the brooding sky and the trees moving noiselessly in the wind.

There was only one place Fletch could have taken Val and that was to the lodge at the reservoir.

Her nurse's training made her rebel at the idea. If he was badly hurt then Val belonged in the hospital, no matter what the consequences. And Fletch was wrong for not taking him there. What could he have been thinking?

Impatiently she went to her own room, changed into a pair of wool slacks and a heavy cotton athletic jersey, selected a parka from the closet, stood for a moment in the center of the room debating whether to get in touch with someone—Dore—then made a glum face at herself in the mirror and went downstairs to get her car out of the garage.

As soon as she reached the lodge she felt certain that she had made a mistake. Fletch's own car, an Imperial, was nowhere around, and the lodge looked exactly as it had when she visited it last in November. Winter storms had uprooted a small tree in front and torn a few shingles from the roof, but there was no sign that anyone had been around, until she went inside and opened the draperies to permit a maximum of murky light to enter the three rooms of the lodge. Then she saw candles in dishes placed on tables and shelves, and smelled the recently melted wax. She went into the tiny bedroom. The covers on the bed hadn't been folded back, but the imprint of a body was unmistakable.

Lucy searched, fearfully, for some sign of her brother

or Val. She went out again to the garage and as far as the pump house at the edge of the thick woods.

If they had been there, they were gone now.

In the lodge she put a pot of coffee on the stove. At least, she thought, shuddering, the gas was connected. When the coffee was ready she poured a cupful. Rain had begun again; it tapped lightly against the windows overlooking the terrace. There was a five-foot wall around the terrace, which blocked a view of the reservoir from inside the lodge, but on the outside, some hundred feet above the shore, the dam and many of the small islands dotting the water could be seen.

One of the doors to the terrace wasn't securely shut and rain was filtering in. Lucy went to close it, looking abstractedly at the empty terrace. Then her shoulders trembled with shock.

At one corner of the terrace, near the wall, a pair of shattered glasses with thick horn rims lay as if they had been trampled on.

She knew they were Fletch's even before she picked them up.

Her face was wet from the wind and rain coming out of the south. She wiped her cheeks and looked over the wall, at the steep slope that started just beneath the terrace.

When she saw the body tumbled among the rocks below she felt only a gradual slowing of her heartbeat and pulse, until she was scarcely aware of them. The tips of her fingers had gone numb. She had the odd sensation of being detached from her own body as she made her way down to the water's edge, oblivious of pain even when she fell, twice, against the rocks. Her eyes were fixed on her brother, a part of her mind willed him to be alive, this *had* to be a mistake . . .

"Fletch—Fletch—please—get up—!"

Her lips were numb, too; there was a droning in her ears louder than the wind as she reached him, tugged at a wet leaden shoulder. So still, so still—but she would wake him.

"Fletch," she said again insistently, kneeling beside him.

And suddenly he raised himself from the dark rocky ground and stared at her, shuddering.

All she could see of his face were the tormented eyes, the bloody lacerated mouth; because he had literally been carved to pieces. His hands had no fingers. His nose, his ears, *gone.* He made a terrible wailing sound and blood came up. It spurted from his mouth and from gaping wounds in his cheeks, spilled over her helping hands.

He shuddered again and died as Lucy huddled against him in a last protective agony, though now there was nothing left that could harm him, only the dark, the wind, the cold seeping rain.

Practice followed the directions of a homemade map taped inside the door of the fuse box and located a switch box on a power-line pole down the road that provided electricity for several houses in the area. The influx of light in the lodge helped a little. Dry clothes, a couple of musty blankets, and hot coffee helped Lucy, although her face was still grim with fatigue. It was incredible that she had been able to carry, or drag, Fletcher Childs's body up that slope, even though it had taken her nearly three hours to do so. Perhaps the extreme physical effort had been as beneficial as anesthesia to her, had helped absorb the shock to her mind and emotions.

She was able to answer Practice's questions lucidly, and only at the end she looked at him with patient inattention and began to pick nervously at the fluff of the blanket and frame the unspeakable question with her lips: Why? Why had Val killed Fletch?

Practice had carried Fletch Childs into the bedroom as soon as he was able; moving Fletch once more wouldn't matter and he couldn't bear to have Lucy near the badly mutilated body. He had made all the necessary calls, and fortunately they didn't have to wait long.

"Like Hugh McAdams?"

"Yes. Were there any weapons in the car with St. George?"

"No mention made. We'll check the car over thoroughly when it comes in. Why? What did you have in mind?"

Practice hesitated. Something suddenly seemed odd and out of focus to him.

"I was wondering if Val St. George had a sword," he said.

17

There was a gray band of light above the treeline of the Capitol grounds as Practice drove toward the old brick building on Center Hill which contained the headquarters of the state highway patrol. He went up the steps and an old man in a pin-striped vest unlocked one of the chrome and glass doors for him. Practice walked across the floor and took an elevator to the office of Captain Mike Liles.

Liles's voice was gruff from three hours of interrogation. He looked up sourly, after inviting Practice in, and rubbed his eyes.

"Where do you have him?" Practice asked.

"Detention room in the basement. Lucy not with you?"

"Lucy's asleep. What has he said?"

Liles made a circle with thumb and forefinger.

"No more than that. He says he won't talk to anybody but Lucy."

Practice slumped in a chair beside the desk and took his hat off.

"He won't admit killing Hugh McAdams and Fletch Childs?"

"As I said, he won't even talk about them. He did give us

The troopers came in with rain dripping from the long black slickers they wore and the brims of their hats; not long after, county officers arrived and stood around idly, while reports were filled out and more questions asked. Lucy responded to the presence of the officers, to the cross-examination and the quiet voices, and was more alert. She told her story again in a firm low voice.

They were interrupted by another trooper with a message for Practice. "Captain Liles is on the radio, Mr. Practice."

He dashed through the downpour and got into the front of the patrol car.

"Jim? I'm sorry as hell to hear about Fletcher Childs. How's Lucy?"

"She's going to make it all right. Quite a shock for her to take." He was surprised by the confusion of feelings that rose to block his throat: tenderness, sympathy, admiration. She was going to be all right. She could take it.

"I thought you'd want to know this right away," Liles said. "Val St. George was picked up an hour and a half ago."

Practice looked away from the glowing ruby of light on the radio receiver to the waves of rain on the windshield.

"Where?" he asked tautly.

"About five miles east of the Kansas state line, on Forty-four. He was driving Fletch Childs's Imperial."

"Did he make any trouble when he was arrested?"

"No. As a matter of fact, he was discovered sound asleep on the front seat, pulled off on a country road not far from the highway. He's being brought in now; should arrive in another hour."

"Near the Kansas line?" Practice asked doubtfully. "Where was he going?"

"Who knows? The important thing is, we got him before he could murder anyone else. How was Fletch killed?"

"We're waiting on the coroner. It looks to me as if he died from the fall. But he was pretty beat up, deliberately mutilated."

his address here in town. We shook the room clean and came up with nothing. There were no weapons in the car. He was carrying a switchblade knife with a six-inch blade on his person when arrested."

"Where was he headed when your men spotted him?"

Liles spread his hands. 'All he said was, 'I knew there was going to be trouble, so I cut out.'"

"How does he look to you, Mike?"

Liles got up out of his chair and stretched, then kicked lightly at the side of his desk.

"He's plenty scared, but damned if he'll show it. He just sits and looks at the wall and questions bounce right off him."

"How badly is he hurt?"

"As soon as he was brought in we had a physician examine his arm. Apparently Fletcher Childs did a good job. The wounds were probably painful, and it's likely he lost quite a lot of blood, but none of them were deep. The worst was a slash on the forearm, which had been closed with five stitches."

"Could he use the arm at all?"

"I know what you're getting at. A one-armed man couldn't have hung Hugh McAdams in that sack. According to the doctor, he could have used the arm as much as he wanted to, if he was willing to disregard the pain."

"Then he could have killed Hugh McAdams."

"Yes, it looks that way. He might have a good alibi from, say, eleven Tuesday night until six or so last night, but if he does, he hasn't condescended to offer it."

"Mike, do you think he killed Fletch and that little boy?"

Liles reached for a cigar on his desk, studied it, then decided against smoking.

"It's this way. Without any statement at all from St. George, we can prove he was at the mansion Tuesday night, killed one dog and seriously wounded another, and was bitten as he tried to get away. We can prove that he went to Fletch Childs for help and that Fletch dressed his wounds.

After that I'm not sure what happened. Maybe Fletch took pity on the boy and drove him to the lodge at the reservoir to gain time to figure out a way of helping him. There, Val may have turned on Fletch and murdered him. He took Fletch's car and drove back to Osage Bluff to carry out a plan he'd had in mind for a long time. His first try at killing Chris Guthrie failed three years ago. But with one murder behind him, he was primed to make another attempt on Chris's life, the most natural form of revenge against Guthrie."

"Up to that point you should be able to make a case. But how could he know Chris and Hugh would leave the school just when they did? If he was waiting in the vicinity of the school in hopes that he'd have a chance to pick Chris up during the day, one of your men would have spotted him."

"Yes, they would have." Liles looked pleased with himself. "The answer is, he didn't have to hang around outside the school. He worked there."

"I never thought of that. What did he do?"

"Assistant janitor."

"How long had he been working there?"

"About six months. The way I see it, he took the job just to be near Chris. I think he went to the trouble of gaining the boy's confidence, and planted the idea of a visit to the old prison in Chris's mind. Chris will be able to tell us about that tomorrow. St. George returned to the school yesterday to murder Chris, and happened to arrive in time to see the boys sneaking away. From that point it was easy. He probably took a length of rope and a sack from the janitor's storeroom, and followed them. Once the boys were inside the prison he made a move for Chris but scared them both, and they ran. Down below it's very dark and the boys looked a lot alike, same height and coloring. St. George got the wrong boy, that's all."

"Chris will identify him, then. After that it doesn't matter whether St. George has anything to say or not."

"We'll have a good case." Liles frowned. "But I want a

confession. That's why I hoped Lucy would come; she might get him started."

"What if I talked to him? Do you suppose it would do any good?"

"I don't know. He doesn't like cops, that's for sure."

"Well, it couldn't hurt. Besides, I'd like to meet him."

Liles called downstairs to have the detention room cleared, and he and Practice went down to the basement in the elevator.

"There'll be a man right outside the door in case he tries something," Liles said. "Are you carrying a gun? Penknife?"

Practice shook his head and entered the room, which was windowless and empty except for a bunk bed bolted into one wall, a small table, and two chairs. Val St. George was sitting on the edge of the bunk; he looked up slowly as Practice entered, stared for a moment, and then looked down at the floor again.

"Who are you?" he asked.

"Jim Practice."

The boy's lips tightened. He looked even younger than his twenty-four years, Practice thought. He was wearing jail denims and a white shirt that was too big for him. The cuffs were rolled back. His left arm was bandaged from wrist to elbow.

"That's your name. I mean, *what* are you?"

"I'm a lawyer and a friend of Lucy's."

Val St. George looked up again. "Is Lucy here?"

"No."

"She send you?"

"No."

His lips curled slightly. "I guess she wrote me off. Why not?"

"I'd say she had good reason."

The boy was silent for a while, his eyes fixed on the floor, his right hand curled around the steel underside of the bunk so that the knuckles were bled white. As Practice had expected, he was tall and much too thin, with the almost-white skin that had cursed him from birth. There were circles under his eyes. He looked tense, frightened, and a little baffled.

"I know you wanted to talk to Lucy," Practice said.

"Just an idea I had," he said bitterly.

Practice put his hat on the table and sat down on one of the chairs, looking at Val St. George. "Maybe you could tell me what you wanted to tell Lucy," he suggested. "We're alone. Nobody can hear what you have to say except me."

Again the boy smirked, without any lessening of his tension.

"Just you and the cops in the next room, taking it all down on a tape recorder."

"That's just in the movies," Practice said, smiling.

Val shrugged. "I suppose I wanted to tell her I was sorry for what I did."

"You mean for killing her brother."

The boy got up suddenly and turned to the wall, then looked over his shoulder at Practice. It was a calculating look.

"Lucy's told me about you," he said. "You asked her to marry you, didn't you?"

"Yes."

"How come she didn't marry you?"

"I suppose she's looking for something that I haven't got," Practice said.

The boy sat down again, blankly, and looked at his bandaged arm. Abruptly he laughed, almost a sobbing sound, and cut it off within a few seconds.

"Say. Was that you in the garden last night? I mean over at the mansion when the dog jumped me?"

"Yes." Practice looked sharply at Val, but the boy's eyes were closed. "I cut him loose."

"That dog might have killed me, mister," Val said with a hint of petulance.

"So could I have. Sometimes I carry a gun."

"How are those dogs? Did they die?"

"One of them's dead."

"I never liked dogs."

"Lucy missed you last night. She waited an hour and you never showed up. Did you forget?"

"No, I didn't forget. I was all tore up; I didn't want her to see me. I had the sweats, the stinking bends."

Practice made no reply to that. So far, Val St. George had been a surprise to him. He had expected some sort of vindictive psychopath, destructive, vicious, unpredictable. The picture he had seen at the state hospital hadn't prepared him for Val St. George in person. True, he was defensive, deeply bitter, and eager to punish almost anyone who tried to befriend him. But Practice sensed the boy's intelligence, and something of the passionate energy that ruled him. Energy that had gone wrong and resulted in two murders, Practice told himself, but for the first time he was aware of a doubt that this could be so.

"The bends are no good," Practice remarked, picking up Val's terminology. "I have my own variety."

Val looked up cynically. "Do you?"

"What made you go to the mansion, Val?"

"I don't know."

"Did you want to see your father?"

Val's lips parted in a grimace of pain and dismay, as if he had been struck, and he put his hands to his face.

"What are you talking about?" he mumbled.

"I talked to your mother yesterday morning, Val."

"Damn her! Isn't she dead yet?"

"Do you want her to be?"

"You get out of here," Val said threateningly. "Who asked you to come around? Who asked you to meddle? Get out of here!"

Practice stood and reached for his hat. "All right."

He was halfway to the door when Val said tonelessly, "Wait."

Practice glanced back. There were tear tracks on Val's stony face.

"I didn't mean what I said about my mother dying. I don't want that."

Practice sighed and stood with his arms folded. Val wiped at his cheeks, then let his hands fall between his knees.

"I wish I could go ahead and be sick," he said softly. "But I can't. I can't throw up." He lifted his head. "I don't suppose she had much good to say about me."

"How long since you've seen her?"

"Years. I don't know exactly."

"I think, more than anything in the world, she'd like to see you, Val."

He tried to feign indifference, but his lips betrayed him.

"Well, that isn't likely to happen, is it?" he said brokenly. "Not now."

Practice sat down again.

"Why did you go to the mansion Tuesday night, Val? Did you want to see John Guthrie?"

"I'd seen him before. Lots of times. Around the Capitol. On days when he was appearing before the Legislature I'd go early and get a seat in the gallery. Man, I've heard him make a lot of speeches. And I've seen him at political rallies. One time he shook my hand and smiled at me. For the rest of the day I didn't know where I was or what I was feeling. Talk about the bends!"

"Tuesday night," Practice said quietly.

"Sure." Val lay back on the bunk, his hands behind his head. "I suppose I had the idea months ago, but I wouldn't admit it to myself. Then gradually it took hold of me, like a spell, until I was walking around in a trance days and dreaming about it at night. I couldn't think of anything else: he was my father and he was betraying me. I had to make him realize what he had done to me, what my life had been like without him."

"How were you going to do that, Val?"

"This is the picture I had in my mind. Right out of a Technicolor movie starring Rock Hudson. He's sitting in his bedroom late at night in a silk dressing gown. Sometimes he's drinking a whiskey and soda and listening to music or sometimes he's writing at a desk, working on a speech or something and using a quill pen." Val smiled sardonically, but his eyes were shining and his hands clenched and unclenched nervously. "How's that for imagination? Hollywood's wasting away without me. I knew something of what his room looked like, because Lucy told me. I knew about the balcony outside. Here's where Val St. George begins to look a lot like Anthony Quinn. He climbs up to that balcony without any trouble at all and then he . . ." The boy bit his lip as his voice became a little shrill. "Then he crashes in, I mean *crashes*. He stands in the middle of the Governor's bedroom, with broken glass around his feet, staring at his father, and his father is pale as a ghost; but he's tough, too. He lights a cigar and gets up, walks over to me, and looks me right in the eye. And he says, 'You're just the man I thought you'd be.'"

Val covered his face with his hands and gasped.

"God, I went over that scene in my mind so many times I *believed* it; I even believed I could pass for Anthony Quinn. So I walked to the mansion and wandered around the streets for about an hour, just staring at it and wondering how I could get in. Finally I went all the way down to the railroad and crawled up that bluff, and by the time I reached the wall I was out of breath. I was dirty as a pig and shaking scared. I didn't think about dogs or anything like that. I shimmied over the wall and dropped down into the middle of some bushes, and there was this German shepherd right in front of my face, barking his head off. I almost passed out. I was so scared I couldn't move. Anthony Quinn! But the dog didn't jump me; he just stood off about three feet and barked. I looked around for a stick to throw at him. As soon as I picked up the stick he leaped and grabbed it. I thought my arm was next, so I—I took out my knife and—I made a pass at him. I just wanted to scare him off. But he was closer than I thought. The blade cut right through his throat. He just fell over and thrashed around and died. I'm telling you, I was almost sick. I never hurt anything before. Never."

"But you sent a drawing to the Governor threatening his life."

"I suppose I—I thought about hurting him sometimes. Kid stuff. That doesn't mean I could have done it."

Practice studied Val. Had his evasive reaction been due to shame or fear?

"Did you know those fingerprints on the drawing were your mother's?"

"Sure, I knew it. I didn't think it mattered. I've had that book since I was a kid. Stupid thing to carry around with me. I used to crawl up in her lap and she'd read me those stories until the pages were nearly worn out. Even when she—she'd had too much to drink and felt bad, she'd try to read to me. Once she broke the glass she was drinking out of and cut her hand, but she went right on reading to me, turning the pages with her bloody fingers and reading. That was a long time ago. I couldn't have been more than four."

"Why did you stay around the mansion after you'd killed the dog? I'd think you would have wanted to get away from there."

For a while Val was silent, but Practice didn't have the feeling that he was searching for some further means of evasion.

"Look," the boy blurted, "it was *his* dog. All I wanted was to talk to him, and already I—I had killed his dog; and I thought, he'll never listen to anything I have to say now. I was in a panic. I looked up at that balcony and the lighted windows and I told myself, now, you have to face him now or you'll always be lost. So I went up the tree and jumped for the balcony and pulled myself over the railing. I tried to open the doors quietly, but they were stuck. I was afraid he'd hear me out there before I could get in, and call the cops, so I smashed the glass and broke the doors down. I called to him so he wouldn't be scared. I called him 'Father,' but I couldn't say it very loud because I was choking to death at the same time.

"Then I saw the room was empty. He wasn't there at all. I was just sick. I saw myself for a fool. I realized what I had done, breaking in that way, and I hated him because I had spent half my life trying to get to him and it had to happen that way, with a dead dog down below on the grass and my hands shaking and my stomach heaving. He wasn't even there!"

"That's when you wrecked the room."

"Yes," Val St. George said despairingly. "I wrecked his room. Then I went down the way I had come in and hid by the wall, where I could see. I wanted to be there when he came in that night. I wanted him to be mad, mad as hell."

"Why did you go to Dr. Childs, Val?"

"What else could I do? My arm felt numb and I was bleeding bad. I knew what would happen to me if I went to the hospital. I didn't trust Childs, but I thought if I could talk him into calling Lucy, she'd help me."

"What story did you tell Fletch?"

"I didn't tell him anything at first. He wasn't around when I got there. By that time I felt too weak to move anymore. I sat down in a corner of the porch where nobody could see me from the street. I think I passed out. The next thing I heard were voices and a car door slamming. There was a Cadillac full of men parked out by the curb, all of them gassed, from the way they were acting. Dr. Childs came up the walk. When I stood up I scared him; he nearly jumped off the porch. I started talking pretty fast, telling him that I was a friend of Lucy's and that a dog had bitten me. He didn't want to let me in the house. Then he said he'd call a cab for me so I could get to the hospital. I must have pulled another blackout about then, but it couldn't have lasted for long. When I came to I was inside, and Dr. Childs was on the porch waving the Cad on. He said he'd catch up to them in a few minutes."

"He took you upstairs to his bedroom and treated the wounds."

"I hurt pretty bad and asked him if he could give me something. He looked through his kit, but he couldn't find any morphine, so he gave me sodium pentothal instead."

Practice leaned forward in his chair.

"Sodium *what?*"

"Sodium—ah—pentothal. I know that was the name of the stuff. I read the label on the bottle."

"And after you were given the sodium pentothal, you went to sleep."

Val was silent for nearly a minute.

"I must have," he said quietly.

"When did you wake up, Val?"

The boy stirred restlessly on the cot.

"What's the use of telling any more?" he said angrily. "You're not going to believe it."

"I believe everything you've told me so far, Val. When did you wake up?"

"Well . . . I wasn't ever really *asleep.* Almost asleep, I think, because I was dreaming. Honest to God, I dreamed my whole life in just a few minutes. At first I was on a soft bed, and I kept trying to lift myself up and out of that bed, but when I raised my head a bright light would hit me right in the face, and I couldn't stand it, so I lay down again. Somebody kept talking to me, and . . ."

"What, Val?"

"A face. His face. I was always seeing the doctor's face near me. His lips were moving, but I didn't hear anything. I just went on dreaming."

"What did you dream?"

"My life. I told you. My mother was in those dreams, and—my . . ."

"Father?"

"Yes. Him, too."

"But eventually you woke up. Where were you when that happened, Val?"

The boy rubbed his forehead. "I've got an awful headache," he complained.

"Please try to go on."

"I woke up on another bed in a paneled room. The light was softer; it came from a candle on a shelf opposite the bed. I must have stared at that candle flame for an hour, until the wax had melted half away. My head was too heavy to lift, and my arm was throbbing under the bandages. I wanted a drink of water, but I couldn't make a sound. Then I heard the voice again, an angry voice this time. There was an argument."

"You mean you could distinguish two voices? Two men talking?"

Val didn't continue immediately. He massaged his forehead with one hand and stared at the ceiling. Practice studied his face intently.

"There was an argument," Val said at last. "But Childs was doing most of the talking."

"Had you ever heard the other man's voice before?"

Again Val was quiet, and Practice felt uneasy, wondering what was in the boy's mind. Had he suddenly stopped telling the truth?

"No," Val said in a low voice. "I never heard it before."

"What were they saying, Val?"

"I was really doped. I don't . . ."

"But you could tell there were two voices. You must have been able to distinguish some of their words."

"I suppose so," Val admitted. "But I don't remember. I was lost, and scared. I just heard a couple of voices; I wasn't trying to . . ."

"Val, are you sure you're leveling with . . ."

The boy suddenly jerked upright on the bunk, his face contorted.

"I don't know, I don't know what they said!" he yelled.

"All right, Val, you're not helping yourself by getting violent."

"Helping myself?" he said in a choked voice. "What chance have I got to prove I didn't kill that Childs and some little kid I never heard of?"

"Right now the best thing you can do is settle back and try to remember as much as you can of what happened at the reservoir last night."

"I don't feel like talking anymore."

"Don't do that to me, boy. You've started a story that involves another man in events directly anticipating the death of Fletcher Childs. That's your story, but you haven't offered any proof at all that someone else was there last night. If you could just recall a few words . . ."

"I'm trying," Val said wrathfully.

Practice let the boy alone. He was sitting on the edge of the bunk, holding his head in his hands.

"One thing," Val said.

"What do you remember?"

Val pursed his lips, and then, in a fair imitation of Fletch Childs's voice, said, " 'I've done everything—but destroy him with my own hands—and you're not grateful. Well, now I'll tell him the truth—and you can go to hell!' "

"Was there a reply?"

Val's lips twisted. "No. Right after that Childs started screaming. And then all at once he stopped. It was quiet. I heard something like a door slamming open. Then I heard the wind. And then footsteps, right outside the room I was in. I froze like I was dead. Someone came in. I didn't even breathe. He came right up to the bed and I felt him standing there, it seemed like five or ten minutes. Then something cold touched my throat, right here." Val demonstrated with a fingertip on his jugular vein. "I knew it was a knife and that he was going to cut my throat, but I couldn't move or open my eyes. I don't know why he didn't do it. Maybe he thought I was already dead."

"The man went away then?"

"I guess he did. I lay there for a long time after, listening, but I couldn't hear a sound. Finally I took a chance that he was gone. I got off the bed and crawled to the door and pulled myself up and went out into the living room. But nobody was around. It was almost dawn."

"Did you search the house?"

"No! All I wanted was to get out of there. I had to sit down for a few minutes because I felt so bad, but as soon as I could walk okay I went out. Childs's Imperial was parked in front of the house and the keys were inside. So I took the car."

"Val, how did you know that Fletch was dead?"

The boy's head sagged. "I just knew, that's all. After hearing him scream, and all. I figured the guy who put the knife against my throat had killed Childs, too."

Practice had a knotted feeling of disappointment in his stomach. In contrast to the way Val had described his visit to the Governor's mansion earlier, the crucial part of his story seemed vague and unconvincing. Practice realized that he was pulling for Val, that he wanted to believe him.

"Where did you drive?" he asked.

"Where?" Val looked surprised. "Here. The city."

"Why come back here?"

"I had some money hid away. About sixty bucks. I needed that money. Then . . ."

"Then you were planning to run."

"I was in trouble. I figured with the car and sixty bucks I could make it to California . . ."

"You're too bright to have figured anything of the sort. You were driving a stolen car. You wouldn't have lasted twenty-four hours on the road in it. You were running because you were panicked silly."

"Wouldn't you have been?"

"Let's leave my emotions and reactions out of this; they aren't relevant. What time did you return to Osage Bluff?"

"I don't know."

"Well, think, Val. You went directly to the furnished room you kept?"

"About eight in the morning. I left the car three blocks away. An Imperial in that neighborhood . . ."

"How long were you in your room?"

"About . . ." Val's eyes shifted away, and he licked his lips. "About an hour and a half, maybe two hours. I wasn't feeling so good. My arm hurt and I had the shakes."

"But you stayed in your room all that time. You didn't go near the Borden school?"

"No. Why should I? That would have been a stupid . . ."

"So you left your room, as near as you can remember, around ten o'clock in the morning. You walked to where you had parked the car, got in, and started for California."

Val nodded.

"And during the two hours you were in Osage Bluff, did anyone see you? Did you talk to anyone?"

"Maybe somebody saw me."

"Who?"

"You know, on the street. Nobody who . . ."

"Let's go back to ten o'clock. You were headed for California. How did you know which highway to use?"

"There were some maps in the dash compartment. I looked them over."

"So it was about ten-fifteen when you started off."

"I guess so. I wasn't counting time."

"And you didn't stop again until you were near the Kansas line. You stopped there because you felt too bad to go on."

Val nodded again.

"What time was that?"

"About two-thirty or three."

"That was your first stop in something like four and a half hours?"

Val shrugged.

"Or did you stop for gas along the way?"

"I had to. The tank wasn't even half full when I left Osage Bluff."

Practice relaxed and sat back in his chair.

"Where did you stop, Val?"

"I don't know. I wasn't paying any attention."

"You must have some idea."

The boy scowled. "I said I don't know. When the tank was empty, I stopped."

"Did you stop in a town?"

"Some small town. I don't know the name."

"How long had you been driving?"

"I don't know. I just drove."

Practice stifled his impatience. "Val, it's absolutely necessary for you to remember where you stopped. Yesterday afternoon, about one o'clock, a small boy was murdered in the old prison near the Borden school."

"I know about that," Val said tightly.

"You worked at the school and you'd been there several months. You had plenty of time to get acquainted with the boys, with Chris Guthrie, the Governor's son. Did you know Chris Guthrie?"

"I knew him."

"Did you ever talk to him?"

"A couple of times. Why shouldn't I?"

"What about?"

"I can't remember."

"Did you ever mention the prison to him?"

Val seemed to have grown smaller and more remote as he sat on the edge of the cot, staring down at the floor.

"Look," he said, "I took that crummy job because I couldn't get anything else. No other reason. So what if his—what if this kid went to school there? I didn't know that. When I found out who he was, I—can you blame me for being curious? For—I spent a lot of time, just—watching him. You'll find that out; the regular janitor caught me at it. Then I—I tried to figure out ways to approach the kid. Once I gave him an old baseball and once a piece of cake. I never talked to him when we were alone; there were always other boys around. I didn't have anything against the

kid. He was—you know, he wasn't a jerk like a lot of them
are. He sounded okay to me. I wasn't—*jealous* of him or
anything like that."

"Weren't you, Val?"

"No!"

"Did you tease him about the prison?"

"What do you mean?"

"Dare him to explore it or something like that?"

Val's hands clenched tighter.

"He'll remember, Val. You might as well tell me."

"Yeah, I did."

Practice sighed almost inaudibly.

"So it was stupid and childish. That doesn't make me out a
murderer."

"I don't know what it makes you out, Val. There was an
attempt on Chris Guthrie's life three years ago. Only a
couple of weeks later you committed yourself to the state
hospital. You're the illegitimate son of the Governor of this
state. You've admitted sending him a threatening letter. You
destroyed one of the Governor's dogs and demolished his
bedroom in a fit of passion. It's reasonable that the feelings
you had for Guthrie could easily be extended to his—
legitimate—son. By your own admissions you made several
efforts to get close to Chris Guthrie and plant the notion of a
rather dangerous escapade in his mind. Yesterday, Chris and
his friend sneaked away from school at the lunch hour and
went to the prison. They were followed by someone who
either knew they would be leaving or happened to see them
as they left. In the prison they were surprised by this person
and ran for their lives. Hugh McAdams was caught, trussed
up in a sack, and nearly cut to ribbons by a long knife or a
sword. Chris escaped by hiding in a well. I don't know if he
got a good look at the killer; the light is poor inside the
prison. One thing he'll remember: it was your idea to go
there. The District Attorney will make sure he remembers.
There's no real evidence yet that you killed either Fletcher

Childs or Hugh McAdams, but the circumstantial evidence is impressive. As far as I know, nothing but your unsupported word stands for your defense. You have no evidence that Fletch Childs received a visitor in the middle of the night at the reservoir. You have no way to prove you were a hundred miles away from Osage Bluff at the time Hugh McAdams was murdered. Oh, you bought a tank of gasoline, but you don't know where."

"I'll remember where!"

"Do that. And then prove you didn't turn around and drive back to Osage Bluff in time to murder that boy. It's a lousy story, Val. You ought to be able to see that."

"If you don't like my story, then make up one to suit yourself, but let me alone!"

Practice didn't reply. He had hoped to jar Val's memory by pointing out to him the need to document every minute of his time for the past twenty-four hours. For someone like Val, a habitual lone wolf, it would have been a difficult task under the most ordinary circumstances. Now he was charged with two deaths, and his inability to provide any sort of adequate account looked only like the desperate evasions of guilt, which, perhaps, was the only answer.

Practice wasn't sure now how he felt about Val St. George. The boy was all but unapproachable. He was bitter and hostile. And yet, in the few moments when his desire to be helped had overcome his innate suspicions, the story he had told sounded like the truth. Practice could believe in the Val St. George who had been forced to kill one of the German shepherds, and had been sickened and angered by his own violence. But the image of Val St. George deliberately murdering a man and a small boy wasn't nearly as persuasive. Logically he could be guilty of both murders. Practice glanced again at Val, who was trembling now on the bunk. He saw a thin, vulnerable youth who had spent the better part of three years living on dreams, stalking the shadow of his father with self-confessed heroic intent.

Practice wondered if it weren't time for John Guthrie to meet his other son. Perhaps if Guthrie talked to Val . . . But the shock might be more than Val could survive just now.

Troubled and uncertain, Practice rose.

"I'm going now, Val. Is there anything at all I can do for you? Would you like some cigarettes?"

Val shook his head. Practice hesitated, thinking that he had something to say.

"She's written me off, then?" Val whispered. "She thinks I killed her brother and she's written me off."

"What else is Lucy going to believe?"

"Tell her I didn't do it. Tell her I didn't kill anybody, and that's the truth. I don't care who else believes it. But tell her . . ."

He didn't seem able to say more. Practice studied the boy's bent head, then walked to the door and let himself out.

Mike Liles was waiting in the hall.

"Has he loosened up any?" Liles asked.

Practice pulled out his pouch of tobacco and began to make a cigarette.

"He told me his story. I don't think any of it can be proven, Mike. But I don't think he'll change it, either. There's something about that boy I could admire, under other circumstances. If his life had been a little less thankless he might have . . ."

Liles yawned and deposited the coffee container he had been drinking from in a nearby wastebasket.

"We'll see if he sticks to his story."

"Mike? Couldn't you let him sleep for a couple of hours? He's worn down to the bone."

Liles shrugged. "Then this is the best time for me to work on him. Christ, Jim, the kid has killed twice. Didn't you get a good look at that McAdams boy?"

"I saw all I wanted to see," Practice said grimly.

Liles gave him a long look. "I think you want to believe St. George is innocent."

"I'd like to believe it."

"But you don't."

"I don't know what to think right now. I'm as exhausted as he is."

Liles shook his head in resignation and walked toward the door of the interrogation room. Another man, in plain clothes, followed, and the door was unlocked by a turnkey. Practice turned away and started wearily down the hall. The sun had just risen and light was flooding through the windows on the east side of the hall.

"Jim!" Liles called; and Practice, aroused by the urgency in his voice, turned and ran back to the detention room.

The other officers were laying the body of Val St. George on the bunk. The boy's head rolled loosely, and there was an expression of shock in his sightless eyes.

"What happened?"

Liles pointed to the foot of the bunk. "He must have got down on his hands and knees on the bed and stuck his head between the mattress and the pipe frame. A real tight fit, and not much give in the mattress. Then he threw his feet over the end of the bed. All his weight was on his neck and he was falling free, so his neck snapped. Just as effective as if he'd put his head in a noose. He was dead when we came in."

Practice stared at the body of Val St. George, unable to believe for a few moments that he had killed himself. And then he remembered what Val had said to him as he was leaving, the urgency in his voice: *Tell her I didn't kill anybody, and that's the truth.*

So Val had already made up his mind what he was going to do, but Practice didn't feel any better about it. Somehow, he should have been able to help the boy, and he had failed.

"I suppose that's as good as a confession," Liles said, nodding toward the bunk. "Jim, I'll want a complete statement from you."

"All right. Can I stop by later in the day? I'm not up to it right now."

"Sure, go get some sleep."

"What's going to happen to him, Mike?"

"The usual. County morgue until somebody claims the body. But who'd want him?"

"I think I know who—a man named Skandy. I'll get in touch with him myself. Mike, what if Val was telling the truth? What if he didn't kill Fletch or Hugh McAdams?"

Liles took the unlighted cigar out of his mouth and wiped a shred of tobacco from his lower lip. He tilted his head to one side and looked calmly at Practice. "Figure it all out. Nobody else could have killed them."

18

The first light of day and the songs of birds in the pale spring trees outside the window awakened Steppie.

She woke with a violent thrashing of limbs, and then lay still, her eyes wide and frightened, focused on the ceiling, the fragments of a nightmare dissolving in her mind. When she again felt capable of movement, she turned her head slowly to one side.

The Major wasn't in bed with her.

Steppie wondered what had happened to him. Of course, the nights he spent with her, he rarely slept, perhaps he didn't even sleep when he was in his own bed. Usually he lay on his back with his hands folded on his chest, not changing his position for hours. If she was lucky enough to drift into a fretful doze when he was with her, when she awoke he would still be in the same position, his eyes open and yellow, his breathing so shallow that she could not hear him at all.

Part of the nightmare she had just escaped came back to her, and she swallowed. The tip of her tongue was raw from cigarettes and she had a bad headache. Probably she had passed out along about dark yesterday. She had been drinking too much; but what else could she do in this place? He wouldn't let her go home.

He needed her, he said.

For what?

He came and went quietly, and sometimes she heard the sound of his car, and sometimes she didn't. She might be sitting in the library with a book, and suddenly she would look up and he'd be sitting opposite her, as if he had suddenly materialized; the experience was frightening enough to make her heart stop beating for a long second.

No one as old as the Major could be so quiet, but somehow he was ageless, weightless, noiseless.

Inhuman.

It would amuse her friends—and her enemies—to know that Major Kinsaker never tried to make love to her. Sometimes he uncovered one of her breasts as they lay together in the night, and put his hard dry lips against her nipple, but he never did anything else. Maybe he couldn't. She had been tempted to find out.

But they wouldn't be amused if she told them why he didn't make love to her.

Steppie sat up in bed, choking on the dryness of her throat. Damn it, she wanted to get out! She had been here for three straight days and was slowly losing her mind.

She got up from the bed, steadied herself with an effort, looked at the sun on the windows. Her eyes watered. She knew that she looked dreadful, and she resented her unseen face that morning.

Thirty-seven, thirty-seven, thirty-seven years old.

Her robe wasn't where it should have been, and Steppie didn't trouble to look for it. She put on a pair of slippers and tried to push her hair off her forehead with one hand.

The connecting door between the two bedrooms was open, and Steppie went carefully as far as the doorway of the

Major's room, leaned against the jamb, and looked inside. The room was cheerful with morning sun. The Major wasn't there, and his bed was untouched.

She stared at the telescope for several moments.

Would he be in his room at the usual time later this morning, sitting in front of his telescope, looking down at . . . ?

Steppie stifled her thoughts impatiently. She didn't care why he should be so interested in the square brick school building below.

She shook her head and her eyes rested for a moment on the portrait of Molly Kinsaker.

For an instant she thought she would be sick. Quickly she closed the door and went downstairs in her nightgown. All the draperies were drawn in the lower part of the house and she barely saw herself flickering over the surface of the mirror at the foot of the stairs.

First she looked into the kitchen, thinking that he might be having his breakfast. But there were no dishes on the kitchen table.

Then she heard a persistent, unidentifiable sound: *slaptick.*

The basement door was ajar. Steppie opened it wider and looked down the stairs. She saw a vague, ghostly light in the room below, and knew immediately what it meant.

She would not, she could *not,* make herself go down into that room again.

For several minutes she remained motionless, listening, her head pounding, but no other sound came to her and the light didn't change.

If he were showing those pictures again, she thought, the light would flicker as the ghastly images followed one another across the movie screen.

Slowly she descended into the basement, and on the last step she reached up to pull the cord of the ceiling light.

The sixteen-millimeter projector was set up on a table facing the portable silver-gray screen. A rectangle of light

was fixed in its center. The ticking sound came from the end
of a reel of film whirling on the side of the projector. The
movie had ended, but still the Major sat in a wooden chair
behind the table, eyes on the screen, shoulders hunched,
hands gripping lightly the long gleaming sword in his lap.

Steppie knew as soon as she saw the sword what her
nightmare had been; it wasn't just wild fantasy, melting from
her mind in the moments of awakening; it was the truth, only
the truth, which her conscious mind could never fully
accept.

Before Steppie could stop herself, a sound that was partly
a sob and partly a scream came from her throat, and she fell
back against the wall, staring at the Major.

He didn't move or turn. His eyes remained, without
blinking, on the screen.

"It's all right," he said in comforting tones. "Everything's
fine, Molly. You go on back to bed."

19

The suicide of Val St. George had almost been welcome
news to John Guthrie.

Practice surveyed him over the rim of the coffee cup he
was holding. The Governor looked rested, decisive, well
groomed. He and Mike Liles had been in a huddle most of
the morning straightening out details of the double murder,
so that it was unlikely that any hint of scandal would be laid
at Guthrie's doorstep.

Now it was up to Practice to see that the boy's funeral
would be swift and discreet. He had already made one
telephone call to Gene Ogden and received a pledge of
cooperation. He understood Guthrie's relief that a danger-

ous situation had been resolved, with no harm coming to him or to his family, but he didn't understand why he was feeling resentful toward the man.

They were sitting in the offices of Guthrie's law firm, which he had seldom visited since his election.

"I got in touch with Lucy this morning," Guthrie said. "Someone from this office and an executive of the bank will see to all the arrangements for Fletch's funeral. Lucy said she was capable of handling the details herself. Maybe so, but I made her realize there was no reason for her to suffer through all that. I couldn't talk her out of resigning as Chris's governess, though."

Practice put his cup aside and noticed with displeasure that his hands were trembling after a not very restful sleep.

"How is Chris?"

"In a bad temper." Guthrie smiled, a fond smile that was unfamiliar to Practice. "He threw a spoon at me when I told him Lucy couldn't come today. The doctor's going to keep him in bed a couple of days until the cold is cleared up. You know, I never realized how much the boy takes after my side of the family: restless, moody, but bright as hell."

Practice let him go on in a similar vein, somewhat astonished that Guthrie seemed just to have discovered the fact that he had a son. That at least was one piece of good news in an otherwise dismal day.

". . . so I promised him a trip as soon as he gets out of the hospital. I thought we might go up to Greenbard County tomorrow afternoon and get in some fishing before the weekend at A.B. Sharp's."

"Where are you going to stay?"

"My great-uncle has a farm not far down the road from the Major's place. Doesn't use it much anymore, except as a private hunting and fishing preserve. Come to think of it, Chris has never been fishing; it ought to be an adventure for him." Guthrie became thoughtful and leaned forward, clasping his hands on top of the desk. "You know, Jim, he doesn't remember much of what happened to him day before yesterday."

"What does he remember?"

"One of Liles's men saw him early this morning, with the doctor, and asked a few questions. He didn't probe too deeply, there was no need and it might have upset Chris pretty badly. Anyway, Chris was talkative enough. They were inside the prison before they knew St. George was following them; he got within a few feet of them and then . . ."

"Wait a minute," Practice interrupted. "Did he identify St. George by name?"

"How could he?" Guthrie said with a hint of annoyance. "He didn't know St. George. Oh, he'd seen him around school, sure. But *we* know who it was."

"How did Chris describe the man who was following them?" Practice asked patiently.

Guthrie took a cigar from a box on his desk and held it in his hand without lighting it.

"He was tall and thin, and didn't have a head. Only eyes."

"Only eyes? You mean he was wearing a mask."

"Probably that's what Chris meant. Anyway, the kids were too scared to stand around gawking at him. Chris did say that he was holding up a big sack, as if he were getting ready to pull it over Chris's head. Chris was closest to St. George, I suppose. The boys ran. Hugh slipped and fell down, losing a shoe, but Chris didn't stop. He said that Hugh got up right away and wasn't far behind him as they went down the stairs. Hugh was screaming that the man was going to get him. The passage Chris found himself in was dark, but he kept running. He doesn't know if Hugh was following or not. He ran until he fell into the water, then he crawled on his hands and knees to the opening of the well and lowered himself inside. He could hear some muffled cries in another part of the prison. Then he didn't hear anything at all for a long time."

"He doesn't remember my pulling him out of the well."

"No. But as I say, Liles's man didn't press him too hard. No reason for it."

Practice rose. "Well, I'll stop by the hospital to see him on my way to Lucy's."

"Do that. I imagine he's getting pretty bored with nobody but Dore for company. Jim . . ."

Practice stopped and looked back at Guthrie.

"Do me a favor and don't hound the boy."

"What do you mean?"

"Well—Liles has the notion that you're not happy with the case against St. George. Hell, man, as a lawyer . . ."

"Val St. George himself proved how weak his story was by committing suicide. As a lawyer, there's no more for me to do. But who says I'm a lawyer anyway?"

Guthrie smiled grudgingly. "Getting ready for a bout of the running fits?"

"Maybe."

"Why don't you take a week or two off, then? Good for the soul to get away."

"You mean after the conference at Sharp's is over."

Guthrie nodded. "I'll need you close to hand until then."

"Thanks very much," Practice said deliberately, and went out.

20

The door at 217 Bartow Street, where Fletcher Childs had lived and raised his sister, was standing open a few inches, and as Practice walked up to the porch he heard the hum of a vacuum cleaner inside. He hesitated at the door, which was neither open wide enough to let him walk in or closed sufficiently so that he felt he should ring the bell. He compromised by knocking, loudly, and presently the vacuum cleaner was silenced and a black woman with a dustcap on her head peered out at him, blinking in the sunshine.

"Miz Childs ain't admittin' no visitors."

"I think she's expecting me. Jim Practice."

The woman looked him over doubtfully. "Well, okay. She's in the liberry. Come on."

Practice stepped into the living room. All the furniture had been moved to one side and the carpets were rolled up. The drapes had been taken down and neatly folded, and the shades were rolled all the way up. Two of the windows sparkled as if just washed; the others showed their winter's accumulation of grime.

He made his way to the library. The furniture here had been shoved into a corner and all the books were removed from the shelves. Lucy was down on her knees in front of the French doors, washing the glass. She saw his reflection in one of the doors and got up, stripping the protective bandanna from her head.

"Hello, Jim," she said quietly.

"What's all this, Lucy?"

She shrugged lightly. "Just my way of doing things. Time for spring cleaning, so we're cleaning house." Her hands were damp and reddened; she wiped them on her apron. "I just couldn't stand being alone in this big empty house, so I'm letting in the air and light. As long as I keep working I don't have time to think too much."

"Lucy, is there anything I can do for you?"

"No, there isn't anything." Her eyes met his briefly, then she looked away.

"John tells me you've resigned as Chris's governess."

She nodded. "I had to. I'm going to miss having Chris around, but . . ."

"Any plans yet?"

"Let's go in the kitchen and have some coffee. We can talk there."

She put the coffeepot on and stood looking out at the garden, while Practice pulled out a chair beside the breakfast counter and sat down.

"I'm going to sell the house as soon as I can," Lucy said. "I don't have any reason to keep it now. Of course, the will has to be probated; that'll take time. I'd like to get away for a few months, but I don't have any idea yet where I'll go." She was grave and composed, but not as if she were on the edge of severe grief. She and her brother had been friends, Jim knew, but they weren't especially close. "Jim, Captain Liles told me this morning that you talked to Val just before he—he killed himself. What did he say? Did he give any reason for . . ." She bowed her head for a moment, wincing, then straightened.

"Val never admitted killing either Fletch or Hugh McAdams. He said that he was innocent. He wanted me to tell you so. It was the truth, he said. He was anxious for you to understand . . ."

"Understand!" she said bitterly. "All I understand is that I trusted him and he killed my brother, for no reason, no reason at all. Fletch tried to help him, and . . ."

"It's done, Lucy. What happened wasn't any fault of yours. There was no reason why you shouldn't have believed in Val."

She shook her head. "I don't understand so many things about him. What did he have against the Governor? And Chris? Was he just so crazy that—no, I don't want to talk about him. I can't stand to talk about him. I was so sure of that boy. He was so sad, and alone, and so determined to be better . . ."

Her voice failed and she went quickly to the stove, removing the pot of coffee. She poured a cup for Practice and stood near him, holding her own cup in both hands, sipping, looking bleakly at nothing.

"Fletch was very interested in politics, wasn't he, Lucy?"

"What—oh." Her eyes focused as she glanced at him with a brief smile. "You ought to know, the two of you never talked about anything else."

"I know he was active in the party. But did he ever say anything to you about running for office?"

"Half of our library is made up of books on political theories, and Fletch's notebooks on politics fill a trunk."

"Was he inclined to be, oh, unhappy because he thought his party had passed him by?"

"Not as far as I know. Why the questions, Jim?"

"I was just curious."

She looked at him blankly. "I'd like to get back to work, Jim. I suppose you know about the arrangements for Fletch."

"Yes. I'll be there, Lucy."

As he rose she was already a step toward the door, and it was easy for him to reach out and catch her by the wrist. He thought she would resist, and then she softened and came toward him, her eyes tightly closed, and huddled against him, her face pressed against his chest. He raised his other hand to the back of her head, hesitated, and let the hand drop. In a few moments Lucy lifted her shoulders and stood free of him, a faintly sad, distantly friendly look on her face.

The funeral next day happened quickly. Nearly 150 mourners were at the cemetery, but Practice was interested only in the man who had not attended: Major Starne Kinsaker.

His absence was inexplicable. After the funeral, as they were walking back to the limousines parked below the hill where Fletch had been buried, Practice was able to question one of the Major's partners in the Osage State Bank. No, he hadn't seen the Major for several days. It *was* unusual for him to have stayed away from the funeral of a friend; perhaps he was ill.

Practice sat in his car until long after the last automobile had driven slowly down the lane to the gates of the cemetery and had been absorbed by the traffic on the highway.

He had lain awake most of the night before, his head filled with contradictions, suspicions, and vague theories. About four-thirty, as the boy downstairs went whistling off on his bike to deliver the morning newspapers, he got up, showered, shaved, fixed himself a breakfast which he wasn't able to eat, and then sat for two hours with a yellow legal pad and several sharpened pencils before him. At the top of the pad he wrote:

Proposition I: That Val St. George was innocent
of the murders of Fletcher Childs and Hugh
McAdams.

He then wrote down all he could recall of his conversation with Val. Since he already had done virtually the same thing for Mike Liles, he felt satisfied that every scrap of information was on his pad. After studying what he had written, testing and rejecting various hypotheses, he tore the pages from his pad and picked up his pencil again.

Proposition II: That Major Starne Kinsaker
murdered both Fletcher Childs and Hugh
McAdams.

He wrote busily for an hour, his eyes clouding thoughtfully from time to time. When he had finished, he read over his pages critically, smoking, and tapping his pencil against the table.

Beneath the last sentence he scrawled, in large capitals, "No evidence."

This is what he had written:

> The death of Molly Kinsaker seems to have been the most crushing blow of the Major's life. Essentially she was all he lived for, because undoubtedly after more than a quarter century of politics his involvement was not acute, nor were there any great challenges left to him in politics.
>
> Molly died in a ghastly and cruel accident. Perhaps his grief would not have been as great if the true facts of the accident had been available to him; perhaps, eventually, he would have recovered from the blow.
>
> But because of Fletcher Childs, he was not allowed to recover. It seems certain that Childs, only witness to the accident which killed Molly, moved the unconscious John Guthrie to the seat behind the wheel of the jeep so that it would appear *he* had been driving at the time. He then filmed every incriminating detail: empty beer cans in the jeep, John Guthrie staggering—with drunkenness, or shock, or both—around the jeep, and Molly Kinsaker lying on the hood.
>
> John Guthrie was then being groomed as his party's candidate for Governor. He had been a close friend, since boyhood, of Major Kinsaker's.
>
> Thus the crime which Fletcher Childs had committed, adding tragedy to tragedy, was very disturbing. He could have had only one motive:

by disgracing John Guthrie, he hoped to succeed him as the party's candidate for Governor.

But Major Kinsaker acted in an entirely unpredictable way. With Childs's assistance—unlikely a third man was involved—he carefully removed all traces of the accident, and had Molly's horse brought from the farm. Then the Major tried to go on as if John Guthrie had been nowhere near his daughter that day. But, strong as he was, eventually he gave way to his grief. (Fletcher Childs would not let him forget it, nor let him forget that John Guthrie was the cause.)

Guthrie and the Major split long before the elections, but the Major continued to work for his election, because he still felt that Guthrie was the only man available who would make an unbeatable candidate. And even as he worked for Guthrie, a need for revenge took shape in his mind. That was the Major's secret, and Fletcher Childs must have spent many sleepless nights wondering what was holding the Major up.

When Guthrie made his attempt to take the party leadership away from the Major, it must have seemed the final outrage, an attack on life itself in the Major's eyes.

The Major is an outstanding marksman, and with his rifle he first attempted to revenge himself on Guthrie by killing the Governor's son. It was easy to see how he could have missed his first shot as he lay concealed in the woods above the lake where Hilda Brudder and Chris sat. But why hadn't he tried a second shot? Was he afraid to make the boy's assassination perfectly obvious, or did he have Chris lined up in his sights when something—a car on the road, a noise in the woods nearby—distracted him?

Or was it only because he couldn't bear to go through with it? Wasn't he able, then, to hate John Guthrie enough to take his only child?

In the next three years John Guthrie inadvertently kept the Major's hatred of him raw, until the Major was literally insane with a desire for vengeance.

How long had he planned his second attempt on Chris's life? Had he ever wished that it might not be necessary: had he ever prayed for John Guthrie to leave him alone with what life he had left?

From his house on Tournament Hill the Major could see the school that Chris attended, and, perhaps, on many of the afternoons when he was in the garden, he looked down at the children playing and thought of his own daughter.

What was Fletcher Childs thinking during the months when the struggle between the Governor and the Major grew more bitter? He knew that with just a few words the Major could bring disgrace to John Guthrie. Perhaps he brought pressure of his own to bear on the Major. He wanted to be in office badly enough to jeopardize his professional reputation, and he wouldn't have been content to sit back and say nothing while the Major stubbornly allowed John Guthrie to go on hacking him to bits.

With so much against him, how long was the Major able to hold on to his sanity?

On the night Val St. George demolished the Governor's room at the mansion, and went to Dr. Childs for help, the doctor administered sodium pentothal as a sedative, and under the influence of this so-called truth drug Val babbled enough of his life to convince Childs that he had what he needed, with or without the Major's help, to ruin Guthrie. So he drove Val to the reservoir for safekeeping and then telephoned the Major to brag about his prize, or perhaps to urge the Major to join him in his plot.

He must have been more than a little taken aback to discover that the Major knew about Val's existence; knew enough, in fact, to thoroughly smear the Governor without any assistance from Val. But by now the destruction of John Guthrie's reputation wasn't enough for the Major; he had bloodier plans. He drove to the reservoir in the hope of heading off Childs, and encountered violent resistance from the doctor.

Was Fletcher Childs upset enough at this point to tell the Major that Molly Kinsaker had caused her own death?

If so, what was the Major's reaction? (Remember what Steppie has had to say about the films of the accident: imagine the Major sitting all these years and running them, studying the face of John Guthrie, the drunken gait, the grinding tragedy that repeated itself night after night.) How could he believe, so long after, that what he had accepted as true, what he must believe, was not true at all?

He could not allow himself to believe Fletcher Childs, because he could only live with hate, not the truth. And so he killed the man who was trying to tell him he had no reason to hate John Guthrie.

That killing sparked his second attempt on the life of Chris Guthrie.

Perhaps he intended to shoot Chris while he was at play in the school yard; the distance was about three quarters of a mile from his house, not a difficult shot for a man of the Major's prowess, and it would be next to impossible for investigators to say exactly where the bullet had come from. Perhaps he sat in his room with a rifle and scope nearby and waited for the moment when the children would come hurtling through the doors for recess. And while he sat with his eyes on the brick school yard, he saw the two boys, Chris and Hugh McAdams, jump down from the window of the washroom and hurry down the bare slopes of the little valley to the prison.

And another idea occurred to him . . .

Practice swallowed hard and picked up a cup of lukewarm coffee. Some drops spilled on his pad as he drank. Wearily he read the last paragraph again, then picked up his pencil and wrote, "But where was Steppie?" after it.

The sun was nearly overhead in the cemetery when Practice shook himself from his reverie and blinked his eyes at the glare of light on his windshield. A flower-scented breeze came down from the heights of the cemetery and swept through his car. The legal pad was still in his hand. He looked down and reread the last sentence.

Steppie, of course.

If anyone could prove that the Major was guilty of murder, it was Steppie. If she had been in the Major's house for several days, then she must have heard or seen him go out the night Fletch was killed. Perhaps she could verify the fact that he had left the house not long before Hugh McAdams's murder.

Practice remembered the look on the Major's face when he had come into the room and seen Chris lying on the bed. He had been severely shocked, but at the time, Practice had passed off his reaction as natural. Where was the Major

when Practice brought Chris up the hill from the prison?
Was there some way he could enter and leave his house
without being observed, either by someone in the house or
in the immediate neighborhood?

Practice reached over and opened the glove compartment, and took out his revolver and a holster. He unfastened
his belt and slipped the holstered gun under his coat, then
tightened his belt again and started the car.

He was ready now to talk to Major Kinsaker.

Between the low-hanging boughs of the oaks in the steep
and uneven front yard of the Major's hilltop house a man
rode a power mower, leaving a green wake of freshly cut
grass behind him. Practice could smell the grass in the still
air, as he got out of his car in front of the granite gateposts at
the foot of the drive. He glanced up at the house, but there
was nothing about it to suggest that anyone had lived there
for the last ten years.

He was halfway up the drive when the engine on the
power mower quit and the man who drove it called cheerfully, "'Fraid you won't find anybody home."

Practice changed course and approached the gardener.
He pushed his hat back on his head with an expression of
disapproval and resignation.

"Now, how am I going to plan a new kitchen if I can't get
in to see the old one?"

The gardener wiped his damp forehead with the back of a
grimy glove.

"I guess you can't. Anyway, the Major left early this
morning, just as I drove up." He waved a hand at a
dilapidated pickup truck parked in the porte cochere.

"That was early?"

"Sunup. About six-thirty."

"Maybe he'll be back soon," Practice said hopefully.

"Couldn't say. I never have conversation with the Major.
He just mails me a check every week and I work on the yard
whenever it needs it."

"Is there a lady of the house?"

The gardener winked. "There is and there isn't, if you get me. But she went with the Major this morning. Looked as if she didn't feel too well."

"How's that?"

"Well, I saw he was leaving, so I pulled up across the street. Major had to help the lady to the car. She didn't seem to have a bone in her body. Laid down right away in the back seat. He got in and drove off without a glance at me."

"Maybe he left the back door open for me," Practice said. "No harm in looking. If I can't get in, I can't get started on his kitchen. Between you and me, I could use the money."

The gardener laughed. "Things is sure tight." He started up his power mower and jockeyed it around expertly.

Practice followed the drive up and passed through the shade of the porte cochere to the rear of the house. There he stood for a few moments, looking down at the heavily planted backyard.

A high fence covered with honeysuckle or ivy surrounded the property and at the bottom of the hill there was a gate in the fence. Outside the gate a narrow tree-enclosed path led into the valley, at the end of which the old prison stood. Half the valley was thick with trees and underbrush, and Practice couldn't make out the course of the path. He followed along and picked it up again, dwindling down a hundred feet through stones and high weeds to the back of the prison. The distance was about two thirds of a mile from the Major's back door to the walls of the prison, and much of the route was concealed.

Practice returned to the front yard and waited until the gardener had cut another swath to within a foot of where he was standing and had stopped his machine. This time he didn't shut off the engine, but looked up at Practice questioningly.

"No luck," Practice said over the noise. "You wouldn't have any idea where the Major was going, would you?"

"Couldn't say." He looked thoughtful. "Probably won't be back today or tomorrow, though."

"Why?"

"After he helped the woman into the car, he loaded up the trunk. Big duffel, then two rifle cases. He was wearing boots and hunting clothes, you know, that green-brown color. He shouldn't go stumping around the woods in clothes like that. Nobody can see him."

"That's right," Practice said, and nodded to the gardener, who turned his machine around and clattered off through the high grass.

He was certain that the Major was driving north to his farm in the country around Greenbard. And Steppie was with him. The gardener had said that she didn't seem to feel very well. Could she have been drunk that early in the morning or was something else wrong, very badly wrong?

The drive to Greenbard would take three hours, and he wasn't learning any more than he already knew by hanging around Osage Bluff.

He went quickly to his car and drove up Tournament Hill, then turned left and headed across town. Near the river bridge he stopped for a full tank of gas, then he was on the road driving north, with a slight headache and a not unwelcome sense of danger thickening his throat.

21

The fence was of a type common to that part of the state, about five and a half feet high,' of whitewashed boards in parallels of three, with big square posts about seven feet apart topped with flat capitals. What was unusual about the Major's property was the hedgerow behind the fence, with only intermittent breaks to reveal rolling pastureland, wood lots, and a good-sized lake with a long concrete spillway. Below the dam, Angus cattle lounged in the grass.

He had been told to look for a gradual beginning of bluff along the road, then a sharp turn to the right. The woods had thickened and the road was soon cut off from the sun by the rise of bluff. He slowed down. A road of limestone gravel met the road he was traveling on through a natural break in the rock. He entered, and after a hundred yards or so came to a bridge with a gate across it, but the gate wasn't padlocked.

Practice got out and opened the gate, then drove through, and followed the road along an unusually clear stream.

The woods ended suddenly and another fence appeared, shining in the sunlight that came across a great open meadow, which rose gradually to a hill overlooking the river more than a mile away. There was a large white house on the hill, with shade trees around it. A stable nearby looked as if it could house a hundred horses.

At the store Practice had been told by a garrulous native that the Major rarely opened his house; when he came to the farm he stayed elsewhere, usually in the house of the farm's supervisor, who lived several miles away.

To Practice's left, just outside the wall of woods, was a

cottage of white brick with a steep gray slate roof. The fence around the house was brick, too, enclosing a small yard, and so high that he could only see the tops of windows.

A gray Cadillac was parked in front of the fence.

Practice stopped his car behind the Cadillac and got out. He could feel the cool woods close at hand, while the sun was reflected brightly from the wall in front of him. He heard the sound of the stream and what might have been a small waterfall back in the woods. An orange cat rose up cautiously from where it had been sunning itself on top of the wall and backed away.

There was no other sign of life. Practice shaded his eyes and looked toward the hill and the main house, but saw no sign of activity there either.

A quail came running quickly around the corner of the wall and then, perhaps seeing the cat, ran off. Practice stood listening for a few seconds, then pushed open the swing gate and walked into the yard of the cottage. He immediately felt the seclusion which the high fence afforded. Behind the house a few towering trees let down their boughs to within a foot or so of the fence. There was dense quiet within the woods, and Practice felt wary, without knowing why. He looked the cottage over carefully, then approached the front door along a moss-covered stepping-stone pathway.

Practice knocked at the door a couple of times, but not hopefully. He didn't think that anyone would answer him. Hesitantly he put his hand on the butt of the revolver underneath his coat, then frowned and withdrew the hand. He tried to open the door and the latch clicked. He let himself in.

There wasn't much light within the cottage, and he reached behind him to push the door open wider. Sunlight spilled across the floor, fanned over a paneled wall, soaked into a blanket thrown across a figure lying on a red leather couch. He could see only her forehead and a wave of blond hair, but he knew it was Steppie.

Something dark and ugly seemed to be squatting in her

hair, like a huge spider, and he shuddered, drawing closer, until he was certain that what he was seeing was dried, matted blood. Under the blanket her breasts didn't seem to be moving at all, and her skin was ashen.

"Steppie?" he said.

He reached down to draw the blanket from her face, and suddenly the light that had been pouring in through the doorway was partly blocked. Practice looked up and saw the Major standing in the doorway with a rifle cradled in one arm. The sun was almost directly behind the Major's head, and Practice could see nothing of his face.

"Did you hit her?" Practice asked angrily.

The Major made no reply. He took two steps into the room, and moved his rifle so that it pointed at the floor only a foot or so in front of Practice. The rifle was a Winchester 70, .30-06, with what looked like a Redfield variable scope mounted. His finger was on the trigger, and the rifle rode comfortably against his arm, positioned for shooting within the sling.

"I didn't know you would come," the Major said then. "But so much the better."

"What the hell do you mean?"

The Major turned his head slightly so that Practice could see one cold yellow eye glittering in the light that outlined his face.

"Half an hour ago John Guthrie arrived at the farm next to mine, which is owned by a relative of his named Crenshaw. The house is about three miles from here by way of the woods. His wife and boy were with him. I was there, watching. You should have been with them, but you weren't. That worried me, and so I came back. You wouldn't have come here unless you had some suspicion of what I might be going to do." His head moved again and he stared down at the still form of Steppie. "I suppose it's of little importance to you whether you die beside John Guthrie or beside your ex-wife."

"You're not going to kill anybody else, Major."

The Major frowned. "I don't want to talk to you. I'm not interested in talking to you. I believe you're wearing a gun on the left side of your belt. Open your coat and take the gun out of its holster."

Practice didn't budge. Nothing changed in Major Kinsaker's face, but abruptly the rifle tilted until the muzzle was centered on Practice's midsection.

"I have no time to play chess with you, Mr. Practice. In an hour the sun will have set and John Guthrie and his family will be at dinner. Twilight is particularly beautiful here at this time of the year. I'm sure they'll throw open the terrace doors before sitting down. If they do, I'll be able to shoot each of them through the head within five seconds. They won't know what hit them. There will be no fear, and death will occur instantly."

"You crazy son of a bitch."

"You may think I'm insane. No matter. I'm perfectly capable of killing them from any distance up to twelve hundred yards. Today I went to some trouble to cut the telephone lines. The Crenshaw farm is ideally isolated; no one lives close enough to hear the shots, and even if the shots were noticed, no one would pay the least attention."

"You have a grievance against Governor Guthrie," Practice said tightly. "But there's no reason for you to murder either his wife or child."

"Every reason," the Major said evenly. "John Guthrie destroyed my daughter."

"That's a lie. He was not responsible for Molly's death."

The Major seemed to flinch.

"I was there. I saw what happened."

"You saw what Fletcher Childs wanted you to see. Come to your senses, Major."

Again the faint uneasiness was evident in the Major's face.

"Fletcher Childs? I don't know any Fletcher Childs."

"You've known him for . . ."

The crack of the gun came as Practice was spinning, his face contorted in pain, a hand clasped to his right arm just above the elbow. He went down on one knee. The fingers of his right hand were shocked and numbed. Vaguely he saw the Major coming, and tried to get at his revolver with his left hand. A blow from the butt of the rifle against his shoulder knocked him flat. He rolled to avoid a second blow, leaving the revolver on the floor. The Major shoved it away with one foot and hit Practice again, this time with the side of the stock, a glancing blow. Practice threw up his hands in an effort to protect his head.

"Shut up, shut up, shut up," the Major said, his eyes glittering as he smashed the butt through Practice's hands. Practice barely felt the blow at all, and suddenly the Major's voice stopped. He couldn't hear, but he could feel the floor under his face. He tried to move, but it was no use, his head was as heavy as stone; six horses couldn't have dragged it an inch.

Hands tugged at one shoulder and he was rolled over on his back. He could see, a little, but his throat was paralyzed and he made no sound. A shadow was moving over him. From a great height the Major's face appeared, and light glinted briefly on glass; then a shower of liquid spilled over his face, stung his eyes, ran into his open mouth. The taste was familiar; the liquid burned his throat and he choked.

Whiskey. He was drunk again, all hope was gone.

He lay still for a few moments, looking up at the beamed ceiling of the cottage, trying to remember what he had wanted here. He was having a drink with Steppie, and that seemed all right. But something had happened, something disastrous, and he had to get up . . .

As he stared at the beams, trying to locate the rest of his body, his mouth seared by the unaccustomed taste of whiskey, the ceiling seemed to waver and go out of focus. Clouds drifted below it. That was odd. A nagging fear took hold of him and again he struggled to rise. Sure, he was drunk. But there was another reason.

The Major . . .

The Major had shot at him and bludgeoned him. And

now the cottage was filled with light, flickering light, deadly firelight, the pungency of smoke.

Get up!

He tried to rise, using his right arm for support, and pitched forward on his face. The floor was hot. He put both hands under him and tried again. The smoke was thicker, biting; he covered his nose and mouth with his sleeve to avoid sucking smoke into his lungs. His eyes wouldn't focus. The crackle of dry, blazing wood scared him.

Overhead the beams were crawling with flame and one entire paneled wall was burning. Everything else had ignited: draperies, carpets, lampshades, furniture.

In the midst of the flames Steppie lay on the red leather sofa. The blanket was smoldering at her feet, and as he stared, it burst into flame.

He crawled to the sofa and snatched the blanket from her body. Dimly he realized that the heat and the smoke in the closed house were reaching the suffocation point. He got to his feet and stumbled across a blazing carpet to the door. His coat had caught fire, and he shed it painfully, noticing the bloody wound above his elbow. But he was using his arm, so the bullet hadn't crippled him.

He tugged futilely at the front door for valuable seconds, then turned and made his way back to the sofa.

Blackened draperies had fallen close to Steppie's head, and he snatched them away, singeing his hand. A tarnished window, not more than three feet square, gaped at him behind the sofa. It was almost head-high from the floor. Coughing, Practice looked around and seized a straight chair. The paint on it was beginning to blister. He lunged for the window and shattered it with the chair, then cleaned the pane of fragments. Fresh air billowed in and he sucked at it greedily, turning in horror as he heard the ominous buckling of the roof. He picked Steppie up in his arms and carried her to the window, maneuvered her awkwardly, feet-first, through the space, and let her go. Then he wriggled out after her and tumbled down a slope into a damp bed of grass. He lay there, semiconscious, until he was able to go back and drag Steppie a safe distance from the house.

He sat with his back against a well, staring numbly at the spectacle, his head pounding, his throat raw from swallowed smoke. His shirt stank of the smoke and spilled whiskey. He wondered if someone had seen the fire yet. There was a fresh evening breeze, and as the smoke rose against the background of trees, it was carried away swiftly. How long had he been inside—ten minutes or an hour? Had he been unconscious for any length of time? He rubbed his forehead and looked up. The sun was not visible and the sky was darkening.

In an hour, the Major had said, *the sun will have set and John Guthrie and his family will be at dinner . . .*

22

Practice forced himself to stand and groaned. He looked down at Steppie. Skull fracture, he thought. Probably in a bad way. I should help her—but soon, in only a few minutes, John Guthrie and his family will be at dinner. And when they sit down, the Major is going to shoot them, one after another.

Somebody would discover the fire, he hoped, and Steppie. But he had to stop the Major.

The next farm, he thought. There would be a road. Three miles. No, that was the distance on foot. Maybe longer by the road. How much time did he have?

He went out through the gate and saw that the rim of the sun was just visible in the west, within a great pink shell of sky. The Major's Cadillac was there. Shakily he got into his own car and for once was happy about his habit of leaving his keys in the ignition. He backed around and roared down the narrow gravel road beside the stream, now with only a twinkling of light on the surface, as it flowed through the darkness.

The highway. He made the turn, skidding dangerously, straightened out, and pushed his foot hard on the accelerator. One minute, two minutes, at seventy miles an hour around blind curves, *three minutes!* The twilight had almost ended. He was aware of the moon in the dark blue sky as he peered through the windshield, searching for the access road to the Crenshaw farm. *Or had he missed it somehow?*

He visualized the Major sitting patiently in concealment with the Winchester at his shoulder, securely held by the leather sling, waiting another few seconds until he was absolutely sure he couldn't miss . . .

A hundred yards down the paved road Practice glimpsed a break in the hedgerow, a passage between trees, and he hurriedly braked. Just as he was making the turn into a lane marked with a discreet "C" on the gateposts, he realized that he had lost his revolver during the scuffle with the Major. He had no weapon at all.

The Crenshaw road inclined steadily toward a woods, and the trees on either side rushed by precipitously as Practice drove on. He was forced to shift down into second to make some of the turns. Abruptly the trees fell away and the house was ahead of him, a two-story frame building with a slim stone chimney on the left. He shoved his hand down on the horn. In a fraction of a second he saw that two of the front windows had lights behind them. He saw the barn situated behind the house, and the abrupt rise of a wooded hill away to the left of house and barn. In the next second the car lurched over a deep rut and Practice's hands were torn from the wheel; he fell sideways in the seat, but his foot was on the brake and he quickly regained control of the car.

As he raised his head, he saw the broken glass of the windshield over the wheel, an area as big as a saucer, with a small hole in the center, and ducked his head below the window line again. This time he heard the small splintering sound as a second bullet pierced the windshield.

Instinctively he swung the car around to make himself less of a target, and with his head still down, opened the door and crawled out. He heard two more bullets strike the car with a precise deadly thumping, and this time he also heard the far-off reports of the Major's rifle.

From the brief look he'd had at the farmyard and the hill beyond as he drove in, he'd decided that the Major was either high on the hill, effectively screened by trees, or in the barn loft.

Practice looked over his shoulder. The barn loft was plainly visible to him, which meant that if the Major were sitting up there, he had a clean shot at Practice. But the bullets had struck the other side of the car. He raised his head cautiously and sighted through the rear windows for an instant, but it was too dark to see . . .

Another bullet smashed through both windows, so close that specks of glass struck his cheek. Practice crouched again, wondering if the Major's bullets could reach through the body of the car for him, and he felt his stomach cramping with fear.

"Jim!"

Again he looked over his shoulder, and this time saw John Guthrie, in a white shirt and denims, standing in the doorway of the farmhouse.

"What the hell is going on out there?"

"Get back!" Practice shouted. "Get in the house!" But the screen door had slammed and he saw the Governor advancing toward him, his white shirt clearly visible in the dark.

"Who's doing the shooting . . . ?"

"No!" Practice shouted, but before he could say more he heard the crack of the Major's rifle, and John Guthrie pitched forward and lay motionless on the grass.

Practice stared at him in horror. The white shirt had given the Major a target he couldn't possibly have missed.

Whether he had chosen to place his bullet a little above the
collar or through the heart was unimportant.

"Daddy!"

This time it was Chris in the doorway, holding the screen
open, and as Practice glanced up he saw Dore's blond head
behind the boy. Again Chris screamed, "Daddy!" And
Practice suddenly broke from cover, running toward the
door which seemed half a mile away. There was no cover at
all. Perhaps the Major would be momentarily off guard. Or
perhaps he was now centering Practice within the scope,
tracking him in his headlong, hopeless run, timing his
heartbeat, waiting for the moment to send Practice into the
dirt with another perfectly placed bullet.

With a groan of fear and anguish, Practice threw himself
toward the ground in a diving somersault, distantly hearing
the crack of the rifle. Then he scrambled to his knees, ran,
dived again, seeing nothing but the doorway and the terrified faces of Chris and Dore. Another bullet whined off the
concrete doorstep just ahead of him.

The door was open. He hurtled through, pushing Chris
and Dore aside.

"Get down, get down," he pleaded, and before he was
finished, the house began to explode, fragment after fragment, windows, table lamps, even the walls. He crawled on
hands and knees to where Chris was standing, staring out at
his father on the lawn. He pulled the child down with one
hand and yanked at Dore with the other.

"What's happening, what's happening?" Dore moaned.
"Who's trying to kill us?"

Practice heard the bullets hitting inside the house, digging
into floors, walls, furniture. As he looked up, a light fixture
over the dining room table shattered with a little puff of
smoke and swayed crookedly on its chain. *Stop it,* he thought,
his teeth gritted. *Enough!* He wondered how long it would be
before one of the Major's volleys found them, flat on the
floor; how long before he heard the unmistakable sound of a
bullet striking flesh.

And then, magically, it was quiet. Chris whimpered on the floor, and Practice moved slightly, holding him. One light remained on, a table lamp in front of the chimney, the one place safe from the bullets that had been fired into the house. They were lying on a diagonal line from the chimney and fireplace to the front door, and now Practice thought he knew approximately where the Major was hiding up on the hill.

Was he changing position now, so that the chimney would no longer be an obstacle to him? Would his next bullets search them out and kill them as they lay helplessly pinned to the floor, unable to move or to run away?

"Dore!"

He heard her sobbing nearby and lifted his head slightly to look at her.

"Tell him to stop—tell him to stop . . ."

"Dore! Listen to me. As soon as you hear the next shot, I want you to scream, 'Chris! Chris!' And then cry as loud as you can. When he shoots again, scream as if you're hit. Can you remember that?"

"Tell him to stop," she moaned.

"Dore . . ."

He lifted his head again and saw, not far away, a chaise with a padded, canvas-covered cushion. He squirmed to the chaise and lifted off the pad, then worked it back to where Dore was lying. He doubled the pad, and covered her. Only her arms and legs were unprotected. The doubled pad was more than a foot thick. He didn't know if it could stop a .30-06, but it might.

Chris was beginning to stir, and Practice crawled back to him and lay down so that he was covering Chris with his body.

They waited.

There were six shots this time, each about three seconds apart. He heard them hitting the floor all around them. After the fourth shot Dore suddenly roused herself and began to scream Chris's name. And then, as suddenly, she stopped. Practice had been listening for the last bullet, but he hadn't heard it hit. There might have been a slight, almost undetectable *thump,* as if the cushions which covered Dore had been struck. But he couldn't be sure. He bit his lip and kept Chris absolutely still beneath him.

Come on, he thought grimly. *Come on, you bastard, and take a look. You have to know, don't you? You have to know!*

He heard his watch ticking close to his ear and tried to gauge the passing of time, but soon abandoned the effort. Was it five minutes since the bullets had stopped? How long could he keep Chris still? What had happened to Dore? He was afraid to make the slightest move. The Major was a hunter; he could stalk like a ghost. He might be outside the screen right now, looking in, his rifle on them, alert for any movement.

Back in the woods an owl hooted. Chris's breathing was labored. Practice held his hand firmly on the back of Chris's head, wishing he could talk to the boy, reassure him in some way.

The screen door opened an inch, a sound that chilled Practice.

He's coming in.

Did any of them look dead? Would the Major recognize the sham and raise his rifle again to place a last bullet in each of their heads?

The crack of the rifle nearby jolted him. He didn't know if his muscles had jumped convulsively at the sound or not. He lay still, wanting to scream to dispel his tension, not daring to . . .

"Get up," the Major said. "Get away from the boy."

So he knew. Slowly Practice raised his head, feeling the stiffness of his neck and the slow noose of fear around his throat. He wanted to plead, to make this fierce, indefatigable man leave them alone, but he was too exhausted with the knowledge of sure death.

"Stand," the Major said; and Practice rose, staring into those implacable yellow eyes. The Major stood directly in front of the screen door, half in darkness, half illuminated by the brightness of the moon outside, the rifle cradled in his arm as steadily as ever.

On the floor, Chris sobbed.

"Stand away from the boy," the Major said.

"No."

"Don't be a fool. I don't want him to die in pain as my daughter died. But I'll shoot through you to get to him."

"I'm coming for you, Major," Practice said. "I know I won't make it. I won't get two steps before you stitch me up and down with that Winchester. But still I'm going to come."

"If you choose to do it that way," the Major said unemotionally, and he adjusted the aim of his rifle with his left hand.

Outside, the motor of Practice's car roared.

The Major flinched, and for a moment his expression was bewildered, but he didn't take his eyes off Practice. He took a step back, and, not losing sight of Practice, turned his head to look out.

The sound of clashing gears was loud and jarring in the night.

Light filled the doorway, and the Major's malevolent eyes glittered. His lips stretched away from his teeth and he cried out, vaguely, but his cry was barely audible over the noise of acceleration as the car raced toward the house.

The rifle arced away from Practice, who snatched Chris from the floor and backed away with him. The Major stood stiffly and calmly within the blinding headlights as the car came on. He fired round after round into the light.

He was still firing as the car jumped the two concrete steps outside and smashed into the house at a speed of more than fifty miles an hour. The Major literally disappeared in the explosive impact of metal and wood, and the whole house seemed to buckle as if it were the center of an earthquake. Practice braced himself for the collapse of the roof and walls that would kill them as surely as the Major's bullets, but miraculously the house absorbed the impact of the two-ton automobile, survived its seizure, and remained standing. There was a huge hole in the front wall, and part of the upper floor had fallen in. Pipes were burst and water spurted upward in a cloud of steam that mingled with the heavy dust of plaster and debris. The car was badly wrecked, but as Practice stared, the door on the driver's side opened with a squawk of bent metal and John Guthrie got shakily out, his eyes fixed intently on Practice.

"All right?" he asked. "Is everybody . . . ?"

"I think so."

Guthrie looked down at the rubble piled up under the wheels of the car. The stock of a rifle was visible and Practice thought he could see one of the Major's arms, but he didn't really want to look.

Blood rolled down Guthrie's left cheek from a long but apparently superficial wound. He dabbed at the blood with his fingertips and leaned against the side of the car he had driven into the house.

"Only way," he said, horrified. "There was nothing else I could do."

"You did enough," Practice told him.

23

The train was late.

Osage Bluff's station, a block below the hill on which the Governor's mansion stood, was an antique, and had never looked prosperous even in the days when trains ran more frequently. Years ago, the parking lot in front and alongside the station would have been packed with cars and taxis, and the waiting room would be full, anticipating the arrival of the eight o'clock from Fort Frontenac; but the airlines gradually had taken their share of the passengers, and now fewer than a dozen people waited outside on the platform under the long roof. They gazed impatiently down the tracks for the headlight of the diesel as the streamliner came around the bluff beneath the penitentiary and slowed to the sound of its great strident bell.

Practice had been able to park only a few feet from the cobblestone walk along the tracks, and he waited fretfully, with one cigarette and then another, looking out at the black river and at the lights of the river bridge. It was summer, and hot. He wiped his forehead with an already smudged handkerchief and wondered if she had really come at last.

He felt and heard the train's approach simultaneously, looked at his watch, grunted, and got out of the car as the diesel bore down on the station, headlights revolving. The lighted cars slid by quickly. It was one of the few luxury trains left on the line. The conductors and porters Practice glimpsed standing behind half-doors were ancient men in starched white or baggy blue suits. He searched the windows of the coaches anxiously for Lucy, but didn't see her.

The train ground to a stop and the porters jumped down quickly from two coaches directly in front of the station. The passengers began to get off, and Practice walked along the platform, eagerly watching them appear.

Lucy was one of the first to get off. She wore a blue traveling suit and carried a small overnight case. The porter pulled a larger white suitcase off the train for her and with a smile set it down out of the way. Lucy thanked him, and as she turned, Jim was aware that her hair was different; she was wearing it in a more sophisticated style. He came up to Lucy feeling slightly disheveled in the heat, and out of breath, and as flustered as he had ever been in his life.

"I'll take that, lady."

She turned quickly, tried to smile, but couldn't. They

looked at each other for an awkward few moments, then she reached out and touched his sleeve and said softly, "Oh, Jim."

Lucy was jostled by departing passengers and she stepped out of the way. Practice picked up her suitcase.

"This way," he said. "How was your trip?"

"Long. I think I ought to get used to flying, but . . ." She stopped and stared up the hill, at the lights of the city and of the Governor's mansion, just visible through the trees.

"There have been some changes," he said. "But not as many as you might think. Cities don't change much in a year and a half. Just people."

They walked side by side to his car, a used Plymouth, and he put her suitcase in the back seat. He had an opportunity to look more closely at Lucy as she got in. Her clothes were expensive. He knew from John Guthrie that Lucy made close to forty thousand dollars a year in Washington. Guthrie had arranged the job for her, and seen to it that she had a full social life almost from the moment she'd arrived. Lucy hadn't had much to say about herself in the few letters she and Practice had exchanged, but it was obvious to Practice that she had prospered in new surroundings. And he was glumly certain that she had all the male attention she could want. He wondered if there was a particular man by this time, one whom she was thinking about even now. He felt years older than he had just minutes ago, uncertain, and a little drab.

He was aware of how shabby the interior of the dusty Plymouth looked. There were crumbs of tobacco on the dashboard, and the back seat was littered with scraps of paper and legal pads.

Lucy took a deep breath and smiled at him.

"Well, tell me all the news. I never hear anything from the Guthries, except for a few lines John sometimes scrawls at the bottom of his letters to Senator Toneff."

"He has this ranch in Montana, seven hundred and some acres in a place called Sourwater Valley, which looks better than it sounds. He's got beef cattle, sugar beets, and wheat, and wants for nothing as far as I know. Dore's happy, too. He bought her six pairs of blue jeans as soon as they moved away from here, and the nearest civilization is thirty miles away in Billings."

"And Chris?" she asked eagerly.

"At first Chris didn't want any part of the ranch. He hated horses and so forth. Stayed in his room and sulked most of the time. But this spring he finally came around to the point where he admitted he might like to climb on a horse. Just a matter of time for Chris."

Lucy laughed. "Do you think they'll ever come back to Osage Bluff?"

"John swears not. But he's a politician, and his politics are rooted here. Maybe in three years, or four, when he has the ranch under control, he'll divide his time between there and Osage Bluff. Now, tell me, before I bust—you write the most uninformative letters, by the way, welcome as they are—how's Washington? What are you doing? Is it—a permanent sort of thing?"

She laughed again. "Let me catch my breath. I love Washington. It was far different from anything I'd known, or thought I could get used to. But John's friends took me in hand and helped me over the rough spots. Senator Toneff is a dream to work for. We have fierce arguments over everything and he's fired me a dozen times. Always apologizes with a big vase full of roses. I'm rooming with a girl from Atlanta who won a lot of beauty contests and speaks an unbelievable language I haven't caught on to yet. The pace is furious, most of the time. That has its good and bad points. Aren't we going to the hotel?"

"Yes. First I had—I wanted to show you—something," he finished lamely.

On a narrow street, just a block from the downtown area, he pulled into a parking place beside an old five-story building with a pitched roof and three gables. He opened the lobby door with a key and they took the elevator, which was not much larger than a telephone booth, to the top floor. Under the sloping roof he led her to a white door set in a red wall. Lucy was smiling in a strange way. On the door, in black letters, was a sign, JAMES TYLER PRACTICE, ATTORNEY AT LAW. He hesitated a moment in front of the door, not daring to look at Lucy, then opened it and turned on the light in the small foyer. There was just room inside for a secretary's cubicle, a couch in yellow, and a small rug on the floor with wide olive and green stripes.

"Jim . . ."

"Wait." He crossed the anteroom and opened the door to his office. There was one big window in the room, framing the lighted Capitol and a portion of the river below it. He didn't turn on the lights but stood looking toward the Capitol. Lucy came into his office and he glanced back over one shoulder at her.

"I pay too much for it," he said. "The kind of business I do, I should have a booth in a lunchroom uptown. Things are slow but gradual."

"It's—wonderful, Jim."

"No. But my own. Oh, not even my own, if I want to be technical. John Guthrie gave me a lot of help. Maneuvered some business my way when he left his own law office in the hands of his partner. That got me started. I've been hard at it ever since."

"Talk about uninformative letter writers!" Lucy said.

"I could have bragged, I suppose. I was desperate enough to write a lot of stuff that hadn't come true yet. I could have kept repeating over and over what a big man I was going to become. I wanted to, but somehow it would have been dishonest. I didn't want you to come back that way, Lucy. I didn't want to lure you back. You know something Lucy? I'm forty-two years old. And I'm starting to lose my hair."

"Oh, shut up," she said softly.

He suddenly felt severely short of words. "Well, this is what I've done. What I've always wanted, Lucy. I can't wait to get down here in the morning and make twice as much work out of the work I have. I hate to leave and go home at night. Because it gets lonely where I live. I'm forty-two years old and a man who's missed a lot of chances. I don't have any right to expect not to be lonely, but that's the way it is."

"There's Steppie," she murmured, and he wished he could look back at her. But he was afraid to.

"Didn't I tell you? She married again about two months ago. The doctor who was treating her for headaches. She told me the other day she was going to get pregnant by the end of this month. Or else."

"I thought you and Steppie would . . ."

"Maybe we tried, Lucy. But there was too much against us, from way back when. And my heart wasn't in it. I didn't really want her, I guess. I wanted you."

"You're forty-two years old," she said. "And you're starting to lose your hair."

"There's something else. I can drink again. Apparently I wasn't a real alcoholic; the condition was mental. So now and then I have a cold beer when I get home, if I feel like it. It means no more to me than a cold beer should. Lucy?"

There were tears in her eyes. "You miserable—bastard. Why didn't you tell me anything? A bunch of polite letters, and I never knew . . ."

"Trying to be honest with you, I guess, Lucy. I suppose that's a part of the way toward saying that I love you."

"It's an important part," Lucy said.

"But I don't know how the rest should go."

She walked carefully away from him, around the other side of the desk, and stood close to the glass, looking out at the Capitol blazing white and beautiful against the sky.

"There always seemed to be something wrong with the one in Washington," she said. "I suppose it's just because I've always been a homegrown girl. Why do you think I came back here, you?" There was a sudden joyful lilt in her voice.

"I—can't even ask," Practice said miserably.

"He's losing his hair," she said scornfully to nobody, and

then she wheeled and faced him, her eyes glinting in the dark. She came slowly toward him, and as she approached, there was a change in her face; she was more than beautiful, she was real and adoring, and more than a little lonely herself.

They raised their hands and touched them together, palm against palm.

"Take me home," Lucy said gently. "I'll show you how the rest should go."